She knew he was naked under the red silk robe. Her breath quickened at the thought.

"I came," he said, somewhat uncertainly, "to return your bedroom door key."

Her voice was low and seductive. "I knew you'd bring it back. Now use it, please. Lock the door and come to me."

Before he could turn away, she threw aside the bed linen to reveal that she too was naked. The key rattled against the lock, betraying either his nervousness or, more likely, his impatience. It didn't matter which to Virginia. She held out her arms to him. He blew out the lamp and then his warm body was pressed against hers and she rode a wave of passion that carried her beyond thinking or caring what the results might be. His impatience and hunger matched hers...

Also by Dorothy Daniels

For Love and Valcour
Sisters of Valcour

Published by
WARNER BOOKS

CRISIS AT VALCOUR

DOROTHY DANIELS

WARNER BOOKS

A Warner Communications Company

WARNER BOOKS EDITION

Copyright © 1985 by Dorothy Daniels
All right reserved.

Cover design by Barbara Buck

Cover art by Max Ginsburg

Warner Books, Inc.
666 Fifth Avenue
New York, N.Y. 10103

 A Warner Communications Company

Printed in the United States of America

First Printing: June, 1985

10 9 8 7 6 5 4 3 2 1

ONE

Virginia Hammond Birch quickly sorted out the mail the maid had brought to her bedroom. From the dozen or more letters she removed the one postmarked London. She tore it open angrily, as if she knew what the contents would be. She scanned the single page, crumpled it, and threw it into the wastebasket.

"Goddamn him!" she exclaimed.

Her elder sister, Nanine, sighed and retrieved the letter and envelope. "You forget that I need this for my bookkeeping," she admonished.

"Look at it!" Virginia said heatedly. "There's nothing in it except the figures for his sales of our cotton. Look at the way he signed it! 'Your respectful servant.' Dammit, he's my husband!"

"He's also our representative in London, Virgie. And he's doing a remarkable job of selling our cotton," Nanine reminded her gently.

"For his fee." Virginia's tone was contemptuous. "Couldn't he at least ask how I feel?"

Nanine studied the envelope. "Virgie, look here—the letter was mailed less than two weeks ago! The clippers certainly live up to their reputation for speed."

Virginia disregarded the attempted diversion. "To hell with him! I'm going to divorce him."

Nanine smoothed out the crumpled letter and replaced it in the envelope. "Now wouldn't that be silly? All Elias would have do is demand that you identify the father of your son. He's not Elias's child—you know full well Elias is sterile. And your demand for a divorce would bring publicity in all the Charleston newspapers. It would kill Mama, humiliate us, and wreck your reputation."

Virginia's eyes flashed scornfully. "It might be worth it. Elias claimed to be in love with me. With love there should be forgiveness, but all he did was leave for England as soon as he found out I was pregnant."

"Perhaps," Nanine reminded her, "it wasn't completely due to the fact that you had cheated on him, but because of the caliber of the man you gave yourself to. A renegade, a murderer and a thief. A man who was later sentenced to be hanged, and still will be, if he's ever caught."

"Whose side are you on anyway?" Virginia demanded. "You're my sister!"

"Now let's stop this bickering," Nanine said. She had moved to one of the windows overlooking the island and its intercoastal-waterway approach from Charleston. "The guests are on their way. Some are here already, and we intend to make this the biggest and best ball ever. We're not even dressed, and Mama will have a fit if she has to greet everyone by herself."

"It would be a better affair if this letter hadn't arrived, but I'll do my part. Run along, Nan. Ivy can help me dress."

"Good. I want to help Phoebe—she's very nervous about how she'll be accepted."

Virginia made no reply, but she looked thoughtful, remembering the day she had first realized that Phoebe, who'd been her servant once, was really her sister. Virginia recalled her hatred of Phoebe and the anger she'd directed at her father, who'd not only laughed at her but warned her not to mistreat Phoebe because she was his daughter as much as Virginia was.

Virginia regarded her reflection in the mirror. Though twenty-seven, she'd changed little in appearance, but she had matured since the flirtatious and giddy days that had ended abruptly when the Yankee army took over the islands off Charleston for the duration of the war. She had fled with her family then, and had endured many hardships in the long years of the fighting, during which she had lost her father, James Hammond. And then, soon after the war ended, Marty, her only brother.

The privations of the war had matured Virginia. She'd become calculating and practical. Her lovely violet eyes could appraise an individual with amazing accuracy, yet still seem to bear an air of innocence, though it was deceptive. Her lips were enticing, her smile devastating. Her long blond hair was like spun gold and shimmered when the sun touched it. Everything about Virginia was beautiful and sensuous. Her firm, well-rounded breasts; her waist, still small, above gently curved hips; and legs that gave evidence of being most alluring when a breeze pressed her skirt against them.

In contrast, Nanine's beauty was subdued. Her wide brown eyes regarded one with interest and reflected an innate warmth. Her dark hair, center parted, accentuated her heart-shaped face. There was a gentle softness about her that was a direct contrast to Virginia's boldness. They were both courageous, but in different ways. Where Virginia allowed her emotions to rule her, Nanine was always under control.

Phoebe had some of the qualities of each sister. She was Virginia's age, for they had been born within days of each other and both had been nursed by Belle. Phoebe was the daughter of a mulatto who'd been the mistress of Virginia's lusty father. Phoebe had been raised in the main house and given the same education as Virginia. Not until the girls were grown had Phoebe been told that she was a slave and could no longer play with Virginia. Though it had pained her because her skin was almost as fair as Virginia's, she'd not become embittered and had proved loyal to the Hammonds throughout the war. So much so that Virginia had forgotten the anger she'd felt when she'd first realized that she and Phoebe were sisters. It had taken the war to bring them close.

Afterward, Phoebe had married an officer in the Union army and gone north with him. Through necessity, she'd secured work in the theater, and with her talent she'd become an instant success. She'd done well until her ancestry was revealed; she'd been subjected to merciless, scathing publicity. She'd then fled back to Valcour without her husband, who had abandoned her.

Virginia gave an impatient shrug and shut out the memories. Her mother would fret because she was late getting downstairs. She called out to the servant in the next room.

"Ivy, come here at once."

The girl who responded was eighteen, slim, with a graceful walk and a mere trace of bronze to her skin; she was not entirely white. She had even features, with a small mouth and nose. Her oval face was topped with thick black hair that curled softly. It was cropped short, so that ringlets framed her face, giving her head a sculpted look.

"Reckon you better hurry, ma'am. Plenty o' boats. An' comin' mighty fast."

"Help me into my gown and don't talk so much," Virginia said sharply. "And be careful with it."

"Sure is beautiful, ma'am." Ivy held up the skirt of the gown. "Goin' to look mighty nice on y'all."

"It better, for what it cost." Ivy helped Virginia slip into the gown, but in her haste a spray of violets attached to the sleeve caught in Virginia's golden hair, loosening a strand. She slapped Ivy's arm. "You're mussing my hair! Be more careful."

As serenely as before, Ivy went about fastening the gown, admiring it as she worked. It was a gown worthy of admiration, for it was a newly arrived and strikingly picturesque Paris import. Virginia knew there would be no other like it. The petticoat was of white silk with a white lace flounce, over which was a skirt of gold satin. There were wide revers on each side, edged with lavender ruches and turned back to reveal the silk petticoat. The overskirt, of puffed lavender satin, was trimmed with a rich fringe of the same color. Long trailing sprays of gold and dark purple pansies with green leaves covered both the overskirt and the petticoat. Similar pansies were arranged at the back of the puffed overskirt. The brief, off-the-shoulder sleeves were touched with gold pansies and edged completely around the neck with pleated gold-satin lace. Virginia's coiffure was embellished with the same gold and purple pansies. She wore a simple gold necklace from which hung an emerald. Dangling from her pierced ears were delicate gold chains at the end of which were small emeralds. Elias had sent them to her on his last trip to Washington. He'd ordered them made especially for her.

She'd written, telling him of their arrival and asking what she could do with them. His cryptic reference to them consisted of two sentences: "Keep the jewelry. It was bought for you." Usually his letters enraged her, but that one had pleased her, mostly because the earrings were so beautiful and would enhance her fair skin and golden hair. Her satin slippers matched her gown, and she wore purple lace gloves that reached halfway to her elbows.

Virginia stepped away from Ivy, who was attempting to soften a fold in the gown, and regarded herself in the full-length mirror.

"Nobody goin' to rival you, ma'am. Nobody!" Ivy said amiably.

"You talk too much, Ivy, but thank you, especially for dressing my hair so attractively."

A trace of a smile touched Ivy's mouth. She'd spent an hour on Virginia's coiffure, but the results were well worth the effort. The fringe of bangs on Virginia's brow accented the pompadour, on which Ivy had arranged the flowers. The soft curls resting on Virginia's shoulders and neck lent further enchantment to her beauty.

"Is there anything else I can do for you, Miss Virginia?"

"Yes. I wish to see my son before I go downstairs."

Ivy hastened to open the door into the corridor, then followed Virginia to the nursery. Virginia went directly to the crib and looked down at her sleeping son. Each time she did, she thought her heart would burst. She'd had no idea that mother love could be so wonderful, so all-consuming.

The child, fathered by Bradley Culver, had been christened James Elias Birch. James had been her father's name. She'd written Elias about the name shortly after the boy's birth. Even though Elias had never made any reference to it, she knew he would never deny paternity. He was too much the gentleman.

She was pleased that the child's hair was the same golden blond as hers, but it was as thick and unruly as his father's. He also had Brad's deep-set, dark brown eyes, beautifully shaped sensuous lips, and strong jaw line. Damn, she thought, why did the child have to resemble his father so closely? The thought of Bradley Culver sent a shiver of apprehension through her. How could a man who had stirred her very being with such wild, uncontrollable passion, and with whom she'd taken daring risks to make love, also instill terror in her? The answer came readily enough. His ruthlessness. He took what he wanted. The thought heightened her fear of him. He must never see his son. Having made that decision, she kissed the sleeping child lightly on the brow, straightened, and turned to Ivy. Although the young girl's expression was noncommittal, she was well aware of the love her mistress bore her son.

"Ivy," Virginia said sternly, "from now on your work here must consist entirely of caring for my son. You will have no other duties or responsibilities. Mind now, you must be very attentive. If anything happens to him, I'll have your hide. Do you understand?"

Ivy nodded apprehensively, for her mistress's manner was threatening.

"See that you take care."

"Sho' will, ma'am. Sho' will."

Virginia was already heading for the door, but she turned suddenly, almost colliding with Ivy, who was hastening to open it.

"Why do you revert to Negro dialect when you speak English as well as I?" Virginia demanded.

"Doan' rightly knows, ma'am."

"Oh yes you do," Virginia retorted angrily. "You're being impudent and I'll take none of it from you. I have to take enough from Belle. And take heed—if it weren't for Moses, she'd have been off this plantation long before now."

Ivy dropped her dialect. "Sorry, Miss Virginia. I won't be, as you say, impudent."

"Then you admit you were."

Ivy gave a barely perceptible nod. "Don't really mean to. It's just that talking properly seems a waste when I'll never be anything but a servant."

"Phoebe was once my servant," Virginia reminded her.

"But she's beautiful and grew up in this lovely house where she learned how to do things as white folks do."

"You can learn too, from watching," Virginia said. "Don't you suppose that's how Phoebe learned?"

"But she has talent," Ivy argued softly.

"I can't stand here debating this with you now," Virginia said impatiently. "Just mind that you guard my son."

"Please stop worrying, Miss Virginia," Ivy said, puzzled by the fear revealed in her mistress's face. "I know how much you love him."

"You couldn't," Virginia said fiercely. "No one could."

Ivy sidestepped to the door. "Miss Lenore will be upset if you don't get downstairs—she was fussing already. I'll stay with the baby. Don't worry."

Virginia's manner softened. She knew Ivy could be trusted. "Thank you, Ivy. I don't mean to be so harsh. It's just that I wouldn't want anything to . . ."

Virginia took a deep breath and walked slowly from the room, head held high. Her lips widened in the merest trace of a smile as she passed Ivy.

When Virginia stepped into the hall, Ivy did also. She'd never seen anyone so beautiful. Even when her mistress was angry she looked radiant. Ivy wondered why Virginia's husband never came home; she knew something was wrong. A few times when she'd entered a room with the baby, Virginia and Nanine, engaged in conversation concerning Elias, paused abruptly and remained silent until she'd left.

Virginia paused at the landing and looked down at the large reception hall. Her eyes passed over several people she knew and paused when they regarded a man of average height, standing alone, smoking a slim, dark cheroot. She repressed a smile as she noticed his eyes surveying the crowd restlessly. His name was Carlos Cabrera. He knew no one, for he was Mexican, here at her invitation. She remained motionless, studying him carefully. Almost as if she willed it, he looked up. Her eyes met his briefly as she reached for the balustrade and started her slow descent. Without taking his eyes off her, he immediately started moving through the crowd, edging toward the staircase. He was a handsome devil, Virginia thought, her blood stirring. Thick black hair with a soft wave; dark brown eyes that openly adored her; perfectly chiseled features and clean-shaven except for a thin wisp of mustache. He was waiting for her when she completed her descent. She extended a gloved hand, which he took, bowed over, and kissed lightly.

He raised his head and gave her an adoring smile. "Señora, you are so beautiful. I ask that you dance every dance with me."

For just a moment she was eighteen again, back in the prewar days, loving to flirt and tease. But as quickly she returned to the present, as she scanned the guests in the reception line waiting to greet her mother. Most were older and not filled with the old gaiety, for the war years were too recent and the memories too vivid.

"Forgive me, Carlos." She slipped her hand from his. "I must join Mama. My sisters have not yet come down and she is alone at the reception line."

He nodded. "So long as I see you later, señora." He was as charming as the Southern gentlemen and Virginia was entranced. She reminded herself to be cautious about her behavior because she was still a married woman. She'd caught a few glances turned her way, some curious, some puzzled. She supposed it was Carlos's bronzed skin that confounded them. She would enlighten them about that shortly. Or could it be because of Elias's continued absence?

She cast the unpleasant thought from her mind and made her way across the reception hall to where her mother stood greeting the arriving guests. Lenore Hammond's furrowed brow was evidence of the cares and agonies of the war years, but during all the hardships and the loss of her husband and only son, she had never forgotten her reputation as a famous hostess. Prior to the war she had given the most lavish balls and dinners in the Charleston area.

She looked older, for her dark hair was now generously sprinkled with gray and jowls were forming on her once-firm jaw line. Yet she was still the gracious and charming hostess and, in private, a chronic complainer. She was also inclined to be sharp-tongued, though, according to her precepts, only when the occasion demanded it.

"It's about time," she whispered caustically when Virginia reached her side. "You always accuse me of being slow and late, but I never knew anyone as careless as you and your sisters. Where might they be on this important occasion?"

"They'll be here in a few minutes, Mama." There was a momentary respite, which allowed them to talk. Through the open French doors, Virginia saw the stream of guests still on their way from the dock to the mansion.

"I hope so. I'm no longer young enough to stand here and perform the niceties by myself."

Virginia eyed her mother admiringly. "You look it, Mama. You look stunning. And you've done yourself proud. Few of your invitations were not accepted. And there are more guests on their way across the channel." Virginia knew flattery always made her mother forget her pique.

Lenore softened. "Our dinner dances were always popular because we knew how to run them. Before the war, I mean. And, beginning now, they will be again. I shall see to it."

"Within reason, Mama. Don't forget we're still recovering from the war, and already we've spent a fortune restoring Valcour. We must be attentive to the fact that we cannot use our money indiscriminately."

"Oh, bother that," Lenore said. Then, as she observed more guests approaching, a warm smile crossed her face and her voice softened. "How do you do, Alice. And Percy. You both look well. How pleased we are that you could come."

"It's our pleasure, Lenore." Percy Larkin, portly and middle-aged, took Lenore's hand and bowed over it. "It's good to see this lovely house restored. And you presiding over it as hostess. With the help of your beautiful daughter, of course."

"Indeed, yes," Lenore agreed, flashing Virginia a veiled chiding glance, then turning her attention to Alice Larkin. "Your gown is charming. Is it from Paris?"

"Oh, yes." Mrs. Larkin was a lady of plain features, which the gown seemed to overwhelm. "Our son Conrad sent it to me from New York City. He married an heiress. A Northerner, but I must say she's been most generous to us. She's even invited us to their home on Long Island. Imagine, a home on Fifth Avenue and another on Long Island."

"And another in Paris, my dear," Percy said, stifling a yawn. "Next thing, Alice will be talking like a damn Yankee."

"Heaven forbid," Alice said. "But you can't deny, Percy, that her money has helped us."

Virginia laughed. "I'm sure you'll enjoy your visit north."

"Thank you, Virgie," Alice said gratefully. "You married a Yankee and you're certainly happy."

"Very," Virginia said, managing a smile.

Lenore had already turned her attention to the next couple and the Larkins moved on. Lenore and Virginia were kept busy for the next half-hour as they greeted the guests. Virginia knew her mother was tiring and wished Nanine and Phoebe would come to lend a hand. She cast a hasty glance around the hall, hoping to glimpse them.

Her attention was drawn to a gentleman who stood out above every other man in the milling crowd. Not only because of his expensive white silk evening clothes or because he was the tallest man in the room, but because there was an almost studied arrogance in his posture and in the way he observed the others in the room. He wore sideburns, a heavy beard, and a mustache, but they were neatly trimmed. He turned then and his eyes met Virginia's.

Her heart seemed to stop momentarily. She took a deep breath as the room began to swim. Her curiosity about him had turned to open fear. As if he was aware of it, his mouth widened in a smile, revealing beautiful, even teeth. His eyes mocked her as he gave a slight bow. The next moment he was elbowing his way through the crowd to reach her.

"What's wrong, daughter?" Lenore asked with concern. "You look faint."

"I have a fierce headache," Virginia said hastily. "I'm going upstairs for a headache powder. I'll send Nanine and Phoebe down."

"Please do," Lenore said crossly. "Of all the times for you to get a headache. I can't afford to get one, here by myself."

Virginia moved swiftly up the stairs, the guests parting to give her room. She caught a glimpse of Señor Cabrera, but gave a brief, negative shake of her head as he headed toward her. His smile was one of quiet resignation.

She headed toward Nanine's room, knowing she'd be the last to dress. But halfway along the corridor she paused and leaned against the wall. Her heart was pounding madly and she was trembling from head to foot.

Phoebe fastened the last hook on Nanine's dress. "Mauve is very becoming on you, Nan," Phoebe said, looking at her sister in the mirror.

"Just as green is on you," Nanine said. "Your gown is gorgeous. They do dress in New York City, don't they?"

"Yes, they do," Phoebe said, as she fastened a cluster of gardenias along one side of Nanine's coiffure. The effect was mildly flirtatious.

"Goodness," Nanine said, coloring. "I don't think that goes with my dull personality."

"You're not dull, sister," Phoebe said, touching her

cheek to Nanine's. "You're a loving and lovable lady. I wish I could have known Miles."

"So do I," Nanine said. "We loved each other dearly."

"I know. Virginia told me how you defied your mother and brought him to the island after the duel in which Martin was killed."

"I had to. Miles was ill and needed me. No—that's not quite right. I needed *him*."

"You needed each other. You gave him what his money could never buy. Happiness."

"It couldn't buy him good health, either," Nanine said sadly. "But at least we had a brief time together."

"I suppose I could say that too." A trace of pain touched Phoebe's voice. "Virginia and I didn't do so well with our marriages."

"As far as Virginia is concerned," Nanine said quietly, "she was completely to blame. Elias worshipped her."

"Do you think he still does?" Phoebe asked.

"You'd never know it from his letters," Nanine mused.

"That's true. I hope she can forget her loneliness. In fact, I think that Mexican may help her."

"He's just here on business," Nanine reminded her. "I think, with his help, we're going to improve our cotton crop. Just now it's so good it commands the highest prices in the world, but crossed with his it will be even better."

"Elias can take credit for his salesmanship," Phoebe said. "I wish Virgie didn't resent him so. He's made the island plantation far more profitable than the big one on the mainland, where more-ordinary cotton is grown."

"Virgie received a letter from him today that sent her into another rage," Nanine said. "And speaking of the mainland, it's time to go there and check the books. We're lucky to have Christopher Savard to overlook the mainland plantation. He's trustworthy and . . ."

The door to the parlor opened suddenly and Virginia

ran into the bedroom. Out of breath, she leaned against the wall, trying to recover her ability to speak.

Nanine went to her. "What's wrong?"

"Is it your mother?" Phoebe asked with concern.

"It . . . it's . . . him!" Virginia managed. "It's . . . Bradley Culver!"

"Here?" Nanine asked in horror. "Are you sure?"

"I'm positive. He smiled at me and bowed. He's grown a heavy beard. A disguise, I suppose. And a good one. But it's Brad."

"Stay here," Phoebe said. "I'll get out of this gown, put on something more practical, slip out the back door, and go directly to the Yankee army authorities on the mainland. They'll come at once and arrest him."

"No!" Virginia shouted. "No, Phoebe!"

"He's a condemned man. He should have been hanged long ago," Phoebe countered. "You can't let someone like that roam the island."

"No, Phoebe!" Nanine said. "Virgie's right. We can't afford the publicity. For Virgie's sake and for . . . Jimmy's."

"But what am I going to do?" Virginia asked. "I hate him! I wish they'd hanged him back when he was condemned. How can I face him? What does he want?"

"I wonder, too," Phoebe said. "He's risking his life coming here."

"The answer is obvious enough," Nanine said.

Virginia nodded but made no reply.

"He wants to see his son," Nanine said to Phoebe. "There's nothing unusual in that. And he's willing to risk his neck to see him."

"I'll never let him see Jimmy," Virginia said, anger slowly replacing her fear.

"If he makes no trouble and removes himself from this island immediately, I don't think we should do anything about him," Nanine reasoned. "He is truly an evil, vindictive man, but he's clever. He'll reveal the whole story if we arrange for his arrest."

"Perhaps all he wants is money," Phoebe suggested.

Virginia was calmer now. "It isn't money—he has no trouble getting that. I'm sure he's wealthy from his ill-gotten gains."

"Find out what he wants," Nanine said. "You can't make any decisions until you know."

"I know what he wants." Virginia sighed. "He wants to see his son. And if I refuse, he'll tell the story. He's merciless when crossed."

"How can you be so certain?" Phoebe asked.

"He did things on this island that hastened the Northerners' departure," Virginia replied. "He burned down a house. Even killed a man who was giving me trouble. A Northerner."

"My God!" Phoebe exclaimed.

Virginia looked at Nanine. "Didn't you tell her?"

Nanine shook her head.

"I suppose you wonder how I could have given myself to such a scoundrel," Virginia said to Phoebe. "I don't know. I—just don't know. But I did. Now I live in terror of him. And of what he can do to this family."

"Then why not let me slip out of the house and go to the mainland?" Phoebe pleaded.

"Oh God, no!" Virginia cried.

"See him," Nanine said in her quiet way. "Find out why he's here. You don't know for certain that he wants to see Jimmy."

"I'm certain he does," Virginia replied. "But you're right. I must see him. I have no choice."

Virginia embraced Nanine and left the suite. Nanine exhaled sharply.

"What next?" she asked. "Phoebe, this is going to be more serious than Virgie thinks."

"In what way? His mere presence here is enough."

"A man like Brad—an infamous scoundrel, to be sure—will not only want to see his son, he'll want him."

"We can't let that happen."

"No, we can't, and we won't. But I fear it's going to take some doing. Brad is no ordinary man. He's a very ominous person and extremely clever. Even though he comes of a fine family, for which Virgie and I are grateful, he's not someone to be trifled with. But come along now. We'd best get downstairs before Mama begins to suspect something."

"I'm frightened," Phoebe said. "And not only of Bradley Culver. This is the first formal affair I will attend as—a Hammond. And everyone knows I was once a slave. That's enough of a problem without Bradley showing up."

"Phoebe, I predict you'll not only be accepted, but warmly so."

"Are you saying they'll accept a Negro?" Phoebe's expression showed her disbelief.

"Perhaps not, but in your case it's different. You're a famous person. An actress. You've already gained acceptance. You weren't asked to leave the show. You left because you were afraid you'd be derided and hated."

"As soon as it was discovered I was a Negro, there were some bad incidents," Phoebe said. "I never talked about them, but they happened."

"In New York," Nanine reminded her. "Let's hope we're more gracious in the South. If one or two turn away, don't be alarmed. Most will accept you. It's Virgie I'm worried about. And that damned scoundrel who fathered her son."

Virginia descended the stairs, this time with no thought of making an impressive entrance. She stifled her irritation when she saw Carlos awaiting her at the foot of the staircase and eluded him with a graceful sidestep as he reached for her hand.

"Not now, dear Carlos. There is an old friend I must greet."

"But, señora, these are all old friends," he protested.

"This one is special." Her eyes were already seeking Brad. He was standing at the entrance to the library. Seeing him so handsome and relaxed annoyed her further. She knew he was fully aware of it, too. Carlos, undeterred, trailed her like a jealous lover.

He paused when he realized where she was headed. "So," he observed, "it is the bearded gentleman. Very handsome and distinguished."

Virginia gave him a sideways glance. "Please, Carlos, go away."

He gave a brief nod. A matronly woman eyed him curiously, then addressed him. Carlos's manner was courteous, but his eyes were still on Virginia. He saw the bearded man take her arm as he smiled down at her. He also observed her unsuccessful struggle to free herself. She disliked the man. Carlos smiled serenely. He was no longer jealous, even when the stranger led her through the French doors into the gardens. The music started up then and Carlos motioned to the ballroom. The matron smiled assent and they joined the others heading there, eager to dance to the lively rhythm of the string orchestra.

Outside, Brad guided Virginia to the area where the formal gardens were edged with tall shrubbery that shielded them from the house.

"You're as maddeningly beautiful as ever," he said, looking down at her. "I'm having a hard time keeping my hands off you."

"Damn you," Virginia said. "If you touch me, you'll regret it."

"I doubt that. You wouldn't dare turn me over to the Yankees. But I'm not here to resume where we left off sc long ago. But admit it, Virgie—we had some memorable hours."

"I scarcely recall . . ." She massaged the arm he finally released.

"Especially in your bed," he said. "Even in the old tool house where we first indulged in what I suppose one would call an amorous situation, though I have a better word for it."

She came to an abrupt stop beside an arbored rose garden. "What do you want? Why did you come here? If you expect me to resume our trysts, your conceit is boundless. I've had enough of you."

"There's a bench," he said. "We can talk better if we're comfortable. And stop glaring at me. Someone might come by and notice."

"That would be dangerous for you. There are many people here who might recognize you."

"I doubt it. This heavy beard is as good as a mask. An excellent disguise." He led her to the bench, but after she was seated he stood before her with one foot on the bench. "I was known as a ruffian, a man in a leftover Rebel uniform. I was skinny, too, with black hair and dirty clothing. I was a renegade and I looked it. Now I'm a gentleman, robust, well dressed, and clean. I spoke to a dozen men and none showed the slightest glimmer of recognition."

"I know all about you. Answer my question. Why did you come?"

He sat down very close to her; she didn't dare move away from him. He regarded her with an intimacy that served only to fuel her anger. If he noticed her reaction, he ignored it.

"Virginia, we were once lovers. Don't tell me you didn't enjoy it as much as I. Right now I'm sorely tempted to ask you to let me visit your bedroom tonight, as I did before."

"If you try that, I assure you I'll have you arrested, no matter what you threaten."

He nodded. "I believe you might. But why should there be any animosity between us? We're the parents of a son. I know how dearly you love him and I'm grateful for that."

"You came to see him, didn't you?"

"That's the main reason."

"If I let you see him, will you go away quietly and never come back?"

"I may go quietly, but I won't promise never to return. This boy is my son, too. Is he like me? Strong and healthy?"

"He's a year and a half old. A mere child. Still a baby, really."

"I'd forgotten that. I've been thinking about him a great deal lately, and somehow, in my mind, he was older. A lively youngster I could romp with. Inquisitive, mischievous, and filled with laughter. One whom I could pick up and toss in the air and listen to him squeal with delight. Whom I could take fishing or teach how to use a hunting rifle. Order him never to take impudence from anyone. Oh yes, I've been thinking about him too much. That's why I have to see him."

"Will you go away once you've seen him?"

"Virginia, he's my son. The only child I have ever fathered. I promise nothing except that for now I'll go away."

She tried to restrain the horror creeping into her voice, for she didn't want him ever to know how much she feared him.

"Does that mean you'll be back? That you'll take my son from me?"

"I didn't say that. For Christ's sake, Virginia, be reasonable. He's my son as much as yours. I have a right to enjoy him as well as you."

"I will never give him up," she said slowly. "Never!"

"Have I asked you to? I'm a man on the run. The only thing that lets me remain free is the fact that I have plenty of money and can pay my own way. I also have certain connections so that I can live in comfort even though I am wanted. Even if my fate is to die by suffocation or a broken neck. I don't deceive myself."

"What if I refuse you? What if I turn you over to the authorities? You don't have the upper hand, Brad. It's I who shows mercy to you. You have no right to make any demands of me."

He was still totally relaxed, unafraid of her threats. Seated beside him, she realized that, despite her anger and her fear of him, he still held a certain fascination for her, and she recalled the first time she'd met him. After the end of the war, he had recruited from desperate, bitter, war-weary ex-soldiers a small band that quickly became outlaws. They preyed on Yankees who came to the South to claim the spoils of war. And they operated against Southerners who cooperated with the Yankees. This band of terrorists became a monumental danger to carpetbaggers. When Bradley and his men were defied, they killed, raped and burned, robbed and looted. She could understand that he was now a wealthy man, for the amount of their spoils was known to have been ample.

He and his men had come to the island on a raiding mission. Virginia had been out riding that day on an inspection tour of the mansions so recently left by the Yankees who had come to the island. She'd been riding alone when she was intercepted by the outlaws, who mistakenly believed her to be a Northerner. They were about to begin passing her from man to man, but Brad had put a stop to it. Then he had pulled her down from her horse and embraced and kissed her with passion; thus had begun her affair with him. A kiss she had never forgotten, for it had aroused in her a passion to match his own, and he had recognized this.

Then, when she identified herself, he had promptly treated her with Southern courtesy and chivalry. But it had not ended there. He'd returned, more than once, and she'd eagerly awaited him by prearrangement. Each time she'd gone willingly into his arms, completely and gladly, as fierce passion ruled them both. His daring intrigued her. His strength and masculinity brought to her a desire she could not resist, until she found herself with child while simultaneously Brad was being sought as a murderer.

All this ran through her mind as she faced him now, long after her passion for him had been drained away by the shattering circumstances that had ended with the flight of her husband.

"I have never before or since met anyone as lovely or desirable as you," he said softly.

"Stop it!" she cried. "If you think there is any chance of resuming our past relationship, you are very much mistaken. And know right now that you will never take my son from me. Think also of the fact that I shall never tell my son who his father was or what manner of man he was. You will one day hang. It's inevitable. Shall I tell him to honor a man executed as a vicious murderer? I never want him to know you. I'm not even certain I shall allow you to see him now. I'm not proud that you're the father of my son."

"You'll let me see him," he said confidently. "You don't dare deny me that privilege, for you've just now admitted to me that you'll never allow him to know who I am or what I was. I can destroy that hope you have now. You'll do as I say—and I say I shall see my son. Now! Today!"

"You will see him for only one reason: that you promise never to come here again and never to—"

"I'll never make such a promise," Brad said angrily. "I've had enough of your histrionics!"

She suddenly realized she had said too much, fallen in a trap, perhaps of his making, for he was a clever man. She restrained an angry retort and softened her voice. "You came here today knowing you would be safe among a great many people. Who told you that we were holding a ball?"

"I don't recall. Charleston is full of gossip."

"You don't live in Charleston."

His smile mocked her. "You're right, but unless it becomes necessary, I'll not tell you where I live. Though it might surprise you some. I do not precisely trust you, my dear Virginia. I love you, but I do not trust you. I warn you, don't try any tricks. You may endanger your family."

"Thank you for warning me," she said coldly, aware that his threat wasn't an idle one. "Now I'll take you to see the child. The dance has already started, so we'll be inconspicuous."

"No rush. I'm enjoying myself. I've always liked being around women who are beautiful, spirited, and passionate. You're all three. And I always did like matching wits with you. You're a worthy adversary. But it took me to tame you."

Virginia restrained her anger with difficulty. "If you want me to say I enjoyed my trysts with you, very well, I'll admit it. You have an enormous appeal. But I'm no longer under your spell."

"I realize that," Brad said good-humoredly. "And I'm sorry. You never held back while making love with me."

"It's over. I don't wish to discuss it."

"Then let's discuss your family. How is Nanine, your older sister? I understand she married a very sick man who died and left her everything."

"Why do you ask? You seem to know all about her."

"And your half-sister, the actress Phoebe. She married a white officer. Too bad it didn't work out. She's quite a beauty."

"How do you know?" Virginia asked angrily. "You never met her."

"No, but I saw her perform in New York. She was blackmailed by one of your former slaves whom you shot."

Virginia's face revealed her amazement. "Where did you get your information about my family?"

His smile was sardonic. "I told you—I have ways. However, that came out in the Northern papers. I read them. I like to know both sides of a story."

"To me you are a blackguard and I wish I'd never had the misfortune of meeting you."

"Strange," he said with an impish grin, "you never told me that when our naked bodies were locked in embrace."

She shrugged. "I'm tired of this banter. If you wish to see your son, we shall go to the nursery."

'I'm ready." He rose and extended his hand, which she ignored. "What's the boy's name? I never asked. Wanted to hear it from you."

"James. I named him after my father."

Brad nodded. "I like the name. It's manly."

"Should I thank you for that?" she asked caustically. "You may be assured I never considered naming him Bradley."

"Now it's my turn to say I've had enough of this verbal sparring. I wish to see my son."

"Brad, just what are you up to?" Virginia asked wearily.

"Nothing really." He looked amused. "I'm puzzled by your behavior. It's as if you hate me. Have you forgotten we have a son born of our intimacy?"

"The brief intimacy is over. I feel nothing when I'm with you. If you were to make love to me—"

"I'm tempted," he broke in with a half-smile.

"It would be rape." She eyed him with frustration. "Haven't you heard anything I've said?"

"Every word, but I don't believe you. You're a passionate woman who enjoys passionate lovemaking."

"I have half a mind to go back in the house and report
your presence here."

"You wouldn't do that," he said confidently. "Just let me
see the boy and I'll leave quietly."

She made no objection when he took her arm, for that
was the courtly way of escorting a lady. She led him to the
kitchen, a building separate from the mansion and reached
by a covered walkway. When they passed through the
kitchen, Belle, the rotund, Negro cook, obediently moved
aside for them, but gave Virginia a disapproving look.

They entered the mansion through the large dining
room, where tables were set up and the banquet would
soon be served. It was closed off from the rest of the house
so that the servants could work unhindered. Those who
were busy at the table paid little heed to them. From the
dining room a door led into a large pantry. At one end was
a stairway that led to the second floor. They ascended to
the sleeping quarters, undetected by the many guests.

Virginia's heart was beating too fast, too hard. She felt
that her brow must be covered with perspiration, though it
was not. She concealed her terror as best she could. He
must never know how much she feared him.

When they reached the nursery, she held up a hand for
Brad to remain where he was, then opened the door and
looked in. Ivy, seated beside the crib, looked up quickly.
Virginia motioned for Brad to step into the room, then
said to Ivy, "Leave. At once. Wait in the hall."

Ivy showed her surprise at the terse order, but she
promptly complied. She glanced briefly at Brad, noting his
handsome features. He favored her with a warm smile, as
if he approved of Virginia's choice of a nurse for his son.
After Ivy closed the door, Virginia beckoned to him. He
approached the crib slowly, for once as unsure of himself

as Virginia was in his company. He looked down at his sleeping son.

"God!" he whispered in awe. "He looks like me."

"A little," she said coldly.

"A lot," he insisted, not taking his eyes off the child. "What color are his eyes?"

"Dark brown, like yours."

He bent over the crib, his hands resting lightly on either side of it. Virginia tensed, fearful that he was going to pick up the child and make a dash for it. But Brad only kissed the boy on the cheek, very lightly. Then one of his hands moved down to rest gently on the covered body. He stroked it reverently, then he straightened and put his arm about Virginia's waist, not possessively but with affection.

"Thank you, Virginia," he said softly. "To think that a part of me is lying in that crib fills me with a humility I didn't think I was capable of. No matter what happens to me, he'll still be here."

"To that I agree," Virginia said, with no trace of bitterness. "We must go now if we don't wish to wake him."

She didn't try to disengage Brad's arm. For a fleeting moment it seemed natural that they should stand this way, like proud parents looking at their sleeping son.

Brad sighed deeply. "My dear, you kept your bargain and I'll keep mine. It was worth risking my neck for this one glimpse of him. Promise me you'll continue to care for him as you have been doing."

"Do you need my word for that?"

"I reckon not. Thank you, Virginia. I only wish . . ."

"Brad, we can never take up where we left off. Those were different days, different times. We were reckless. I was irresponsible."

"Don't say that," he said fiercely as he gripped her shoulders and turned her toward him. "We were lovers. It was worthwhile and wonderful."

Her eyes dueled with his. "Only the baby is wonderful."

He drew her to him and pressed her hard against him. His face lowered and their lips met. His kiss was passionate, but Virginia did not respond. He released her.

"It was only for old times, Virginia. Don't be angry."

"It meant nothing to me, so I'm not angry, but I shall be if you don't leave here immediately. I presume you have some way of getting off the island and reaching the mainland without being observed."

"I have a boat hidden. I'll go. I don't dare risk any more delay. I believe there was one person in Charleston who may have thought he recognized me. He was unsure, but he may have had second thoughts."

"Please go, then. Now."

He nodded, looked back at the crib, then stepped up to it for one final glance. The baby stirred but didn't wake. They heard running steps outside. Brad reached under his coat for the gun in his back pocket. Virginia tensed.

It was Nanine who entered; she closed the door and set her back against it. "There's a contingent of Yankee soldiers just arrived, with a Lieutenant Johnson in charge. They're looking for you, Mr. Culver."

"Damn!"

"Nan, we have to hide him. We must!" Virginia said. "Where's the lieutenant?"

"Phoebe brought him to the library, but he insists on talking to you."

"The attic. They'll not go there. Nan, take him to the attic!" She turned to Brad. "I'm protecting you only for our son's sake."

"Come with me, Mr. Culver," Nanine said urgently. "Virgie, please go downstairs. Talk to the Lieutenant. Convince him there's no need to order a search of the house. I think they came only to warn us; I don't think they suspect he's on the island."

"I hope you're right," Virginia said. "Brad, don't come back. Please. I'll pray for your safety, but if you love your son and want no scandal to touch him, never come back."

Though he nodded, he remained silent. Nan grasped his arm desperately, and they headed down the corridor, observed only by Ivy. She pressed herself against the wall as they passed, to give them room.

He followed Nanine to a narrow back staircase that led to the large attic, where the only light came from two fan windows. The air was stale and hot.

She sighed with relief when they reached this hiding place. Brad showed his relief as well. He removed his coat, hung it over the back of a chair, and leaned against a stack of trunks.

"Thank you, Nanine," he said. "You likely saved my life."

"If I did," she said quietly, "it was to save my family the embarrassment your arrest would have brought us, Mr. Culver."

"I know. But it was worth the risk. I saw my son."

"Did you come to take him away?" Nanine asked.

"Would you blame me?"

"Yes. You're not fit to be a father to Jimmy, or any other boy."

"I know it's difficult for anyone to change his opinion of me after what I was. But I have changed. Completely, with no desire to go back to what I was."

Despite the gravity of the situation, Nanine managed a smile, though she spoke in an undertone. "You've certainly changed in appearance. You no longer look like a ruffian. I recall your appearance that day in court when you were on trial for your life."

"I owe you an apology for what I did to you." Brad also kept his voice low.

"You were being gallant," Nanine said. "And I'm glad

you identified me as the woman you came to see at Valcour, instead of Virgie. It worked out very well, especially since she was carrying your child, though she didn't know it until later that day, when she visited Dr. Hawley to learn the reason for her fatigue."

Brad nodded. "She visited me that day also. It gave me a lift, knowing I was leaving a son behind."

"You couldn't have known it would be a son," Nanine chided.

Brad smiled. "I told Virginia not to dare have anything but a son. Did she tell you? I mean, after she left me?"

Nanine shook her head. "I had to return to Valcour. There was a note at the hotel awaiting me, informing me that Miles, my husband, had taken a turn for the worse."

"I'm sorry he died," Brad said sincerely.

"So am I," Nanine said. "But the time we had together was glorious for both of us."

"You're a very courageous lady, Nanine. And a very good one. Would you consider me impertinent if I asked you a few questions about Virginia?"

"Not unless I think she would object to my answering them."

"All right," Brad said. "I'll ask you again—did Virginia tell you immediately, once she learned she was with child?"

"Not immediately," Nanine replied quietly. "She followed me back to the island the next day and told me then. I asked her to return to the mainland immediately and ask Dr. Hawley, our family physician, to come and do what he could for Miles. When she reached the doctor, he told her that Elias had returned from Washington and was at the hotel. Dr. Hawley suggested she go there. She did—and her world caved in."

"What do you mean?"

"Before she could tell him she was with child, in the hope he'd believe it was his, he told her he was going to

England, where he would handle the sale of our cotton. He has done very well for us, but he never returned."

"Why?" Brad asked in genuine surprise.

Nanine put a cautioning forefinger to her lips. "He knew about her condition and knew the child could not be his."

Brad looked perplexed. "I still don't understand."

"When you fought with Elias that night on Valcour and he captured you, you kicked him. He'd been shot in the groin during the war. The bullet was never removed. Your kick dislodged the bullet, giving him constant pain. He went to Washington for surgery to remove it. Following the surgery, he was given a letter from the surgeon, which he showed to Dr. Hawley. The letter stated that the only permanent damage was that he could never become a father."

"But you said that before Virginia could tell Elias she was pregnant, he informed her, in so many words, that he was abandoning her."

"Dr. Hawley, not knowing that my sister had a lover, believed Elias to be the father. You see, before Elias showed Dr. Hawley the letter, the good doctor congratulated him on his impending fatherhood."

"Oh, my God. Now I understand her bitterness toward me."

"Does she know you've reformed?" Nanine asked. "That is, if you're speaking the truth."

"I swear it, Nanine," Brad said with deep feeling. "No, Virginia doesn't know. And I doubt she'd care."

"She'd care as far as little Jimmy is concerned. That's one thing that has bothered her—the fact that her son's father is an outlaw and a murderer."

"I wish there were something I could do to wipe that out, but there isn't. I'm a wanted man for my past crimes.

They'll never show me mercy. All I hope is that the truth of the baby's paternity is never exposed."

"We hope that too. Before Elias left for England, he told Dr. Hawley that he wanted his name to be put on the birth certificate."

Brad spoke in an undertone. "If I ever see him, I'll thank him. If I don't, will you please thank him for me?"

"I will. And I'll tell Virginia you're leading a respectable life now."

"She'll never believe it."

"In time she will. If it's any help to you, I believe you."

He walked over, bent down and kissed her lightly on the cheek. "Thank you, Nanine. Thank you for telling me the story. It must have been one hellish day for Virginia."

"I didn't know the baby was yours until Elias walked out on her. That was the same day you were sentenced to be hanged. The only other person, besides Dr. Hawley, who knows the true identity of the baby's father is Phoebe. And Elias."

"I appreciate his acknowledging the child as his," Brad said. "I just wish he would forgive Virginia and come home."

"Why?" Nanine asked.

"So Jimmy could have a father," Brad said irritably. "Four women in the house. Not a single man. It's unnatural. Not the proper environment for a boy to be brought up in."

Nanine agreed. "We'll see to it that he has playmates."

"I'm sure you will," Brad replied. "But it's not the same as having a father who can help him grow up in a manly fashion."

He noticed Nanine regarding him cynically and said, "I know what you're thinking. Try to forget what I've been. I'd like you to know, and to tell Virginia, that my grandfather was a three-term governor of the state of Georgia. As for my parents, who are now dead, my father was a senator and a lawyer. He was born to wealth, as was my mother. She was a renowned hostess in Georgia and Washington. She also did a lot of charitable work for the underprivileged. I was attending West Point when the war broke out. I became bitter because the South lost."

"We know all that," Nanine said, much to his surprise. "Virginia told Phoebe and me. She also told Dr. Hawley."

"Who told Virginia?"

"Captain Delaney. He admired you, even though he wanted to see you punished for your crimes."

Brad was amazed. "I had no idea. Well, thank God she knows something good about my background, even if not of me." He paused. "Does she grieve for Elias?"

"I have no idea," Nanine said. "It's not always easy to know what's in Virginia's mind. I had no idea you and she were lovers. Certainly Elias didn't suspect." She looked thoughtful. "All I can say is that whenever she receives a letter from Elias, she goes into a rage. It's because his letters are so impersonal. Nothing but business."

Brad smiled. "I can picture her. She's a spirited woman. and a damned persuasive one. I can see her even now, using her womanly attributes to persuade the lieutenant I'm not here."

Nanine gave him a chiding look. "Be grateful she has them."

Virginia remained in the nursery, walking back and forth until she had composed herself sufficiently to hear from the lieutenant his reason for coming to the island with a contingent of soldiers. She went over to the child's bureau and bent down to check her coiffure in the small mirror. She tucked a few strands of hair back in place, then opened the door to summon Ivy, who was still in the hallway a short distance from the door.

"Stay with my son," Virginia ordered. "And should you be questioned by soldiers, say nothing about the gentleman I brought to the nursery."

"I promise," Ivy said, her concern matching Virginia's, though she had no idea why her mistress was so upset.

Virginia went directly to the library. She was pleased to see that the lieutenant was young and reasonably handsome. He looked extremely strong and confident, and she wondered if she would be able to convince him that Bradley Culver was not on the island. At the same time, she knew she had to be cautious not to let him know that she suspected Brad was the reason why the lieutenant and his soldiers had come.

Phoebe made the introductions and excused herself, knowing Lenore would be fuming because she was alone again.

Virginia extended a gloved hand. The lieutenant took it and bowed. "Mrs. Birch, I apologize for the intrusion, but we believe an outlaw named Bradley Culver might have come to the island. At least, the rumor in Charleston is that he's been seen there."

"Please sit down, Lieutenant," Virginia said graciously, motioning toward the fireplace. "May I order you a julep?"

"On any other occasion I'd be most grateful," he replied, walking over to one of the two chairs before the fireplace. However, he remained standing until Virginia had seated herself, clasped hands resting demurely in her lap.

She looked directly into his eyes as she asked, "What is the problem, Lieutenant Johnson?"

He studied her just as intently as he replied, "Bradley Culver, ma'am."

"The outlaw?" She gave a good imitation of surprise and concern. "I do hope not."

"So do I," he replied. "I feel very bad about this

intrusion, especially when you're giving such a grand affair."

"I'm sure you do," she replied sympathetically. "Though I must say I'm puzzled as to why you've come here. I'm sure that it's concerned, in some way, with your duty."

"Yes, ma'am. As you know, Captain Delaney is no longer the commandant in the city, but I was instructed to refer to Bradley Culver's files if there were rumors that he was in the vicinity. There have been. I checked the records and learned he was captured here by your husband."

"Yes," she replied quietly. "But he escaped."

The lieutenant smiled wryly. "He's clever, extremely intelligent, and very ruthless. He even escaped from us when he was about to be hanged."

"I know his reputation, Lieutenant. However, I must say his behavior the first time I met him was gallant. But then, I'm a Southerner and he hated only Northerners. Still, I can't imagine why he'd want to return to the island. The people who owned homes and property here before the war now have them back. The Northerners couldn't make a go of it, and I purchased their homes for the back taxes—which is exactly how they got them."

"I understand that in some cases you did more than was necessary." The lieutenant was obviously under Virginia's spell.

"Very little." She leaned forward slightly, aware that the low décolletage of her gown would fall free and reveal much of her full, well-formed breasts. Her tone became more intimate and grateful as she said, "I take it you came to warn us."

Color slowly suffused the lieutenant's face as his attention was distracted by the generous display of Virginia's bosom. He was obviously affected; he seemed not to have heard her.

"I said, Lieutenant," Virginia repeated, "that I assume your reason for coming to the island was to warn us."

"Th-that's correct, Mrs. Birch," he said, composing himself. "He may have come here to seek revenge against your husband, who's a Northerner."

Virginia leaned forward a little more, aware, though seeming not to be, of the lieutenant's quickened breathing. "If you wish to search the house, you may. I'm sure our guests won't mind the inconvenience. But are you aware that my husband has been in England for well over a year?"

"I didn't know that, Mrs. Birch." The lieutenant stood up. "I won't inconvenience you further. However, I'll have my men make a sweep of the island. We must ascertain that he isn't hiding somewhere on it. This would be a perfect sanctuary for him."

"I appreciate your thoroughness, Lieutenant." Virginia rose slowly. "And I thank you for considering our guests. I know I would recognize Mr. Culver, and if I should hear of his being sighted here, I'll send you word immediately."

"We'll be beholden to you, ma'am."

She extended a hand. "Good luck, Lieutenant Johnson. And good day."

He saluted smartly and let his eyes rest briefly on the white skin swelling above Virginia's gown. What he didn't know was that before Virginia had sat down, she'd lowered the brief off-the-shoulder sleeves so that the neckline of her gown would fall open. She was pleased that he didn't wish her to escort him out; she couldn't leave the library without adjusting the gown. Her bosom was almost completely exposed. She was glad she'd chosen the more friendly tête-à-tête before the fireplace with them facing each other, rather than sitting behind her father's large mahogany desk. Her demure manner belied any boldness on her part, and using her charms to distract him gave Brad a chance for more time. How much longer would his luck hold, she wondered. A few moments after the lieutenant had left, Phoebe entered the room. Obviously she'd been watching the closed door.

Virginia was standing before a wall mirror, raising the sleeves of her gown and adjusting the bodice so that it would be less revealing. She addressed Phoebe's reflection in the mirror. "Go to the attic and tell Nan and Brad the house won't be searched."

Nanine moved to one of the dusty fan windows and cautiously peered out. She saw the soldiers ready to sweep the island.

"I don't believe the Yankees are going to search the house," she said. "They're going to search the island, however. They're positioning for it now. Will they find your boat?"

"No. I tied it up on one of the other docks alongside the boats belonging to the island. I'll go as soon as it's dark."

"I wish you good fortune," Nanine said. "And I hope we never see you again."

"You will," he said. "If my luck holds out."

"I pray that it does, and I also hope that something happens to scare the daylights out of you so you'll never find your way back to this island."

The door leading to the attic opened and closed, alerting them both. They heard muted footsteps ascending the stairs. Nanine remained where she was. Brad concealed himself behind the stack of trunks, drawing his gun as he did so.

Nanine breathed a sigh of relief as soon as Phoebe stepped into view. "It's all right, Brad," she said. "It's our sister. Phoebe, this is Brad Culver."

Phoebe gave him a mere nod as he stepped out from his

hiding place. "Virgie sent word the house won't be searched, Mr. Culver. However, the island will."

"Thanks, Miss Phoebe," Brad said. "This is scarcely the time to mention it, but I want to compliment you on your performances in New York City. I saw you several times."

"Thank you," Phoebe said graciously. "Nan, you'd better come downstairs."

"Mama must really be fussing," Nanine said.

"She is, but our continued absences might arouse suspicion among our guests."

"Do they know whom the lieutenant is looking for?" Nanine asked.

"No. Naturally, with the lieutenant's presence and seeing the soldiers through the windows, the guests were curious, but I told them the soldiers were searching for an escaped prisoner. You know your mama would be upset if she thought it was Mr. Culver."

"May I bring you some food?" Nanine asked Brad.

"No, thanks," he replied. "It might arouse suspicion if you were seen. I'll leave as soon as darkness falls and the island quiets down. I have a good view of the water and I can see the soldiers leave."

Nanine sent Phoebe on ahead and paused at the nursery to instruct Ivy not to leave the room. Nanine added that she would bring food up for her and Jimmy.

Virginia walked swiftly down the covered walkway to the kitchen. She was nervous and worried. So many things had happened, and so many more were likely to if Brad was seen by the soldiers. She entered the steaming, noisy kitchen, where a dozen girls were bustling about under Belle's supervision.

"Whut yo' wants?" she demanded as Virginia approached her. "Sho' gots mo' trouble'n I kin handle now, 'thout yo' bustin' in heah."

"I only wish to be sure everything will be ready on time, Belle."

"Yo' evah knowed when it ain't? Goin' to say right now, yo' git to fix any mo' big soirees like this one, I gonna quit."

"Five or ten years ago, I'd have had you whipped for saying that," Virginia snapped.

"Ain't no whuppin' no mo'," Belle said confidently. "Yo' evah says that again, I sho' gonna quit."

"If dinner isn't served on time, and if it's not up to expectations, you won't have to quit. I'll fire you."

Belle laughed heartily. "Ain't worried none. Yo' fires me an' my man gonna leave too, an' yo' sho' cain't do 'thout Moses. He run the place an' yo' knows it, so wants no mo' fancy talk from yo', missy. That all I gots to say."

Virginia walked out into the coolness of the walkway. The banquet would be perfect. Belle had never turned out a poor meal.

Virginia was tempted to risk a quick trip to the attic to be sure all was well, but she decided against it.

Belle's impudence did nothing to ease Virginia's raw nerves, but she knew that a lot of Belle's talk was bluster. She loved Valcour, and she loved the soirees. It gave her a chance to wear the red satin uniform Virginia had ordered for her. She was so huge that all her uniforms had to be specially made.

Virginia knew she should have had more sense than to go to the kitchen, for Belle made a habit of riling her, but she couldn't remain still and she needed a few moments to calm down before she rejoined her mother. Her spirits rose when she saw Phoebe approach, obviously in search of her.

Phoebe said, "Brad is safe and won't leave until after dark, when the soldiers have departed and the house is quiet. As you know, he has a good view of the water from the fan windows."

"That's a relief," Virginia said. "Will you please rejoin Mama? I want to mingle with the guests. I'm still shaken by Brad's appearance, and since so much time went into planning this affair, I'd like to enjoy it. Besides, it may help to calm me."

"A little champagne would help more," Phoebe said. "Pick up a glass on your way to the ballroom."

"I'm not interested in dancing," Virginia said. "I just want to mingle."

"I hope you have a chance. Carlos's eyes haven't stopped searching for you. Nanine believes his interests concern only the cotton you grow on the island. I believe it concerns you."

"He's very gallant," Virginia replied, managing a casual tone. "And whatever his interests are, mine concern the cotton he raises. Don't forget, I'm a married woman, and I'm certain that, like all Mexicans, Carlos is a deeply religious man and would respect my marriage vows."

"A gentleman can respect a lady and still desire her," Phoebe said. "And speaking of gentlemen, Bradley Culver gives every evidence of being one, even with a gun in his hand."

"He's a brigand," Virginia said sternly. "And he usually has a gun in his hand. I'll be glad when he's off the island."

"So will I," Phoebe agreed. "He said he'd leave when the place quieted."

"The question is, how soon will he return?" Virginia said tensely.

"Do you think he will?"

"I know he will." And I'm terrified he'll kidnap Jimmy."

"You could be wrong, Virgie. I believe he's a wanderer. Also, a man who has a strong desire for a variety of women."

"I'm certain of that. I just wish his interest stopped with

women. But he was deeply affected when he saw Jimmy in his crib."

"Virgie, you must relax." Phoebe brightened. "Oh, Carlos has spotted you. I'll return to your mother. Take him around and introduce him to the folks here. And stop worrying."

Virginia gave her a reassuring nod and turned to Carlos. "Thank you for seeking me out," she said, managing a pleased smile. "Will you have a glass of champagne with me?"

"Ah," he beamed, "I can scarcely believe my ears."

They paused at a long table set against a wall. It was covered with a gleaming white lace cloth. On it were enormous cut-glass bowls of punch and sterling-silver trays on which were crystal glasses filled with sparkling champagne. He took two and gave one to Virginia. She sipped hers gratefully.

"Exactly what I needed to relax," she said, managing a smile.

"You seemed to have a lot on your mind." He eyed her over his glass, which he'd yet to touch. Virginia's champagne was half-gone. If he noticed, he gave no sign of it, but when she emptied her glass, he took it from her and handed her another.

"The gentleman you saw me with is a friend of my husband, who, as you know, is in England. Mr. Davenport brought me the unsettling news that my husband has been ill with a cold that settled in his lungs."

"I knew you were upset," Carlos said quietly. "But I thought it was because you were angry with him. I couldn't help but notice the possessive way he took your arm, and your unsuccessful effort to free yourself."

"I am impetuous," Virginia admitted. "And my seeming anger was really impatience because I thought he wasn't being completely honest with me. I feared my husband's

illness was more serious than Mr. Davenport stated. I
hadn't heard from Elias in several weeks. Naturally, when
I learned he'd been seriously ill, I felt Mr. Davenport could
have contacted me sooner."

"Perhaps he was unable to," Carlos reasoned.

"I doubt that," Virginia said, managing an injured air.
"He'd been in this country for at least two weeks.
Unfortunately, I never cared to have my husband associate
with him. He has a rather unsavory reputation. Not only
because of gambling, but with the ladies."

"In that case, I hope you put him in his place."

"I'm not certain," Virginia said, pleased that the lie
slipped so easily off her tongue. "But at least he's gone."

"I'm delighted," Carlos said. "I was beginning to think
I'd not have a moment in your company."

"We have only a few moments before dinner, and I'd like
to introduce you to some of the guests."

"If I must," Carlos said, chiding her gently.

"We'll have time to talk later," Virginia said, giving him
a flirtatious glance. She took another sip of champagne and
set her glass on a table; Carlos placed his beside hers.

She made a point of introducing him to the islanders,
who were charmed by his gracious manner. She wanted
them to know the man who was going to make them
wealthy beyond their wildest dreams.

She caught sight of her mother being escorted into the
dining room by a white-whiskered gentleman wearing a
Confederate uniform. Virginia recognized him as Colonel
Zachary Spires, whose plantation was only a few miles
from the Hammonds' on the mainland.

Lenore had forgotten her irritation at her daughters in
the pleasure of having a gentleman pay her attention. The
other guests followed, and the bustle and laughter soon
quieted as each sought out his name card. Once the guests
were settled, the servants began serving the meal. The

tables were placed to form a U. Virginia sat next to her mother at the head of the table. The colonel was on Lenore's right, where Nanine was supposed to have sat. Carlos sat between Virginia and Nanine. Phoebe was also seated at the head of the table, as were two couples who lived on the island.

Dinner was a brilliant affair. The servants, in their red coats and white gloves, served the best food obtainable in the postwar months. At the close of the meal, Virginia rose to introduce Carlos, their guest of honor.

"Ladies and gentlemen, since my father is no longer with us to make the usual speech, I will take his place and do my best. Valcour is our island now, all of it. The Yankee soldiers who forced us to flee have now gone.

"As you know, the soldiers were assigned here to conduct an experiment. They wished to see how the slaves, now free, would manage without the supervision they'd always known. It was an abysmal failure. Many of the slaves thought freedom meant they no longer had to work, even for themselves. Perhaps that was our fault—I'm not sure. Anyway, the island soon became spoils of war, with those unsavory people from the North who came here to buy our homes for back taxes. They, too, believed they could get on here, grow cotton and become rich. They failed as miserably as the ex-slaves. It became necessary that we get them off the island so that the families who belonged here might return and restore Valcour to what it once was—a small paradise and a successful series of plantations growing the finest cotton in the world.

"Once again, we're on our way to great success. We are about to engage in producing a new type of cotton that will be superior to what we now know. With the experience and willingness of our good neighbor from Mexico, Señor Cabrera, and his type of cotton, we will very soon begin improving cotton over the entire South. It will be our salvation in these times of stress and poverty resulting from the war.

"Every family is now back on our beautiful island of Valcour, and I assure you this social affair is only the first of many. We are very proud of how we regained and once again restored the island after the carpetbaggers left. We intend to make it even better in the future. Mama wishes me to tell you how pleased she is that you could come. My sisters, Nanine and Phoebe, are also. As you probably already know, Phoebe has joined us after a very successful career in the New York theater.

Lonzo Parker, a florid, white-haired man, stood up. "Saw her in New York. Cost me two dollars and fifty cents and the same for my wife. We went back three more times. Couldn't keep my feet still when she danced. Swear I never saw anything so pretty in my life. Made me feel twenty years younger. And Helen felt just the same."

"Yes, Phoebe," Helen Parker added, "your singing was as good as your dancing. You're extremely talented."

"Why not give a performance now?" Lonzo suggested.

Phoebe, stunned that Virginia had made it a point to call her "sister," stood up. She was no longer afraid.

"Thank you, Mr. and Mrs. Parker. I'll dance for you as soon as I collect my orchestra."

Phoebe left the table and called one of the red-coated servants to her side. "Go down to the quarters and get me anybody who can play music. Have them bring tambourines, bones to clack, and banjos. Drums, too. And hurry!"

The guests returned to the ballroom and lined the walls for the performance. Within twenty minutes the musicians appeared, uncertain and uneasy. Phoebe had them stand next to the string orchestra.

"Yo' plays yo' kin' o' music," she said, reverting to her slave dialect, "an' I follahs yo' if I kin. Or yo' follah me, whatevah yo' likes. Goin' to do Rockin' de Heel, some taps, an' if it go good, yo' plays the music fo' de cakewalk."

They wasted no time. To the accompaniment of the discordant music, Phoebe began the wild steps to Rockin' de Heel and went into the exaggerated limp that was part of the dance. The string orchestra joined in, improvising with their instruments and doing it well. At the end of the dance, there was a smattering of applause at first and then a wave of it as those who were reluctant succumbed to the music, the dancing, and the gay mood it had created.

A few were heard to comment sarcastically at the idea of a girl with Negro blood dancing at a ball. Someone else mentioned the fact that the Hammond family practically controlled the island and had restored it with their own money, so it might be well to accept this girl. In any case, the food, drink, and high spirits overcame any objections to Phoebe.

Phoebe began to tap, something at which she was expert, and now the music created a still-livelier atmosphere. The clacking bones, the shaking of the tambourines, the rhythm of two drums, makeshift affairs but wholly in keeping with this kind of dancing, and two banjos carried the melodies. The strings of the white orchestra found the rhythm and followed it.

Phoebe stopped to catch her breath. "I thank all of you," she said. "Dancing is the most fun in life, I think. I'll prove it to you. Please—let's everyone do a cakewalk. There's no cake, but whoever wins will be given a bottle of fine brandy. All you do is line up in couples and move your feet any way you wish. Whoever dances the most intricate steps or the most exaggerated steps, wins. Good luck. Here we go."

She took Carlos's arm and he quickly fell into the rhythm of the dance. Since he was Virginia's guest, the line quickly formed. Sometimes laughter drowned out the music. Virginia and Nanine stood aside to act as judges.

They selected one couple, almost at random, for the dancing was so bizarre that it was impossible to pick the best pair. At the end Phoebe was applauded long and loudly. A few, no more than a half-dozen, did not join in, but the rest of the party accepted Phoebe without question. Carlos bowed and kissed her hand.

The dancing ended the party. Lenore had completely forgotten her pique at her daughters and enjoyed Phoebe's performance as much as most of the guests. She took her place at the door after saying good night to Colonel Spires. Virginia, Nanine, and Phoebe joined her to help with the farewells.

When the last of the guests departed, Lenore excused herself and went upstairs. The girls followed the few stragglers to the dock and watched the last of the boats slip away in the darkness. They turned then and strolled slowly back to the mansion.

Virginia felt a warm glow of pride as she looked up at the house, named Willowbrook, still aglow with lights. She glanced warily at the fan window, which was visible from this side of the island, and was relieved to see it was dark. It would be like Brad to have some kind of light. She was certain that he was still as daring and reckless as ever. His audacious visit to the island, dressed as an invited guest, was proof.

Phoebe broke into her thoughts. "I'm grateful to both of you for calling me sister in front of all those people. It was daring."

"They'll accept you," Virginia said placidly.

"Perhaps," Phoebe admitted. "Though it will be reluctantly, and mostly because of the fact that you're so influential—and wealthy."

"So are you," Nanine countered.

"Ill-gotten gains," Phoebe said soberly.

"Oh, I don't know," Virginia said. "I'm certain that every gentleman who patronized your mother's fancy house felt he got his money's worth. I met your mother. I'm sure she would have seen to it."

"I expect she would have," Phoebe agreed with a smile.

"I'm sorry I never had the opportunity to meet her," Nanine said. "I'm sure, Phoebe, that once she saw you when you went to visit her, she loved you."

"She certainly helped us out of a tight jam," Virginia said. "And she left you a wealthy young woman."

"Yes," Phoebe admitted. "Mama and I became close in her final days. I was with her the five weeks before she died. Sam is still running the whorehouse she willed him."

"I wonder if Brad is still in the attic," Virginia mused.

"God forbid," Nanine said. "Want me to go up and find out?"

"No. He'll go this time. It's his return I dread."

"He may have more sense than to come back," Phoebe reasoned.

"He'll be back," Virginia insisted. "I know him."

"Does he still love you?" Phoebe asked.

"I doubt he ever did," Virginia replied matter-of-factly. "He would never be faithful to any woman. He's a wanderer, to put it kindly."

"Did he notice Señor Cabrera?" Nanine asked.

"If so, he didn't mention him," Virginia replied. "However, Carlos noticed Brad. I said Brad had just returned from England where he'd seen my husband and learned Elias was very ill."

"Good heavens, Virgie," Nanine exclaimed. "Why did you tell such a lie?"

"Carlos saw Brad take my arm and my unsuccessful attempts to free myself. I had to think of something. I told him I was annoyed because he hadn't called on me sooner. I also gave his name as Mr. Davenport."

"You haven't changed," Nanine said, shaking her head.

"As far as Brad's concerned, I have," Virginia said.

"What about Carlos?" Nanine asked. "I may as well refer to him as Carlos since I expect he'll be around quite a bit."

Phoebe smiled. "I think so too."

"I'm very excited about our deal with him," Virginia said.

"I think you should consult Elias," Nanine said.

"Never," Virginia said heatedly. "And don't spoil my evening by referring to him. He can't even write a civil letter."

"I almost think you still love him," Nanine said.

"So do I," Phoebe added.

"You're both wrong," Virginia said. "If I were to think seriously about remarriage—and first I'd have to get a divorce—I have someone else in mind."

"Carlos," Nanine said in her quiet way.

"Yes. He'd be a good father to Jimmy."

"That's one point Brad made in the attic," Nanine recalled. "He was upset that his son would grow up in a house full of women."

Virginia felt fear clutch at her heart.

"When he said that," Nanine went on, "I couldn't help but smile. He was quite upset."

"So am I, after hearing that."

The women had reached the house and paused to admire it.

"Where's Mama?" Virginia asked.

"She went upstairs," Nanine said. "Happy as a clam because of that wonderful Colonel Spires."

"That really made the ball a success for her," Virginia replied. "Why don't you both go upstairs? I'll lock the doors."

"Thanks, Virgie. I am tired. In spite of Brad, it was a beautiful soiree. Phoebe really livened it up."

"Thanks to Phoebe, we sent everyone home in good spirits," Virginia added.

"I was terribly frightened, but I didn't want you to know," Phoebe said. "I got a few snubs when I tried to engage in conversation with some of the guests. And I suppose I'll meet more of it, but I think I can cope with it now."

"We'll help you," Virginia said with quiet assurance. "Just remember, you're Papa's daughter. James Hammond was as much your papa as he was ours. Papa told me that once. And remember too that Nanine and I love you. Now run along. I want time to do some thinking."

Virginia lingered on the grounds until she was certain that Phoebe and Nanine had gone upstairs. Her thoughts switched from Brad to Elias and then to Carlos. She wished, in a way, that she could write to Elias about the steps she was taking regarding the cotton, but she'd not give him the satisfaction of having any part in the success she was certain would result from the transaction with Carlos.

The house was quiet when she went in. After she put out the lamps and candles and locked the doors, she went into the dining room and poured herself a generous brandy. She drank it quickly, refilled the glass, and headed for the stairs. She knew that she'd been doing this too often recently, but she needed sleep and the spirits would help her attain it.

Upstairs, she paused long enough to check with Ivy, who lay on a cot that she had placed beside Jimmy's crib. She told Virginia that no one had come except Nanine when she brought up supper for her and the child. She'd also stopped in a few minutes ago. Reassured, Virginia planted a light kiss on her sleeping son. Then, after cautioning Ivy to scream if any intruder should enter the room, she went to her suite. There, she consumed the generous contents of the glass while she prepared for bed. The brandy relaxed her, and in minutes she was in a deep sleep.

TWO

Virginia awakened early, alert and eager to head for the mainland. She donned a morning gown and lace cap, then went directly to the nursery. Jimmy, already dressed, was running about the room, his legs strong but not always certain. He was a good-natured child, and when he fell he picked himself up with a squeal of delight. He was carrying a good-sized soft rubber ball when she entered, but tossed it aside at the sight of her and ran to her outstretched arms. She gathered him close and rained kisses on his face. He babbled unintelligibly as she talked loving nonsense to him for a few minutes, then set him down and turned her attention to his nursemaid.

"You look tired, Ivy. Didn't you get any sleep?"

"No, Miss Virginia. I wanted to make certain Master Jimmy was in no danger."

"Thank you." She made a mental note to bring Ivy back a little gift as a reward. "Nanine and Phoebe are sleeping late; but I'm sure they will spell you so you may get some rest. "I must hurry now—I'm going to the mainland."

"I'll be taking Jimmy downstairs now," Ivy said. "We'll have breakfast in the play area outside."

"Splendid," Virginia approved. "He has his sandbox and enough toys to keep him busy. You, too, I dare say."

"The fresh air will wake me up," Ivy replied politely.

Virginia gave her son a farewell kiss and hastened to the stairway. She was halfway down, her mind concerned with

49

the day ahead of her, when she became aware of Carlos smiling up at her.

"Good morning, Carlos," she said, delighted to see him. "Have you breakfasted?"

"No, señora," he replied, his bow courtly. "I wanted the honor of being at your side."

She laughed. "Are you always so gallant?"

When she reached him, he took her hand, kissed it lightly, and slipped it around his arm.

"Are you?" she persisted.

"Only when the lady is as beautiful as you," he replied lightly. "And that is rare."

"I'm famished," she said when he seated her. "I think I was too excited yesterday to eat. At least, I don't recall eating. I hope you did."

"You may be assured of it." He sat down beside her. "Come to think of it, you took only a few bites of food. I got the impression you had something on your mind. You mentioned your husband's illness, but I felt there was more."

"Nothing serious," she lied. "My son had an upset stomach yesterday and I was concerned."

"You wouldn't be a devoted mother if you weren't," Carlos said.

"Well, I can't be with him today," she went on. "I'm going to the mainland to check with our overseer, Chris Savard. He's very competent and trustworthy."

"That is always a relief."

One of the kitchen girls entered with a large tray on which was a platter of freshly fried eggs and ham. The aroma of biscuits, still steaming, filled the room. A large silver pot of coffee was already on the table.

Carlos sampled the contents of his plate, nodded approval, then spoke. "How soon will you leave?"

"In an hour. I'll pack enough to see me overnight. I always stay at a hotel, even though our home is available."

"I suppose it has stood a long time."

"No. It was burned down by Union sodiers and had to be completely rebuilt. My husband, Elias, found the plans to the original dwelling and worked with an architect to restore it."

"Since there is so much work here, why would your husband wish to conduct business in England?" Carlos paused. "Or am I intruding on something very private? An estrangement, perhaps?"

"Oh no." Virginia dismissed that with an airy wave of her hand "The cotton we grow on this island is superior to anything on the mainland. You've seen it, so you know I'm speaking the truth. Elias felt that in order to get the best price, he should be there."

"I can see his logic, but once that was accomplished, couldn't he have found someone trustworthy to carry on for him? What I am saying—"

"What you are saying, my dear Carlos, is that I seem to be a passionate woman and you don't understand how I can do without the love and comfort of a man."

"What really puzzles me, señora," Carlos looked directly into her eyes, "is how he can content himself in London, knowing he cannot savor the bliss of taking you in his arms."

"I'm afraid you are intruding." Virginia reached for the silver coffeepot. Carlos held his cup while she filled it, then she half-filled her own. His inquisitiveness made her uncomfortable, but she cautioned herself against getting angry; he must never have even the slightest suspicion regarding Elias's absence.

"Forgive me, señora." His smile was apologetic.

She decided to elaborate. "However, it is not for the reason you stated—an estrangement. It's business. As for my loneliness—I have far too much to attend to here. When I'm lonely, I turn to Jimmy—our son."

"Yes, señora—I can see how the boy brings you close to your husband, even though an ocean separates you. Forgive my curiosity."

Virginia decided to direct the conversation away from her. "I'm surprised you aren't married."

"When I marry," he replied, "I will wish to have the time to give my wife the attention she deserves. You see, I come of a large family and I am the oldest. I have the responsibility not only of the business but of seeing that all goes well with my sisters and brothers."

"Are they grown?"

"Oh yes" he replied. "Four sisters, three of them married. I had that to attend to. And four brothers, two of whom are married. Their problems are my problems."

"I should think they would want to live their own lives, once they've married," Virginia ventured.

"Oh, they do, but they have their homes on the family ranch and it is a custom to discuss all problems. It keeps the family close, Since my parents are dead, I am the patriarch."

Virginia realized it wasn't so different from what went on in her own family. They, too, shared one another's problems.

She and Carlos had a second helping, then she excused herself and went upstairs. Carlos assured her he would be at the dock with his baggage, awaiting her.

True to his word, he was. Virginia's baggage had already been brought to the small dock by a houseboy, as had Carlos's. She'd made a swift change from her morning gown to a traveling dress of sea-foam green. The tiered skirt was piped with pink, as was the ruffled bustle. Her straw bonnet was edged with pink and green silk rosettes.

It was held firmly to her head by a satin bow tied beneath her chin, giving her a coquettish look, but her manner when she reached the dock was almost formal. A servant stood in the boat to help them aboard. Carlos managed without help, then turned to extend both hands to Virginia. She handed him her silk-fringed parasol, then let him assist her.

Once they were seated, the servant started rowing. He was a tall, strong, husky Negro, and the sinewy muscles of his arms bulged beneath his white cotton shirt. There was plenty of water traffic and they limited their conversation to talk of that until they reached the dock at Charleston. The servant transferred their baggage to a carriage that Carlos rented. As Carlos drove; his attention was riveted on the burned-out buildings and other scars of the war. As in other sections of the city, not a great deal of restoration had been done. The South was bankrupt, and in the aftermath of a lost war, there was not a great deal of ambition to set things right.

There were rows of gutted warehouses, residences, and stores. A large part of the city had been set afire by Rebel officers who wished to leave nothing for the Yankees to acquire.

"It looks as if the war ended yesterday," Carlos remarked with distaste as he viewed the blackened ruins.

"Charleston will once again be a beautiful, bustling city," Virginia said confidently. "Though the progress may not be visible, it has already started. It will be even bigger than before. And our cotton will sell better than ever. There's nothing ahead for us, Carlos, but a bright future."

"Your attitude is proper and pleasing to hear. I shall be honored to be a part of it."

They left that area of the city and Carlos slowed the horse so that Virginia could point out places of interest. She told him of life here during the war and of how

various families had fared. She pointed out chimneys that
stood alone, mute testament to the destruction perpetuated
by Union soldiers. She cried out with excitement when
they approached a white-pillared plantation house set in a
park.

"Do you recall the gentleman who was with Mama,
wearing a Confederate uniform? He held the rank of
colonel during the war."

"Oh yes," Carlos said. "Your mama introduced us. I had
a brief but pleasant conversation with him."

"He lives there. Aren't the grounds beautiful?"

"Most unusual. Intriguing, really," he said, noticing that
the topiaries lining the drive were cut to resemble children.
"The arrangement of shrubbery and flowers reminds me of
a fairyland."

"I believe it's deliberate. He designed every bit of it
himself."

"Does he have grandchildren to enjoy it?"

"No, but he's always allowed parents to bring their
children to enjoy it. In the rear, there are picnic tables and
another arrangement of plants cut to resemble characters
from fairy tales."

"I'd love to see it," Carlos said.

"If he's home, he'll be outside," Virginia said. "We can
stop, but only for a few minutes."

The colonel's house was on Carlos's side and Virginia
moved closer to him, hoping to catch sight of the Colonel.
In doing so, her breast pressed against Carlos's arm. The
contact made her blood quicken. Carlos turned quickly
and their eyes met. Without taking his eyes off her, he
guided the horse to the side of the road, let the reins drop
and pulled her to him. When his lips sought hers, she
didn't fight him; she was as hungry for his closeness as he
was for hers.

A convulsive cry escaped her as one of his hands moved

up from her waist and gently enclosed her breast. His lips, moving against hers, further aroused her, but the barking of a dog nearby caught her attention.

Her hands, which had tightened on his shoulders as her passion heightened, moved down to his chest as she tried to push him from her.

"Please, Carlos," she whispered, not trusting her voice, "let me go. I beg of you. Please."

He did, though reluctantly. "My dear señora," he said, the passion in his voice stirring her anew. "I could not resist you. I felt your breast against my arm when you pressed against me. It sent the blood coursing through my veins. Please forgive me if I offended you."

"It was my fault." Her voice was steady now, and she widened the distance between them. "I was hoping to catch sight of Colonel Spires."

"Then you forgive me, señora?" Carlos had also gotten a grip on his emotions, but his eyes still held a hungry look.

"There is nothing to forgive. We won't refer to it again."

"Thank you, señora." He turned, picked up the reins, and urged the horse into motion.

They were silent until they came in sight of her family's plantation. Carlos marveled at the impressive mansion and extensive acreage. The covered porch, which extended around three sides of the house, was two stories high. Wide pillars added to its imposing appearance. Lace curtains dressed the windows, which sparkled with cleanliness. Virginia knew the interior was just as pleasing to the eye, for everything had been purchased new.

A tall, thin Negro who had been doing yard work saw them, dropped his rake, cupped his hands to his mouth, and gave out a shrill yell as he ran toward the fields.

In the distance, Chris Savard, riding a sleek Arabian, heard the cry and galloped quickly across the fields. A short distance from them, he slowed the animal and rode up to the carriage. He removed his wide-brimmed straw hat and bowed slightly as he stopped on the side of the vehicle where Virginia sat.

"This is a pleasant surprise," he said.

"Thank you, Mr. Savard," she replied. "I'm eager for you to meet Señor Carlos Cabrera from Mexico. I think Nanine told you some time ago that he grows a very strong-fibered cotton and we're going to experiment with it on Valcour. If it improves the cotton there, we'll bring it here."

Chris shook hands with Carlos. "I'd not heard of crossing types of cotton before Miss Nanine told me about it. It sounds interesting and challenging. I'll be pleased to work with it if you find it meets your expectations."

"It will work," Carlos replied. "It will be a sensation. I have dreamed of this for a long time."

"Then we'll do our best to make your dreams a reality," Chris said. "Would you care to inspect the fields?"

"Sí," Carlos said. "That is why we came."

Carlos and Virginia rode the carriage to the fields, with Chris riding beside them.

"Have you had any trouble with the help?" Virginia asked.

"None. Our people work harder as free men and women than when they were slaves. Of course, you pay them more than the other planters do but that's not their fault—they're broke flat from the war."

They walked through the fields. The former slaves did not stop their work.

Carlos was clearly impressed with what he had seen and stated so on their return ride.

"I had no idea your plantation and cotton fields were so vast."

"It was even bigger before the war," Virginia replied. "Papa had almost a thousand slaves there."

"And I must say your husband made an excellent choice in Mr. Savard as overseer."

"Elias took his time in finding one. Mr. Savard is a West Point graduate. He was an officer in the Confederate army and saw service in several important battles."

"I'm surprised such a handsome gentleman isn't married."

"I'm sure the war is responsible for that," she replied thoughtfully.

Chris Savard was handsome, she reasoned; tall and slender, lithe and muscular. Despite the wide-brimmed hat he wore, his face had tanned in the sun, making his blue eyes seem bluer. He had a generous mouth and a finely shaped face.

Carlos's soft, seductive voice forced Chris Savard from her mind.

"Virginia, I asked, if you went to the plantation often."

Surprised laughter escaped her. "That's the first time you've called me Virginia."

"I could think of no other way to get your attention," he said, joining her in laughter. "I asked you three times before you heard."

"I don't go there often," she replied seriously. "Nanine attends to the bookkeeping and she goes there more frequently. Phoebe usually accompanies her. They chaperon each other."

"I notice your sisters are together most of the time," Carlos observed. "They're closer to each other than you are to either of them."

"It may seem that way, Carlos, but it isn't. We're a closely-knit family."

"You may be assured that I thoroughly approve of that," he said. "And now, will you do me the honor of dining with me tonight?"

"I'd like to," she replied. "We can discuss our plans still further. Do you feel certain that crossing the cotton will be a success?"

"Yes. Have you doubts?"

"Not really." She frowned slightly. "Somehow I got the idea that Mr. Savard wasn't altogether enthusiastic about it."

"He didn't express such an opinion," Carlos said thoughtfully.

"Perhaps he's uncertain, Virginia mused. "And he's not a gambler."

"Are you?" Carlos asked.

"I must be," she said gaily, "to be a party to it."

"Then tonight we will drink a toast to two gamblers."

Virginia's dinner gown was of green and violet silk. She'd have liked a new gown, but there'd been no time to purchase one. Besides, this one had been worn only a few times. They were given a corner table partially shielded by palms. A large bouquet of gardenias, set in a silver bowl in the center of the table, scented the air. Virginia commented on its beauty, adding that she'd not noticed any on other tables.

"I ordered them special—for a special lady," Carlos said.

"Thank you." Virginia smiled across the table and raised her champagne glass to touch his.

"To two gamblers," Carlos said. "May our daring project flourish. And may our friendship ripen with time."

Virginia sipped her champagne and lowered her eyes. His were openly adoring her. She felt a stirring of passion. She'd managed to quell that while she was carrying Jimmy and after his birth. She wanted no hint of scandal to touch the child; she knew she would do anything to prevent that. But her passion had been stirred with Brad's return. And today her passion had been aroused again, when her breast had pressed against Carlos's arm. His lips, moving against hers, and his hand cupping her breast and gently squeezing it, had sent sheets of fire through her. And on their return from the plantation, her mind had kept reverting to thoughts of Chris Savard.

It was probably the seductive scent of those damned gardenias, she thought. She managed a shaky smile and lifted her glass to her lips. Carlos was regarding her curiously. She wondered if he could guess what was on her mind. The idea unsettled her. Yet, she hungered for the love of a man. Not just a few stolen kisses, but the ecstasy of wild abandon and complete surrender.

"What are you thinking of, my dear?" Carlos asked. "You look a little frightened."

"I'm thinking of Elias," Virginia said quickly. "I'm wondering if he'll approve our business deal."

"Haven't you written to him about it?" Carlos looked surprised.

"No. I feared he might not approve."

"Shouldn't you let him know anyway?" Carlos asked seriously.

"What if he said no?" she asked.

"Then I would be the loser," Carlos said forlornly. "But you would be an obedient wife."

"I'm afraid I'm too independent to be completely subservient. You see, during the war, my sisters and I had to live by our wits. I learned to do a lot of things I never thought I'd have to do. But in the process, I grew up. I was a spoiled brat. Once I learned to think and make decisions, I knew exactly what I wanted and I determined to get it."

"That is part of the heritage of being an American," Carlos commented. "And in that respect, it doesn't matter whether you come from the North or South. It also makes you very desirable. A woman with spirit is a challenge to most men."

"What do you mean?"

"I could fall in love with you," he replied quietly. "In fact, I already have."

"I suggest we discuss the quality of the food. The waiter is about to serve us."

"You're also very adroit at making a man keep his distance."

"I remind you again, I'm a married woman. With a son."

Carlos gave a shrug of resignation. "I'm defeated before I can even begin to woo you. Forgive me. I shall be most discreet for the rest of the evening. But you mustn't expect me to regard you as if you were a stranger."

"Just a dinner companion," she replied, emptying her glass, which the waiter immediately refilled. "Tell me about your plantation."

"I'd like to say I find your son quite adorable."

"Please, Carlos. Your plantation."

"Very well, I have four hundred peons at work for me," he said. "Far fewer peons than you have Negroes. But then, I am not quite as wealthy as you, my dear. I plan to be, and the thought occurs how wonderful it would be if we not only blended our cotton but . . . ourselves. I think of you in my arms. I am driven mad by the dream. You are the most desirable woman I have ever met. I cannot help talking this way. I want to hold you. I want to disrobe you. I want to . . ." he closed his eyes, "have all of you."

"Carlos," she said quickly, "you promised—"

"I cannot help myself. You must not blame me. All my life I have disciplined myself. But now that I have met you, I can't seem to control my emotions."

"Carlos, you promised . . ." She tried to stop him, but he knew she was wavering.

"You are a woman of great passion. I can tell that. Your

husband has been in England for many months. You are not one to be alone this way. It is not good. I know, for I too have been long without love."

"I think, Carlos, that we should pay more attention to our supper. I'm amazed at the tenderness of the beef."

Carlos sighed. "I speak of love and you speak of food." He gestured hopelessly. "Very well. We'll eat the tender beef."

"You're angry," she said, amused.

"Outraged," he agreed, trying to make light of it. "Here I have unburdened my heart to you and . . . you would rather pay heed to a steak." He looked at her and set down his knife and fork. "It is a fine supper, sí. None better. I thought the Confederate states were being starved to death."

"Oh no. We're eating far better than we have in years. Didn't you notice that at last evening's banquet on Valcour?"

He kissed the tips of his fingers and his eyes teased her. "None better in my life. It was almost like love. But I must not speak this way."

"No, you must not," she said sternly, though she wanted him to continue. It was becoming an effort to maintain a discreet formality. She pushed her plate away and she finished what was left in her glass. The coffee, served as they talked, was hot and strong, and it seemed to heighten the effects of the wine. They'd consumed two bottles.

They ascended the grand staircase to the second floor of the hotel, where their rooms were located. Carlos studied his key and hers. "The rooms are too far apart," he said with a resigned smile. "But then, does it matter?"

"No, Carlos." Virginia managed a casual tone. "Sleep well. I'll accompany you to the station in the morning and see you off."

"That is no consolation, if you wish the truth," he said. They reached her room and he unlocked the door. "Good night, *cara mia*. May your dreams be of me."

He caught her hands and kissed her palms and then her wrists where her pulse already throbbed. Before she could turn, his hands enclosed her waist lightly. He held her close to him as his lips touched hers. It was a brief embrace, but sufficient to leave her breathless.

This time he freed her before she could protest. He stepped aside as she entered the room and didn't move until she closed the door. Inside, she pressed her lips tightly together to hold back a cry of longing. Her legs felt weak and her breathing was rapid from the emotion his closeness had again stirred within her. She pressed her palms against her cheeks. Her skin seemed to be on fire, her pulse was throbbing, and her body trembled with desire.

She kicked off her shoes and raised her skirts as she sat down. She unfastened her garters, pulled off her silk stockings, and tossed them aside. She straightened and let her hands come to rest on her bare thighs. Her feet moved slowly back and forth on the silky pile of the rug, further arousing her. She squeezed the flesh of her thighs until she winced with pain. She was growing mad for the ecstasy of fulfillment, and the only man she would care consort with was leaving in the morning. He'd said nothing about returning, although she imagined he'd not remain away long. She released the painful grip on her legs, got up, and walked unsteadily to the bathroom to draw a cool bath. She was trembling from head to foot and needed something to quiet her.

When she finally slipped into her nightgown, she was relaxed and pleasantly sleepy. She turned down the bedcovers and remembered she hadn't locked the door. She looked on the bureau for the key and went through her reticule but did not find it. It occurred to her that Carlos kept it. She was a trifle irritated, but there was a bolt she could turn. She reached for it . . . then hesitated.

If he had deliberately chosen not to surrender the key, it meant only one thing. She removed her fingers from the bolt lock and walked slowly to the bed. She stacked the pillows so that she might sit up, and she drew the bedcovers close about her, for the cool water had left her skin chilled. It had also helped, to a mild degree, to relax her. All she had to do, she reasoned, was get out of that bed, walk a dozen or so steps to the door, and lock it with the bolt.

She was undecided; she trusted Carlos, but she was hesitant to have him come to her in the night. Then she recalled the letter from Elias and again hated him for his coldness and formality. She thought of Bradley Culver and shuddered, for he was a man she feared. And yet that old magnetism about him was still there. She even recalled the handsome Chris Savard at the big plantation. She wondered if he had sleepless nights because of lack of a woman. Or did he go to a brothel to satiate his desires as most men did?

She swung her legs to the floor and sat on the edge of the bed for a few moments before she reached for the bedside lamp. She knew she should blow it out, but instead she turned it down until the room was barely lighted. As she did so, she realized that she had already surrendered to Carlos, and the waiting became maddening.

There was a discreet tap on the door, which she answered with a whispered invitation to enter. Carlos, in the red silk robe he had worn at Valcour, walked slowly to her. The robe was short and there was no sign of a nightgown beneath it. He was naked under that robe. Her breath quickened at the thought.

"I came to return your key and apologize for having forgotten to give it to you," he said uncertainly.

Her voice was low and seductive. "I knew you'd bring it back. Now use it, please. Lock the door and come to me."

Before he could turn away, she threw aside the bed linen to reveal that she, too, was naked. The key rattled against the lock, betraying either his nervousness or his impatience. It didn't matter which to Virginia. She held out her arms to him. He blew out the lamp, and then his warm body was pressed against hers and she rode a wave of passion that carried her beyond thinking or caring what the results might be. His eagerness and hunger matched hers.

Through her mind flashed the thought that the last time she had made love was when Bradley Culver had stolen into the mansion in the middle of the night and made his way to her bedroom. Unlike Carlos's courtly way of seducing her, Bradley had simply awakened her and flung himself upon her, though not before she had awakened sufficiently to tighten her arms around him and welcome him.

Carlos lay back, his breathing still rapid, like that of a man who'd been too long without the comfort of a woman. Virginia's breathing matched his, as she basked in the bliss of a fulfillment she had madly desired and needed for so long.

Carlos kissed her breasts and drew her to him.

"I love you, *cara mia*. I ask for your hand in marriage. You will divorce your husband, of course."

"Of course," she said dreamily, still filled with ecstasy, reliving the act in her mind.

"I must return to Mexico in the morning as I planned, but I will be back soon. Tell me you love me."

"Didn't I prove it by giving myself to you?"

"But do you love me? Unless I loved you truly, I could never have done this."

"You're a liar," she said lightly. "You've been planning this ever since we met."

He laughed and caressed her thigh. "You are an observant woman. I thought my behavior so decorous that you believed my interest in you was restricted to business."

"Am I that ugly?" she asked, feigning indignation.

"Your body, your face, your eyes—everything about you drives me mad." His voice grew husky as he repeated his question. "Do you love me? I demand to know."

"If I didn't, Carlos darling, your little trick with the key would not have worked. I'd merely have turned the bolt and not answered your knock."

"Then we'll waste no more time talking, *cara mia*. This is our last night together for some weeks. We must make the most of it."

Virginia pressed her body against his and her mouth sought his. This time she was as much the aggressor as he, for she knew that after tonight she would have to bank the fires of her passion until his return.

THREE

For the sake of propriety at the crowded depot, they shook hands formally before Carlos boarded the train for the first part of his journey home.

"In two months, I will be back," he vowed, "and before I leave we shall be married. I will bring you home to meet my sisters and brothers."

"I'll be waiting, my darling," she said. "Make it sooner if you can."

"I love you . . . for the first time in my life, I am in love."

"Be careful, darling," she said.

He swung aboard the car, then turned around on the platform. "You will take care of the little matter of money, of course?"

"I intend to go directly to the bank from here. Goodbye, Carlos."

"I will remember the wonderful beauty of you until I return," he said as the train began to move. He raised his voice to a shout. "And I will never forget . . . last night." He said more, but the hiss of steam from the locomotive drowned his words.

She lowered her head to hide her laughter, then raised it again and waved. She turned back to the waiting carriage and was assisted into it by the driver. During the brief ride to her bank, she thought about Carlos and the night before and, for the first time, divorce. The thought frightened her, for such a step would not be taken lightly. She was

66

sure she loved Carlos. He was courtly and made her feel like a queen. Of course, she didn't know him well, but he was honest and sincere and they had much in common with their experiment with their two breeds of cotton.

It would be convenient to marry him. She would not go to Mexico, despite his desire that she meet his family. She would talk him out of it. For all she cared, he could sell his plantation or let his brothers run it. It didn't matter if he was troubled financially, for she had more money than she needed and her sisters were even wealthier. She believed she was on the verge of beginning a new life. The thought cheered her.

And it would be very satisfying to write to Elias, telling him she was suing for divorce and would marry again as soon as the decree was issued. Maybe that would bring him to life. She wanted him to display anger in his letters. She would feel a personal triumph in that. She would also see to it that he no longer represented her family's plantations in England. That, she was sure, would hurt him. She was just as certain that Carlos would agree with her. That, too, pleased her.

Nanine would be shocked when she learned the news. Phoebe would be tolerant; if she disapproved, Virginia would never know. No matter. Her mind was made up. She dreaded the scene her mother would make, but that, too, would have to be faced. She would not back down. She was in love. Carlos was a man whose company she enjoyed. His passion equaled hers, and in the company of others, he had eyes only for her. However, the thought of divorce disturbed her, for it was not taken lightly anywhere, but she would handle that. Elias would probably be happy to be free. She brightened as the answer came to her: she would claim that Elias had met another woman and wanted his freedom to remarry. In that way, pride would demand that she get a divorce. Sympathy would be entirely on her side. She'd not fool Nanine—she never had been able to—and Nanine would be shocked at such deceit, but she would never betray her.

Her thoughts drifted back to Carlos. They'd made love all night, with a bare hour's sleep just before dawn. Yet she'd never felt more alert or more vibrant than at this moment. She was close to thirty and she felt twenty. She must have laughed aloud, for the driver cast a glance over his shoulder and regarded her with a smile. She had to get a grip on herself. She had business to attend to and there was no more time to think of love or lovemaking.

She dismissed the carriage at the bank, for she could walk the three blocks back to the hotel and check out. She entered the bank, the city's largest, and already partially restored from the ravages of war. She was well known here, for she and her sisters were the bank's largest depositors.

Henry Tyler saw her enter and quickly rose from behind his desk. They met halfway along the lobby. From behind their grilled windows, tellers smiled their welcome. Tyler escorted her to a chair beside his desk and resumed his seat.

"It's always a delight to see you, Miss Virginia. I trust your mother and sisters are not too exhausted from the ball. It was an outstanding affair. Your sister Phoebe is a very talented young lady. Her performance was most enjoyable."

"Did you resent the fact that she has a drop of Negro blood?" Virginia asked, genuinely concerned.

"I think it's high time to disregard that in one so . . . well . . . almost white and so wealthy. It's a shame she quit the stage. She should return, you know."

"She wants to, I'm sure, Mr. Tyler. But most folks, even Yankees, believe a colored shouldn't try to attain the fame and wealth Phoebe has acquired."

"I'm sure she's aware of that, but she's also intelligent

and will learn to cope. I assure you that in this bank she'll be treated like the lady she is." Henry paused and frowned. "I hope it isn't concern for that which brought you here."

"No. My business here concerns the plantation owner, Señor Cabrera."

"Oh yes, the gentleman helping you develop a new strain of cotton."

"We have great hopes for it."

"Do you wish me to send him the amount of money you designated the last time you were here?"

"Yes. I hope you have the papers ready."

"Miss Virginia, you speak of considerable sums. You have already sent him a great deal of money."

"Of course I have," she said testily. "Why shouldn't I?"

"In cases of this kind, the bank likes to make certain its customers are not being cheated and deceived. One of the valuable services we offer. Also, you're James Hammond's daughter. He trusted our judgment."

"What do you mean by that, Mr. Tyler?"

"We took it upon ourselves to make an investigation of Señor Cabrera. What we learned is not good."

"He has a very large plantation," Virginia said indignantly.

"It is quite small and he is heavily in debt. If it had not been for your advances to him, he would have been bankrupt long ago."

"Are you sure of this?" she asked with growing dismay.

"We do not divulge this kind of information unless we are certain. Señor Cabrera is a noted spendthrift. Besides that, he has sired seven children by his first wife and five by his second, from whom he is already estranged. He's quite a philanderer. He's being forced to pay for the upkeep of his large family and was even jailed once when he missed payments to his first wife. As you no doubt know, his church frowns on divorce. Since his divorce and remarriage, he is a social pariah among his countrymen."

Virginia exhibited none of her consternation. "If there is no doubt of the truth of this, Mr. Tyler, you must not forward him the sums I have designated. Please see to it that he gets not a dollar more. I was not aware of his true nature."

"I can't say I blame you for that. I watched the man at your ball, and he is indeed handsome and suave. This has enabled him to have many alliances with women. He is a knave and a scoundrel."

"Thank you for making me aware of this," she said. "It seems to conclude my business here today. Thank you again, Mr. Tyler, and good day."

She walked serenely out of the bank, praying that no one had cause to notice the turmoil within her. She was sure that Mr. Tyler suspected nothing. In almost a daze, she walked back to the hotel, claimed her key, and went upstairs to her room. There she locked the door, removed her hat and gloves, and flung herself on the bed. She began to beat her fists against the pillows. She tossed and turned on the bed, stifling her sobs, hating herself for having been taken in by an impostor. The fact that he'd so easily seduced her fueled her anger. She'd trusted him; she had made elaborate plans and sent him a great deal of money because she'd believed him to be a man of good character.

It was a bitter feeling to have been trapped and violated by a man like him. She was sure he'd have returned with the same charm, with the same skill in lovemaking, and she'd have gone into his arms again, mad with desire. Now it was ended, done with—painfully. She'd been made a fool of, and she was sure that if he had walked into the room at that moment, she'd have killed him.

Now she would have to find some reason for never allowing him to return. Nanine had been skeptical, had tactfully cautioned her to move slowly. If only she'd listened.

It wasn't going to be easy, this explanation, and Virginia

knew Nanine would see through it, but there was no other way. Virginia would have the satisfaction of keeping his cotton and crossing it with her family's. At least she would get that much out of the encounter. Perhaps it might even become a very profitable venture.

She got off the bed and washed her face with cold water. There was nothing more she could do here in Charleston. She was in no mood to buy gifts for Mama and Ivy. All she wanted to do was return to the security of Valcour.

Phoebe had seen the approach of the boat and was at the dock to greet her. She offered Virginia a hand as she stepped onto the dock, then looked into the craft for packages, which Virginia never failed to bring back.

"No gifts," Virginia said. "I was too damned mad to buy anything."

"What went wrong?" Phoebe asked.

"Carlos is a fake. A cheat, a lothario who ought to be hanged. In the first place, he hasn't any money, and his 'beeg' plantation is a small one and on the verge of bankruptcy."

"Oh dear," Phoebe said. "Are we deeply involved?"

"Mr. Tyler at the bank had the wisdom to investigate Carlos before sending him any more money. What we've spent is gone, of course, but we did get his cottonseeds, and he'll no longer share in anything we make when we cross it with ours. It may also amuse you—Nanine will be shocked—that Carlos has almost a dozen children. He's been married twice and is well known as a philanderer."

"Oh, Virgie, I'm sorry." Phoebe embraced Virginia tenderly. "I know you were fascinated by his charm."

"Even that's phony," Virginia said. "Though I fell for it. He proposed last night. I made no commitment, wanting time to think about it. Since he's already married, I'll forget the proposal."

"He is a charlatan," Phoebe agreed.

"Well," Virginia's smile was bitter, "I shan't be fooled again."

"Good. Did you really believe his interest in you was restricted to business?"

"Why do you ask that?" Virginia managed a light tone.

"He couldn't take his eyes off you," Phoebe replied. "Surely you must have noticed."

Virginia gave a light shrug. "His attention pleased me, but I didn't take him seriously. Not even when he proposed. After all, sister, I'm still a married woman. Small consolation, really. A marriage in name only."

Phoebe nodded but made no comment, knowing her situation was identical.

"Enough talk about me," Virginia said briskly. "We must see Nan so I can tell her about Carlos, but I do have something nice to relate to you. Mr. Tyler enjoyed your performance yesterday. He believes there will be little prejudice against you."

"Oh, there will be prejudice," Phoebe contradicted. "I know that. But not in this family. You've proven your love for me, and you know I love you, too. I feel I belong here, and your caring will ease the pain of whatever bigotry I encounter."

"I'm proud of you, Phoebe," Virginia said. "Mr. Tyler did make the comment that you'd meet up with bigotry, but not from everyone. He added that he felt you'd be able to cope with it."

"That was kind of him," Phoebe said gratefully. "The most bigoted person I've known is Tom Sprague, my husband. I was reluctant to marry him here and go North, but he swore that my having Negro blood wouldn't matter. I found out it mattered a great deal when I read a letter he'd received from his parents, asking why he hadn't brought me to Boston to meet them. He kept using the excuse with me that he had to stay in New York and find a teaching position. They even told him that with his father's influence, he'd have no trouble getting work there and would even get promotions that would place him at the head of the education system."

"You had a difficult time there, didn't you?" Virginia asked gently.

"The success I attained in the theater eased the pain. The money did also, until I discovered there wasn't as much as there should have been."

"Because Tobal, the slave I shot and drove off Valcour, went North," Virginia said.

"And blackmailed me. That was when I knew Tom would go to any length to keep anyone from learning I was part Negro. But I went to the police, and they set a trap for Tobal. When the story was published, Tom walked out, along with his clothes and most of the money that was left in the bank."

"I'm sorry it happened that way for you," Virginia sympathized. "I deserved to lose my husband."

"I suppose I'm lucky I lost mine," Phoebe said.

"How is Mama today?" Virginia asked.

Phoebe brightened. "At present, she's in a euphoric state of mind over the success of the ball. Colonel Spires made quite an impression, so everything is now perfect. She's back at what she dotes on—dances and dinners and balls. I doubt she'd even hear you if you told her that Carlos is a scoundrel."

Virginia laughed. "I want to go upstairs first and freshen up. Then I'll join you and Nanine. Tell her what I've told you about Carlos."

"She's in the library. We'll see you there."

Nanine had caught sight of her sisters approaching the house and had sent for iced lemonade and cucumber sandwiches. Virginia had changed to a white voile dressing gown with a violet lining. She'd taken the pins from her hair and given it a light brushing, then let it hang free. There was no outward sign of the torment and humiliation she'd suffered a few hours ago.

After drinking a glass of lemonade and eating a sandwich, Virginia said to Nanine, "I assume Phoebe has already told you the news regarding Carlos?"

"Yes," Nanine replied quietly. "I'm sorry, Virginia. But you're well rid of him."

"Oh, I'm not going to get rid of him," Virginia said, to her sisters' amazement. "We still have the seeds."

"How do you know that his cotton is what he says it is?" Nanine ventured.

"He brought samples of it. You saw it."

"Are you certain it came from his plantation?"

Virginia frowned thoughtfully. "I'd say so."

"I hope so," Phoebe cut in.

"I believe he has excellent cotton," Virginia reasoned. "What he's looking for is someone with a lot of capital to help him enlarge his holdings. He has quite a family to support."

"I'd like to see something turn out well for you, Virginia," Nanine said. "That must have been quite a shock."

"It was. But it won't defeat me."

"After what we went through in the war," Phoebe said encouragingly, "I think we can surmount any obstacle."

"At any rate," Nanine said, "it's been a busy twenty-four hours. We learned that Carlos tricked us; Phoebe knows she wasn't shunned at the ball; and Mama has been restored as the best hostess in the South."

"And we'll be richer," Virginia added. "I prophesy that our new cotton plants will provide a fiber that will never be rivaled."

"Just a minute now," Phoebe said. "With all our talk of

good fortune and bad, we neglected one item. A man named Bradley Culver."

"He could become a menace," Nanine said, "because he presents a problem that isn't going to be easy to solve."

"What do you mean?" Virginia asked in sudden apprehension.

"You both know that in hiding Brad when the Yankee soldiers came, I spent some time with him in the attic. He talked to me freely. We must not misjudge the man. We know he's highly intelligent, his family background is excellent, and his days as a marauding Rebel outlaw are over. He talked quietly to me and earnestly."

"About what?" Virginia demanded. "My son?"

"His son also," Nanine reminded her. "As we know, Brad is all male. Both in appearance and in his thinking. He worries that his son, being raised in a household of women, will turn out to be a sissy. His expression, not mine."

"Damn him!" Virginia said. "I should have known. We must never forget that he's a murderer, a confessed rapist, a thief, and the leader of a gang of ruffians that terrorized half the state. And, I might add, a man who has been tried and sentenced to hang. He got away, but they'll find him eventually. He can't escape the law forever."

"I'm not favoring him, except that his son is my nephew," Nanine said. "We have to keep that in mind as well."

"At least Jimmy is too young to know about these matters, for which we should be grateful," Phoebe said.

"Nan," Virginia said with obvious worry, "did he ever say anything about wanting to share Jimmy?"

"Not exactly. But I believe it's on his mind."

"How in the world could he do that?" Phoebe asked. "He's a wanted man, a criminal in hiding."

"Brad wouldn't worry about that," Virginia said. "He

wouldn't give a damn. Not if he wanted Jimmy badly enough, and I think he does. It frightens me."

"He could never take him legally," Nanine said.

"Do you think that would bother him? For years he's never done anything legal."

"I'll say this much, Virgie," Phoebe said. "He'd have a fight on his hands if he ever tried to take the boy by force. Tough as he may be, three women are tougher."

"Well," Nanine said, "we can't spend our lives living in fear of him. We've many things to do. Raising cotton is the most important, so let's devote ourselves to that."

"Who is going to take charge of the mainland plantation?" Phoebe asked. "The way I see it, you'll be concerned with the new type of cotton, Virgie. And you, Nan, handle the business end of both plantations. That leaves me free to see to the mainland farm. I want to do something in this family. I know Mr. Savard doesn't need any supervision, especially from an ignoramus like me, but I think the family should be represented there. At least some of the time."

"Could that be because Chris Savard is there?" Nanine asked lightly.

"Nan, I'm a married woman," Phoebe said indignantly.

"So is Virgie!" Nanine laughed aloud. "Be warned!"

Virginia laughed with the others, but not as heartily.

FOUR

With a well-founded intuition of what would happen, Virginia resolutely made her way to the kitchen to tell Belle about plans for a Fourth of July social.

Things had gone well at Willowbrook. A calmness had descended over the house and its people. Nanine was kept busy with her books, each month facing another onslaught of anger when Virginia received her estranged husband's financial report from London. Virginia too was very busy, exploring the possibilities of the new type of cotton to be grown only on Valcour.

Phoebe and Nanine visited the mainland plantation but found little to do, other than checking on the house to make certain the servants kept it up. Phoebe liked it there, however, due mostly to Chris Savard, whose manner was friendly. Only one incident marred the calmness of Phoebe's life: she was served with papers for a divorce suit instituted by Tom Sprague, her husband, now in Boston. She was neither surprised nor unhappy about it, for she'd been expecting it for a long time and had even contemplated beginning a legal action of her own.

With things running so smoothly, Virginia felt little inclination to suffer Belle's anger, for there was no pressing reason why she could not be replaced. As usual, she was astride a tall stool that accommodated only a meagre portion of her ample figure. She was supervising preparations for the evening meal, issuing orders to her girls and doing little more than that.

She wiped her wide, black face with the edge of her apron and glared at Virginia. "Whut yo' wants heah? Cain't yo' sees I'm busy."

"Belle, the Fourth of July will be celebrated next week and we're planning a picnic. . . ."

"Like hell yo' is! I ain't cookin' fo' two hundred folks any mo'." Belle slid off the stool and from her five-foot height defiantly looked up at Virginia. "Tol' yo' befo', ain't right to make me wuk like that no mo'."

"You supervise. The servants you're in charge of do the work. This is a picnic for the people who live on Valcour. We'll seat about seventy, and it won't be a formal ball."

"No, ma'am, ain' cookin' fo' seventy folks." Her physical confrontation with Virginia over, she hoisted herself back on the stool.

"As you wish. I shall place Veronica in charge of the kitchen beginning today," Virginia said.

"Veronica!" Belle sniffed in contempt. "She cain't cook no mo' than one o' them gals I gots wukkin' fo' me. Veronica don' knows nothin' 'bout cookin', 'less all yo' wants is grits. She do her thinkin' wit' her ass."

"I shall write a check for your wages to date. You may stop by the library before you leave Valcour to get it. You no longer work here, Belle."

"My man's goin' wit' me. Warns yo'! This heah plantation cain't run 'thout him."

"A boat will be waiting at the dock in an hour," Virginia said. "Goodbye, Belle."

She turned and walked out, followed by Belle's loud, high-pitched curses. Somewhat shaken, Virginia returned to the library and sat down. Nanine, behind the desk, looked up.

"What's happened?" she asked. "You look like you're spoiling for a fight."

"I've had the fight. I just fired Belle."

Nanine leaned back in the leather chair. "It was coming to that, I suppose."

"She's impossible. She refused to cook for the picnic. This is one of the times when I wish we were back in the days of slavery. I'd have her whipped right now. She thinks we can't run the place without Moses, and perhaps we will find it hard to do without him, but I wonder if he'll put up with her cantankerousness."

"I'll wager he won't. And unless he goes, Belle won't. She's shrewd enough to know she won't be able to get along in the city. Even for someone as good as she at cooking fine meals, there are mighty few jobs. Even if she got one, her ill-nature would do her in. What if Moses makes her change her mind?"

"Perhaps she won't be quite as ornery. I'll take her back, but with that understanding. I surely don't know where we'd fine a suitable replacement, and the invitations to the party have already gone out."

"You won't have to wait long to find out," Nanine said. "Now, Elias reports in his past letter that one of our newer accounts in London is on the verge of defaulting, and perhaps we shouldn't ship the last order to that firm."

"Bother Elias! Can't he handle a simple thing like that?"

"He's not authorized to make such decisions, Virgie. I think we should cut them off."

"Then do it, for heaven's sake. Did Phoebe get back from the mainland last night?"

"She's sleeping late. Before Chris rowed her back to Valcour, they had a late supper in town. I haven't talked to her beyond learning that, but I doubt there are any problems on the mainland."

"So Savard is becoming that friendly with her. I hope it doesn't go too far."

"Why not?" Nanine asked candidly. "They're young. I think it's good for both of them."

"I don't want Phoebe hurt again."

"You mean, of course, that if Chris discovers she's not lily white, he'll turn his back on her."

"Savard is Southern. He fought for the South. Do you think he'd accept her?"

"Virgie, practically everybody in Charleston knows Phoebe has Negro blood. They know, too, that at the last soiree she was accepted. Besides, she's a talented actress and could go back on the stage whenever she wanted to. She could overcome any unfavorable publicity, in time. Also, she's rich!"

"I'm not so sure, and I don't want her hurt," Virginia reiterated. "I'm going to Mama's suite and talk to her about the picnic. She's excited about it, as she usually is about anything social. Then I've got to read up on transplanting cotton. I don't know. Sometimes this whole business of trying to improve our cotton bothers me. I can't find any references to that sort of thing having been done before."

"Let me know how it progresses," Nanine said.

Virginia walked to the window. "I declare, Belle's wasting no time. She's on her way to the fields to tell Moses. Oh, please prepare a check for her. I told her it would be ready. If she goes, we're done with her. If she stays, we can show her the check so she'll realize we meant business. I'm tired of her. I hope she goes."

"You won't feel that way when you're eating supper tonight," Nanine said with a laugh. "I'll see to the check."

Belle, walking to the cabin she shared with her husband, was still seething with anger. Once in the cabin, she changed into a street dress, stretching the material to accommodate her ever-increasing girth. She was laying out her clothing when Moses returned for what he expected would be his noonday meal.

Moses, a powerful man, as black as Belle, with white hair and an unwrinkled face despite his age, needed no explanation for Belle's packing. She'd done this before.

"Yo' leavin'?" he asked. "O' yo' jes' takin' a vacation?"

"Leavin', an' yo' kin put yo' things in one o' them burlap bags out back. Leavin' right now."

"Who tol' yo' I'm leaving'?" he asked. " 'Cause I'm tellin' yo' I ain't. An' neither are yo'. Ain't no jobs in Charleston o' anywhar else. War ain't been oveh long 'nough, an' they's six million nigguhs lookin' fo' wuk. They ain't any 'cause the white folks ain't got money 'nough to pay 'em. Not like heah, wheah the pay is good an' on time. Yo' gots to be crazy to run off like that."

"I's runnin'." She continued stuffing clothing into the ancient carpetbag.

"Belle, I'm askin' yo' polite, don' do this."

"Yo' comin' with me o' ain't yo'?" she demanded.

"Ain't goin' no place an' yo' ain't either." He seized her arm and turned her about to face him. "I says yo' ain't goin'."

"I says I sho' am."

His big, callused hand struck her hard across the face. The side seams of her dress split as she stumbled back and fell against a chair. She held up her hands to avoid any more blows. When she was sure there would be no more, without a word she began removing her few possessions from the carpetbag.

"We belongs heah," Moses said. "Ain't no otheh place fo' us. Now yo' goes to see Missy Virginia an' tells her yo' ain't leavin'."

"Whut makes yo' think she'll take me back?" Belle asked, but with only a touch of her former determination.

"'Cause yo' is the bes' cook in the worl', an' Missy Virginia sho' knows that."

When Belle, wearing a freshly laundered apron over her uniform, entered the library, both Nanine and Virginia were there. She faced Virginia, who was seated beside the desk.

"Changes my min'," she said. "Ain't leavin'."

Virginia regarded her indifferently. "What makes you think I've changed mine? Nan, give Belle her check so she can clear out."

Nanine removed the prepared check from a drawer and extended it to Belle, who hesitated a moment and then finally examined the check.

"Ain't nothin' extra heah, I sees."

"We don't give extra pay to people we fire," Virginia said. "The boat will be at the dock in half an hour."

Belle let go of the check and it fluttered to the top of the desk. "Says I ain't leavin'."

"You say. Or is it Moses speaking?" Nanine asked in her quiet way. "It's not easy to tell, because your face looks a mite swollen. Is that Moses talking?"

"Hits me good," she admitted. "Hurts mo'n gittin' whupped."

"Not very likely," Virginia scoffed. "Not the kind of whipping I'd have ordered. What about the picnic? You refused to do the work."

"Gets it ready. Bes' suppah yo' evah eats."

"You surely have changed your mind," Nanine observed. "Shall I tear up the check?"

"Yes'm. Begs yo' does. Don' wants no mo' gettin' hit by Moses. 'Sides, seein' this heah picnic is fo' the folks livin' on Valcour, reckon ain't so bad doin' fo' neighbors."

"Then get to the kitchen and see to our supper," Virginia said. "And remember—no more shirking and no more arguments."

"Yes'm." Belle lowered her eyes as in the slavery days. "Goes now."

She was halfway across the dining room, on the way to the kitchen walkway, when she stopped. "Yo' kin kiss mah ass," she said loudly enough to be heard in the library.

Nanine and Virginia burst into laughter. "All we have to hope for now," Virginia said, "is that she won't poison us. I'll go tell Mama that Belle isn't leaving and will supervise the kitchen for the picnic."

It was mid-afternoon when Phoebe called out from the drawing room, "There's a big boat ready to dock. Are we expecting anybody?"

"Not that I know of," Virginia said. She hurried from the library to join Phoebe, who was already standing on the veranda, observing the activity at the dock.

"They're unloading some boxes," she said. "Lots of them. Did you order anything for the picnic? Or some clothes?"

Virginia's puzzlement equaled Phoebe's. "I haven't even been to the mainland. I'll get some of the hands to go down and fetch whatever it is. From the size of some of the crates, I'd say it was furniture."

Four field hands were dispatched to carry the boxes to the house. They placed them on the veranda and, at Virginia's order, pried them open. She dismissed the men, then knelt to examine the contents of one crate. She removed old newspapers used for packing and lifted out a colorful rocking horse. Not one for a toddler, but a nearly life-sized pony on rockers.

With Phoebe's help, and Nanine's as well when she was drawn by her sisters' excited voices, they unloaded the remainder of the large crates and lined up the toys. There were blocks, wooden trains, and even a depot. They found carved animals, one of them a hide-covered cow with a bell hanging from its neck; it was on a rolling platform and moved its head and mooed whenever it was pulled by the attached cord. There was a large fortress to be surrounded by wooden soldiers in Confederate uniforms, complete with a cavalry unit, caissons, and horse-drawn cannon. There was even a small Rebel uniform with a wooden rifle for the boy to wear when he played soldier.

"Guess who sent these," Virginia said uncomfortably.

"Brad, of course," Phoebe said. "I never saw so many toys."

"Or such expensive ones," Nanine added. "Jimmy is going to be in heaven with these."

"Most are too old for him," Virginia snapped.

"Virgie," Nanine said, "at least Brad thinks of the boy."

"Too much and too often," Virginia said. "Besides, it could prove embarrassing as he grows older."

"True," Nanine agreed. "But Brad couldn't be expected to think of that."

"How can I explain packages that will arrive for him as he grows older?" Virginia asked. "Packages that contain no name of the sender."

"You can always say they came from you," Nanine said.

"That would be deceitful," Virginia replied in all seriousness.

She was busily gathering up the crumpled papers that had fallen from the crates, so she didn't see Nanine regarding her with amusement.

"Another thing," Virginia said impatiently. "There isn't a tag or merchandise slip of any kind to tell us where these toys came from."

"What you're saying," Phoebe reasoned, "is that Brad doesn't wish you to know his whereabouts."

"Exactly," Virginia retorted. "He must have ordered the store not to include anything to locate them, but he never thought about the packing and neither did the store, I suppose." She'd already spread out three pages, taken at random, on the floor of the veranda. "These are from the *New Orleans Picayune*, dated about two weeks ago."

"So he's hiding in New Orleans," Phoebe said. "At least he knows the best place. May I bring Jimmy down to see his gifts?"

"Yes," Virginia said, "but don't hurry. I want to put some of them away. This is too much to give a child at one time. And he's too young to appreciate most of these. Help me put them in the closet with Papa's records, Nan."

Nanine immediately joined Virginia in the task of secreting the toys. "Just remember, Virgie, if Mama or anyone wants to know where they came from, you were the donor."

"I imagine Brad is having hysterics," Virginia said behind a stack of repackaged toys she was carrying into the closet. "He knows his gifts have arrived about now and is well aware of what my reaction will be. On top of that, I'll have to lie to my son. I hate that."

"I think you're rather good at thinking up tall tales," Nanine said as she neatly stacked the cardboard boxes.

"I only do it because it's necessary," Virginia said pointedly.

"It will be necessary the rest of your life," Nanine replied serenely. "Just remember to do it in good grace. And don't get angry each time something unexpected happens."

"I just pray it doesn't happen too often."

The two had everything put away and had dispatched two hands to place the empty crates in a storage shed before Phoebe returned with Jimmy. Lenore accompanied her, having been in the nursery when Phoebe came in and learned that there was a surprise awaiting Jimmy downstairs.

He insisted on walking to the stairs, at which point Phoebe swept him up in her arms and kissed his cheek. He accepted her embrace as willingly as he did Virginia's, and he babbled all the way to the drawing room, where

Virginia and Nanine had placed the toys they'd selected for him to see.

For a few moments he was speechless after Phoebe set him down. Then he let out a happy cry and ran at once to the rocking horse. Virginia picked him up and placed him carefully astride the animal. He had to be strapped into it, and there was a metal bar for him to hold on to. His cries of joy swept through the house, even bringing Belle from the kitchen. Her face lit up with pleasure as she watched the child moving slowly back and forth on the wooden rocking horse. Perverse as she was, she loved him, and her loyalty extended to Nanine and Phoebe. Her vituperousness was directed solely at Virginia, and she never lost an opportunity to vent her displeasure on her mistress.

Belle never forgot that her own son—Moses's son too—had been taken from her and sold so that she could nurse Virginia and Phoebe, the daughters of the master of the house. Phoebe, begot of Fannie, a slave whom James Hammond had manumitted and set up in a high-class brothel in New Orleans. He'd kept Phoebe, who was almost as white as Virginia, and had educated her. Not until Virginia had told Phoebe to try on one of her ball gowns, so that she could make a decision as to which to wear, had Virginia realized that the slave who'd been raised in the house as a playmate for her was really her sister. It was when they stood side by side before a full-length mirror and Phoebe had, in a thoughtless, moment, arranged her dark hair exactly as Virginia wore hers, that the resemblance revealed itself to Virginia.

She'd gone to her father in a rage and demanded to be told the truth. He'd laughed at her anger and admitted he'd sired Phoebe. He'd even revealed how he'd provided for Fannie, added that he'd frequented the place himself. She'd hated Phoebe from that day on until, in the course of the war, Phoebe had risked her life to return with

Virginia to Valcour, where a Yankee garrison was stationed. They wanted to retrieve the family silver so that it could be sold, but they'd been captured and brought before Major Elias Birch, military commander of Valcour. He and Virginia fell in love. They had a double wedding, with Phoebe marrying Lieutenant Tom Sprague.

Lenore and Ivy had joined the group and observed the other toys placed so that Jimmy could examine each one. He tired of the rocking horse and turned to Virginia and extended his arms. She set him on the floor. He ran to a toy on which sat several figures holding sticks with which they beat a drum in front of them. Nanine showed Jimmy how to press a lever so that the drums would play. He reveled in that for a while, then went to a large ball, almost as big as he. When it was pushed, music played inside, and once again he shrieked with glee.

When he tired of playing, Ivy picked him up and turned to Virginia. "It's time for his nap, Miss Virginia. He was about to have it when Miss Phoebe came for him."

"I know it is, Ivy." Virginia's smile was grateful. "He'll probably dream about his new toys."

Lenore suppressed a yawn. "I've grown tired watching him. The toys are certainly fascinating. Virgie, but why did you buy so many? You know there's such a thing as spoiling a child. Your papa spoiled you."

Virginia nodded. "True, Mama. But I think I'm unspoiled now. I grew up with the war."

Lenore regarded her daughter thoughtfully. "Of you three sisters, I think you grew up the least."

Virginia was shocked. "How can you say that, Mama?"

Lenore sighed. "I suppose because I have never understood you. You say one thing and I get the feeling you're thinking something quite different."

"Just now, Mama," Nanine broke in quickly, "Virginia's mind is occupied with raising a new breed of cotton."

"I hope you know what you're doing." Lenore adopted her injured tone. "It would be dreadful if anything went wrong and we lost this plantation."

"Don't worry about that, Lenore," Phoebe said. "Everything I have belongs to this family."

"And that goes for me too, Mama," Nanine said. "We love you. We wouldn't let anything happen to you. We know you're happy now that we can give parties again."

"Thank you, girls." Lenore brightened perceptibly. "Which reminds me, we're giving a picnic. I'm sending Colonel Spires an invitation and I must plan the menu. Thank heavens Belle didn't leave."

After she left the room and was safely upstairs, Virginia said, "Sometimes I find it difficult to hold on to my patience when Mama starts on me."

Nanine laughed. "You're going to have to acquire a lot of restraint."

"In fairness to Mama," Virginia reasoned, "I'll admit I'm impulsive. Our brother, Marty, was like that, and it proved to be his undoing."

"Did your mother know he drank?" Phoebe asked.

"If she did," Virginia replied, "she would never admit it. He couldn't accept the fact that the South lost the war, just as Brad couldn't. Brad became an outlaw and broke every law set by decent citizens. Marty would never have caught that bullet in his duel with Miles if he'd been himself; but he'd been drinking, and although he was sober at the time, his body had taken too much abuse."

"Ironic how he fought a duel with the man I fell in love with and married," Nanine reminisced. "Miles suffered terribly because his bullet killed Marty."

"He would, because Miles was a gentleman. When he told us he deliberately aimed the gun to one side of Marty because he couldn't bear the thought of killing another human being, we know he told the truth. We also know that Miles spoke the truth when he said Marty deliberately stepped into the path of the bullet."

"Marty had a sense of humor," Virginia said. "I think he'd have appreciated the irony of what Miles did and the way it turned out."

"I hope so," Nanine said. "Because I never knew such happiness as the precious few months I spent nursing Miles and marrying him. Supreme bliss."

"You deserved it," Virginia said kindly. She remembered how Miles had told her of his love for Nanine, yet his reluctance to marry her because his health was such that the marriage could never be consummated. Virginia had told him that for Nanine, the marriage would be consummated the moment he slipped the ring on her finger. He'd proposed then, and they'd married immediately. Nanine had brought Miles back to the island and had done everything possible to nurse him back to health, but there was no cure for his blood condition and he grew steadily weaker until death claimed him. He had willed everything to her and she had become a woman of great wealth.

"I wish I could have known Miles," Phoebe said. "He was a noble man who deserved a woman like you, Nanine. A pity you had to lose him."

Virginia said, "We lost ours, too, Phoebe. We were unlucky in love."

"There are times when I think you and I deserved to be," Phoebe replied.

"How can you say such a thing?" Virginia asked indignantly.

"Because I wanted to live a lie," Phoebe replied earnestly. "I went North with the thought that no one would ever know I wasn't white."

"Tom encouraged that," Virginia scoffed.

"Perhaps. But I didn't discourage it. And you deceived Elias. I know that when you look at Jimmy, you believe it was worth it. I agree with that. Nevertheless, it doesn't erase what you did to your husband."

"You're right, of course," Virginia admitted. "I have a headache. I'm going upstairs to lie down."

Phoebe and Nanine didn't speak until they heard Virginia's door close.

"Poor Virgie." Nanine's tone was compassionate. "Her life won't be easy. She'll always be on the defensive for her son, even when there'll no longer be a need."

"And she'll have to live with the fear of Brad slipping onto the island and kidnapping his son," Phoebe said.

Nanine nodded. "It's as if she'll have to pay the rest of her life for having been unfaithful to Elias. If only he could forgive her. Really forgive her."

"How?"

"By coming back."

Phoebe eyed Nanine hopefully. "Do you think he will?"

"No," Nanine said without hesitation. "I used to hear them quarreling at night. Virgie told me it was because he wanted a family. But she wanted to bring the island back first."

"But since he couldn't have a family," Phoebe reasoned, "why couldn't he forgive her and accept Jimmy as his son?"

Nanine stood up. "He gave the boy his name. I think that was noble of him. Especially when he'd already learned that he could never father a child. I'm going upstairs now. I have a headache, too. I think the significance of what these toys portend upset me as much as Virgie."

FIVE

The Fourth of July picnic was a great success, as were all the soirees hosted by Lenore. Belle complained, but not too vehemently, and she furnished a superb supper. As the party was restricted to those who lived on Valcour, it was smaller. Because of that, it was possible to conduct some of the business of the island. After the guests assembled in the house, Virginia assumed the role of spokesman.

"We're on the verge of the greatest boom in cotton sales in all of history." She spoke from the center of the drawing room. "As you have heard from my husband in England, the Valcour cotton is the most expensive in the entire world. And we're going to make it even better—and more expensive. In the spring, we'll plant the Mexican seed," she took a quick breath as she proceeded headlong into the necessary lie, "which was furnished to us by one of the largest plantation owners in Mexico. We shall then endeavor to cross it with out cotton next year, and from the new plants obtain fiber that is just as silky as what we now grow, but strengthened by the hardier and stronger Mexican variety."

There was total agreement on the brilliance of this enterprise and Virginia was praised for her resourcefulness.

"Particularly," she told Nanine and Phoebe later, "since I lied about Carlos's damned plantation, which is far from the biggest, and more likely far from the best, because the man is lazy and no doubt spends more time chasing women than attending his fields."

"Under the circumstances, I can see why you had to do it," Nanine conceded. "We'd certainly built Carlos up, prior to sending him packing."

"Do you think he'll ever come back?" Phoebe asked.

"If he does, he'll be met by the muzzle of a shotgun," Virginia said. "I'll have nothing more to do with that bastard. Please excuse the vulgarism, but when I think of him, that kind of language seems the most fitting."

"I wish the planting had already been done," Nanine said. "We have to wait a year for Carlos's seeds to grow, then another year to perform the transplanting."

"Is there any guarantee it will work?" Phoebe asked. "Carlos might well be some kind of confidence man."

"I'm certain it will work," Virginia said. "I know enough about growing cotton to be sure there's a chance that cross-planting will succeed. Though I admit I really don't know how it's done."

"Then it's never been done before, as far as we know," Nanine said.

"Other plants have been greatly improved by this method. Why not cotton? At any rate, we can't afford not to try. Somebody else may think of it and succeed. We have to be first."

"Then we'll hope and pray for success," Phoebe said.

"All I hope for," Virginia said, "is a few peaceful years. With no Carlos, with Brad in hiding so he's out of my life, and with our plantations flourishing as they never have before. That, and my darling Jimmy staying healthy and strong."

"He's nearly worn out Brad's toys," Phoebe said. "He thoroughly enjoyed them. Evidently Brad had a good idea of what his son would like."

"Purely guesswork," Virginia said disparagingly. "He

knows nothing about children. How could he? He fought the war and afterward turned bandit. He never had time for children. Now let's forget those men and get to work."

It was April when Carlos returned. Though he arrived early in the evening, he sent his boat back to the mainland before going to the house, so there was little Virginia and her sisters could do about sending him back.

It soon became apparent that he came as a thoroughly chastened man, for his manners were impeccable. He explained that he was there only to fulfill a contract he had made with Virginia.

She was taking a stroll on the grounds, basking in the spring air, when she caught sight of the boat leaving the dock. She met him halfway down the path to the dock and made no pretense of her anger.

"You have an exceptional amount of gall, sir, coming here after what happened."

"My dear Virginia," his reflective smile was easily observable in the moonlight, "I have no regrets about that. And I doubt you have."

"I'm not referring to what you speak of. I mean you cheated us. You lied, exaggerated, and placed us in an embarrassing position. We trusted you and we were foolish in doing so."

"You wounded me mortally," he said, "when you cut off the money due me. I was far more embarrassed than you, señora. But I have come to straighten everything out and to make full restitution for whatever harm I did. Please believe me."

"I wouldn't believe you under any circumstances," she said. "Since we can't very well send you back in darkness, we'll put you up for the night."

"*Gracias*, señora."

"And if you leave your room in the middle of the night, I'll likely kill you. Is that clear?"

"I have no intention of leaving my room. Now will you listen to what I have to say?"

"Not until my sisters are present. Though I doubt they'll believe your reason for your return any more than I."

"Do they know of our—little—assignation, señora?"

"If they did, you'd be on your way back to the mainland right now, even if you had to swim. Do you think I'd want them to know how I was victimized by such as you?"

"*Gracias.* I now know how to handle the situation with no further embarrassment for any of us."

When they reached the mansion. Phoebe and Nanine were in the drawing room. They received him as coldly as Virginia had. Carlos, recognizing this, realized that he must immediately state his business before he was turned out of the house.

"Let me say first that I am sorry I did not tell you the exact truth about the size of my plantation. I thought it necessary to impress you so you would listen to my proposal, which I still say will make us rich. Despite its limited size, the cotton is the best."

"Very well, Carlos, Nanine said, "get to the point of your visit and be done with pretty speeches."

"When I first came to you with the proposition of crossing my cotton with the type you grow, I meant every word. I did not lie about the prospect of success. I furnished you seed, but on thinking it over, I realize that growing my kind of cotton from seed will only delay what we are really after. So, down at the dock are enough seedlings well along in their growth, so that if you plant them, in a matter of a few months you will have cotton and mature plants ready for crossing with yours. These are prime plants, the best I grow, and no matter what else I may be, I am an expert in growing cotton. You will find no one who will deny that."

"And just what do you expect in return?" Virginia asked.

"Only what we agreed upon as my share in the profits."

"It will speed things up if we have growing plants," Nanine admitted.

"We will keep our end of the bargain," Virginia said.

Only then did he revert to the slyness by which he lived and operated. "One small thing. In order for my plantation to exist, I must have financial help. You might consider it an advance."

"On the profits we hope to make?" Nanine asked, eyeing him cynically.

"*Sí*, señora," he replied blandly. "There will be no risk then."

"How much?" Virginia asked.

"Three thousand dollars. A pittance, señora."

Virginia glanced at her sisters and saw them nod slightly. "Very well. Early in the morning I'll give you a check and send you back to the mainland. In consideration of this—advance, as you call it—you must agree never to return to this island again. Our sole contact will be in writing. Is that clear?"

"*Sí*, it is clear. Undeserved treatment, I must say, but very clear."

"I would advise you to retire now and arise at dawn so we may be rid of you," Virginia said.

"*Sí*, señora. I am travel weary. May I have your check now?"

"Come with me to the library," Virginia said.

Nanine moved to follow, but Virginia gestured. "I can handle him. We'll be right back."

Belle entered the drawing room before Virginia led the way to the library.

"Sees yo' gots comp'ny," she said with surprising docility. "Thinks maybe I gits somethin' fo' you'."

"That won't be necessary," Virginia said.

"Yes'm," Belle replied. "Maybe I gits breakfus' fo' this heah gen'mun?"

"You may serve him a very early breakfast," Virginia said. "That's all, Belle."

She nodded and waddled out of the room. Virginia led Carlos to the library. He closed the door and sat down, feeling quite at ease with Virginia. She was already seated behind the desk, checkbook open, quill pen in her hand.

"One thing more," he said. "The check will be for ten thousand. You may falsify the books any way you wish to account for the added seven thousand."

"You're completely mad," she said angrily. "Just because I let you get the best of me once doesn't mean you can do it again."

"Oh, come now," he said pleasantly. "The evening with me was worth seven thousand."

"You damned egoist..."

"Because if you pay me, I shall not let your sisters know what happened that night. With your pride," he laughed softly, "you never told them. As you say, the night you made a fool of yourself. And..." he held up his hand to stifle Virginia's angry answer, "I shall not talk of it in every bar and café and hotel, naming your name. Seven thousand is not too much to pay."

"You can go straight to hell, you filthy-mouthed skunk. And you'll not wait until morning to leave the island. Much as I hate to expose any of my help to the risk of an hour and a half's row to the mainland by night, I shall not hesitate to arrange it. Do you want three thousand for your damned plants—or nothing?"

"Virginia, don't be so angry," he chided gently. "It will get you nothing, and in the end, you may have to pay me more than ten thousand. I warn you, I am not a man to be trifled with."

"I believe that. It's you who does the trifling, with any woman you can seduce. It won't work again with me. You can't prove anything. And my word will count for far more than the word of a lying, cheating bastard like you. This is the United States, señor, not Mexico."

"Virginia," he said, still genially, "the night we made love so passionately—and my God, you do know how to arouse a man—I paid two bellboys in the hotel to witness me entering your room and leaving it. I have no doubt they also listened outside the door. We did grow a bit... shall we say... physically active and made certain recognizable noises in the night. Plus certain words of love. Though, I suppose, prudes would say 'lust.'"

Virginia broke out in a cold sweat, first from fear, then anger. She held back her temper with difficulty, but she managed, for she realized that Carlos was telling the truth. It was exactly the way he would have operated that night. She could not afford to be placed in the position of defending herself against his accusation. Not with Nanine or Phoebe. She had an idea that they had long ago suspected what happened that night, but she did not want her family's social status to be compromised. There were plenty of people in Charleston and Savannah who would relish such a story, even if they did not fully believe it.

"Well?" he asked.

"I hate myself for agreeing to give you this money. Likely I could get you put in jail for the fraud you perpetrated on everyone who lives on Valcour. But I realize your lying tongue could cause us trouble."

"Señora," he said with a small laugh, "it would not be a lie. Surely you know that."

She pulled open the drawer. She signed a check for ten thousand, entered the stub for three thousand, then crossed it out because she decided not to deceive her sisters about the reason for the amount she was paying.

"You will be gone in the morning before any of us wake up. I shall have a boat and an oarsman waiting at dawn. If I see you again, I shall surely be so revolted that I will not hesitate to use a shotgun on your miserable hide."

He folded the check and placed it in his wallet. He rose and bowed. "You are angry now," he said. "But that night you were not angry, and if I say so myself, you are paying me seven thousand dollars for the pleasure of the night. And I am very certain, when you recall our lovemaking, it was worth that amount. Possibly more. *Adiós*, señora. I will be gone in the morning. But when this cotton grows and you also grow rich, I will have my share, and do not forget that. I strongly advise you to be generous."

She stood up and regarded him contemptuously. "Get out! Get out before I change my mind and take a gun to you. I'm inclined to do so right now."

He seemed to believe that, for he exited promptly, and as he went through the door, Ivy stepped aside, for she'd been about to enter.

"May I come in, Miss Virginia?" she asked.

"What do you want?" Virginia demanded.

"Your son is ready to be tucked in and he keeps calling for you."

Virginia was suddenly contrite. "I'm sorry I was cross, Ivy. It wasn't your fault. I'll be up in a few minutes."

"Thank you, missy."

"Thank you, Ivy," Virginia said, managing a smile, "for taking such good care of him."

Virginia returned to the drawing room, where Nanine and Phoebe were patiently waiting.

"What happened?" Phoebe asked. "Carlos almost ran past the drawing-room door and went upstairs as if he were being pursued."

"Would you two consider taking a gun with me and going upstairs and executing that bastard?" Virginia paced the floor nervously.

"Good Lord!" Phoebe exclaimed. "What did he do?"

"I'll say it for you," Nanine said. "You slept with him that night in Charleston, didn't you?"

"Yes. It was my own choosing. What's the matter with me? I ask that of you both. What's wrong with my judgment of men? Of Elias, my husband. Of Brad, that murdering man who fathered my child? And now..." she pointed at the ceiling, "that scum upstairs. The first two I don't mind so much. I was in love with Elias."

"You still are," Phoebe said.

"The hell I am! But I did love him, and when I met Brad I was lonely. Elias was never around and I felt frustrated. But Carlos? I was the world's biggest fool to have let him have his way with me."

"Is he blackmailing you?" Nanine asked.

"I had to give him a check for ten thousand. I'll transfer seven of that from my own account."

"Oh, Virgie," Nanine said worriedly, "you shouldn't have."

"How could I do anything else? He has proof he spent the night in my room. He arranged that like the sly, conniving slime he is. I can't afford to have the story gossiped around the city. I deserve to lose that money. A fool has to pay for the consequences of her idiocy. And I was a fool."

"How can you be sure he'll stop with that amount?" Nanine asked.

"I can't. But at the moment I felt there was nothing else I could do. Even now I don't."

"I think you used proper judgment," Phoebe said. "There was a great deal of blackmail paid on account of me. My husband, Tom, paid it to avoid the scandal of having me exposed as possessing Negro blood. The poor man, to have been so overcome by fear that he'd pay all that money."

"Tom paid it," Virginia replied. "But as I recall, you never paid a dollar. So how can you say I was using proper judgment?"

"Virgie, when I knew what Tom had done, I went to the police, and the men who blackmailed us are now in prison. But look what happened to me. As soon as the news came out, the producer of the show immediately got the idea that because I was part nigger, he could have me when and where he wished. Believe me, he had a sore ankle for a few days afterward, but . . . I was out of the show. Out of the theater. That's what happened when I defied a blackmailer. Carlos can do as much harm to you. People don't have to fully believe the story to snicker at how you were fooled. If just the story gets out, that's enough to make things difficult. It's worth all the money to shut Carlos up."

"And if he doesn't shut up?" Nanine asked in her sensible way.

"We'll handle that when it happens," Virginia said. "*If* it happens. I sent him packing. He'll be gone before Mama wakes up. She doesn't have to know anything about this. Not even about his return to the island."

"If he isn't gone," Phoebe said, "I suggest the three of us light into him so that he'll never forget his departure and never dare come back. The old whips are still in the whipping shed. We could give him a taste of what slaves got in the old days."

"If he isn't gone, I'll agree," Virginia said with a dry laugh. "For now, I'm going to bed after I tuck in my son."

"I'll send someone down to bring Carlos's seedlings to the big shed and we'll see to them in the morning," Nanine said. "Good night."

"Virgie," Phoebe said with an impish gleam, "when you pass the guest-room door, don't knock."

Virginia managed a smile. "If I knock on that door, there'll be a shotgun in my other hand. Good night, and my thanks to both of you for understanding and not making me feel even worse because of what I did. I'm ashamed of myself and I hate myself for having been so damned—"

"Lusty," Nanine broke in. "Remember, Papa was like that."

"Forget it, Virgie," Phoebe consoled. "It's not worth remembering. As for Carlos, I hope he chokes on the money he got."

Carlos didn't sleep well that night. He was fearful. On this island, in this house, his life could be in jeopardy. He knew what an angry woman was capable of, and there were three of them here. He half-expected an invasion of his room before morning.

He was up at dawn. He ate a heavy breakfast, served by Belle, who stood at the table to serve him. He was about to tell her she could be excused when she spoke.

"Suh, know yo' goin' back to the mainland right soon. Gots to go theah myse'f fo' some shoppin'. Yo' reckon I kin go back wif yo', suh?"

"No reason why you can't. I'll be leaving in about twenty minutes."

"I sho' be ready, suh, An' I thanks yo'. Kin git myse'f back heah in time fo' suppah 'cause o' yo' kin'ness, suh."

"Just be at the dock on time," he warned. "I won't wait."

Carlos made the trip to the mainland in complete silence. He had nothing to say to the heavy, coal-black woman who sat facing him, her eyes studying him until the boat reached the dock. He felt like throwing her overboard, but he doubted he could lift her.

Ashore, he promptly forgot about her. He started for the bank to cash the check, then realized that the bank wouldn't open for some time yet. So he went into the dining room of the hotel, read the morning newspaper, drank a healthy portion of brandy, and felt very much at ease with himself. He'd put it over. He'd gotten the money without too much trouble, and he would get more. When Virginia had surrendered to his ultimatum, she had revealed that she could never stand any publicity about their night together. Carlos prided himself on the preparations he'd made for the blackmailing. Virginia had been easy to sleep with and would now be easy to get money from. It had been a profitable adventure and an enjoyable one.

He became so engrossed in his thinking and his brandy that he didn't leave the hotel until after eleven.

At the bank, he had some difficulty cashing the check, for the banker was openly suspicious, but there wasn't much he could do once he'd made certain that Virginia's signature was valid. With an envelope filled with money tucked into his inner coat pocket, Carlos walked to the depot and reached it half an hour before train time.

There were few passengers. Not many people were traveling now, for the war was not yet two years old, and few had money enough to indulge in business trips, and even less for pleasure.

Carlos settled himself in his seat, making sure his window was closed because the soot grew heavy during the long ride. Once the train was under way, he discovered that there was a saloon car recently installed on this rather famous train to New Orleans. He entered the car, ordered brandy, and sat down at one of the small tables. He toyed with his glass, feeling bored and restless.

A handsome, bearded man, well dressed and obviously just as bored, was playing solitaire, a glass of brandy at his elbow. He picked up his glass just after Carlos had done so. Their eyes met. The stranger raised his glass with a slight smile. Carlos responded.

"It is a long ride, señor," Carlos said. "And the cars are so hot.'

"I travel all the time," the stranger said. "I hope traveling improves before too long. But we're lucky it's as good as it is, after what happened to the railroad during the war. At least we have a Pullman and a saloon car."

"I understand the Yankees tore up and bent every rail they came across."

"That's right, and those they missed, we Rebs finished. Care for a game of poker? Just to pass the time. Penny stakes."

"I would be pleased, señor." Carlos moved over to the stranger's table.

"You are Mexican, of course, sir?"

"*Sí.* I grow cotton on a great plantation below the border. Do you know anything about cotton growing, *amigo*?"

"All I know is that it makes very good cloth. I'm a manufacturer. Farm equipment."

Carlos dealt the cards. "But you do not look like a farmer, señor."

"Glad to hear it. Farmers are a gullible bunch. You can sell them anything."

"True." Carlos threw in a penny, lost the hand, and the stranger began to deal. In a matter of minutes, the stakes had risen to half a dollar and then a dollar, which pleased Carlos, for he was winning consistently. He was also drinking rapidly. He'd already consumed two large glasses of brandy.

When the porter began to light the oil lamps, the stranger said, "It's dusk already. Let's delay the rest of the game and have our supper now. I know there's a dining car aboard."

"Now that you remind me," Carlos said, "I am hungry, and I shall pay because I have been winning."

On their way to the dining car, Carlos regarded his

companion more carefully. "Have we met somewhere before, señor?"

The stranger shrugged. "I'm a gambler. I travel a lot. It's possible. Though I don't recall our ever having met."

"It seemed, just for a second when you turned your head," Carlos tapped his temple, "that you looked familiar, somehow."

The stranger smiled. "I think you have me confused with someone else."

Carlos laughed. "No doubt. No doubt."

In the dining car they were served steaks—and more brandy. Carlos was rapidly becoming loose tongued.

"When we return to the game, shall we make it five dollars, *amigo*?"

"If you can afford it," the stranger said.

Carlos patted his jacket over the inner pocket. "I can afford anything, and there is more where this came from."

"You're a handsome man, sir," the stranger said. "I have an idea your wallet contains money from a woman."

Carlos looked offended in a half-drunken way and then he began to laugh.

"You are a shrewd man, señor. How did you guess?"

"Because that's how I get my money, too. You'd be surprised how farm wives can influence their husbands— after I have influenced them."

Carlos laughed. "You are a man after my own heart, señor. Perhaps we should get together and plan some small thing. For profit, of course."

"Let's go back and start playing again," the stranger said. "My name, by the way, is Lawrence Williams."

"Señor Williams, it is a great pleasure." Carlos extended his hand. "The ride is no longer boring."

"We'll keep it that way, eh? I'll buy a bottle of brandy, since you're paying for our supper."

The game resumed as soon as they settled in the saloon car. Before long, Carlos was playing with unsteady hands.

The man who called himself Williams laid his cards face down and sat back, as if to rest a moment or two. "Could we, by chance, go back to where you got that fat wallet and perhaps improve the size of it?"

"No, no, señor." Carlos chuckled. "I would be shot the moment I showed my face. Some time must pass before I go back. But I will. Surely I will, for it is so easy to fool women."

"Tell me how you do it," Williams urged. "Then I'll tell you my methods. Between us, we may come up with something very good."

"I sold them some seed and told them that if crossed with their own, it would produce the best cotton in the world. How does one cross cotton from seed? I don't know. The beautiful one didn't either. Though she thinks I do."

"Very clever," Williams said. "But they'll find out, and then what happens?"

"Nothing, señor." Carlos shook his head in an attempt to clear his eyes. "They found out about me, and a great deal of money they had promised me was cut off. *Dios*, I almost went bankrupt."

"Then how did you get what you are carrying now?"

"I brought back seedlings this time, instead of seeds. And the beautiful one—ah, such golden hair—was happy to give me—hold your breath, señor—ten thousand dollars."

"You must have effective methods."

"It was not only easy, it was pleasurable. This woman's husband has apparently abandoned her. She was starved for a man. What passion, what love. But I had only one night with her before she found out about me and cut off the money I was promised."

"I'm afraid you work too well for me," Williams said.

"I have not yet finished, señor. I was betrayed. I lost a fortune. This ten thousand is a pittance compared to what I was promised. I do not like being cast off, threatened. They are going to pay dearly for that. I have already arranged it."

"Arranged what?" Williams asked.

Carlos waved a finger unsteadily before Williams's face. "I will not tell even you, but they *will* pay. As they have never before paid."

"You look very pale," Williams observed. "You've drunk too much, my friend."

Carlos picked up his cards and blinked at them. "It is true, *sí*. I have trouble seeing the cards, señor. I do not feel well."

Williams helped him up. "We'd better go out to the platform so you can get some air."

"*Sí*, if you will help me. I don't believe I could reach the platform without help."

Williams took his arm in a firm grasp and pushed him along the aisle and out onto the platform. Carlos's head seemed to clear then, and in the light flowing through the glass top of the door he regarded the stranger with sudden recognition.

"You fool me, señor," Carlos said. "I know you now. You were at the ball on Valcour. Virginia told me your name— Davenport... yes, Davenport. From England."

The stranger's laugh was cold and deadly.

Carlos lurched with the swaying train, his head again swimming. Williams held him against the door frame. Carlos's eyes filled with fear as he sensed danger, and he tried to take in a deep breath to clear his brain. Then he gave a sharp cry, but it was smothered by the rattle of the fast-moving train. The point of a knife had penetrated his clothing and pierced his flesh.

Williams yanked open Carlos's coat, removed the wallet and dropped it into his pocket.

"You bastard!" Carlos cried out. "You thief!"

"Carlos," Williams said, "you are the lowest skunk I've ever met. You not only cheat, but crudely. And you are scum. Filthy scum, living off the women you seduce. You are no asset to this world, Carlos, and you do not deserve being a part of it. *Adiós*, señor."

The knife sliced into his body and through his heart. Carlos died with no more than a brief cry of surprise and a grunt of pain. Williams calmly supported the body against the car while he managed to open the platform gate. He dragged the body around, gave it a violent shove, and sent what was left of Carlos hurtling out into the night.

He then wiped the knife with his handkerchief, threw the bloodied rag off the train, put the knife back in his pocket, and walked sedately back to his seat, where he gathered up the cards and shuffled them for a game of solitaire.

Four days later, a package was delivered to Virginia on Valcour. When she opened it, she discovered ten thousand dollars inside. There was no note—nothing to identify the sender.

She knew from whom it came. She knew also that the menace of Carlos was gone forever. But she shuddered in anticipation of what Carlos's murderer was capable of.

SIX

"What are we to do with all this cash?"

"Did you inquire of the bank where Carlos cashed the check?" Nanine asked.

"Yes. There's no doubt that this is the money given to Carlos."

"Brad's work, of course," Phoebe said.

"If this is the money given Carlos, and Brad came across him somehow, then Carlos is dead," Virginia said.

"How can we be sure?" Phoebe asked. "We've seen nothing in the papers."

"Carlos would never have given up the money," Virginia said. "It must have been taken from him by force, and there is no doubt in my mind who took it from him and returned it to us. Brad. And I assure you, Brad would have killed him. It may have happened so far away from here that the story never reached our newspapers. Or perhaps Carlos's body has not yet been found."

"I agree that's what must have happened," Nanine said. "Nobody else we know would have reason to kill Carlos and take the money from him."

"True," Phoebe said. "But tell me, how could Brad have known that Carlos had been here and blackmailed us for ten thousand dollars?"

"I can't imagine," Virginia said. "The only explanation I have is that perhaps Brad never disbanded those outlaws he commanded. They were fiercely loyal to him. He may still retain some of his men, and perhaps he has posted one or two here at Valcour to keep an eye on what's happening. Oh, my God," she exclaimed suddenly, "what if he has learned about my assignation with Carlos and uses it to take my son from me? No court of law in the country would take my side."

"You're forgetting that Brad couldn't go into a court of law," Nanine said calmly.

"For a moment I did." Virginia's face revealed her inner torment. "However, I know this—Brad has his own court. He deals with justice in his own way."

"It could even be his way of protecting his son," Phoebe said. "By having spies here."

"Even so," Nanine said, "how could a spy find out what had happened? The blackmail occurred behind a closed door. Even Phoebe and I didn't know the facts until you told us, Virgie."

"Yet, Brad must have boarded the same train . . ." Virginia ventured.

"How do we know Carlos even left Charleston?" Phoebe asked.

Virginia had an explanation for that. "The package of money was mailed in Atlanta the day after Carlos left here. I don't understand how Brad knew. But, knowing Brad and knowing Carlos, I'm sure Carlos will never bother us again."

Nanine said, "If Brad knew about the money we paid Carlos, he must have had some idea of why it was paid, and he'd not let Carlos again intimidate the mother of Brad's child. That's the explanation of why. *How* doesn't really matter."

"I hope you're right," Virginia said. "But I wish I knew how Brad found out."

"It's likely he knew some of the facts—enough to confront Carlos," Phoebe said. "But it's not possible that he

knew about...the blackmailing. Unless Carlos was fool
enough to tell him."

"At any rate," Virginia said, "we're rid of Carlos."

"And we have the seedlings he brought," Nanine said.
"Moses says they seem to be flourishing already."

"I'm going to call a meeting of the island and invite
everybody to inspect the seedlings," Virginia said. "We
must decide how we'll share the plants when they mature.
And there's the cross-pollination to be considered after we
harvest those plants."

"That will keep you busy," Nanine said. "Phoebe, are
you going to the mainland plantation to check on how
Chris Savard is coming along with this year's crop?"

Phoebe smiled. "I know, without going there, that everything is running smoothly. You do, too."

"Mama's already thinking about our annual Fourth of
July celebration," Nanine said. "Which keeps her busy,
too. For now, things are going well, so I suggest we take
advantage of this to handle the problems that crop up."

"It worked out well last year," Phoebe said. "Tomorrow
I'll go to the mainland and stay there a few days. If there's
banking or shopping to be done, I'll do that, too."

Serenity descended over Valcour, but while Virginia and
Phoebe accepted it, indulged it, Nanine was still worried.
She had no doubt that Carlos was dead. But she feared
that when his body was discovered and identified, it might
become known that he had had business on Valcour and
had been murdered on his way home. Even in death,
Carlos might somehow be able to bring trouble to Valcour.
And so could Brad, who was still very much alive.

Phoebe left for the mainland plantation the following
morning. She spent a few hours making purchases, then
hired a carriage for the journey to the plantation.

"I'm delighted to see you again, Miss Phoebe," Chris

Savard said when she arrived. "Your rooms are ready, and a very capable girl has been assigned to see to your comfort."

"Thank you, Mr. Savard. I'm to inspect the books and inspect the plantation to see how everything is going, though I know it's quite unnecessary. We're fortunate to have you as overseer."

"I appreciate your trust and confidence in me and I welcome your visits," he replied graciously. "However, I firmly believe you and your sisters should keep a close watch on things here. How else can you reassure Elias? He put his heart and soul and every ounce of energy he possessed to turn this plantation into a profitable enterprise."

"I know," Phoebe agreed. "I wish he could see that you've done him proud."

"You're very kind, Miss Phoebe. But it's work I love, and naturally I'm pleased to be entrusted to the running of this plantation and to have a room in the house. It just seems a shame that such a beautiful place stands empty. It's a house built to be lived in."

"True," Phoebe said. "But my sisters love Valcour."

"That's understandable. I imagine you do, too."

"I grew up there, though I spent time here also. But I feel more at home on Valcour."

"I must be getting back to the fields." Chris mounted his horse. "If I can answer any questions, you know where to find me."

"I shan't bother you today. I'll attend to the books after I freshen up. I would like you to join me at dinner tonight— that is, unless you've made other plans."

"I'll be very pleased. Good day, Miss Phoebe."

He urged his horse into motion and the animal galloped back to the fields. Phoebe watched his lean figure, noting how well he sat the animal. She was also aware of how her heartbeat had quickened when he had dismounted to greet her. His easy smile and warm blue eyes as he regarded her had almost made her tremble with delight. She hadn't felt that way since Tom had courted her.

With a reluctant step, she went upstairs to the suite that had been assigned her. The rich mahogany furniture glistened from the care it received. The sitting room had a chaise-longue in front of the small fireplace. Over it was a painting of Willowbrook, done by a former slave who had shown an aptitude for painting. When Virginia had realized how talented he was, she'd sent him North to complete his education and attend art classes. She had left the details to Phoebe, who had written to Captain Malloy of the New York City police.

He was the officer Phoebe had gone to when she discovered that Tom had been paying blackmail to Tobal, the ex-slave Virginia had shot and forced off the island when he'd attacked Elias. Tobal had gone North, seen Phoebe's picture in the newspaper, and realized she was passing herself off as white. Captain Malloy had warned her that if she refused to pay the blackmail and wanted Tobal exposed, she would suffer advserse publicity once it became known she was part Negro. Everything Captain Malloy had told her had come true: she'd been reviled, scorned, and insulted, and finally had fled the city.

Captain Malloy promptly answered Phoebe's letter requesting information, telling her of a tutor who could evaluate the extent of the education Lincus had had and place him in the proper school. There was also the name of an artist who took an interest in talented beginners. He would evaluate Lincus Hammond's work. The sisters allowed the ex-slaves to use the family name of Hammond. Captain Malloy also cautioned her to be certain that the young man brought his drawings and paintings with him.

Phoebe had insisted on paying for his trip North and for his education. Captain Malloy had assured her he would meet the young man at the depot and get him established in a suitable home in a Negro neighborhood, where he would feel more at ease. The three sisters had sent Captain Malloy a gold watch as a token of their gratitude.

It was working out very well, Phoebe thought. Lincus wrote her once a week and related in detail how his education and painting lessons were proceeding. In the few months he'd been North, his handwriting and spelling had improved enormously. He was beginning to express his feelings on paper with surprising smoothness. It made Phoebe feel good to know she was helping, but she gave Virginia the credit for recognizing Lincus's talent and wanting him to have his chance in the world.

A smile crossed her lips as she thought of spirited, headstrong Virginia, who could also be a thoughtful, compassionate woman. Phoebe could understand why men were attracted to Virginia for more than her beauty. She was intelligent, magnetic, flirtatious, and passionate. If only she could see through the men to whom she had given herself. A rogue by the name of Brad Culver; Carlos, a confidence man and a roué; and her first husband, Wade Le Garue. He'd died in the war, but not before he'd stolen the silver hidden on Valcour, which she and Virginia had risked their lives to get.

A young girl dressed in a soft gray uniform and a lace cap tapped lightly on the door. Phoebe opened the door and told her she'd not need her now, but would later when she would like to bathe and change into a dinner gown. Without being told, the maid knew her mistress would dine with Master Chris.

The maid's name was Tessa, and she could scarcely contain her excitement at the thought of helping her mistress with her toilette.

"Did yo' bring a lot o' clothes, Miz Phoebe? Loves pretty clothes."

"I brought only one dinner gown, Tessa, because my stay here will be short."

Tessa looked disappointed, but she regarded with approval the deep green dinner gown stretched across the bed. The long skirt was deeply ruffled. The overskirt had three rows of ruffles, and the bodice had a standing ruffle that outlined the heart-shaped neckline and would conceal the partially exposed bosom. It was daring for just a dinner for two, Phoebe reasoned, but she wanted to look her best for Chris. Unless he had a lady friend in the city proper—and he might well have, she cautioned herself—his life here must be dull and lonely.

Phoebe looked at the gown again. Though she'd purchased it in New York, she had no aversion to wearing it. She especially liked the pink satin bows that decorated the shoulders and sleeves, which ended just below the elbow and were also ruffled. Tessa dressed Phoebe's dark brown hair with a center part and a low coil at the base of her neck. Her long, thick hair had just the right texture to be worked with ease and hold in place.

Phoebe had covered herself with eau de toilette and the room was filled with its fragrance.

"Yo' smells real good, Miss Phoebe." Tessa breathed in the fragrance. "Mistuh Chris gonna be real s'prized an' happy to have dinnuh with a beautiful lady like yo'."

"Oh, I'm sure Mr. Chris has lots of dinners with lots of beautiful ladies," Phoebe ventured.

"No, ma'am, he don'. He jes' wuks an' reads all he kin 'bout cotton. Teaches the han's 'bout it, too. They respec's him."

"Doesn't Mr. Chris attend socials?" Phoebe asked in pretended surprise.

"No, ma'am," Tessa said seriously. "Awful lonely heah.

Loves it, though. All the pretty new things in the house. Eve'ythin' smell so clean. But no one evah heah. Sho' is lonely fo' someone young as me."

"Perhaps you'd like to work in the house at Valcour," Phoebe said, knowing the girl wouldn't leave.

"'Deed not, Miss Phoebe," Tessa protested. "Jes' wants to stay heah. Likes a li'l 'citement, though. All yo' pahties at Willowbrook. Nevah have none heah."

"You know," Phoebe said seriously, "you're right, Tessa. I'll speak to my sisters about it. Perhaps they'll give a ball here one day."

"Hopes it mighty soon. Sho' would like some music, dancin', an' lots o' people movin' 'bout."

Phoebe laughed. "Well, I'll see what I can do."

Tessa stepped back and regarded her mistress. "Yo' sho' looks purty, Miss Phoebe. Mighty purty."

"I hope Mr. Chris thinks so," Phoebe replied. "Do you know if he's downstairs?"

"Yes'm, he is. He dressed up fo' yo', Miss Phoebe. All spit an' polish, but please don' say I tol' yo'."

"Not a word, Tessa. Not a word."

Phoebe put on a simple gold necklace, earrings, and a bracelet before she went downstairs. Chris was awaiting her in the drawing room, which had been decorated by Virginia in delicate French Regency furniture. Twin settees flanked the fireplace, and chairs and tables were arranged in tête-à-tête fashion around the room. The chairs and settees were upholstered in pink moiré satin, and the filmy lace curtains were framed with cherry-red moiré satin draperies. Colorful vases of varying size decorated the room. Paintings adorned the walls. Some were of Valcour, painted by Lincus. Phoebe had brought him here to see them before he went North. He'd beamed with pride, seeing his work gracing the Hammond mansion.

Chris was seated in one of the chairs, his long legs

stretched full length and crossed at the ankles. His pale blue jacket above white trousers and shoes complimented the blue of his eyes. His black string tie was a stark contrast to his white shirt. He was freshly shaved and smelled faintly of bay rum. Phoebe felt her heart miss a beat as he stood up and came directly at her. He took her hand and raised it to his lips.

"You look enchanting, Miss Phoebe," he said, smiling at her. "You have no idea how pleasing it will be to sit opposite such a beautiful lady. A festive occasion, really. And your gown is magnificent."

"Thank you, Chris." A mere smile touched her lips. "May I be less formal?"

"I'd like it very much." He offered her his arm and led her to the dining room.

"And I'd like you to call me Phoebe." She looked up at him, her smile widening.

There was open admiration in his eyes. "I think this is going to be a very pleasant evening."

"I'm sure of it," Phoebe replied.

Sterling silver candelabra decorated the sideboard, and twin silver candlesticks graced the center of the table on either side of a silver bowl filled with roses from the garden. The crystal was finely etched, and the china was the most beautiful and delicate Virginia could find.

"How beautiful," Phoebe exclaimed. "Who did that?"

"Tessa," Chris replied. "I was lucky to get her. She's well trained."

"She is indeed," Phoebe agreed. "Just one criticism. The table is so large, I just wish we weren't at opposite ends."

"That can easily be remedied."

He picked up the silver bell and rang it. Tessa appeared immediately, her round face eagerly awaiting orders.

"I summoned her, Phoebe," Chris said. "You tell her the change we would like."

Phoebe laughed and told Tessa to set two places halfway down the long table. Tessa obeyed, and, in short order, the two were toasting each other with champagne.

"Tessa really is a gem," Phoebe said. "And she's so happy to please."

"She's happy tonight because the house is lit up and graced by a beautiful hostess," Chris said. "I'd like to drink to that."

Phoebe repeated what Tessa had said about the house being lonely and her desire to have parties in it.

"Yes," Chris agreed. "She is young, and I've been afraid she might leave. However, now that you've started with this dinner, she may believe there will be more of them in the future."

"Perhaps I should talk to Virginia about having a dinner party here," Phoebe said. "She knows so many people in Charleston. And Lenore loves to hostess."

"I like this sort of evening better," Chris said. "Candlelight, a beautiful lady, pleasant conversation, and good food. I hope you'll like it. We have a good cook who is awfully tired of preparing food for just a bachelor."

"Virgie, Nan, and I must have a little talk about this big house. As you say," Phoebe warmed to the subject, "it's a house made to be lived in. A shame it's empty most of the time."

"That's the way it seems," Chris said. "Just who is supposed to be in charge of this plantation?"

"I am," Phoebe said. "But there's so little for me to do. I come once a month and get the figures and bring them back to Nan. As you know, she had that task until I returned to Valcour."

"Then I think," Chris said, "in fairness to this house, and to the servants whom I'm ever fearful will leave because there's nothing for them to do, you should spend more time here."

Phoebe laughed. "I'll think about it."

Tessa was standing in the background, her expression serious, but when Phoebe nodded for her to serve dinner, she beamed and headed for the kitchen. Phoebe and Chris chose topics of general interest during the excellent dinner prepared by a woman who'd been hired by Elias while he was overseeing the replanting of cotton and the rebuilding of the large house. She'd proven herself so competent that he'd asked her to stay on. Now she had charge of the kitchen and wished, as Tessa did, that there were people to cook for and bring the house to life.

Chris suggested that they have a glass of port on the veranda and watch the sunset. Phoebe agreed, but first went to the kitchen to compliment the cook on her dinner. Phoebe had met Callie before, but neither she nor her sisters had had more than snacks when they came, since they'd wanted to spend their time shopping in Charleston. Callie beamed when Phoebe entered the kitchen. The woman was heavy, as Belle was, but Callie had the height to carry it.

"Thank yo' Miss Phoebe. Yo' sho' lookin' beautiful. A real pleashuh to haves yo' heah. Please come mo' offen."

"I will, Callie," Phoebe promised. "And my sisters will also."

"Sho' hopes so. Big house like this an' nevah used. Ain' right. Jes' glad we gots Mistuh Chris to looks aftuh. On'y thin' is, he don' needs much lookin' aftuh."

"We're very fortunate to have him," Phoebe agreed. "And to have you and Tessa. Do you have any problems overseeing the others who came in to help you keep up the house?"

"No problems, Miss Phoebe. If they is, yo' can bets Mistuh Chris takes keer o' them."

"Good." Phoebe turned to Tessa, who was standing

behind her. "Please bring the port outside. And perhaps some nuts?"

"Sho' will, Miss Phoebe," Tessa replied happily.

Phoebe felt as if she were hostessing a party, everyone was treating her so royally. She returned to the dining room, where Chris awaited her. He again held out his arm, and she slipped hers around it. They stepped out onto the large veranda and walked around to the west side, where the sun had almost set. There were several groupings of wicker chairs and tables. Chris led her to a corner where potted plants had been placed to provide a degree of privacy. "This is where I spend most of my evenings."

"Don't you get bored?" Phoebe asked.

"I'm too tired at the end of a day for that," he said. "Though I get lonely. Very lonely."

"You never married," Phoebe said. "Does the thought of it frighten you?"

"On the contrary, it has tremendous appeal."

"Has work consumed you to the point where you feel you don't have the time to share your life with the right woman?"

"That's it," Chris said. "The right woman."

"Why don't you get around a little?" Phoebe asked. "You'll never find her in this isolation."

"Oh, I've been around," he replied. "I've attended a few soirees. Enjoyed them, too, but never met anyone with whom I wished to become serious."

"I'm sure you've been pursued."

Phoebe nodded her thanks as she took her glass from the tray extended by Tessa.

"No. Perhaps because I've never wanted to be. Oh," he gave a slight shrug, "a few ladies have visited me here, but I can be a rather taciturn man when I want to be. And, in those cases, I wanted to be. I know you were an actress in

New York City. Elias told me you'd met with great success. Weren't you happy?"

"At first." Phoebe knew he didn't wish to talk about himself further, so she turned the discussion to herself. "But I had problems and left my career to come home. It's nice calling Valcour home. Though it's always been home to me."

"I know." He regarded her over his brandy snifter.

"Did you know I'm an ex-slave?" she asked, having decided to be blunt about what was most on her mind.

"Yes. Did you know I have no idea who my parents were? My real ones, that is. I was adopted by two wonderful people who raised me. They're both dead now."

She smiled. "To be honest, Chris, I know nothing about you except that you're competent and a gentleman."

"Thank you. I'd also like to say that though my sympathies were with the North, I fought on the side of the Confederate army, because I felt I owed it to my father. My mother died before I was grown."

"I know you were a student at West Point when the war broke out," Phoebe said.

He nodded. "I liked it there and was doing very well, but as I just told you . . ." He didn't finish the sentence. There was no need.

Phoebe took a sip of her port. "My ex-husband—he's already divorced me—was ashamed of the fact that I was part Negro."

"How could he have felt that way if he loved you?" Chris asked, perplexed.

"He didn't love me. I think he was mesmerized by Valcour. Or the loneliness of war caused him to believe he loved me. I didn't deceive him, though I could have. He swore that the fact that I wasn't all white would make no difference. We weren't North very long before I knew it did. When I asked how soon we'd meet his parents, who lived in Boston, he always had a reason for delaying it. One day I found a letter from his mother asking when he was bringing me to Boston. That's when I knew our marriage had never been on firm ground."

Chris set his glass down on the table. "Would you like to take a walk in the dusk?"

"Very much," she replied. "It's so beautiful. The perfumed air, the quiet, the distant strains of music and singing coming from the cabins."

"Elias fixed them up and rented them very reasonably," Chris said. "But then, you know that. I go down there some nights and watch them perform."

"It was with my own people that I learned to do the dances that took the audiences in New York City by storm."

"Elias said you're extremely talented." Chris took her arm and led her off the veranda and onto a path to the gardens. "I hope one day to see you dance. Professionally— if you intend to resume your career."

"I may never do that." Phoebe's voice held a note of uncertainty.

"Why not?"

"I'm content being here now," she said. "I don't know if I ever want to return to the theater."

"What do you want?"

"Marriage. And children. Yet, I must be honest. I'm frightened that they might not be white."

"Wouldn't you love them if they were black?" he demanded.

She looked up at him, her eyes tortured. "Of course I would. But would my husband? You see, Virginia and Nanine love me. I know they do, just as I love them. They're my family and they're white. If I married, it would have to be to a white man. But I couldn't go through with another man what I went through with Tom. I'd rather die than be humiliated as I was."

"Oh, Phoebe." His features softened as he looked down at her. "No one as beautiful and as good as you should have such a problem."

"I'll always have it," she said. "And I may as well admit it. I did a lot of thinking when I was with my mother."

"I know you were with her the last weeks of her life." Chris paused and turned to her.

"How do you know so much about me?" She was suddenly consumed more by curiosity regarding his knowledge of her than by the problem that beset her.

He regarded her soberly for a moment. "After Miles died, Nanine used to come here quite often. He did leave her this plantation, as you know. We became quite friendly. She talked a lot about you. I'd read about your success in the theater, and when Elias was here he used to tell me whenever they got a letter from you. They worried about you, you know."

"I tried not to let them know about the hard time Tom and I had in New York," she said. "But I suppose that, knowing me, they could read between the lines."

They'd reached a path that led directly to a gazebo. "We've had quite a walk," Chris said. "Would you like to sit in there for a bit?"

"Yes. Please," Phoebe said, already leading the way. A half-moon lent sufficient light for them to see clearly. There were a few chairs, a settee, and a chaise-longue, all in wicker, with well-upholstered chintz cushions made especially for the furniture. The sisters had spared no expense on the furnishings.

Chris's arm encircled Phoebe's waist as he guided her to the chaise-longue. She felt a wave of weakness and desire at his closeness. She knew it wasn't just because she was seated beside a man, but rather because she was in the presence of Christopher Savard. She loved him. She'd never dared think of it before. She wondered if she dared now. She felt certain that he wasn't a trifler of women, and he seemed sincerely interested in her.

As if to reassure her, he said, "I love you, Phoebe. I've loved you for some time. In fact, since the first time I saw you. I think Nan knows. She's a very perceptive lady. I used to ply her with questions about you. I suppose some were foolish. It was really to get her to talk about you. I hungered for news of you, even before I'd ever laid eyes on you. When I finally met you, I had to stifle that hunger, because I worked for you."

"I should say you worked for Nan, since Miles left her the plantation, but Virgie, Nan, and I share our wealth. Please don't let that come between us. Not tonight. You've made me feel so wonderful. So alive."

"I'm going to kiss you, Phoebe, he said. "Unless you'd rather I didn't."

Without a word, she lifted her arms and wrapped them around his neck. Their lips met, and the passion they'd kept in check for so long seemed to explode. A soft moan escaped Phoebe as he rained kisses on her neck, her chest, and her breasts, which were forced almost free of bodice, for she was bent back.

"Oh, God, Phoebe, I love you. If you care, please say so." His voice was hoarse with emotion. Hers trembled when she answered.

"I love you, my darling Chris. I realize now I've loved you for some time. Perhaps that was why I didn't come as often as I wanted to. I was fearful you would notice. I couldn't bear to reveal that I cared and have you scorn me because I was part Negro."

"Damn the color of your skin," he said harshly. "It's you I love. Your body, your soul, your mind, your skin. Just for you to walk in the room sets me on fire. I'm half-mad now. I want to possess you. Please let me, my darling. And don't ever mention the fact that you're a Negro again. I don't give a damn. I love you. I'll love our children, whatever their color. I want to marry you, but just now I want you."

He spoke with his head pressed against her bosom and his words were muffled, but Phoebe reveled in what he'd said. She had neither the will nor the desire to deny him. She wanted him as much as he wanted her.

She slipped free of him and started to undress. He sat there watching her shed her clothes. When she was nude, he dropped to his knees, kissing and caressing her body, murmuring endearments.

Phoebe bent, slipped her hands under his arms, and urged him to his feet. She undid his string tie and slid her arms into the sleeves of his coat, freeing him of it. He took over from there, and when he was nude, he picked her up in his arms and carried her to the chaise-longue. He set her down gently and lay beside her, gathering her close. Phoebe's arms enclosed him and her mouth sought his. In the perfume of the night, they made love, plighted their troth, and planned their future.

Afterward, Phoebe made him promise to keep it a secret for a while. He demurred at first, stating that he wanted the world to know.

"Let's not share our love with anyone for a few days," she urged.

"You're afraid of Virginia." His statement, so unexpected, startled her "Admit it."

"She likes you," Phoebe said. "I don't believe she loves you, but she's spirited."

"She's also a married woman," he replied, rasing himself enough to cover her. "Elias is my friend, and I love you. Your body and your hands just about drove me mad. Thanks, my darling."

Phoebe's hand rested on his thigh. She squeezed it gently as she spoke. "You'll sleep tonight, won't you?"

"No, dammit. Not with you here. And I'm not sleeping in the house tonight. I couldn't stay there, knowing you were a few doors away, and not come to you."

"I should hope not, she said primly. "And I shall be very hurt if you refuse to share my bed with me."

"You hussy," he exclaimed as he gathered her close.

Their laughter was smothered when their lips met. She broke the embrace, saying that they would be more comfortable in bed. They dressed hastily and returned to the house. She went directly upstairs. Chris joined her after he had put out the lamps.

SEVEN

Virginia, riding her brown Arabian, led the way along the narrow, forest-lined road. Phoebe, riding behind her, felt slight stirrings of apprehension. She wondered if she'd been wise in not telling Virginia and Nanine that she and Chris Savard were engaged. But she had wanted to keep it a secret for a few days, at least. She'd appropriated Chris's black string tie before she left, and from that time on it had nestled next to her breasts. It kept him close to her, and when she touched the area with her hand, pressing the fabric to her skin, her heart soared, though she was flooded with the weakness of desire.

Usually Virginia chose to ride alone, but today she'd asked Phoebe to come with her. Phoebe wondered if it was to question her about Chris. But she doubted that Virginia had the slightest suspicion of what had transpired at the plantation.

Phoebe turned her thoughts to the caressing warmth of the early summer day. The bright sunlight seemed to make the dead, naked trees come alive. The Spanish moss, hanging in great lengths from the tall branches, gave the trees a majestic beauty. Two herons, startled at the approach of the horses, left their nests in the tall trees. It was a perfect day for riding. Perhaps that's why Virginia had invited her to come along, for she turned and smiled, motioning to the two herons circling high above. Phoebe nodded, returning the smile.

Where the forest ended, a brief expanse of marsh grass led to a rocky shore. They skirted the grass and moved farther inland. Soon they came upon the white-painted schoolhouse. It had been built by the Yankees for the purpose of educating the Negroes who in slavery had been kept illiterate to quell their rebellious tendencies. The expenses of maintaining the school and the salaries of the teachers were paid by the Hammond sisters.

They continued until they rode alongside the old slave cabins, now converted into comfortable homes for the Negro farmhands. The clotheslines were heavy with the morning wash. Several slim, proud black mothers waved and called out greetings. Virginia and Phoebe answered but didn't stop.

It was like a vacationer's tour of the island, for Virginia, leading the way, seemed intent on covering both the busy sections and the quiet areas, like the two cemeteries, one for the graves of the island's Negroes, one for the whites.

Still, Virginia did little talking, and that intensified Phoebe's apprehensions. When they reached the white graveyard, they dismounted. The sisters walked to the graves of their father, their brother, and Miles Rutledge, Nanine's husband. The fact that Virginia held Phoebe's hand softened her apprehension.

"We don't come here often enough," Virginia said.

"Even so, the graves are well tended," Phoebe remarked.

"Thanks to Nanine and Moses. Isn't it odd how things turn out?"

"What do you mean?"

Virginia pointed to two graves. "There lies our brother next to Miles Rutledge, the man who killed him."

"I think they'd both approve of being buried this way. We know neither one meant to kill the other, even if it was a duel."

"We must get small Confederate flags for their graves.

Papa died in the service, and Marty was a brigadier with a fine record."

"It's lovely here," Phoebe said. "Especially so this morning. If you turn slowly to your left, there's a family of deer studying us and wondering if they should run."

"I see them. It's an enchanting spot, Phoebe. I think this island is the most beautiful place on earth. And we brought it back from the shambles caused by the war."

"Your dedication and hard work made it possible," Phoebe said.

They returned to their horses, mounted, and rode even farther inland, where the other plantations were located. Here the fields were in full operation. These plantations were smaller than the vast acreage owned by the Hammond family, but they provided a rich livelihood for the forty-odd families on the island.

A game of croquet was in progress on the expanse of lawn between the two mansions owned by Robert and Alice Benson and Mary Lou and Alan Cartwright. Two other couples were engaged in the game with the Bensons and the Cartwrights.

"They seem to have guests," Phoebe said.

Virginia's interest heightened. "Let's go over and meet them."

Phoebe was hesitant, but she stifled her uneasiness and dismounted with Virginia when they reached the lawn. Phoebe supposed she would always have these moments of fear when she was confronted with new faces, wondering if she'd be accepted. An attractive couple, still carrying their croquet mallets, accompanied Mary Lou Cartwright. She introduced them as Mr. and Mrs. Douglas Farrel.

"They're Yankees, Virgie," Mary Lou said. "From New York City."

"My sister Phoebe and I are pleased to meet you."

Virginia assumed the role of spokesman. "I trust your visit is pleasant."

"Indeed it is," Mrs. Farrel exclaimed. "We're completely captivated by the island. And delighted to meet you. Mary Lou told us how you helped the islanders regain their homes."

"You're to be congratulated, Mrs. Birch," Mr. Farrel said. "That was quite an undertaking. In fact, you also made a name for yourself, Mrs. Sprague. Both Lorraine and I saw you perform on the stage in New York City. You were excellent."

"I'm quite in agreement," Mrs. Farrel said. "Did you know the show closed shortly after you left it? I don't blame you for doing that. What you had to contend with was ghastly."

"Quite," Phoebe agreed. "But I'm very happy back with my family."

"I'm sure you are," Mrs. Farrel replied.

Phoebe wasn't certain whether Mrs. Farrel's friendly manner was sincere, but there was no time to dwell on it, for Alice and Robert Benson joined the group to introduce their guests, Gladys and John Bishop from Oklahoma.

John Bishop acknowledged the introductions, adding, "I by no means intend to boast, but I've traveled extensively and been to all the well-known vacation spots in the world, but none can compare to the charm and tranquility of Valcour. This island has everything. We had no idea it was such a perfect vacation spot."

Mrs. Bishop agreed, saying, "I told John I'd like to move down here and live out my life."

"It's very kind of you to speak so highly of Valcour," Virginia replied. "You already know how I regard it and the residents who have been our friends for decades."

Mrs. Bishop said, "I know Mary Lou and Alan think highly of you. They said you're a rebellious and rather unconventional family, except for your mama and your sister—is her name Nanine?"

"It is," Virginia replied lightly. "Phoebe and I would like you to meet them. Mama loves to play hostess, so if you have the time, we would be most happy if you would be our dinner guests tomorrow night."

The guests looked to their respective hosts and hostesses, who readily agreed. After a few more moments of light talk, Virginia and Phoebe said goodbye and rode off.

"How odd," Phoebe mused, "to hear Valcour called a vacation spot. I never thought of it in that way, but you know, it's true."

Virginia smiled. "I suppose I didn't think of it as a place where one could lollygaggle, because I worked so hard to bring it back to what it once was."

"It exceeds what it once was," Phoebe said. "Thanks to you."

She also wanted to give Elias credit for the work he had done, not only on Valcour but on the mainland. However, there was no point in doing so. The mere mention of his name angered Virginia.

"I guess you could say we've been on vacation all our lives. Let's ride over to our fields, visit Moses, and see how the Mexican plants are coming along. There's nothing rebellious or unconventional about that."

They laughed as they exchanged glances. Then they quickened the pace of their horses, for both were eager to visit their fields. When they came upon them, the sight made them pull up and sit in silence, marveling at the beauty of the area.

The cotton was not yet in sufficient blossom to create a white blanket, but the green of the plants was bright in the sunlight.

In the distance, the two-story mansion built decades ago by the Hammond family looked like an ancient castle with its chimneys on slanted roofs and its tall windows glistening in the late-morning light.

Moses came riding from the fields to greet them. As he approached, he swept off his large, battered straw hat and nodded to both women. He was a large, muscular man, still in prime condition despite his white hair and his black, wrinkled face.

"Mo'nin', ladies," he said. "Nice o' yo' to stop by."

"How have you been, Moses?" Virginia asked. "We don't see much of you these days."

"Been right busy, Miss Virginia." Moses chuckled. "Sho' gots one fine crop growin' this yeah. Keeps a man busy seein' to it."

"We couldn't do without you," Virginia admitted. "And I want to thank you for keeping Belle in line."

"Simmered down some, reckon. Ain't been complainin' lately, an' nevah says she goin' to quit. Knows bettah, reckon."

"She's afraid of you," Virginia said. "And she's a trial to me. But she's very good in the kitchen, especially when we have guests. I'm glad you put her down, Moses."

"She give yo' mo' trouble, yo' lets me know, an' I takes keer o' that woman."

"How are the Mexican plants doing?" Phoebe asked.

"Mighty good, Miss Phoebe. Gots part o' them in one big patch an' the rest scattered 'roun' to see if they grows bettah in some spots than othahs. Seems they all doin' real well."

"I'm glad to hear that," Virginia said. "We expect great things of those plants."

"Yes'm. Sho' don' knows much 'bout marryin' two cotton plants, but reckon kin be done."

"We'll find out how," Virginia said. "We depended on the Mexican planter to show us how, but he won't be back, so we have to attend to this ourselves."

"When yo' gets ready, jus' lets me know," Moses said. "Maybe I kin sort o' he'p then. Mo'nin to yo', ladies. Gots wuk to be done."

He bowed again, replaced his hat, and rode off astride the old farm horse he had ridden for so many years.

"Carlos certainly was generous with the seedlings," Phoebe said.

"It was a pleasant surprise when I saw them," Virginia said, smiling. "Possibly he thought that when I realized how generous he was, I'd forget his duplicity."

"It sounds reasonable," Phoebe agreed. "He did have charm, and those brown eyes could make anyone melt."

"I'm sure he had a lot of practice seducing women," Virginia said with a trace of bitterness. "Certainly I was taken in by him."

"Are you sure that getting cotton seedlings from his plantation had nothing to do with it?"

"He brought us seeds, if you remember," Virginia said remindfully. "Bringing the seedlings came as a complete surprise. Nonetheless, a welcome one. I can't wait until they grow larger. I'm getting impatient."

Phoebe laughed. "That's part of your personality."

Virginia's brow furrowed. "I just wish there was someone I could contact to help me with crossing the two breeds."

"Why not write Elias?" Phoebe ventured. "If he knew, he'd certainly tell you."

"I doubt it." Her mood turned cold. "He'd tell me nothing."

"Aren't you being unfair? He's made a lot of money for us since he went to London."

"For himself also," Virginia retorted. "And I'm certain it isn't all work and no play."

"For the sake of fairness, it hasn't been with you, either."

"Very well. I had one night with Carlos. I was foolish,

but I was also starved for love. I'm not reserved like you and Nanine."

"Leave me out of it," Phoebe said quickly. "I'm as hot-blooded as you."

"If you are, you hold yourself in check quite well. Getting back to the subject of cotton, do you suppose Chris Savard could help us?"

"It's still early," Phoebe said hastily. "I can go there and discuss it with him."

"No. You've just come from there," Virginia said thoughtfully. "No need for you to go back. I'll go."

"What about Jimmy?" Phoebe was desperately searching for a reason to make Virginia change her mind.

Virginia brightened. "I'll take him with me."

"I'll tell Ivy to pack for both of them," Phoebe said, realizing that nothing would deter Virginia from going to the mainland plantation.

"I'm not taking Ivy," Virginia said.

"What if Brad should learn you're at the plantation with Jimmy?"

Virginia brought her horse to halt and reached over to pull the reins on Phoebe's. "What's gotten into you? You're acting as if I shouldn't go. It's only to talk with Chris. Certainly I have the right to."

Phoebe smiled uncertainly. "Of course you have. I'm sorry I was acting so foolishly. However, I'll say this. I asked Chris about crossing our cotton with the Mexican and he replied that he'd never heard of doing it with cotton, though he supposed it could be done. He also said that since you were so set on doing it, he hoped you'd meet with success."

"I intend to," Virginia said coldly. "I think it's about time he and I had a talk. It almost sounds as if he disapproves of the idea."

"No, Virgie," Phoebe said quietly. "He's very fair. You

know that. And very competent. You know that also. You needn't take my word for it. Nan will tell you that. He likes Nan very well. He has a lot of respect for her because of the way she handled herself with Miles and after his death."

"You seem to have done a lot of talking with Chris." Virginia paused and eyed Phoebe carefully. "And your face is suddenly suffused with color. I hope he treated you respectfully."

"He did," Phoebe said. "We did a lot of talking. I talked to him of my experience in New York. And of how much I love Valcour and being a part of your family. And of how fearful I was of falling in love and marrying again, lest my children be born black."

"What did he say?" Virginia asked sternly.

"He asked if I'd love them if they were black."

"And your answer?"

"It was yes. He said that then there would be no problem. He also asked me if I didn't have enough faith in you and Nan to know you would never reject me."

"That was quite a confidential talk—usually one connected with lovers."

Phoebe managed a smile and looked directly into Virginia's eyes. "He wasn't even holding my hand. I suppose I just got carried away. He was kind. I'd never had a talk like that with him before."

"Did you dine together?"

"Yes. Callie and Tessa were delighted that they could at last serve a dinner. I asked him to dine with me since he has dinner in the house every night."

"He's always used the breakfast room," Virginia said. "I had a snack there with him a few times."

"I suppose Nan did also," Phoebe replied. "Virgie, please don't be angry with me. Nan did ask me to go there and check with Chris and also to make some entries in the books. You had no objection to my going."

Virginia suddenly relaxed and reached out to squeeze Phoebe's arm lightly. "Forgive me. I swear for a minute I was jealous. I'm acting like a silly schoolgirl."

Phoebe knew that this was the time to confess that she and Chris were betrothed, but the words wouldn't come. She feared Virginia's temper, and she knew that Chris Savard was on Virginia's mind. Nonetheless, she decided to be frank.

"You don't have the right to be jealous of any woman, Virgie. Not when you're still married."

Virginia stiffened. "Damn you for throwing my marriage in my face. Especially when the man ignores me completely. I'm no wife to him and he's no husband to me."

"Why don't you relent and write to Elias?" Phoebe asked, her eyes pleading. "You hate him so much that you must love him."

"I loathe him," Virginia retorted. "And I loathe you for trying to force me to do something I never will."

"Because of your pride?"

"Call it what you want," Virginia said through clenched teeth. "But don't ever tell me to write to that monster again. Not after what he did to me."

"Need I remind you of what you did to him?"

"I know what I did," Virginia said.

"Did you ever tell him you were sorry?" Phoebe demanded, amazed at her daring.

"No," Virginia retorted. "Nor will I. The result of that illicit alliance with Brad is a son whom I love dearly. He makes up for my lack of a husband."

"Jimmy deserves a father," Phoebe said. "Elias could fill that role. I believe he'd come to you if you wrote him."

"He wouldn't," Virginia retorted. "Nor will I ever write."

"I'm sure the hurt he suffered when he learned you had been unfaithful to him and were with child by another man—an outlaw—was as great as the shock you had the day the doctor gave you the news."

"You never spoke to me like this before," Virginia said heatedly. "I almost wish you were a slave and I could order you brought to the whipping shed for a thrashing, which I'd administer myself."

Phoebe smiled. "You don't mean a word of it, Virginia. You love me as much as I love you. You're angry, stubborn, even hateful, but nothing you say will frighten me—or hurt me, because we love each other."

Virginia relented. "We've been through too much together for me to turn my back on you. But I've done so with Elias, and I'll never allow him to set foot on this plantation or this island again. Nothing will ever make me change my mind about that. So don't ever bring up the subject again."

Phoebe's eyes pleaded with Virginia, but she was unyielding.

"I mean it, Phoebe. Remember that."

Virginia urged her horse into motion. Phoebe sat motionless until she was certain that Virginia had reached the house and handed over the horse to a stable boy. She was ashamed that she hadn't confessed to Virginia that she and Chris were engaged. It had been cowardly of her not to.

She touched her horse's flank with her quirt and let him amble slowly back to the house. There, she sought out Nanine, who was in the library working on the books.

Nanine took one look at Phoebe's tortured features. "What happened?"

"Everything."

"Was your ride unpleasant?"

"It was wonderful—until the end."

"Tell me the wonderful part first," Nanine said, putting

down her quill pen and sitting back, resting her head against the softness of the leather chair.

Phoebe told her that they'd stopped at neighbors and invited them and their guests for dinner, then had gone to the cotton field.

"We were talking about the breeding of the two cottons," Phoebe went on, "when Chris Savard's name came up."

"That shouldn't have caused any unpleasantness," Nanine reasoned.

"I know." Phoebe lowered her eyes as she spoke. "It probably wouldn't have if I'd spoken to you both when I returned from the mainland plantation. But I chose to remain silent about what happened there."

"What did happen?" Nanine asked.

"Chris and I fell in love and became engaged."

"I'm very happy for you, Phoebe," Nanine said quietly. "And you know I wish you a wonderful future."

"Thank you."

"What did Virgie say when you told her?"

"I haven't told her."

"Oh, my God," Nanine said, a trace of panic in her voice.

"She's going to the plantation to talk with Chris regarding the crossing of the Mexican cotton with ours. That's what upset me. I tried to dissuade her with the only argument I knew—Elias. I suggested first that she write him and ask his advice. When she refused, I told her I'd tell Ivy to pack a bag for herself and Jimmy. But she said she isn't taking Ivy with her."

"Go on," Nanine said, knowing there was no telling what would happen once Virginia learned of the betrothal of Phoebe and Chris.

"Then I brought Brad into the conversation, asking what might happen if he learned that she was alone in the house with Chris."

"I'm sure that made her even angrier."

"Yes. But she got her emotions under control, and said that she had actually become jealous of me. Obviously, she's thinking about a liaison with Chris."

"Obviously."

"I didn't really mean to be deceitful," Phoebe said. "I wanted to keep the good news to myself for a while."

"You're not being completely honest, though, are you?" Nanine, in her wise way, knew that Phoebe feared Virginia's temper.

Phoebe reluctantly met Nanine's gaze.

"No completely," Phoebe admitted. "I know Virgie is intrigued by Chris. But I doubt she's in love with him."

"I doubt it too," Nanine agreed. "Virgie's in love with love. She's a good woman, but one who must know the comforting feel of a man's arms about her. Who is eager to consume him and be consumed by him. Who wants to match his passion with hers. She's very possessive and determined to have what she wants. She'll not allow anyone or anything to stand in her way. That's why you were afraid to let her know about you and Chris, isn't it?"

"Yes." Phoebe's voice was barely audible.

"I don't know what advice to give you."

Both women were silent for a few moments. Then Nanine spoke again.

"I don't think you'd better tell her now. She might fire Chris. We can't allow that to happen. Let her go there. If Chris is the man I believe him to be, he'll reject her advances, for that's what they'll be. She has no claim on him. God help us when she gets back. But perhaps it will help her wake up. It's about time she learned that she can't have every man she wants. As for Brad, I'm concerned about him also. He's unpredictable."

"So is Virginia," Phoebe replied. Then she rose. "I'm going upstairs to freshen up."

Nanine said, "At least Virgie can't confront you with having been intimate with him."

Phoebe had reached the door. She turned slowly. "I was. He spent the night in my bed." She opened the buttons of her riding blouse and slipped her hand inside to retrieve the black string tie. She held it up for Nanine to see. "At night it's under my pillow. It keeps Chris close to me."

"I pray to God that Virgie doesn't suspect," Nanine said. "I don't know how she'll react."

"Even if Chris was attracted to Virgie, he respects her marriage vows and, just as important, he respects Elias."

"I know," Nanine agreed. "I know Chris. I suspected he cared for you. He had a habit of bringing the conversation around to you when I went over there—after your return, of course. He hadn't met you, but he informed me that Elias had told him about the family's concern that all wasn't going well with you in New York City."

Phoebe nodded. "He told me all that. He also talked with me about my being part Negro. He gave me more confidence. I believe I won't be so fearful about meeting people now, though it wasn't easy this morning when we stopped to talk."

"Did it go well?"

"I think so," Phoebe replied, dubious about Lorraine Farrel, but not wanting to give Nanine further cause for worry.

"Good." Nanine leaned forward and picked up the quill pen. She dipped it in the crystal inkwell and touched it to the side, saying as she did so, "Run along. I must get this completed before supper. Thanks for bringing me back such an orderly set of figures. Virgie was always so impatient with the bookwork."

"Thanks, Nanine." Phoebe turned and headed for the stairs, replacing the black string tie inside her blouse. She pressed her hand to her bosom as she ascended the stairs.

EIGHT

Virginia awakened late. Lenore had hosted the dinner for the guests of their neighbors on Valcour, and it had gone well, but it had been lengthy because the conversations were interesting and spirited, concerned mostly with the island and its rare beauty. They'd compared it with European spas, with Bar Harbor in the North, and with Fort Lauderdale in the South. Despite some dissenting voices, Valcour won out.

So Virginia had retired quite late and had slept well, and when she rose she felt refreshed and ready for the early-summer day. She slipped into a peignoir and started for the nursery, where Jimmy slept soundly. But before she left the bedroom she paused to glance into the bureau mirror. She was instantly attracted to a folded, crumpled, smudged piece of paper that had been slipped under a corner of the mirror's wooden frame.

She removed the paper and unfolded it. It was a note written on a small, roughly torn out piece of paper from a ruled pad. It was brief and to the point, and it created in her a fear that made her gasp and reach unsteadily for the edge of the bureau to maintain her balance.

My dear Virginia,

On Monday next you will go to the only hotel in Falmouth, a village just outside Charleston. You will

register as Mrs. Paul Chandler. I will meet you there on a
matter of grave importance. We shall talk about our son, but
I assure you there is something of even greater concern that
may affect Valcour, or at least your plantation. I strongly
urge you not to disappoint me.

As ever.

She reread the note, removed her peignoir and dressed
quickly, and left her suite to knock briskly on Nanine's
door. She received no answer there and remembered that
her elder sister was always an early riser. But she found
Phoebe in her suite, dressing her hair.

"Come downstairs quickly," Virginia said. "It's urgent. I
must talk with you and Nan. Never mind breakfast for
now. Just hurry."

Virginia found Nanine in the library, working at the
books. "Look at this," she said worriedly, holding out the
note.

Nanine paled as she read it. "There's no doubt of who
sent it. What do you propose to do?"

"I'd like to tear that note into a thousand pieces. I don't
want to see him."

Nanine extended the paper to Phoebe when she entered
the room.

She read it and said to Virginia, "This is frightening."

"Very," Virginia agreed. "I'm terrified that he wants
Jimmy."

"The only way you'll find out is to see him," Nanine
reasoned. "Where was the note?"

"Tucked in the frame of the bureau mirror."

"Which means someone entered the house," Nanine
said. "Yet, each night I take pains to see that the windows
and doors are locked."

"One of us always does," Phoebe said. "Which means
Brad couldn't have gained entry into the house."

"Locked doors and windows wouldn't keep Brad out," Virginia replied, remembering the night he'd awakened her and demanded her body, which she'd given eagerly.

"It was daring of him to come here," Phoebe said.

"Brad will dare anything," Virginia said. "But I don't believe he placed the note there."

"Who, then?" Nanine asked.

"If I knew, I'd shoot whoever did," Virginia said angrily. "I can't imagine anything concerning Valcour that Brad could warn us about. He has only one purpose in mind—my son."

"It may be more than that," Nanine said thoughtfully. "We know he must have come in contact with Carlos, and he may well have learned something. I suggest you see him. If only for Jimmy's sake. You can't fight the man when you don't know what his plans are."

"You're right, as usual," Virginia said. "But if he thinks I'm going to let him have Jimmy, he's very much mistaken."

"Brad seems unafraid of moving about," Nanine commented. "For a man under sentence to hang, that takes nerve—or foolhardiness."

"Brad's not a fool," Virginia defended him. "But he's not the brigand who used to terrorize the carpetbaggers. Besides, he's a well-educated man. He knows how to dress and has the manners and the background of a gentleman. The authorities are looking for a grubby outlaw."

"You'll have to meet him tomorrow," Nanine said. "Do you think one of us should go with you?"

"No. Brad's a strange man. He might resent your presence. I'm not afraid of him. All I'm afraid of is what he wants. The note states we're to talk about Jimmy."

"Well," Phoebe said, "the sooner you meet him, the faster you'll know what he's up to. He knows that if you start screaming, he'll have to run or get caught. You have the advantage over him there."

"I doubt I have the slightest advantage if he has his mind made up to take Jimmy," Virginia said. "Brad has proved many times that he's absolutely ruthless."

Phoebe said, "I'll go to the mainland with you, and if you don't return in a reasonable length of time, I'll get help from the Union army. Wasn't it Lieutenant Johnson who came here?"

"Yes, but I wouldn't advise that," Nanine said. "I doubt Virgie has anything to fear from Brad. Physically, I mean. He's no longer an outlaw."

"I think he has his old band of outlaws ready to help him—what's left of them, anyway. Maybe that's how the note got into my bedroom." Virginia shuddered at the thought. "To think I was sleeping and someone just walked in."

"When will you leave?" Nanine asked.

"Late in the morning, so I won't have to sit around some old hotel worrying. I know where Falmouth is. It's not even on the map it's so small, but a road goes through there. I only hope the hotel is reputable. I'll take one of Papa's revolvers in my bag, just in case."

"Do you believe that's wise?" Nanine asked.

"Wise or not, I'm taking it, and I hope Brad never comes into this house to take Jimmy or I'll use it. I mean that."

"For the moment, I doubt we have anything to fear. At this stage, probably all he'll do is tell you what he wants."

"Phoebe, think up something to tell Mama," Virginia said. "And please arrange for two men to row me ashore and wait overnight. In case something goes wrong."

"Everything will be ready," Nanine promised.

Just before noon, Phoebe and Nanine accompanied Virginia to the dock. Her small suitcase had already been placed in the boat, which was manned by two brawny oarsmen. Phoebe and Nanine waved a farewell as the boat started its trip to the mainland, then they turned and walked back to the house.

"What excuse did you give Mama for Virgie's sudden departure?" Nanine asked.

"I said that she had some business at the bank," Phoebe replied.

"You didn't lie. Virgie told me she was going to stop there to have a talk with Henry Tyler. She wants another confirmation besides the one I got that the money we received is the same as what they gave to Carlos."

"I think she's wise, especially since she's going to see Brad."

"At least your confrontation with Virgie will be posponed for a while," Nanine said.

"I hope it won't come to that," Phoebe said. "I did wrong in not telling you both when I returned. I realize now that the best thing is to face up to whatever problem you have."

"Never mind," Nanine consoled. "I feel certain that Chris will handle it in a sensible manner. Though I doubt he'll spare Virgie's feelings. That's why I didn't want you to tell her after you came back from your ride two days ago."

"You mean his frankness might cause her to fire him?"

"Exactly. And that's something we can't afford. I don't know whom we could get to replace him."

"As far as I'm concerned no one could," Phoebe said with pride.

Nanine laughed. "I thought that after the war and once we got the house enlarged and restored, we'd find peace and tranquility. I fear we have a long way to go."

Virginia stopped at the bank before hiring a carriage to take her to Falmouth. Henry Tyler, the banker, confirmed that the money Carlos had obtained from the cashed check was the same as that which Nanine had brought back to the bank after Virginia had received it.

"There was no mistake," he said. "As you know, our former money, Confederate money—shinplasters—is not used anymore. The North has sent in bills, many of which are new. That's how I'm sure this is the same money. Some of the bills are in sequence, and I took care to make note of the numbers. There's absolutely no question about it, Miss Virginia. And I think you were wise in returning it to the bank. That was far too much money to keep around the house, especially when there's no man to protect you ladies."

"You're right, of course, Mr. Tyler," Virginia agreed, although she didn't feel the least bit fearful or reluctant to use a gun should it become necessary. She'd done it before and would not hesitate to do so again.

"Has he given you any trouble?" Mr. Tyler asked with concern.

"We've not heard a word from him, and I hope we never do. Frankly, we never expected him to return any part of that money. It was quite a shock to receive the entire ten thousand."

"If you ask me, I'd have sworn he never would. I almost refused to cash the check, but of course there was no way to reach you quickly enough, so I had to take the risk. I'm glad it turned out well."

Virginia reached the hotel shortly after four that afternoon. Located ten miles out of Charleston, it was a fair-sized establishment. For some reason, it had been spared during the war; it showed no signs of damage or rebuilding. It was a two-story structure with a small foyer and a dining room, and it was both attractive and clean. She was pleased that it hadn't turned out to be a cheap rendezvous that Brad might have used during his days as an outlaw.

Her room was comfortable and scrupulously clean. No one eyed her suspiciously or asked any questions. She unpacked and then lay down to rest for an hour. At six, she slipped out of her dress while she freshened up and restyled her hair. She applied a touch of rouge to her cheeks and a fine layer of powder to her face. She put on a simple voile walking dress—a soft blue that gave her an air of girlish innocence. She liked the effect and hoped that Brad would not only be impressed but would be charitable regarding Jimmy. She knew she would have to exercise care not to antagonize him.

She went down to an already well-filled dining room. She saw him immediately at a table in a far corner. He was an imposing figure with his bearded face and thick, unruly hair touched with gray—a handsome devil, too. His dark gray suit fitted him to perfection. It was surprising how different he looked with the beard. She realized that if he exercised care, he might never be caught. She'd not have recognized him if she hadn't already seen him at the house.

He rose as she approached the table. He held her chair, bent down as she seated herself, and kissed her gently on the neck. Then he gave her a warm smile and sat down opposite her.

"I couldn't resist that. You're as beautiful and desirable as ever, Virginia. I wish the circumstances were different. I want to fall in love with you. I've matured. I'm even ready to settle down."

"With whom?" she asked tartly.

"You, of course."

"Need I remind you I'm a married woman?"

He looked amused. "Why haven't you divorced him? You're not the kind of woman who can go without a man for any length of time."

"There's been no man in my life since Elias walked out."

"Not even Carlos Cabrera? I saw him at the ball you gave. He was following you around like a puppy."

"That was business."

"Not very ethical business," Brad said gently. "He took you good."

Virginia started to push back her chair. "I didn't come here to be insulted."

"Then let's change the subject. I don't want to talk about that rat. I'll lose my appetite. I want a pleasant dinner and serious talk afterward."

"I would like that," Virginia said, managing a smile. "I'm starved."

"So am I." Brad's eyes captured hers, and, despite herself, she couldn't look away.

More to make small talk than because she was interested, she said, "You're looking well. I hope your style of living has changed from what it was."

"Not completely," he smiled, "but you know that. Lieutenant Johnson paid you a visit the day I was at Willowbrook."

Virginia sobered. "Yes. They want you, Brad."

He shrugged. "And one day they'll get me. In the meantime, though, I'm healthy, at ease, and enjoying life. I live very well, under the most comfortable of circumstances, and I feel completely safe where I stay. You know, I've spent days trying to figure out some way I can see that Jimmy gets my money when they finally string me up. Thus far, I haven't come up with an answer."

"Brad, I wish you hadn't said that. I've little regard for you, but I honestly hope they never find you."

"Well now," he said, brightening considerably. "I like that, coming from you."

Before it could go any further, Virginia summoned the waiter and gave her order.

"Oh, come now, Virginia, that's a mighty meager bill of fare for two people celebrating their meeting for the first time in years," Brad said. Then he turned to the waiter. "Bring roast beef and everything that goes with it. And a bottle of champagne, if you have any."

"We've a few bottles, sir. It's not asked for very often these days."

"Good," Brad said. "Cool it well."

"I wish you hadn't done that," Virginia said. "I don't regard this as a meeting of old friends. You said you had information about Carlos."

"I have, and it may be of great importance. We'll talk later."

"If you have any idea of doing this talking in my room . . ."

"We can't do it here. I'm not comfortable exposing myself in public this way. There's always a chance someone might recognize me and call the authorities. Have a heart, Virgie."

She knew there was no way out. "All right. But only if you agree it will not be personal."

"I wouldn't be so offensive," he said, almost too blandly, yet she could do little about it.

The champagne was cold and refreshing. She lifted her glass as he did. "Oh, Brad," she said, "I don't want you hurt, or caught. I don't hate you, but obviously you can't expect me to renew our friendship. I have a son."

"So have I. We'll discuss that later."

"As far as I'm concerned, there's nothing to discuss."

"You're wrong there, but I want nothing to mar our dinner. I relish having you across the table from me. I'm going to ask you a question, and I don't mean to be obnoxious. Just be honest with me. When you were in my arms and you gave yourself to me, did you do it out of hatred?"

Virginia blushed. She'd not expected him to ask such a thing.

"Did you?" he asked quietly.

"No." Her voice was tremulous as her mind went back to that time. "I reveled in it as much as you. Possibly more, because for you it was just another conquest."

"You're wrong, Virgie. I may have said that—I don't remember—but I want to tell you this now, before we begin the serious business that I have summoned you for. You're ravishingly, indecently beautiful. I'm sure every man who looks at you hungers for you."

"Please, Brad . . ."

"Hear me out, Virgie. It won't take long." He leaned forward and lowered his voice. "I know what I used to be, but even then I fell in love with you, though I denied it because I was the tough, ignoble bandit. I wouldn't let myself think of love—of loving anyone—for I knew that my stay on this earth was going to be short. So don't judge me too harshly. And if my eyes grow too intent as I look at you, or if I move too closely to you, forgive me." He straightened and resumed his normal voice. "Now, let's drink some more champagne and enjoy our supper."

They spent two hours over the meal. The conversation turned to Jimmy, and Brad had a hundred questions about his son. The more questions he asked, the more nervous Virginia became, though she took care not to show it.

Finally he paid the bill and they went up to her room. He pointed down the hall. "I'm in the last room. If you need me."

"How long will this take?" she asked.

"Not long. We'll leave tomorrow. Of course, if you become fascinated with my presence, we can stay longer, but I warn you, I can't hold out forever."

"It will be best if we get this over with tonight," she said. She unlocked the door and he followed her into the room and closed the door. She removed her hat and gloves and sat down on one of the two chairs. Brad had already seated himself. She was no longer afraid of him, and that eased her mind.

"First," he said, "the business of Carlos."

"Yes," she said, relieved that he didn't want to talk about Jimmy quite yet. "What happened to Carlos, and how did you come into possession of the money you returned to me? Thank you for returning the money, Brad. But I wouldn't have objected if you'd kept it."

"Thank you, but I believe it best not to ask questions about what happened to that cheating, conniving Mexican. He talked too much; he bragged too often. As for my keeping it, I don't take money from women."

"Before we go further, Brad, how did you know Carlos was carrying ten thousand dollars of my money?"

"I didn't. He told me, though I suspected as much. Why did you give it to him?"

"Everyone on the island has been engaged in trying to improve our cotton by crossing it with a Mexican type that would strengthen the fibers of our more delicate kind. Of course, it was my idea."

"How did you meet him?"

"He came to the island uninvited, a perfect stranger. He mentioned the name of a family in Charleston who knew Papa well. They suggested he see our cotton. You know, the cotton we grow on Valcour is like none other in the country."

"I know all about it," Brad said. "My interest in you compelled me to learn everything possible about you and your family."

"Anyway, it was his suggestion to improve the cotton, and I like it."

"What does Chris Savard think about it?"

"I didn't consult him. I felt no need for that."

"I hope you know what you're doing. Has Elias been told?"

"No, and he won't be."

Brad looked suprise at her tart tone. "I take it you're not close?"

"He walked out when he learned I was pregnant."

"Yet you gave our son his name."

"He told the doctor I could."

"I admire him for that," Brad said.

"I have no admiration or liking for him," Virginia said coldly. "Nor does he have for me."

Brad looked amused. "You were telling me about Carlos."

"I'd given him several good-sized checks in the expectation that he was going to help. Also, I believed in his sincerity. I discovered from our banker, who took the trouble to check, that Carlos had married twice and had separated from his second wife."

"He was a scoundrel," Brad agreed.

"The worst kind. Deceiving helpless women."

Brad nodded sympathetically, but his eyes held a mischievous gleam. "So you canceled the check you were to send to him?"

"Upon Mr. Tyler's advice. However, Carlos returned to the island one night. He brought with him a large number of seedlings, stating that the work would progress much faster with seedlings. I agreed, but I told him he was not to contact me again. In return, I gave him a generous check."

"To buy his silence because you'd been bilked?"

"To be rid of him," Virginia said firmly.

Brad nodded, but she knew he didn't believe her. He said, "I'll tell you a little more about me. The band of men who worked with me have never completely disbanded. Those who are left have turned to legitimate ways of earning a living, but they still regard me as their leader. And I'm grateful for that."

"Will you explain how someone managed to enter my

bedroom and slip your note into the frame of my bureau mirror?"

"Virgie, twice I came to your home in the night so quietly that no one knew. The second time, I didn't wake you. You were carrying our child. I kissed you, placed my hat on your pillow, and left."

She gave up her questioning, knowing that he wouldn't tell her how he'd gotten the note into her room.

"It's strange," he said. "Here we are, alone in your room, talking like civilized people. I like that. But—back to this Mexican cheat. He drank too much while we were playing cards. I admit to cultivating his company. He was cheating me too, sometimes crudely, sometimes very cleverly. The more he drank, the more he boasted, though I did lead him on. He told me how he had deceived a beautiful woman on one of the islands. Of course I knew he was referring to you. He told me he had taken full advantage of you—for which I could have killed him on the spot. Well, he said he'd been kicked off the island, that money you'd promised him had not come forth, and that he was angry about this, so he had gone back, uninvited. He said he used the excuse of turning some cotton plants over to you and had managed to swindle you out of ten thousand dollars."

"You did say he mentioned something about making trouble?"

"Yes. He said he would get even for being told to leave and that you were in for a considerable surprise that would make you remember him forever. That's all he said. I tried to draw him out, but time was growing short. Also, I couldn't stand any more of his filthy talk in mentioning you—without naming you. If he had, I'd likely have killed him on the spot."

"Thank you. But what happened to him? People knew

he'd been on the island. I was fearful we might be questioned, if he was found."

"He won't be found. The train was passing through a large swamp area where nobody ever goes. He lost his footing and fell off the train. He was very drunk."

"I'm sure he was drunk. I don't suppose you had anything to do with that?"

"Now, Virgie..." Brad's face was the picture of innocence.

"Or that you might have caught him when he lost his footing?"

"You don't believe me."

"Oh, I believe the story," she said with gentle sarcasm. "I have a good picture of it in my mind. But I'm puzzled about what he could have meant about the considerable suprise I was in for."

"So am I," Brad replied. "That's one reason why I wanted to see you. His words kept spinning around in my brain. I thought you might be able to figure it out. I also thought he might be planning to continue to blackmail you. Did you bed with him, Virgie?"

"Of course not!"

Brad gave her a knowing smile. "Your indignation assures me you did. It's all right. God know, I'm aware of what a passionate woman you are. I just hate thinking of your being intimate with such a rat."

"I wouldn't say you were the picture of respectability," Virginia retorted.

"I don't blackmail women, and I've never lied to one. I'm referring to his marital status. I'm sure he fooled you about that."

"In any case, I sent him packing."

"I'm sorry I hurt Elias that night he found me on the island and beat me up. Nanine told me about it the day she hid me in the attic."

Virginia yawned, pretending sleepiness. "I suppose, now that you've told me about Carlos, our talk is ended."

"Like hell it is. This business with him is very much a side issue. But it'll have to wait a few minutes. I'm very uncomfortable dressed up like this. I'm going back to my room to change. Won't be a minute—and then we can discuss the main topic that concerns us both."

She had no reason to deny his request, but when he returned, dressed in a nightshirt covered by a silk robe, she grew angry, but she refrained from any comments, fearful that she might antagonize him. So she remained silent, though her eyes never left his face.

He lit a cheroot. "Virgie, I want the boy."

"Never," she said sharply, coldly. "This ends our conversation."

"Not by a long shot it doesn't. Relax. I intend to be reasonable about this. I only want him for a while. I pledge he will be taken care as well as, or better than, he is on Valcour."

"No."

"Listen to me. I'm a man afflicted with a deadly disease—namely, a hangman's noose. I may not have long to live. He is my son. You've done wonders with him so far, but he's in the company of too many women. Females! You mean well, but a boy needs a father—a man who's close to him. At least for a while. I'd never forgive you if Jimmy grew up to be a sissy."

"We'll not discuss Jimmy. If you have any regard for me, you'll leave this room and never see me again."

"It's my turn to say no. Be reasonable. I swear that I'll return the boy."

"What if you're arrested and he's with you? What then?"

"I'll make very certain that never happens. I know how it can be done."

"Brad, I said I didn't hate you. Don't make me change that."

"I want him for, say, six months."

"Never!"

"He's my son. I have the right to share him. If you don't agree to let me have him for a short time, then I'll take him, and you'll never see him again. It's your choice. And I don't give a damn if you defy me, because then I'll have Jimmy all to myself—forever."

"What if I report you? Or report my son missing?"

"You won't. You wouldn't want it known I'm his father."

"Brad, you wouldn't!"

"Don't tempt me, Virgie. You're the one who doesn't want it know that I'm Jimmy's father. I'm proud of the boy. I'd love the world to know he's my son."

"You're as big a knave as Carlos."

"Perhaps I am—where my son is concerned."

"Isn't there any way I can appeal to you?" she cried.

"Yes. I already told you. Give me the boy for six months."

She bent her head and wept. He sat there in silence, making no move. She raised her head and he handed her a handkerchief. She dabbed at her tears.

"Brad, I can't let him go. His life with you would be too uncertain. Too dangerous."

"You heard my offer. Take it or leave it, Virgie."

"If you come for him, Brad, I'll turn you in. It will break my heart, but I swear I'd rather see you hang than allow you to take Jimmy."

"I expected that," he said. "You're making a big mistake. You can call in the police and the Yankee military occupation forces, but all of them put together will never find me—or Jimmy. I've offered you a better way out and you've refused, so you'll be to blame for whatever happens."

"I could summon the police now, by screaming."

"You could scream, and the authorities could come, but they wouldn't catch me, and you'd have one hell of a hard time explaining why you and I were together. Think of that."

"I don't have to. You think of everything. I won't give him up, Brad. Not for one minutes."

"It's your problem now. Whatever happens, you can be assured that Jimmy will be cared for as no little boy ever has. Where I stay there is all the help any little boy would need for his health, his safety, and his enjoyment."

"Please get out of my room," she said.

"You're upset now, but if the circumstances were different, you'd be sitting there hoping I'd take you to bed with me. And you'd keep your mouth shut while I talk. I'm having a hard time not taking you to bed, but I do profess to be a gentleman these days, so I'll resist temptation. But don't sit there and claim you'd hate it."

"I hate you. At last, I hate you!"

He smiled. "You don't hate me that much. Calm down and ask yourself what good it is to be in bed alone. You don't really have a husband. I've known other women, Virgie. Lots of them in my heyday, though after I had you I could never touch another woman. Would you like to know why?"

"No!" she shouted.

"I'll tell you anyway. Because you're so damned attractive and so warm in bed, and so gifted in what a woman does best, that I'd mentally compare any other women with you and promptly lose interest. What do you think of that?"

"I don't give a damn."

"I think you do. So I'm going to sit here, and you're going to realize how much you want me. But I won't make the slightest effort to satisfy you. Why don't you go to bed? It's getting late."

"With you here?"

"I'm not going to touch you. I may even fall asleep in this chair, and you won't like that. As soon as you get over this news I've brought, you won't hate me. Not tonight, you won't. But it will do you no good, my darling ex-lover. Go to bed!"

She rose angrily, defiantly. She removed her shoes, her blouse, and her skirt. She used a cream to soothe her face, then brushed her teeth and combed her hair. Finally, she removed all her clothes and stepped into her nightgown, in full view of Brad. She buttoned it slowly, turned down the bedcovers, and got into bed.

All during this, Brad smoked, said nothing, and never took his eyes off her. She turned her back on him, but he stayed where he was. For a few moments she felt like crying, but anger and an uncontrollable urge made her sit up suddenly.

"Come then," she said. She raised the bedcovers to receive him.

He rose, crushed out his cheroot, walked to the door, opened it, and left. For a few moments, Virginia was too stunned to move. She'd deliberately undressed in front of him, believing her charms were too much for him to resist. she knew he must have been aroused, yet he'd turned his back on her and walked out.

Her disbelief turned to rage and she beat her fists against the pillows, then wrapped her arms around one and wept. Tears of anger, frustration, and humiliation. Once again, a man had rejected her. Not just any man. The man who had fathered her son.

She'd listened in amazement as Brad related how his love for her had left him indifferent to other women. She'd never even known he loved her, though he'd said so when he learned that she was carrying his child. But the knowledge he'd imparted tonight had given her the courage to appeal to his better nature and ask him not to insist on taking Jimmy from her. She'd thought that once she was locked in his arms, he would weaken and relinquish his demands regarding their son. But he'd proved her wrong. He was far stronger than she.

She had no idea how long she'd slept but as she awakened, her arms extended in welcome, for she was already aroused. She touched warm flesh and her eyes flashed open. The soft lamplight had been turned low, though she didn't recall having done so. Brad was already covering her. Her body was aflame from contact with his.

She whispered his name several times. He was smiling down at her, his eyes soft with desire.

"How did you get in?" she asked.

"You left the door unlocked. You must have known I'd come back."

"Had I thought of that, I'd have locked it." She was once again defiant. "What are you up to now?"

"I came to make love to you, unless you want me to leave." While he spoke, his hands were caressing her body. "Just say the word and I'll go."

She knew he meant it. She gave a brief, negative shake of her head, then raised her lips to his. A soft moan escaped them both at the contact, and the burning desire each felt for the other flamed anew. The night was spent satisfying the hunger that each had kept stifled for so long.

Not until dawn was their passion spent. They lay side by side, in silence and motionless until Brad stirred and started to sit up.

Virginia turned swiftly, covering his body with hers, forcing him down.

"Don't go. Stay with me a little longer."

His hand cupped her face. "My dear Virgie, you are the mother of our son. I want no hint of scandal to touch him.

Therefore, I must be off. Thank you for this night. It may have to last me the rest of my life—however long or short that is."

"You always think of that, don't you, Brad?"

"Every second that I'm awake. I didn't used to, but then life wasn't so precious. Only now do I realize what I missed."

"When did you first realize that?" She was stalling for time.

"When you told me you were carrying my child. That's when I wished I could wipe out my past and start anew."

"Since you know how wicked you were, won't you please forget about Jimmy?"

"Not as long as I breathe," he replied. His smile was tender, and the kiss he planted on her lips was gentle and filled with love.

"You know you're an outlaw. You know you've killed, yet—"

He covered her mouth with his hand. "Yes, I know. But I want my son with me for a while. I want the thrill of loving him, of holding him in my arms, of knowing that he is part of me and that I helped to create him."

"I don't want you near him," Virginia said almost timidly. She didn't want to antagonize him. And, strangely, neither did she want to hurt him.

"Then why were you so willing and so passionate?"

"You've always had that effect on me," she said quietly.

"We're very good together," he replied. "Because we're very much alike. Not exactly, though. You're the only woman on this earth I want to bed with. You can do without love for just so long and then you'll look around and seek a dominant male. That was Elias's weakness—not standing up to you. He could, but I can understand why he didn't. He loved you so much that he always gave in to you."

She'd used up all her emotion; she could only entreat him not to mention Elias's name.

"You don't really hate him, Virgie," Brad said.

"I do. With every breath I breathe."

Brad laughed softly. "It's your pride that's hurt. When Elias walked out of your life, it was the first time he ever stood up to you. You never thought he'd do it. In fact, if it hadn't been for that gabby doctor, you'd never have let Elias know that the child wasn't his."

"You think of everything, don't you?" She looked away from the eyes that mocked her.

"I know you, my darling," he said, then pressed his mouth against hers, hungrily this time.

She felt the same surge of passion as he, and both forgot the few words that had passed between them. Once they were sated, Brad left. Virginia sighed contentedly and drifted off to sleep. It was late morning when she awakened.

She bathed and dressed quickly, then went downstairs to pay her bill. The desk clerk told her courteously that it had already been taken care of.

She couldn't return to Valcour now. It was too late, and she knew she was aglow with the fulfillment of her passion. Nanine and Phoebe would be sure to notice. Despite the fact that she'd lost her arguments regarding Jimmy, she felt a warm glow of satisfaction that Brad had come to her. That his body had hungered for hers.

NINE

Instead of returning directly to Valcour, Virginia went to a hotel in Charleston. Despite her fear of what Brad intended to do, their night had been a glorious one. She didn't remove her hat or gloves when she reached her room. Her mood was pensive and she sat down for a few minutes to decide what to do for the remainder of the day. She knew she would purchase some gifts for her mother, sisters, Jimmy, and Ivy. She glanced at her reflection in the bureau mirror and noted the high color of her cheeks and the sparkle in her eyes. Damn Brad for bending her to his will! She should have ordered him out of the room when he came to her in the darkness and woke her with his caresses. Especially since she had offered herself to him earlier in the evening and he had walked out.

Her mind drifted back to when he'd awakened her, his hands moving gently, skillfully over her body, fully aware of the areas that would most arouse her. The pillow cover was still damp from tears she'd shed, not only because of the humiliation she'd suffered, but because her whole being cried out for a fulfillment only he could give her. She had cried out with desire and drawn him to her.

She knew her one big weakness was her passion. She could no more control it than her father had controlled his. Yet, she felt that if she had a husband to whom she could turn at night, who could comfort her and requite her passion, she would be faithful to him. She was certain she'd not move from man to man.

Small comfort that thought was, she thought bitterly, with Elias in England never to return. At least, not to her. She hated him. The very thought of him made her compress her lips tightly to keep from cursing him soundly. She was well aware that he'd suffered humiliation because of what she'd done, but he'd made her suffer, too. And it was a long-drawn-out pain. She'd felt it ever since he'd left, and she supposed she'd feel it for the rest of her life. She sometimes wondered if bedding with Brad and Carlos and even Chris—for she knew he would be next— was her way of getting even with Elias. She remembered the time she'd gone to the mainland plantation because she craved his body, but he'd been too tired to make love.

She got up and went to the door. She didn't want to stay in the room, brooding over her weaknesses and mistakes. She was certainly paying for them. She was crossing the lobby, heading for the door, when she heard her name called. She stiffened with apprehension, for the voice was not familiar, though it was a man's, deep and cultured.

She turned when she heard her name again, spoken directly behind her.

Relief flooded through her and a gracious smile touched her mouth when she recognized Colonel Zachary Spires.

She extended a gloved hand. "How nice to see you, Colonel Spires."

"The pleasure is mine, Miss Virginia," he replied, smiling. He was the picture of southern courtliness in his white suit and wide-brimmed straw hat. He bowed as he took her hand, and his eyes regarded her with a warm friendliness. "My dear, is Lenore—rather, your mama—with you?"

"I'm alone, Colonel," she replied. "I had to come to the mainland to do some shopping."

"Are you remaining at the hotel tonight?" he asked.

"Yes. I'll return to the island in the morning."

"Then will you dine with me?" he asked. "I've never really become acquainted with Lenore's daughters."

Virginia had no desire to spend any time with the Colonel or anyone else. She had too much on her mind—all of it concerning Jimmy and the fear that his father might kidnap him.

"Please," he entreated, "unless you have other plans."

She made a sudden decision. "It's kind of you to invite me, Colonel. I'll be happy to. What time?"

"I'll meet you here in the lobby at six o'clock. I think we'll find much to talk about."

"I'm sure we will, Colonel," she replied, eager to be off on her shopping tour.

She went first to the couturier where her mother had her wardrobe made. Being ample of girth and sometimes a little careless about being tightly corseted, she'd taken to more flounces, ruffles, and overskirts to conceal the fact that her figure was no longer trim. Virginia decided that she would surprise her mother by ordering a new dress for her.

Mrs. Keefe, the head saleslady, was conversing with a patron but excused herself and came at once to Virginia.

"Good afternoon, Mrs. Birch. I suppose you came about the dresses and gowns your mama ordered." The saleslady adopted a more intimate tone. "Naturally, my employer was delighted to receive such a large order. I only hope your mama hasn't partaken too generously of sweets. Always before, she came and we made measurements, because each time we've had to make adjustment."

"I know," Virginia said, completely in the dark about the order. "Don't worry about it. If any alterations are needed, I'm sure my elder sister can attend to them."

The saleslady looked relieved. "I'm please to hear that, because your mama likes her garments to fit perfectly."

Virginia sympathized with Mrs. Keefe's uneasiness, knowing how demanding her mother could be. But she was more curious as to how her mother had been able to place such a large order without informing anyone in the house. Certainly Nanine or Phoebe would have relayed such information to her.

"Is the order ready?" Virginia asked. "If so, I'd like it delivered to the hotel today. I'm leaving for the island early tomorrow morning."

"Oh yes, Mrs. Birch. We'll package everything and have it delivered immediately."

"Thank you. If you'll give me an itemized receipt, I'll give you a check."

Mrs. Keefe went off in a rush, happy she'd be able to tell her employer that the order for Mrs. James Hammond was being called for. The Hammond ladies had been the mainstay of the establishment when it had opened following the war. Now they enjoyed a large clientele, but they favored their first customers.

She returned with the itemized bill. Virginia was seated at a small desk in an alcove that was partly concealed by lustrous fabrics draped across the arched entry and fastened with a huge tasseled cord. She dipped the quill pen into the china inkwell, touched it to the side, and glanced at the total sum for the purchases. She almost exclaimed aloud, for it was over one thousand dollars.

She scanned the list. Mama had included every kind of costume, even a promenade dress. There were also two moiré satin peignoirs and a silk nightdress. Virginia managed to hide her surprise when she came to three parasols and six bonnets to match the costumes. Mama rarely went outside, preferring to say in her room when she wasn't giving a picnic or a soiree. Apparently she intended to entertain on a grand scale. But the fancy peignoirs were beyond Virginia. Nonetheless, with a casualness she was far from feeling, she wrote out a check for the entire amount. Mrs. Keefe thanked her and Virginia left the shop. She was glad she hadn't intended to order gowns for Phoebe, Nanine, or herself, for she'd have forgotten about it in the shock of learning what her mother had bought.

Virginia then went to a candy store to purchase sweets for Jimmy and her mother, She, too, hoped that the wardrobe would fit, for wardrobe indeed it was. The peignoirs and nightgowns were what really puzzled Virginia. Her mother always wore very fine cotton gowns and peignoirs, not silk or satin. She'd disdained them in the past, believing they were for women who were interested only in arousing their husbands, and she'd had no interest in that.

In another specialty shop, Virginia selected beaded reticules for her sisters, plus a brown silk parasol for Nanine and a violet one for Phoebe. The colors would match their eyes. Virginia smiled, thinking of Phoebe's eyes, which were the same shade of violet as hers.

For Ivy she chose a gold chain from which hung a heart-shaped locket with a small diamond in the center. The girl deserved it for the love and attention she bestowed on Jimmy. In a further burst of generosity, she purchased a bottle of eau de toilette for the girl. She had the gifts wrapped and tied with a ribbon.

She returned to the hotel with her packages, a little weary but still feeling good will toward the world after her satisfying evening with Brad. If only she could think of some way to dissuade him from wanting Jimmy. She would discuss it with Nanine and Phoebe when she returned to Valcour.

It was a relief to reach the hotel and retire to her room.

Now that she had agreed to join the Colonel for dinner, she looked forward to it. He was a gracious gentleman, and he would make the evening hours pass quickly. She might even have another night of glorious sleep. In any case, it would be a change. She knew Phoebe and Nanine must be as restless as she, in a house without men. It was certainly not a normal situation. She could remedy hers only through a divorce from Elias. But Nanine and Phoebe were free. A pity they couldn't each meet a gentleman with whom they could fall in love and marry.

There was no time for a nap and she suddenly realized that she was starved. She'd breakfasted late and so had felt no desire for a midday repast. But she would certainly enjoy her evening meal. She glanced at the clock, noting she had a bare hour. She undressed, bathed, took down her hair, and brushed and styled it. leaving the back hanging in curls.

Virginia was pleased that she'd chosen to dress, for the Colonel's eyes lit up with pleasure when he saw her. He was awaiting her at the foot of the stairs, and his greeting was courtly.

He held his arm for her and they went into the dining room. Obviously he dined there frequently, for the waiters bowed whenever he spoke to them, which he did several times on the way to their table in the center of the room.

There was champagne chilling beside the table. The Colonel motioned for the bottle to be opened before they were presented with their menus. Virginia was grateful, for she wanted to retain the stimulating feeling she'd enjoyed all day.

They were given their menus and the Colonel ordered, after consulting her regarding her tastes. Then he raised his glass.

"To you, Miss Virginia, the most beautiful young lady

in the room, and one whose charm is exceeded only by her lovely mother, Lenore."

Virginia was unable to stifle her surprise. Charm was one quality she hadn't thought her mother possessed.

The Colonel smiled as he regarded her, still holding her glass in midair. "Drink your champagne, my dear."

"Of course," she said hastily. She took three good sips of the sparkling beverage before she set down the glass.

"I know that including your mama in the toast puzzled you," he said. "But I was once a rival for your mama's hand. Naturally, I couldn't stand a chance against James Hammond. No man could. He was the most dashing, devil-may-care figure around, but a brilliant man for all that."

"Thank you, Colonel," Virginia said. "Papa would have liked hearing you say that."

"I've always regretted that I wasn't here when your family went through so much," the Colonel ventured. "I didn't know your lovely home was burned down until the war was ended."

"Don't worry about it," Virginia replied graciously. "I know what you did for the South."

"I always felt guilty that my home remained standing when all the others around were destroyed."

"I'm glad yours was spared," Virginia said kindly. "Its so beautiful. And so are the grounds. I would like to bring Jimmy there when he's a litte older and can apreciate the topiaries. I never saw them cut in the form of humans before."

The Colonel beamed. "It is novel, and I take great pleasure in seeing children shriek with delight when they see them."

Virginia searched her mind for another topic. "It was good of you to come to the ball. Mama asked especially that you be invited. I didn't know you were one of her swains."

"She had several, my dear, but once she met your father, it was as if a train came along and bowled the rest of us over." The Colonel laughed. "As for the ball, I was delighted to be a guest. It's lonely for me, too, you know. Of course, Lenore has the three of you, so her days are full. And even fuller with a grandson." He raised a forefinger as if a sudden thought occurred to him. "By the way, why don't you and Lenore pay me a visit? And bring Jimmy. You must have named him after your papa."

"We did," Virginia said. "His middle name is Elias."

The Colonel nodded. "Your husband. Sorry I never met him. After the war, I went to Washington to visit friends and to rest. Also, I was recompensed for the wear and tear on the mansion. Part of it was used to refurnish the house. After the number of military men who bivouacked there, it needed it."

"I'm sure it did," Virginia agreed. "The slaves ransacked Willowbrook, although Elias, who had charge of the troops while he was stationed on Valcour, did manage to salvage some of it, because Nanine, Mama, and I were allowed to live there until the war ended. We had a difficult time up until then."

"I'd like to meet Elias when he returns," the Colonel said. "I want to thank him for looking after you."

"I'll tell him when I write," Virginia said, managing a gracious tone. "He'll be pleased."

"You didn't answer my question about paying me a visit," the Colonel said. "The sooner the better."

She hadn't intended to answer it, because her concern at this time was solely for Jimmy. Yet, she found the idea intriguing. The child might be safe there. Brad had no idea that she was acquainted with Colonel Spires. In truth, she hadn't given him a thought since the ball, until her mother had mentioned she was inviting him to the picnic. If her mother hadn't yet sent out the invitations, the picnic could wait. If only she could convince her mother to accept the Colonel's invitation...

"That's very kind of you, Colonel, but are you certain you'd want the bother of having a little boy around? He's at the stage now where he's under your feet most of the time."

The Colonel beamed. "I'd love it. Nothing would sound more delightful then the happy shouts of glee of a child in the house."

"Then I accept, temporarily. I have to speak with Mama. There are days when she doesn't feel so well."

"I think she's lonely," the Colonel said. "In fact, I would imagine all four of you are lonely."

"You're very observant, Colonel."

"I prefer to think I'm very human," he replied kindly. "I thought Lenore looked radiant at the ball. In fact, I thought she looked beautiful. Just sitting next to her made me feel young. Don't tell her, though. She'd probably think me a foolish old man. I always stood in awe of her, you know."

"I didn't know," Virginia said. "And you might be wrong about Mama thinking you silly. She's now planning a picnic and she said an invitation would be sent to you."

"That pleases me enormously," he said, beaming. "But why not suggest she picnic on my plantation. Tell her Jimmy deserves it. A change would do him good."

"I'm certain it would," Virginia said, warming to the idea. "When would you like us to come?"

He leaned across the table. "How about the day after tomorrow?"

"Are you serious?"

"Completely."

"I don't know if Mama would come without a written invitation from you," Virginia said hesitantly.

"When are you returning to Valcour?"

"Early tomorrow morning."

"As soon as I escort you to your door, I'll write the invitation and leave it at the desk for you. Please give it to Lenore the first thing."

Virginia wasn't feigning her pleasure when she said, "I know she'll be as excited about it as I."

"I hope so," the Colonel exclaimed. "Though I believe I'll be the happiest."

Virginia looked at the table. "You know, I can't believe we've finished our meal. Even the dessert. I must confess I was famished, not having eaten since breakfast. I only hope I didn't wolf my food."

The Colonel laughed heartily. "You're a delightful dinner companion, my dear. Please do your best to persuade Lenore to come."

"You care for Mama, don't you?"

There was no doubting Colonel Spires's sincerity when he said, "I love her, Virginia. I never stopped loving her. But please don't tell her. I doubt she's ever thought of me in that way."

"You're a very dear gentleman, Colonel."

The two men who had rowed Virginia over were awaiting her in the boat. They'd left it only to purchase food. They loaded Lenore's purchases, which had been packed in several boxes of varying size, plus those Virginia had made, onto the boat and helped her into it. Lenore's purchases took up almost every inch of space.

Virginia kept a firm grip on her reticule, which contained the Colonel's note. She wondered if her mother would accept the invitation to visit him, and if she was aware that he felt more than a deep affection for her.

Virginia was certain her mother would have nothing to do with romance. She was too settled in her ways and enjoyed the privacy of her room, plus her headaches—real or imagined—which helped her to feel neglected.

The gentle rock of the boat as the men plied the oars, was relaxing and Virginia was pleased she'd chosen to stay over. Her evening with the Colonel had been pleasant, and she had enjoyed another excellent night's sleep. Also, the Colonel's invitation seemed a ready solution to her concern for Jimmy's safety. She would discuss it with Nanine and Phoebe.

At the dock, Virginia left orders for the men to bring the packages to the house. She hastened up the path and waved when Nanine and Phoebe stepped onto the porch. Their anxious expressions relaxed when she told them that, thus far, all was well.

"Aren't you going to tell us about it?" Nanine asked. "We don't want to pry, Virgnia, but we've done nothing but worry since you left."

Virginia embraced Nanine. "Don't you know me well enough by now to realize that I can take very good care of myself?"

"We also know what Brad is capable of," Phoebe said. "Was he kind?"

Virginia hoped her face didn't flush as she said, "He's always been kind to me, Phoebe. It's just his demanding way."

Nanine smiled. "Anyway, you certainly look rested. From the packages I see coming up to the house, I gather you went on quite a shopping spree."

"I bought you each a little something, but most of it belongs to Mama. You didn't tell me she ordered practically a new wardrobe from the couturiere."

"What are you talking about?" Nanine asked.

"No time now." Virginia headed for the stairway. "I'll

tell you when I come down. We have a lot to talk about. Also, I have to deliver a note to Mama from Colonel Spires."

Virginia gave a fleeting glance over her shoulder and laughed at the puzzled expressions on her sisters' faces. She went directly to Lenore's suite. Lenore was stretched out on the bed, propped up with myriad pillows.

"Another headache, Mama?" Virginia asked solicitously.

"Yes, my dear. If my daughters gave me a little more attention, I doubt I'd be as plagued with them as I am."

"I'm sorry, Mama." Virginia opened her reticule and took out the envelope. "This is for you, from Colonel Spires."

Lenore's eyes widened with interest. "Did he mail it?"

"No, Mama. I saw him at the hotel in Charleston."

Virginia remained standing at the foot of the bed, waiting for her mother to open the envelope and read its contents.

Instead of doing so, Lenore regarded Virginia. "Did you get your business attended to?"

"Yes. I also stopped in at the couturier. I was going to order you a new gown, but I learned you had ordered a complete wardrobe."

Lenore bristled. "Do my daughters deny me the privilege of doing so? After all, it's the first time I took advantage of being able to. At least, I thought I would be allowed to do it."

"It isn't a question of being allowed, Mama," Virginia replied, trying to quell her irritation. "It's just that there was really no need for secrecy. You know you may have anything you wish."

"I should think so, I do believe Willowbrook is mine, though at times I feel like an intruder. I am never consulted about anything."

"You should never feel that way, Mama. Anyway, I

brought back your purchases. You might like to try them on. They're on their way up now."

Lenore brightened slightly at the news. "Thank you, my dear. I hope you like my selections. It isn't always easy ordering by mail."

Virginia nodded in agreement, her high spirits already dashed by her mother's manner. "I'm going to freshen up. I hope your purchases will meet your expectations."

"I hope they'll fit." Lenore replied, her eyes on the still unopened envelope.

Virginia left the room quickly. She wished she knew how to converse with her mother without ending up in an argument. Virginia gave a discouraged sigh as she thought of the Colonel. What a shock he would be in for when he received Lenore's reply to his note—if she deigned to write one.

Virginia went to her room. Lenore had succeeded in destroying the buoyant feeling she'd had during her stay in Charleston.

She slipped out of her dress and her corset, massaged her pinched waistline, and took deep breaths of relief as her torso expanded and relaxed. She donned a lacy peignoir, smiling as she recalled the two lavish ones her mother had ordered.

The purchases she'd made had already been brought to her suite. Virginia picked up the gifts and went to the nursery. Jimmy had just awakened from a nap, but he was still sleepy. She placed the packages containing the toy and the candy on his bureau and instructed Ivy to open them when she finished dressing him up, because he was fussing and it was all Ivy could do to handle him. She placed Ivy's packages on the bureau and told her to open them when she had the time. The girl beamed her thanks and looked longingly at them, then turned her attention back to dressing the child, now squirming impatiently in his crib.

Virginia picked up the packages for Nanine and Phoebe, which she'd left on the hall table, and went downstairs. The sisters were in the drawing room, where Nanine had sandwiches and iced lemonade awaiting Virginia's arrival. She gulped down a glass and Nanine refilled it.

"One thing about Belle," Virginia said appreciatively, "she makes delectable lemonade."

Both sisters laughed and nodded agreement. Then they opened their gifts and exclaimed appreciatively. They kissed Virginia, thanked her, and placed the gifts in the hall. Then they returned and moved their chairs close together so they'd not be overheard if their mother came downstairs.

"Well," Virginia began, "Brad wants me to let him have Jimmy for six months. I refused." Calmly, she reached for a second sandwich. "Brad was his usual handsome self. The hotel was spotlessly clean, with good food and the room nicely furnished. The establishment was a pleasant surprise. Lots of charm."

"How can you be so cheerful?" Nanine said impatiently.

"Because something happened there that has given me an idea as to how we might foil him."

"You think that can be done?" Phoebe's tone was doubtful.

"It's a gamble," Virginia reasoned. "But I think it's one worth taking."

"Then it doesn't resolve the problem," Nanine said.

"Only Brad's capture would resolve that," Virginia said.

"Suppose you tell us what happened," Nanine said. "If you can stop eating sandwiches."

"One more," Virginia said, wolfing it. She wiped her mouth, finished her second glass of lemonade, and sat back. "As you know, I stayed over an extra day. In Charleston, of course."

"What about Brad?" Nanine persisted.

"Very well," Virginia said. "Let me begin at the beginning.

I already told you about the hotel. I had dinner with Brad and afterward we went to my room."

"Oh, Virgie," Nanine said. "You didn't."

"Don't jump to conclusions, sister," Virginia said archly. "He insisted we talk in my room. He was businesslike and unrelenting. He stated emphatically that he must have six months with Jimmy."

Phoebe said, "Perhaps you should let him have the child for that length of time. It really might be all he wants."

"That's a gamble I'll never take," Virginia said firmly. "He's a wanted man. Should the Union army, or any other law force find him, there might be shooting. That thought alone terrifies me. If anything happened to Jimmy..." She shuddered.

"She's right, Phoebe," Nanine said. "If for no other reason than that, Brad must never be allowed to have the child. I saw the gun he carried. So did you."

"Besides," Virginia went on, "If he had him for six months, he'd never let him go. He'd love him as much as I do."

"He probably does already," Nanine said. "I talked with him only briefly in the attic, but I knew then that he regretted his past. He said the thing that had made him turn respectable was the fact that he has a son. Fatherhood forced Brad to do some deep thinking."

"Strange," Virginia mused, "How much good a child can do."

"A pity the man can't soften toward you," Phoebe said. "You're the mother of his son. It seems he should give you some consideration."

"I suppose his reasoning is that I'll have Jimmy the rest of my life," Virginia mused.

"That and the fact that he doesn't like his son being raised in a houseful of women," Nanine replied. "And frankly, I don't blame him. It isn't a normal life for a little boy. But continue with your story, Virginia. Did you see Brad after that night?"

"No. But I have a feeling I will.",

"I suppose you went back to Charleston," Nanine said.

Virginia brightened. "Yes. And I met Colonel Spires in the lobby of the hotel. He invited me to dine with him last night."

"What a pleasant surprise." Nanine said. "Did you tell Mama?"

"I brought a note back to her from him," Virginia said. "But before I go into that, I must mention Mama's new wardrobe."

"An entire wardrobe?" Nanine asked in disbelief.

"Practically, including two peignoirs, one silk, one satin. Two silk lace nightgowns. A promenade dress. Parasols. Bonnets. It's unbelievable."

"Very puzzling," Phoebe said.

"A promenade dress," Nanine interjected. "Mama never goes walking."

Virginia continued. "I forgot to bring down the bill— staggering! Anyway, I went to the shop intending to order a new gown for her. However, when I went in, Mrs. Keefe told me that Mama's order was ready for her. Of course, she was apprehensive as to whether it will fit Mama, since her figure changes—as we all know."

"When did she order it?" Nanine asked, perplexed.

"That's what I wanted to ask you," Virginia said.

Phoebe took a sip of her lemonade. "Perhaps Lenore is changing."

Virginia disputed that. "She's upstairs now with a headache. And complaining that we give her no attention and that she certainly should be allowed to order a wardrobe—as if we'd stop her. No, Mama isn't changing. She never will."

"You said you brought a note from the Colonel," Nanine reminded her.

"I had a most pleasant evening with him. He told me he was one of Mama's swains until Papa came along. I gather she had several—though it's hard to believe—but Papa won out. Anyway, he gave me a note to bring Mama. It contains an invitation for her, Jimmy, and me to visit his plantation."

"So that's it," Nanine said thoughtfully. "You think it's a safe place for Jimmy."

"Don't you think it's worth a gamble?" Virginia countered.

"Do you think Lenore will go?" Phoebe asked.

"I'd say she won't," Virginia replied sadly. "Yet, it's my only hope until I can think of something more permanent."

"You could take the child to England," Phoebe ventured. "Elias would protect him."

Virginia glared at her.

"You must admit it would be far enough away," Phoebe insisted. "And Brad could never get out of this country."

"It makes sense," Nanine agreed, "but Virgie will never agree."

"Never!" Virginia replied firmly. "What I must do is try to convince Mama that a change might help her get rid of her headaches."

Nanine smiled. "Good luck. If the Colonel still loves her, his desire might be for something more than merely a friendly visit."

Virginia nodded. "I feel sorry for him, because he does still love her."

"If, by some miracle, Mama should accept, what are your plans?" Nanine asked.

"We'll discuss it when I find out," Virginia said. "I'm going upstairs now. If her answer is no, I must send word to the Colonel. He wants us there tomorrow."

"Good heavens," Nanine exclaimed. "He moves fast, doesn't he?"

Virginia laughed. "You should see his eyes soften when he talks of Mama. He kept calling her Lenore all through dinner."

She stood up, took a clean glass from the tray, and filled it with lemonade. "I'll bring this up to her."

"Even if she should accept and the Colonel tried to hold her hand," Phoebe said, "she'd probably pack and leave immediately."

Virginia nodded agreement and left the room.

Nanine turned to Phoebe. "I have no idea when Mama ordered that wardrobe. Nor why she even wanted it."

Much to Virginia's surprise, her mother's door was open. Her mother motioned her into the room and said, "Please close the door, Virgie."

Virginia offered her mother the lemonade. Lenore thanked her and drank half of it, then wiped her brow, moist with perspiration.

"The clothes fit." Lenore said excitedly. "Everything. I got Ivy to help me try them on. Jimmy played with the boxes. That's why everything looks so untidy."

"I'm glad you're pleased, Mama," Virginia said pleasantly. "I hope your headache is better."

"It's gone, my dear. About the Colonel's note. It said that if we were coming, we need not reply."

"You mean you'll accept?" Virginia kept her voice casual, managing to conceal her shock at the change in her mother.

"It would be rude not to," Lenore replied. "Surely you know that."

"I suppose it would. How long will you stay?"

"My dear, you and Jimmy are invited also."

"I know, Mama. I was quite excited about it, but I told the Colonel you had been troubled with headaches and might not be able to accept."

Lenore came over, rested her hands on Virginia's shoulders,

and her cheek. "I'm accepting. I think it would be a very good tonic for me. Even Zachary said that—in the gracious note he wrote me. I'm so pleased you met him at the hotel. Now I won't have to give the picnic. I wasn't eager to, anyway. It was just something to pass the time."

"Please don't tell the Colonel that. I told him you were planning one and intended to invite him. That was when he said to forget the picnic on Valcour and have one at his plantation. He wants very much for you to come."

"We're going," Lenore said firmly. "I sent Ivy downstairs a short time ago to ask a maid to come up and help me pack."

"Mama, we'll need two boats if you take your entire wardrobe—I mean the one you just bought—plus other things you'll want to take. Then there are Jimmy's and my things. Also, Ivy will come.

"It was thoughtful of the Colonel to invite you also," Lenore said. "Naturally, I couldn't have gone alone—even at my age."

"I'm sure you'd have nothing to fear," Virginia replied seriously. "The Colonel is a true Southern gentleman."

"That I know, My dear. How well I know. Your papa was a rascal." Her smile was one of reminiscence. "But Zachary was always the gentleman. I think I'm more of the Zachary Spires type than the James Hammond, I'm thinking back to when I was young, of course."

"Of course," Virginia said, trying to hide her delight at the change in her mother. Amazing, she thought, what an attentive man could do for a woman. She only hoped the Colonel's intentions didn't include making love. She felt certain her mother wouldn't tolerate that.

"Well, Mama, I'll tell Phoebe and Nanine that we'll be leaving tomorrow. Then I must pack."

"Do that, my dear," Lenore replied gaily. "I'm so excited I don't think I'll sleep a wink tonight."

"Try, Mama," Virginia said, joining her mother in laughter. After all, you want to look your best for the Colonel tomorrow."

"I'll make it a point to, my dear. Run along now. It's so long since I planned a visit to anyone, it will take me quite a time planning what to take. Oh," she retrieved the Colonel's note, which she'd slipped into the pocket of her peignoir, "let the girls read it. And—I suggest we use two boats. These new clothes shouldn't go to waste."

Virginia rejoined Nanine and Phoebe downstairs and related in detail the change in their mother. They listened in stunned silence.

"I'm astonished," Nanine said. "But I'll do my best to control it. Now—suppose you tell us your plans."

"We'll leave tomorrow morning," Virginia said, holding up the Colonel's note. "He told Mama that if he didn't hear from us today, he'd have his carriage awaiting us at the dock tomorrow."

"Well, one thing's for certain, if Brad comes here he'll not find Jimmy," Nanine said with relief.

"Nonetheless, we must make him think Jimmy's here," Virginia said. "So we must carry on inside and outside the house as if everything is the same and only Mama and I are away."

"How will you manage that?" Phoebe asked. "Particularly since you're leaving in the morning."

"Ivy will be leaving with us," Virginia said. "She'll return to Valcour each night carrying a bundle that resembles a sleeping child. If Brad should be watching the island, or having someone do it for him, he'll see Jimmy leave, but he'll also see what he believes is Jimmy returning."

"It might work," Phoebe said reflectively.

Virginia placed the Colonel's note on the desk. "Mama wants you both to see it."

Nanine glanced at it but made no attempt to pick it up.

"Virgie, why don't you go to Lieutenant Johnson? After all, this is a terribly serious matter."

"I'm aware of that," Virginia said briskly. "That's why I feel I should get my son off the island. Besides, what reason could I give to the lieutenant for making a complaint?"

"But you saw Brad. You know he's in this area," Nanine persisted. "He poses a threat to your son. His son also."

"That's exactly it," Virginia said sternly. "I don't want anyone other than you and Phoebe to know Jimmy's true paternity. Certainly not Lieutenant Johnson."

"Elias knows," Nanine said.

"Damn Elias," Virginia said impatiently. "Why must you and Phoebe always bring him into the conversation? He's no part of this."

"He's a large part," Nanine argued.

"He's out of my life. Please, Nanine, I don't want to quarrel with you."

"Nor I with you," Nanine said sadly. "But I must say this. I feel you don't want Brad caught."

"I don't." Nanine's statement had caught Virginia off gaurd, but she tried to amend it. "After all, he is Jimmy's father. I don't want him hanged."

Nanine eyed her ruefully. "Did he spend the night in your room?"

Virginia looked away.

"Did he?" Nanine persisted.

"Not the entire night."

"But you were intimate?"

"Yes," Virginia said reluctantly. But that doesn't concern you."

"True," Nanine agreed. "I'm just trying to figure out what goes through your mind. You're such a complex woman."

"I'm weak, I suppose."

"Not weak, Virgie," Nanine disputed. "Spirited, stubborn,

and you have an intense desire for passionate lovemaking. Especially with someone like Brad."

"Very well, I admit it. But that doesn't lessen my resolve not to let him take Jimmy for six months. That six months is only a sham. Brad is now respectable—or thinks he is. He'd like to live out his life as a gentleman and a benevolent father. I don't really care how he lives it out, but he can't have Jimmy under any circumstances. Please, Nanine, stop questioning my motives."

"I'm sorry." Nanine rose and embraced Virginia. "May I help you pack?"

"No, but I'd like you to help Ivy. Jimmy is getting to be almost too much for her."

"He's a healthy, lively child," Nanine agreed. She picked up the note, read it, and handed it to Phoebe. "We'll give it back to Mama, Virginia. I have a feeling she'll treasure it, even though her feelings toward the Colonel extend no further than friendship."

"If only he'll be content with that," Virginia said quietly. "He still loves Mama. He told me he always has and has never even kissed her. I just hope she won't be repelled if he should become—affectionate."

"He's intelligent enough that he would sense it if Mama wasn't interested," Nanine said. "I'll stop in to see her wardrobe on my way to the nursery."

"Please do. We'll tell her how happy we are that she's going to have a change."

"You know," Phoebe reasoned, "this might just be the thing Lenore needed to give her a new interest in life. I think her presiding over social affairs was only a temporary relief from her boredom."

"You could be right," Virginia replied. "Well, I must pack. I don't know how long we'll be gone, so I'll have to bring enough to last a while. Mama suggested two boats. I hope the Colonel has enough room."

Nanine laughed. "I'm eager to see Mama's wardrobe."

"So am I," Phoebe said.

Virginia laughed. "Come to think of it, I haven't even glimpsed it. The bill was sufficient to startle me. But I'll see it at the Colonel's. I'll leave the receipt on my bureau, Nanine."

"Fine," Nanine replied. "I'll balance the checkbook."

Only one thing marred their preparations. Nanine came to Virginia's suite late in the evening to tell her that their mother had given Belle permission to accompany them.

"She can't come to the Colonel's," Virginia said angrily. "It's gotten to the point where I can't bear even to look at that woman."

"She doesn't want to go to the Colonel's," Nanine explained patiently. "She just wants to go to the mainland to buy herself a trinket."

"So that's it. She's jealous because I brought Ivy back a gift."

"That's it," Nanine agreed. "Don't make a fuss with Mama. After all, it's what you wanted, and you never really thought Mama would accept."

Virginia relented. "You're right, as usual. I suppose I can endure Belle for the duration of the boat ride."

"The men in the boat that will bring the baggage will wait to bring her back."

"I'd like to tell her to stay on the mainland, "Virginia said.

"And you don't have to worry about being near her. She told me she knows there are going to be two boats and she'll go in the one with the baggage."

"Good," Virginia said firmly. "I won't have to listen to her fuss."

"She claims that's the reason she wants to ride alone— that you'd fuss at her all the time. She said she knows you hate her."

Virginia laughed, despite herself. "I don't, Nan. It's the other way around."

Nanine's laughter mingled with Virginia's. "I know. But I'm glad she's going in the other boat. We don't want anything to upset Mama."

"I'm beginning to doubt that anything could," Virginia said. "I've never seen her so energetic. It's as if she had drunk from the fountain of youth."

"I'm happy for her," Nanine said. "I'm afraid we were too wrapped up in our own problems to realize just how lonely she was."

"Yes. Growing old without a mate must be absolute hell."

"Even at our age it is," Nanine said.

"You still miss Miles, don't you?"

"Yes, of course. Love does something wonderful to each of us. I wish Mama could care for the Colonel."

"That's like wishing for a miracle," Virginia replied. "Nanine, will you and Phoebe be frightened here?"

"No. We like the idea. We hope it will confuse Brad—if he's watching Valcour. Especially if you send Ivy back in the evening. But what will Mama think?"

"She won't know more than that Ivy is returning to get a well-earned rest from caring for Jimmy."

"Does Ivy know?"

"Yes. I told her that my husband wants me to bring the child to England and live there, and that I'm fearful he might have Jimmy kidnapped if I don't go."

"Oh, Virgie," Nanine said worriedly. "Why do you tell such lies?"

"At the moment, I have to do what I feel is best for Jimmy. Elias wouldn't mind."

"I doubt he'd like your being so underhanded."

"He'll never know anything about it, so stop worrying."

"That's not so easy," Nanine replied soberly. "Both

Phoebe and I are worried about you and Jimmy. We don't think you can cope with a man like Brad. He's proven how clever he is by evading capture. He's both resourceful and wily."

Virginia didn't disagree. She just wished that Nanine wasn't so perceptive. She was sure her ruse would work, but for how long? She dared not think of the answer.

TEN

The trip to the mainland was uneventful. Two men rowed each boat to hasten the journey. Lenore was wearing a new traveling suit and a matching bonnet. She would have raised her new parasol, also matching, but there was a fairly brisk wind that would have snatched it from her. There was color in her cheeks and a sparkle to her eyes that Virginia didn't recall ever having seen before.

Belle sulked in the other boat, which sometimes rowed alongside them. Whenever she looked their way she glared at Ivy, who averted her eyes.

Virginia noticed and said in an undertone, "Don't be afraid of her, Ivy. She's all bluster. Besides, she's jealous of you because I didn't bring her back a gift. Perhaps I should have, since I'm the only member of the household she dislikes, but I didn't feel she merited it."

Ivy nodded but made no reply.

"If she makes any trouble for you, come to me at once," Virginia said.

"I will, Miss Virginia. Thank you."

Virginia felt a trace of embarrassment as she recalled her father warning her not to make any trouble for Phoebe because she was as much his daughter as Virginia was. His statement had enraged her, but now she realized how right and how fair-minded he had been. She knew she'd inherited her high spirits and passionate nature from her father. She wished she had inherited his other qualities. Perhaps she had, she thought hopefully, casting a side glance at the girl.

The Colonel awaited them on the dock and beamed when he saw Lenore. He bent over her gloved hand and kissed the back of it. She smiled graciously, and after he had greeted Virginia, he gently pinched Jimmy's cheek, gave Ivy a friendly nod, and led them to the carriage. Belle bade Lenore farewell and went her way. Lenore rode in the front of the carriage with the Colonel, while Virginia and Ivy sat in the rear, with Jimmy between them. The four Negroes who had rowed them over placed their luggage in a wagon that the Colonel had thoughtfully provided, so everyone rode in comfort. Jimmy was very excited with all the activity. He chattered endlessly and pointed to the wagons, horses, and people he saw. Virginia found she was having as much fun as her son. Ivy, too, was entranced by everything she saw.

"This is good for the child," she said to Virginia. "Young as he is, he's attracted by the excitement and activity. He's never seen anything like it before."

"You're right," Virginia said, "he hasn't. Do you like it?"

"Very much. But I love Valcour the best."

Virginia smiled. "We all do, Ivy. And we appreciate your loyalty to the family."

"I'm wearing my locket, Miss Virginia."

"Good. You need not worry about the metal turning green. I wanted you to have something very nice."

"Thank you, Miss Virginia. You've been very good to me."

"I haven't forgotten about your education," Virginia went on. "Do you read?"

"Oh yes," Ivy said enthusiastically. "Miss Nanine said I might take any book in the library and read it. I don't think I could live long enough to read them all. But it's wonderful to be allowed to take what I choose."

"Continue to do that," Virginia said. "You'll learn a lot about life from reading. You'll learn a lot about people, too." She found herself liking Ivy more each time they conversed and was struck by her good diction and her intelligence. She was sorry that Belle was making Ivy's life difficult. "What do you like to read?"

"I like to read books about people who do something," she said.

"Do you mean like Miss Phoebe?"

"Not exactly. I mean like a lady doing work of some kind and getting paid for it."

"The way you're paid for being Jimmy's nursemaid?"

"Yes. Only not like being a nursemaid. Like being in charge of something. Like being a housekeeper and having to see that the house is kept clean and the meals served on time."

"Do you mean something where you'd have a great amount of responsibility?"

"Yes. It would make me feel that I'm doing something important."

"You mean a house larger than Valcour?"

"Oh—much larger. But not a house. Something bigger."

"What, for instance?"

Ivy gave a delicate shrug of her shoulders. "I don't really know. I know what I would like to do, but I don't know what to call it. Or how to get work in such a place."

Virginia laughed. "You'll have to learn the kind of establishment you're interested in first."

Ivy agreed, joining Virginia in laughter. Their attention was soon taken up by the countryside, for they were nearing the Colonel's plantation.

"Have you ever seen Colonel Spires's place?" she asked Ivy.

"No, Miss Virginia. I've never been to your large plantation, either."

"Then you're in for a pleasant surprise at the Colonel's. I wish Jimmy were older so he'd enjoy it."

They finally turned in at the driveway leading to the house. Ivy exclaimed at the topiaries, but Jimmy was more interested in a bird that kept flitting across the path of the wagon and chirping incessantly. His excited cries mingled with those of the bird. Obviously it had a nest in one of the topiaries and it didn't like the intrusion of the carriage. Throughout the ride, the Colonel and Lenore had kept up a conversation, mixed with cries of surprise or gay laughter. Virginia couldn't believe how her mother had changed.

The house was quite a surprise, though a pleasant one. The main floor was decorated with Chinese furniture, some of it very heavy, with ornate and intricate carvings. Bronze screens served to divide the large drawing room into cozy niches in each of which were groupings of chairs and tables. There were enormous cushions on the floor, and Jimmy was fascinated by them, tumbling onto the floor as he tried to climb on them. Huge brass urns, heavily etched, were placed here and there. Lenore was fascinated by the unusual atmosphere, which was almost sensual. At least it seemed so to Virginia. Persian rugs of every design covered the floors.

"Zachary," Lenore exclaimed, "I had no idea your home looked like this."

He laughed. "It didn't always. I hope you're not displeased with it."

"Indeed not. Isn't it unique, Virginia?"

"Yes, Mama. Unique and beautiful. I've seen pictures of furniture from China."

"It belonged to my sister," he said. "She was married to a ship's captain who traveled worldwide. He always brought back furniture. When the war ended, she died and left everything to me. Since I had to refurnish my place—or the army agreed to—I suggested they move my sister's possessions down here from Maine. For me, it relieved the boredom. Also, it offered an education in another culture."

"Those enormous pillows—did they come from China?"

"No, Miss Virginia," the Colonel replied, pleased at her interest. "They're from Turkey. Other countries are represented also. As I said, for me it was a welcome relief from loneliness."

"I'm afraid I'll have to ask where we'll be staying, Colonel," Virginia said. "It's time for Jimmy's nap."

"I have your rooms ready. I hope you like Jimmy's. The furniture was in my sister's attic. At the time, I wondered why I took it. Now I know."

He summoned a maid from the rear of the house by ringing a small gong with a clapper that sat on a high table in the center of the reception hall. Virginia and Ivy followed the maid upstairs. A second maid relieved Lenore of her parasol, then escorted her upstairs.

Virginia was pleasantly surprised with the nursery. The crib resembled a ship and was made of bamboo, as was the rest of the furniture, which was bright and cheerful. Virginia was as excited as Ivy was, and both exclaimed with pleasure. On the walls were silkscreen prints of children watched over by their parents.

Jimmy was getting tired and fretful. Ivy told Virginia she would undress him and get him ready for his nap, after which she would unpack his clothing.

Virginia thanked her and let herself be escorted to her room by the maid, whose name was Lurie. She was middle-aged and soft-spoken. As gracious as the Colonel, Virginia thought.

Virginia's room was another surprise. The bed was of mahogany and rosewood, very delicately made. It was heavily netted with very fine lace that looked as if it had been spun of gossamer silk. The pillowcases were also made of silk, with lace flounces at the hems. The chairs were delicate and upholstered in a fine print fabric.

"Will I unpacks now, Miss Virginia, or does yo' wish to res' awhile?"

"I believe I'll rest, Lurie," Virginia said.

"Fine, Miss Virginia. I'll waits a bit an' then brings yo' up some iced tea an' san'wiches—'less'n yo' wants to join yo' mama an' the Colonel in the dinin' room."

"Mama isn't resting?" Virginia asked in amazement.

Lurie smiled. "No, ma'am. She an' the Colonel doin' a lot o' talkin'. Guess they got lots o' talkin' to catch up on. Sho' glad the Colonel got visito's. He mighty lonely. Ain't seen him so 'cited since he comes home fum the wah."

"He and Mama are old friends, Lurie."

"Yes, Miss Virginia," Lurie replied dutifully, though the lowering of her eyes gave proof that the colonel, in his excitement, had told her about the lady whose hand he had once sought.

Ivy and Jimmy had dinner in the nursery. Downstairs, Virginia joined Lenore and the Colonel. He had donned a light blue silk suit for the occasion. The table was beautifully set and candles highlighted the gowns Virginia and her mother wore. Lenore's was a deep cerise that flattered her fair skin. Virginia had to admit that her mother looked at least ten years younger. She and the Colonel kept up a lively conversation at the table, with Virginia contributing only briefly. She was content to watch the two of them enjoying each other's company. Only near the end of the meal did she interrupt their reminiscences.

"Colonel, I was wondering if I might borrow a carriage to take Ivy back to the dock. One of our boats is awaiting her there."

"Of course, my dear," he replied graciously.

For the first time, Lenore turned her attention to Virginia. "Why is she returning, Virginia?"

"She needs a rest, Mama. She insisted on coming with us so that she could see Jimmy settled, but while he's here with us, I think it would be wise to let her have a little time to herself."

Lenore nodded. "An excellent idea. He does wear you out. But he's a healthy boy."

"Indeed, yes," the Colonel agreed. He rang a bell, and when the maid came he told her to send word to the stable to get a carriage and driver ready.

Virginia excused herself and went upstairs. Jimmy was already settled for the night, and Ivy had a shawl around her shoulders, prepared to leave. The wrapped figure that was supposed to be Jimmy was resting on the floor. If anyone in the house saw it, they'd believe it to be part of Ivy's packing. If they noted her quick return, they were so well trained they'd give no sign of it.

Virginia accompanied Ivy to the stable and waited until she was in the carriage and on her way to the dock. Virginia cautioned Ivy in an undertone to carry the bundle as if she were carrying Jimmy, so that even when she got to Valcour, anyone who might be watching would be certain she had returned with him. The idea was to have the watcher—if there was one—believe that the child was being returned to the island under cover of darkness.

Virginia prayed that the subterfuge would work. She returned to the house and listened at the foot of the stairs as the voices of the Colonel and her mother drifted out. On the hall table was a silver tray containing a decanter of brandy and three glasses. Virginia couldn't imagine her mother sipping brandy, but Lenore had been a surprise so far, so perhaps she would try it. Virginia poured a generous portion into one of the glasses and carried it upstairs.

She looked in on Jimmy, who was sleeping peacefully. She went to her suite and closed the door quietly.

She set the glass on her bureau and undressed in the darkness. She retrieved the brandy and sat in a chair by the window to catch the gentle night breeze. She looked out into the darkness and silence. Virginia sipped her brandy and watched the lightning bugs with amusement. It was almost as if they were performing a dance for her. She gazed into the distance toward where their plantation was located and immediately thought of Chris.

A wave of warmth and desire swept through her. She'd hoped she was temporarily free of her body's craving for physical gratification, but her heartbeat had already quickened and her flesh felt hot all over. Even the soles of her feet were damp against the coolness of the floor. She emptied her glass and wished she'd brought the decanter up with her, though that would have caused talk among the servants and embarrassed her mother if the Colonel questioned its location.

She got up and lit a lamp, turning it low. It was obviously Japanese, made of iron, with a temple roof, pierced sides, and a movable door. She paced restlessly about the room, glad she was in her bare feet; the floor was bare except for scatter rugs, and if she'd worn slippers her pacing might have been heard. Perhaps tomorrow she could take a ride over. She quickly dismissed the idea, knowing she'd have to watch Jimmy. She couldn't leave him in charge of Lenore or the servants. None of them knew about Brad and the threat he presented. She thought of Elias and cursed him for not being here. He'd always satisfied her, but he'd turned his back on her, and he would never bed with her again. She gripped the bedpost and pressed her hot brow against its coolness.

A man's voice outside caught her attention. It was followed by some dogs barking. Her emotional turmoil was replaced by sudden fear. She went to the window and looked out. There was no further sound. She thought of the servants, who were housed separately. Nonetheless, she made a hasty trip to Jimmy's nursery. He was sleeping soundly. She sat there awhile, then returned to her room. She went to bed and tried to sleep, but she was too tense. She returned to the child's room, settled herself on the floor, and lay there until daylight cast a gray shadow through the window. Only then did she return to her room for a few hours' sleep.

Even as she drifted off she was aware of the tension in her body. She couldn't relax, wondering if Brad was on the prowl. She hoped that if someone was watching the island, he would report that the child had been returned to Valcour. It might even be, she reasoned, grasping at straws, that Brad had no one to help him now. Though it didn't seem likely.

Despite only a few hours' sleep, she woke early, her first thought of Jimmy. She slipped into her peignoir and went to the nursery. Even before reaching it, she heard voices. Lurie was there, completely in command of the situation, and Jimmy was, as usual, babbling happily.

"I already fed him, Miss Virginia," Lurie said. "I was wonderin' if yo'd let me take the chil' outside where he can romp in the garden. The Colonel made it fo' children. He even wuks on it hisse'f. Sometime all day."

"So I've heard, Lurie," Virginia said. "And I'd be delighted to have you bring Jimmy outside for fresh air and play. Let him burn off some of that energy."

"He sho' gots it." She already had the child in her arms. "I takes good care o' him, Miss Virginia. An' the Colonel say if yo' lets me, I be his maid an' yo's a'so."

"Very nice, Lurie. Thank you. I didn't sleep well last night, so I'm going back to bed."

Virginia was relieved, for she had a terrible headache. She returned to her room, where she slept until noon.

Lurie was in the room when she woke, and in answer to Virginia's question, she informed her that Jimmy was being looked after by Benjie, her husband, who was completely reliable.

"Good," Virginia replied. "I'll take my bath now."

"Feel bettuh wif yo' sleep?" Lurie asked as she went to fill the tub.

"Much," Virginia replied. "I suppose Mama and the Colonel wonder if I'm ill."

Lurie laughed and called back to Virginia, who was brushing her hair, "I doubts they even knows yo' slep' late. They went fo' a ride this mo'nin'. Stops by yo' plantation an' saw Mistuh Chris."

Virginia's interest heightened. "You know Mr. Chris?"

"He heah quite a lot," came the friendly reply. "He an' the Colonel gets to be mighty good frien's. Mistuh Chris have dinnuh heah three o' foah nights a week. Both gen'mun's pretty lonely."

"I suppose so, since they're both bachelors."

"Colonel tell Mistuh Chris he should marry an' have a fam'ly 'fo' he too ol'. I 'grees."

"Doesn't he have a lady friend that he visits?"

"No, ma'am," Lurie called back firmly. "That one man who don' do no messin' 'roun'. He like the Colonel. A'ways the gen'mun."

"That's nice to hear," Virginia said pleasantly. A contemplative smile touched the corners of her mouth. She wondered if she would have an opportunity to visit Chris. It might well be that his standards were so high that he'd not consider visiting a brothel.

She donned a pink dotted-Swiss dress with a double overskirt. The bodice was cut low, so she wore a lace fichu. She had to wear something cool because she would spend the remainder of the day outdoors with Jimmy, except for the hour or so of his nap.

She went downstairs and outside to meet Benjie. He was a younger version of Moses, with a warm, friendly nature. He was of medium height, but his muscles bulged beneath his white skirt, a fact Virginia noticed with satisfaction. Certainly he'd be able to protect the child should Brad or anyone else come to abduct him. Virginia felt that Brad would come himself for that purpose. He'd not want anything to happen to Jimmy.

She kissed the child, talked with him for a little while, and returned to the house. She was famished, but had to lunch by herself, as her mother and the Colonel were having their meal in the gazebo. She was still amazed by her mother's change and delight at being here, and she hoped that nothing untoward would happen to induce her to return to Valcour.

Virginia left the table and was on her way upstairs when a note arrived for her.

The handwriting on the envelope revealed that it was from Nanine; it had been delivered by one of their workers. However, he'd not waited for an answer, so Virginia had no way of questioning him.

She withdrew the letter from the envelope.

Dear Sister,

Brad was here last night. I chose to sleep in the nursery. I'd placed the form Ivy returned with in the crib, covered it, and settled down on the floor.

Unfortunately, I fell asleep, and was shaken awake none too gently. In the low lamplight, Brad hovered over me. His face was contorted with rage. He stated that he knew you'd left, but felt you were up to some kind of chicanery, so he came here and hid. He saw Ivy return and he believed she was carrying Jimmy. He waited until the house was darkened and gained entry. He wouldn't reveal how, and I cannot guess.

I'm certain he knows where you are, though I don't know who could have informed him. Nonetheless, we must now assume there's a spy on the island, though I have no idea who it could be or how we can uncover his identity.

I didn't dare scream, because of Brad's intense anger. He had straddled me and his hands had my shoulders pinned to the floor. His ankles, covering mine, held me secure. I feared at first he might rape me, but he had only one thought on his mind—getting his son.

I still think your only hope is to inform Lieutenant Johnson. You may tell him that I sent word that our home was broken into. I confronted Brad but certainly could not overpower him. That's the truth. Whatever you do, don't remain at the Colonel's. If Brad knows you went to the mainland, he must know where you are. That makes sense, since he never asked your whereabouts.

When Brad got to his feet, he looked down at me and, still straddling me, told me to send word to you that he was determined to get his son and nothing you could do would deter him.

After he left, I wakened Phoebe and related what happened. We sat up the remainder of the night, though we weren't further bothered. Nor will we be, since he now knows you fooled him and Jimmy is on the mainland.

Phoebe discussed the perilous situation with me and agrees about going to see Lieutenant Johnson. He's your only salvation. You can't outsmart Brad. He's dangerous. And quite terrifying when angry. I was completely at his mercy. I fear the man may have contracted a sickness as a result of the war—one that affected his mind, in some way, and over which he has no control.

Please, Virgie, both Phoebe and I entreat you to seek the help of Lieutenant Johnson. You fear Jimmy's paternity may

*be revealed. Both Phoebe and I feel that's a risk you must
take. The decision is yours, but we hope you will give it deep
thought and conclude that our reasoning is the only correct
course for you to pursue.*

*Lovingly,
Nanine*

Nanine's note struck fresh terror into Virginia. She
began to perspire heavily. She knew that Nanine was
right. She should notify Lieutenant Johnson immediately.
She could use the reason Nanine had suggested—that
Nanine had been awakened by an intruder, whom she'd
confronted; she'd then recognized him as the outlaw Bradley
Culver. Yet, Virginia hesitated. Brad hadn't gotten Jimmy.
Perhaps he never would get him. It was the fear of having
her son branded a bastard that caused her to reject notifying
Lieutenant Johnson. She knew she would do anything to
prevent that. She would gamble on her success in foiling
Brad, but she would follow Nanine's advice in leaving the
Colonel's mansion. But where could she go?

The answer came quickly: the Hammond plantation.
Chris was there, and he would do everything to protect
Jimmy. She also felt that he would be a good match for
Brad. He was probably in far better trim, though Brad's
physique was still lean and hard. He might have become
respectable, but he hadn't weakened.

She went to the kitchen and learned that her mother and
the Colonel hadn't returned to the house. She obtained
directions to the gazebo and went there directly. Virginia
was too unnerved to be aware of her mother's laughter
drifting from the gazebo. She hadn't heard laughter from
her mother in years.

A look at the tension on Virginia's somber face brought
a stop to the conversation between Lenore and the Colonel.

He stood up as she ascended the stairs and paused before their table.

"Won't you join us, my dear?" he asked.

"No, thank you. I had a letter from Nanine. She's coming to the plantation this afternoon and wants Jimmy and me there with her."

"Why don't you leave Jimmy here, dear?" Lenore asked. "The Colonel and I will look after him."

Virginia thought quickly. "I'd like to take him with me, Mama. I'm enjoying him. I did neglect him, you know. I depend too much on Ivy, and I want him to know that I'm his mama."

"She's right, Lenore," the Colonel said. "Virginia should have her son with her. Besides, Chris will enjoy taking him horseback riding."

"Jimmy will love that," Virginia said.

"Very well," Lenore said. "I'll go back to the house and pack. I may as well go with you."

"That's not necessary, Mama. It's much more pleasant here. The Colonel has been a tonic for you."

"My dear Virginia," he said gallantly, "it's the other way around. Lenore has made me come alive."

"Thank you, Zachary," Lenore said, blushing, "but I can't think of anything I've done that would lift your spirits."

"Just being here," he said. "Please don't leave. After all, we're mature people. It would be foolish to suspect any wrongdoing on our part."

"He's right, Mama." Virginia was terrified that Lenore would insist on coming, and she didn't want the true reason for her leaving the Colonel's to come out. "Please stay. You'll be bored at the plantation, and you'll be just as bored if you return to Valcour."

Lenore thought a moment. "Do you really think it won't seem unconventional?"

"No one had better even suggest such a thing," the Colonel said gruffly.

"Thank you, Colonel." Virginia planted a light kiss on his cheek.

Lenore looked as pleased as the Colonel. "I guess you both really want me to stay," she said.

"Yes." Both Virginia and the Colonel uttered the word at the same time.

"Please tell Nanine I'm having a most enjoyable holiday," Lenore said.

"I will, Mama." Virginia bent and kissed her mother's cheek.

"Thank you, my dear."

"I'll have a carriage and driver ready for you," the Colonel said.

"Thanks, Colonel," Virginia said. "I'm going to pack immediately. I want to be there before Nanine arrives."

"Take good care of my grandson, dear," Lenore called as Virginia ran back to the house. She half-turned to nod and wave agreement.

Chris Savard was his usual gracious self when Virginia arrived. Since he wasn't surprised to see her, she knew he'd been told by the Colonel or her mother when they'd visited the plantation that she was also a guest at the Colonel's.

Jimmy had missed his nap, so she settled him in the nursery, which she had decorated before his birth. Lurie had fed the child before they left, so he'd not need to eat until six o'clock, at which time Tessa would take over as nursemaid. Chris had excused himself to bathe and change before their talk.

Chris suggested the breakfast room for their discussion because it was on the shaded side of the house. It was furnished with white wicker furniture with upholstered chintz cushions and back rests. Plants hung from the ceiling, making the room restful as well as cool. Callie brought in two mint juleps and told Virginia how pleased she was to see her.

"Thank you, Callie," Virginia replied. "It's a nice change for both my son and me."

"Was upstairs a'ready to looks in on him, Miss Virginia," she said, her smile wide. "He sho' a healthy chil'."

"An armful, too," Virginia said.

After Callie left, Virginia sipped her drink appreciatively. "This is delicious. Callie put enough bourbon in it to make it palatable."

Chris smiled mischievously. "I hope there's enough mint."

"Perfect." Virginia took another generous swallow and grew serious. "I suppose you wonder why I came here."

"I shouldn't, since you're one of the owners," he replied. "However, you looked concerned when you arrived."

"I am," she said, setting down her nearly empty glass. "Jimmy has been threatened with kidnapping."

Chris eyed her with disbelief. "Are you allergic to mint juleps?"

"I'm serious, Chris. My son is in danger of being kidnapped. I've been warned."

"One doesn't usually receive advance notice of a kidnapping."

"I did." She reached for her glass and emptied it.

"Did the kidnapper also tell you his name?"

"He didn't have to. I know it. But he told me to my face he was going to take my child."

"What's his name?"

"Bradley Culver."

Chris almost choked on his drink. "The outlaw?"

She nodded.

"Why did he choose your son? He's robbed, pillaged,

and looted, so he must be wealthy. Of course, he came of
wealth, though I read that his parents are dead."

"Being an outlaw, he couldn't claim any of his parents'
wealth," Virginia pointed out. "If they had any—anything
following the war."

"They had two factories in the North, plus other proper-
ties there."

"He hates the North so much he probably wouldn't
touch them," Virginia reasoned.

"I know he did some outrageous things," Chris said.
"But I never thought he'd stoop to kidnapping."

"Well, he has," Virginia retorted. She looked at Chris
and saw his eyes studying her. "You look as if you don't
believe me."

"I want to, but I don't find it easy." He emptied his
drink and picked up the bell. "I think we could stand
another one. Or would you rather not?"

"I would. I'm quite upset."

Virginia removed the envelope she'd slipped inside the
bodice of her dress and handed it to Chris. "Perhaps this
will convince you. It's from Nan."

Callie returned with two drinks, picked up the empty
glasses, and left quietly.

Chris read the letter, replaced it in the envelope, and
handed it back. "All right. I believe your story. But I can't
believe the motive is ransom."

"It could be that he needs money to get away from this
area."

"Culver is a resourceful individual. He could get away
from this area if he wanted to. He's been sighted in the
North several times."

Tears filled Virginia's eyes. "Very well," she said
reluctantly. "I'll have to tell you. Bradley Culver fathered
my son. He wants to have him for six months. He said
he'd return him after that time. I don't believe him."

"I do," Chris said. "But I can understand your reluctance to let him have the child."

"I refused pointblank," Virginia said heatedly. "He's an outlaw. Suppose the army caught up with him and there was shooting. Jimmy might get hurt, or worse."

"True," Chris said. "What do you want me to do?"

"Help me protect him."

"Here?"

"Of course."

"Did you notify the Union army?"

"No." Virginia looked dismayed. "How can I explain to them? You didn't believe me until I broke down and told you my secret."

"So that's why Elias went to England so abruptly." Chris's statement shook Virginia.

"Yes," she replied, her eyes lowered. "Please don't hate me."

"I don't," he said in his quiet manner. "I hope we can outwit Bradley Culver, but he's had lots of practice in raiding and leaving before anyone can get into action. I'll do my best, though I still think you should follow Nan's advice and notify the army."

"No."

"Do you know the name of the officer in charge in Charleston?"

"Lieutenant Johnson, but I'll not go near him."

"I know him too. In fact, I was at their headquarters last night. Two of my men came down with a fever two days ago. It was raging last night. I could have gotten an old doctor in these parts, but I wanted an army doctor to look at them."

"I don't blame you," Virginia said, thinking of how ill Nanine had been before an army doctor diagnosed her illness and prescribed the proper food that would start her back on the road to good health.

"Anyway, he took them back and put them in the army hospital. So if I seem a little slow or dull, you'll have to understand. I got no sleep."

"That's of no help to me," Virginia said, discouraged.

"I told you I'd do my best."

"You hate me because of what I did to Elias."

"I don't hate you, Miss Virginia. At the moment, I'm very sorry for you. I know the anguish you must be going through. However, if you really love your son, I should think you'd want to be assured of his safety. The army could do that."

"I told you . . ." she began, her tone firm.

"I know what you told me," Chris said. "You haven't touched your drink. I suggest you do so. It will help to relax you. I want to ask you another question. If your child's paternity should be found out and revealed to the public, would you cease to love him?"

"Never!"

Chris smiled. "Then what are you going to do—pamper him all your life? Make a sissy of him?"

"You're as bad as Brad. That's what he thinks."

"He could be right." He paused, then added, "I take it you're seeing him."

"I'm not. He visited Valcour when we gave a ball. I knew then, from what he said, that he was going to make trouble. I begged him to stay away from the child, saying that I wanted nothing more to do with him. Recently I received a letter demanding that I meet him at a hotel in Falmouth. There he demanded that I let him have the child for six months. I refused. He said he'd get him even if he had to reveal the story of Jimmy's paternity. You read what Nan said about the war doing something to his mind. I'm beginning to get that same opinion."

"That has no meaning now," Chris said. "All we can do is station men about the grounds. I'll patrol, too. If I keep

Callie and Tessa in the house all night, I'll have to give some reason for it."

"Then don't have anyone."

"You'll be alone."

"The first floor will be locked, won't it?" Virginia asked. She finally picked up her drink and took a deep swallow.

"Yes. If you think that will keep Culver out."

"Do you have a gun? It won't be the first time I shot a man."

"I'll give you a gun. Just be certain the child doesn't get his hands on it."

"I'm not that irresponsible."

"Good. I suggest we go in for dinner. Unless you want to dress."

"Not tonight," she said.

"I'm glad. As I said, I had no sleep last night or the night before. I'm sure I won't get any tonight either."

"Perhaps he won't come," Virginia said hopefully.

"Does he know you're here?"

"I hope not here," Virginia said. "But he apparently knew where Mama, Jimmy, Ivy, and I were going. I sent Ivy back to Valcour last night after dark. I had a boat waiting for her. She carried a wrapped bundle that looked as if it were Jimmy."

"How did you explain the situation to her?"

"I'd rather not say." She averted her head and finished her drink.

"I think I can guess," Chris said soberly.

During the evening meal, Chris talked at length about the plantation and the excellent cotton crop that would be produced. When he asked about the cotton on Valcour, Virginia informed him that the seedlings Carlos had brought looked good.

"Is he coming back to help you cross the plants?"

"Oh no," Virginia said lightly. "I gave him an outright sum for them."

"Do you know how to go about it?" Chris asked.

"I wish I did," she replied. "The fact is, I didn't care for Carlos's manner. To me, it was a business proposition. With him, it was quite another matter."

"I think you were wise. He's probably an adventurer."

"I got that feeling," Virginia said almost primly. "Do you know how it's done, Chris?"

"I haven't the faintest idea. Nor would I want to experiment with the cotton you have. It's of such superb quality; I'd be afraid to tamper with something that's so outstanding."

"My hope is to get something even more outstanding."

"Don't you think that's a little like wishing for the moon?"

"No," she replied firmly. "I have great faith in my idea. And I'm certain I'll find someone who can help me. Or at least tell me how to accomplish what I want to do."

Chris's eyes held a trace of amusement. "You're a very reckless woman."

"I suppose I'm a gambler," Virginia mused.

"One who plays for high stakes."

"You disapprove of me, don't you?"

"On the contrary, you're fascinating. A willful and spirited lady. A man might fear becoming involved with you, but he'd never be bored."

"You make me sound like an ogre," Virginia said, her expression somber.

"I'm sorry, Miss Virginia. Tell me, do you think Nanine and Phoebe are safe on Valcour?"

"Yes. Don't you?"

"I hope so. At least, Bradley Culver didn't inflict any bodily harm on either of them."

"He has the child on his mind, though I don't believe he would hurt any member of my family."

"You should know, and it's reassuring to hear." He took a final sip of coffee, wiped his mouth with his napkin, and set it on the table. "I'm going to assign men to patrol the grounds, so you'll have to excuse me. As soon as Callie and Tessa leave, I suggest you lock the doors and windows."

"Where will you be?"

"I'll be on watch close to the house. After I've assigned the men, I'll go to the gazebo, where I'll stay until dark."

"If I should need you, I'll go there."

"If you do, make certain you lock the door behind you."

"I will."

She watched him walk from the room, her expression reflective. She still felt that he disapproved of her. Small wonder, since she'd had to confess that she'd been Bradley Culver's mistress and had given birth to his son. She was well aware of the close friendship that Elias and Chris had formed. And she was just as aware that Chris had the same sense of morality as Elias had. He would never have been unfaithful to her, so even though Chris had denied that he disapproved of her, she knew otherwise.

She went to the kitchen to thank Callie for the delicious chicken dinner, then went upstairs to attend Jimmy. Tessa had already settled him in his crib for the night.

"I fed him, Miss Virginia," Tessa said. "He a good li'l boy." She was looking at Virginia with admiration.

"Didn't he tire you, Tessa?" Virginia asked, smiling.

"No. It was fun, an' it nice havin' a chil' in the house. He sho' have a right purty mama. Yo' is beau'ful, Miss Virginia."

"Thank you, Tessa. You'd better go downstairs now and have your supper."

"Will yo' wants me fo' anythin' else?" she asked hopefully.

"Not tonight. Tomorrow you may look after Jimmy if you wish."

"I sho' wish," she said eagerly. "I bathe an' dress him too. I knows how."

"Good. I'll see you then."

Virginia returned to her room, removed her fichu, and sat by the window. In the gathering dusk, she caught a glimpse of Chris talking to a Negro who was all muscle and brawn. The black man nodded from time to time and pointed in various directions. Obviously, Chris was giving him instructions on where to place the men who would guard the grounds against intruders. The Negro went off at a half-run and Chris disappeared behind some tall shrubbery.

Virginia got up and glanced at her reflection in the mirror. Despite the gravity of the situation, her eyes held a sparkle and her skin was slightly flushed. Chris had done that to her. His presence at the table was like a stimulant, even though he disapproved of her. Yet, he'd admitted he was fully aware of her appeal. She undid the two top buttons of her bodice, almost freeing her breasts. She smiled at her reflection and returned to the window. She saw Callie and Tessa walk down the path to the small houses that had been done over, under Elias's supervision.

She went downstairs and locked the doors and windows, then returned to her vigil by the window. Twice she left it to look in on Jimmy. Each time she looked at his sleeping form, she said a prayer of relief. A worrisome frown touched her brow as she wondered how long this could go on. How could she hope to outsmart Brad when the Union army hadn't been able to? The answer came readily enough. It was impossible.

Nanine's argument was right, of course. Even Chris had agreed that the army should be notified. She realized that the odds were insurmountable. She was a mere woman, and Brad was bound by no code of ethics. He made his own rules. She had no defense against him. She suddenly remembered the gun; Chris had forgotten to give it to her. She went downstairs to see if there was one in the house. She'd not given a thought to a gun case when she had redecorated and refurnished the house, especially since the house had never been occupied.

She had to find Chris and learn where the guns were. On a hunch, she went to his rooms, but there was no trace of a gun there. Darkness had settled over the plantation and the house. She would get a lantern from the service room so she'd not be mistaken for an intruder by the workers assigned to watch the grounds. She didn't want to leave even a single lamp on in the house. In darkness, should Brad come, he might believe the house empty. Also, she was fearful of leaving a lamp burning with Jimmy alone in the house. Should it somehow topple over, it was certain to cause a fire.

She used a candle to light her way to the rear of the house, where she found a lantern. The swish of oil as she shook it was reassuring. She found matches, lit the wick, blew out the flame, and went to the front door. She unlocked it, went outside and closed it softly behind her, then relocked the door and dropped the key into her skirt pocket.

She went down the few steps, crossed the stone driveway, and headed for the gazebo, hoping that she'd find Chris there. She moved effortlessly across the soft grass, keeping as much in the clearing as possible.

She reached the gazebo, but she saw no sign of Chris, nor was there any whispered greeting. Holding the lamp aloft, she went up the steps. Only then did she glimpse him. He was sprawled on the chaise-longue, sound asleep. Stifling the curse that rose to her lips, she set the lamp on the floor, partially under the table, where it gave subdued light. When she bent over to wake him, she was struck by his relaxed features. Her eyes slowly moved the length of his body. One of his legs had slid off the chaise and rested on the floor.

Slowly, almost hesitantly, one of her hands moved to his groin and rested lightly on it. She bent down and covered his mouth with hers. Her lips, barely touching his, were in slow, constant movement, while her hand gently caressed him. She'd forgotten the reason for her mission and the fact that she'd unbuttoned the two top buttons of her bodice. Unhampered, her breasts slipped free and touched Chris's chest.

He stirred slightly, then awakened slowly, almost reluctantly. As consciousness returned, so did an awareness that he was physically aroused. He reached out and grasped Virginia about the waist, pulling her down onto him. His lips responded to hers and their kiss grew more passionate. His hands rose to her breasts and he manipulated them gently, causing her to cry out as her desire became more intense. His hands moved down to her buttocks and held her to him as he turned her over so that she was beneath him. He was fumbling with her skirt, trying to pull it up. A tortured cry came from his throat. Their bodies were now in frenzied motion and he was as much the aggressor as she. Her free hand slipped around to the front of his waist to undo his trousers. As the same time, she was reveling in the ecstasy of their passion, which was almost ready to peak.

Then Chris spoke, his voice sounding tormented. "Phoebe. Oh, my darling Phoebe. How I needed you. Thank God you're here."

"Phoebe!" Virginia was so shocked that her body froze.

Chris was as stunned as she. Motionless, he raised himself, looked down at her in the dim light, and blurted, "You harlot. You damned harlot."

"You damned bastard," she retorted, enraged. "You damned, dirty bastard. I'm not Phoebe."

He got off the chaise and turned his back while he rebuttoned his trousers. Virginia was still too stunned to move. Her breasts were fully exposed and her skirt was above her hips, her legs spread wantonly.

He turned around. "You're damned right you're not Phoebe. She's the woman I love. The lady I'm going to marry. *And she is a lady.*"

Virginia threw down her skirt, shifted to the side of the chaise, and buttoned her bodice. Her breath was rapid and deep, but from anger now, all of it directed at the man she thought had hungered for her as much as she had for him. Instead, it had been for Phoebe.

"What are you doing out here?" Chris asked.

"You forgot to leave me a gun," she replied in disgust.

"I didn't forget. You're too emotional to be trusted with a lethal weapon."

"You're a damn fool."

"Possibly," he replied. "But I'm certain there would be no need for a gun, since Culver only wants his son."

"And you'd let him take him, I suppose."

"Not if I could help it."

"You couldn't do much to stop it if you were asleep—and you were."

"I'm sorry about that, but I told you I'd not been to bed for two nights and worked in the fields all day."

"You weren't too tired to respond to me," Virginia taunted.

"I was in deep sleep, which you managed to penetrate. Any man would have reacted to it. I thought you were Phoebe. The lantern wasn't sufficient to light up your face."

"Did you know that Phoebe isn't entirely white?" Virginia asked.

"Yes. Long before she returned to Valcour. Elias used to keep me informed about her career in New York City."

"I suppose you lusted for her then."

"No, Virginia." Chris had regained control of his emotions and addressed her now in his normal manner. "I admired her. I hoped she would be a success. If she'd stayed, I believe she might have overcome the prejudice. I'm honored that she prefers a life with me."

"Do you think she'll be accepted here?"

"She has been so far. Of course, I know the Hammond name is all-powerful. I also know that she deposited a goodly sum of money—none of which I want—in the Charleston bank."

"Are you planning on having a family?"

"Yes, ma'am." Chris adopted a subservient tone.

"Suppose they're black?" Virginia's temper was still explosive.

"Frankly, ma'am, I don't give a damn. We'll love them and we'll do our damnedest to help them learn to live with the prejudice. If we won't be accepted here, we'll go West. There are tremendous possibilities in California."

"Phoebe wouldn't leave her family," Virginia said defiantly.

"After what you've just said about her, I gathered she wasn't acceptable to you."

"You are impudent," Virginia stormed. "I love her."

"Then behave yourself."

He stepped forward, grasped her arms, and pulled her to her feet. "Now you listen to me. If it's any comfort to you, you did stir me up. And if it's of any more comfort to you, if Phoebe didn't possess my every thought, I'd have succumbed to your charms. You're one hell of a woman. Any man who has tasted your lips, felt your body close to his, and been aroused by your skillful and practiced ways, would agree to that. But I love Phoebe. I always will, and I'll be as faithful to her as she'll be to me. As for you—I suggest you get back to the house, where you belong. Your son is alone."

"Oh, God!" She pulled free of Chris. In her haste, she forgot the lantern as she headed for the stairs. She lost her footing and plunged off the gazebo into the darkness, shrieking in terror as she fell. The crash of her body hitting the ground knocked out whatever fight was in her and broke off her cry. Chris was there immediately and helped her to her feet. She meekly asked him to give her the lantern.

"I'll go back to the house with you," he replied.

He took her arm, and, with the aid of the lantern, the two made a swift return. She was holding the key when they reached the door. He took it from her shaking hand, opened the door, and followed her inside. He lit the lamps while she went upstairs, lantern in hand, to check on the boy.

A piercing scream confirmed Chris's worst fear. He cursed himself for not having provided her with a gun, but he knew in what an emotional state she was.

Chris ran up the stairs, her screams still piercing the night. He took the lamp from her hand, glanced at the crib and saw it empty, and led her from the room.

"Calm down, Virginia," he said in a soothing tone. "We've got to go into the city. You can no longer refuse to tell Lieutenant Johnson what's happened."

Her screams had faded, but she was on the verge of hysteria. Chris placed an arm around her waist and led her downstairs. His manner was gentle, for she was scarcely aware of where she was. There was a blank stare in her eyes, her shoulders sagged, and her body trembled from head to foot.

Downstairs, he eased her into a wing chair beside a table on which were a decanter of brandy and two glasses. "I keep this handy because Colonel Spires and I like to finish off dinner with it," he said. "Now you and I will have a drink."

Virginia made no answer. Chris doubted she could, but she did accept the glass and she drank its entire contents. He didn't refill it, nor his own, which he emptied quickly. He hoped his fatigue, which had caused him to fail her, wouldn't return. But he was shaken by what had happened and needed the drink to steady him and help him think.

"I think Valcour would be the best place for you," he said. "You'll be with your sisters."

"My baby. My poor baby." She started to cry. Chris let her. It would release the tension that had built up in her. He brought her two man-sized handkerchiefs, and when her tears were exhausted and she'd dried her eyes and blown her nose, he moved his chair closer. Before he could talk, a man's voice called to him. There were sounds of other voices, too.

"That's Marcus, my head man," he said. "Obviously, they heard your screams, even though they were stationed quite a distance from the house."

He went to the door and told them there'd been a little trouble and there'd be no further need to watch the house. He returned and resumed his seat facing Virginia.

"Now you listen while I tell you the best thing I think we can do. Under the circumstances, it's the only thing."

"I don't even know where to look for my baby," she said dully.

"We'll find your son." Chris maintained a calmness he was far from feeling. "We've got to notify the Union army headquarters that Jimmy's been kidnapped."

"We can't have publicity or we'll never find Brad. We must let him think he's gotten away with this."

"I agree," Chris said. "So we'll tell Lieutenant Johnson that Brad left word with one of my help that the price would be twenty thousand dollars and that he would collect it at a time and place he would designate. We'll tell the lieutenant that there must be no publicity for the reason you state. They know how crafty he is and will agree. I'll tell Johnson that I believe Brad wants the money to leave these parts."

"And then what do we do?" Virginia said dully, still in shock.

"The first thing is to find out who gave Culver information regarding your movements."

"Where do we go to find that out?"

"Back to Valcour. The spy has to be there. With your permission, I'll go back with you. Marcus is a good overseer."

"Please stay here—or in Charleston." Virginia was beginning to come out of her daze. "Stay close to the army. They may have ways of finding out. You may be able to supply them with information. Nan, Phoebe, and I will work on uncovering the culprit."

"Since you have no idea where to look for him, it's wise to move slowly. Do you feel able to ride into town now?"

Virginia stood up. "I'll get a shawl. The ride over to the island will be cool. Not that I'll notice."

She turned to head for the stairway, then went back to Chris. "I'm sorry about my behavior tonight. I'm ashamed of myself. Not only for what I did to you, but because of what I said about Phoebe. I really do love her. I was angry with you for rejecting me. If I'd known you were betrothed to Phoebe, I'd not have tried to seduce you."

"It never happened, Virginia. Now get your wrap. There's a man outside. I'll send him to the stable to have a horse and buggy hitched up."

As he moved to the door, he wondered if Virginia was speaking the truth. He had to admit that she was quite a woman, but then, so was Phoebe, and he was impatient to see her again.

Chris made very good time on the ride to Charleston. First, he drove Virginia to the dock, where he hired a boat.

He told her he would have her clothes packed and returned to Valcour. He also added that should her mother question her absence, he would say that she had returned to Valcour. He ordered her not to worry, but to concentrate her efforts on uncovering the spy and questioning him, in an effort to learn Bradley Culver's whereabouts.

ELEVEN

Virginia reached the island about three o'clock in the morning. She saw moving light as she neared the dock, and when the boatman reached it, Moses was there.

"Yes, Moses. There's no further need to have men patrolling the plantation. Come to the house tomorrow morning. We'll want to talk with you."

"Yas'm, Miss Virginia." He held up the lantern. "Yo' look real peaked, missy. Sho' yo' don' need a doctuh?"

"I'm sure, Moses. Thanks."

She turned and headed for the house. Apparently Phoebe or Nanine had been awakened by the voices, for Virginia saw lamplight begin to appear in the windows upstairs. By the time she reached the house, the downstairs was fully lit.

She heard the lock turn and the bolt pushed back, and then the door opened, revealing both Phoebe and Nanine, each holding a lamp.

"You look ill, Virgie," Nanine exclaimed with concern.

"What happened?" Phoebe asked. "Where's Jimmy?"

"He was kidnapped," Virginia replied, fighting to hold back her tears. Nanine and Phoebe weren't quite as successful, but they quickly got their emotions under control.

"Brad won," Nanine said sorrowfully. "Did you notify the Union army, as I suggested?"

"No. I was wrong. I admit it. Chris is doing that." She

217

turned to Phoebe. "He told me you were to be married. You know I wish you happiness."

"Thank you, Virgie," Phoebe said uneasily. "Please forgive me for not telling you."

"I understand," Virginia replied. "You were afraid to, lest I fire Chris. Well, I won't. Anyway, I'd have to consult both you and Nan, and I doubt I could muster a majority vote."

"Thanks, Virgie, for making light of it." Phoebe said.

"Would you like some hot tea?" Nanine asked.

"Nothing, thanks," Virginia said. "What Chris suggested, and I agree with, is that we try to uncover the spy who has to be here and must have contact with Brad."

"I don't know where to start looking," Nanine said. "Both Phoebe and I tried to figure out who on the island would wish us ill. We just can't imagine who it might be."

"Besides," Phoebe added, "no one knew you and your mama were going to visit the Colonel."

"True," Virginia agreed. "I can't think. My brain won't work."

"Small wonder you look ill," Nanine said. "I think you should go to bed for a while. The rest will help you think."

"I couldn't sleep," Virginia said.

"I'm sure of that," Nanine agreed. "A sleeping draft will help."

"First I must tell you what happened," Virginia said, settling in a chair and resting her head against one of the wings. "I realized yesterday after your letter came that I must leave the Colonel's. I didn't want Mama to know about Brad having entered the house, so I told her that you were going to our mainland plantation and I was going there with Jimmy. I felt that he'd be safe there with Chris and the men to guard the grounds."

"Why didn't you notify the army?" Nanine asked softly.

Virginia closed her eyes. "I wish I had, but Brad threatened to reveal Jimmy's true paternity if I didn't hand him over for six months or made any trouble. I may sound mad, but I'm afraid of him. I know he can be completely ruthless when he feels the occasion demands it. I don't want anyone to know that Elias didn't father Jimmy."

"Is it all that important?" Phoebe asked gently.

Virginia sighed. "Chris asked me the same question, in so many words. He wouldn't believe that Brad would stoop to kidnapping, so I had to reveal Jimmy's paternity. At the time, I didn't know you and he were engaged. I didn't want anyone outside the immediate family to know about Jimmy. Only you two and Elias know who his true father is."

"Speaking of Mama," Nanine said, "is she at our plantation?"

A fleeting smile touched Virginia's mouth. "No. She's still at the Colonel's."

"I can't believe it," Nanine said.

"She was a little unhappy at the prospect of having to accompany me. So the Colonel and I convinced her to remain. The Colonel said no one had ever better say one disparaging word against her character."

"And Lenore was convinced," Phoebe said, also smiling.

"You wouldn't believe the change in Mama," Virginia said. "She and the Colonel don't know anyone else is around."

"Do you suppose a romance is budding?" Phoebe asked.

"I doubt it," Virginia said. "Anyone else, yes; Mama, no. With her, it's the attention she loves."

"Please tell us everything from the time of your arrival at our plantation," Nanine said.

Virginia related the story in detail, omitting only what she'd done when she'd found Chris asleep. Not that she wished to spare herself, for she was still filled with self-loathing that her carnal desire had been so great that she had forgotten about the safety of her son. But there was no sense in hurting Phoebe.

Phoebe and Nanine listened attentively, interrupting only to ask questions about points that weren't clear to them.

"How did Brad gain access to the house?" Nanine asked.

"I don't know," Virginia replied soberly. "I never even thought of it. I almost went berserk when I saw the empty crib."

"We would have also," Phoebe said.

"No more talking," Nanine said, standing. "Virgie looks terrible. We'll give you a sleeping draft. After you've rested, we'll try to figure out who Brad has on the island to keep him informed of our comings and goings."

Phoebe went over to Virginia's chair. "Come sister. We'll tuck you in."

Virginia got up slowly, then cried out in pain and fell back in the chair.

"What is it?" Nanine asked, running over to her.

"I told you how I went to the gazebo to tell Chris he'd forgotten to give me a gun," Virginia said. "He chided me for leaving Jimmy alone and I realized he was right. I turned and slipped off the landing and went flying into the darkness. I was terribly shaken, but not hurt. I expect I'll be stiff for a few days, but none the worse for it. However, my muscles feel outraged."

Nanine and Phoebe assisted Virginia upstairs and helped her undress, noting how her torso and upper legs were covered with bruises. Nanine prepared a sleeping potion; which Virginia dutifully drank.

When she informed them she'd told Moses that there

was no further need for the men to guard the island, they decided to remain up until dawn. In any case, neither of them could have slept. Brad had carried out his threat. They had no idea where he'd taken Jimmy, but they knew that Chris was correct when he'd told Virginia that the first thing they had to do was uncover the spy who had supplied Brad with the information that had enabled him to take the child.

Early the next morning, Marcus, the overseer at the mainland plantation whom Chris had placed directly under him, came to the island. He carried a large envelope containing letters and bookkeeping pertaining to the plantation.

Phoebe brought him into the library, where Nanine was seated in the large chair behind the desk. Her head was resting against the back of the leather chair, her eyes closed, but she opened them quickly at the sound of footsteps.

"Mo'nin', Miss Nanine,' he said, his leathery face widening in a smile. He extended the large envelope "Mistuh Chris say I should bring this to yo'."

"Thank you, Marcus." He turned and saw Phoebe standing behind him. He stepped to one side, saw that the library door was open, and said, "Yes, Miss Nanine, I close the do'."

Nanine regarded him with surprise. So did Phoebe.

After glancing into the hall and closing the door softly, he came back to the desk. "Mistuh Chris say yo' mus' be careful not to lets no one heahs yo' talkin'. Mighty sorry to learn what happen to the li'l boy."

"Thank you, Marcus," Nanine said.

He took a small envelope from his pocket. "This heah from Mistuh Chris. He say you not to answuh. He rathuh I don' take back none case'n they ambushes me."

Nanine took the extended envelope and slipped it into her skirt pocket.

"I wants to ask—an' Mistuh Chris wants to knows—if Miss Virginia doin' bettuh."

"She's sleeping, Marcus," Nanine said. "She was exhausted when she came back last night. We wouldn't let her talk longer than to tell us what had happened. We gave her a sleeping draft and she hasn't wakened yet."

"A res' be good fo' her," Marcus said. "She scream somethin' awful las' night. We scared someone gittin' killed. Don' wonduh. Aftuh Mistuh Chris come back fum Charleston, he tell me someone got on the plantation an' stole the chile. We watches real careful, but man too smaht fo' us."

Nanine, impatient to read the note, addressed Phoebe. "Please take Marcus to the kitchen and tell Belle to give him a meal."

"Thanks yo', Miss Nanine. Sho' 'preshates it. Be some time befo' I gets back."

Phoebe brought him to the kitchen, where Belle was seated on her stool. She regarded Marcus with open disgust. "Whut he doin' heah?"

"Don't be so rude, Belle. I want you to prepare him a plate of food. It's to be hot and he's to have all he wants, plus some of your cake and pudding if he wants it. And he's not to take any lip from you."

"I gives him food, Miss Uppity, but I ain't takin' any lip from yo' eithuh. Yo' is nuffin' but a nigguh jes' likes me. I feeds yo' from this breas'." She placed her hand over her left breast. "An' I feeds Miss Uppity still sleepin' upstayuhs, from the othuh. Massa takes our son an' sells him so I has 'nuff milk to feeds the two o' yo'. I allus good to yo' 'cause yo' one o' us. But now yo' thinks yo' bettuh."

"I think nothing of the kind," Phoebe replied. "And if you give me any more back talk, I'll tell Miss Virginia about you. She fired you once. She can do it again. And this time she won't take you back."

"Don' worry me none. I gits wuk elsewhayuh. So do whut yo' wants."

Phoebe eyed her with disgust, turned and walked from the room. As she went, she heard Belle's voice, hard and demanding, ask Marcus, "Whut's yo' oveh heah foah?"

"Ain't non o' yo' bizness, woman."

"Mistuh Chris, he nevuh sen's anyones heah befo'. Miss Nanine an' Miss Phoebe, they goes theyah."

"Well, this time, woman, Mistuh Chris sen's me heah wif buzness papuhs."

"That all?" she demanded.

"That all," Marcus replied. "Now git me my vittles. I gots to gits back."

Phoebe relaxed. Marcus was a good match for Belle. Phoebe returned to the library. Nanine was still occupying the chair, her brow furrowed in thought.

Phoebe closed the door, remembering the caution Marcus had exercised. "Is there any news about Jimmy?"

"None." Nanine handed the letter to Phoebe. "He told Lieutenant Johnson exactly what he told Virginia he would. The lieutenant said he believed that Bradley Culver was still seeking revenge against Elias for capturing him and turning him over to the Union army. The lieutenant is greatly concerned about the safety of the child."

"I don't believe Brad would harm the boy," Phoebe said.

"Nor I," Nanine agreed. "But the lieutenant doesn't know the real reason for Brad's action."

"I hope there'll never be any need for him to know," Phoebe said. "For Virginia's sake. I have no legal father. It hurts, but I'm not letting it spoil my life. I know it's harder for white folks. There's a stigma attached to being born out of wedlock. But not among the Negroes, since we weren't allowed to marry."

"I have a feeling Virginia's sole concern now is getting Jimmy back," Nanine reasoned. Then she asked, "Did Belle feed Marcus without a fuss?"

"No," Phoebe replied. "But Marcus gave her back as good as she handed out. She snapped at me, too. Told me I was as much a nigger as she and that I needn't get uppity with her. That she fed me from one breast and Virginia from the other and she always favored me because I was one of them."

"She's always resented Virginia," Nanine said. "I know our sister is spirited, but she's done a lot of nice things for Belle."

"I know," Phoebe said. "She has for me, too. But Belle doesn't like me anymore. She never talked to me like that before."

"She's not worth wasting a thought on," Nanine replied. "We have more important things to do." She pointed to the note that Phoebe still held. "You haven't even read Chris's note."

"You told me what he said," Phoebe replied.

"Is there something on your mind?" Nanine asked, noting Phoebe's troubled frown.

"Yes. But I'll read Chris's letter. You seem to think I should."

"It's not a letter, just a note, but there's something in it that should interest you."

Phoebe's features relaxed and she scanned the letter. A sudden cry of delight escaped her lips and her cheeks flushed delicately.

"He loves me!" she exclaimed. "The note was to you, but he said, "Please tell my darling Phoebe I miss her terribly and hope she'll soon be with me. I know this isn't the time to think of anything but the return of Jimmy, so I'll be patient. Just tell her I send my eternal love. Chris.' Did you hear that, Nan?"

Nanine laughed. "I know. I read it first."

"May I have it?" Phoebe asked. "I'll carry it next to the shoestring tie that's pressed against my bosom."

"I was concerned about Lieutenant Johnson coming here. I'm relieved to read that he isn't. If Brad has someone watching the island or this plantation, that would tell him we've informed them. And yes, you may keep the note."

"Thanks. Did you look in on Virginia?"

"An hour ago. She's still sleeping soundly. Let her awaken herself. She looked haggard last night. I was more than a little frightened by her appearance after I learned what had happened. Thank God she didn't have a heart seizure."

Phoebe again looked pensive. "I'm going outside to wait for Marcus. I have a couple of questions I want to ask him before he leaves."

"Don't you want to write a note to Chris for Marcus to bring back? I know he'd like to be reassured of your love."

"I don't think he needs that," Phoebe said softly. "But you're right. I do want to tell him I miss him and love him. And add that he's right about now not being the time for us. We must concentrate on getting Jimmy back."

"Run along," Nanine said. "I'll study the contents of the large envelope and busy myself with that. Anything but just sitting here and wondering. I hope Virgie wakes soon, and then again I dread it. The memory of last night will come back with a rush. I just hope she'll be able to endure the pain."

"She will," Phoebe replied. "Virgie is strong, though she has been coddling Jimmy too much. Out of fear, of course. But she couldn't go on protecting the child like that. It wasn't normal for him or for her."

"You're right, of course. Run along. I don't believe Marcus will dally. He's a very conscientious man."

*   *   *

Virginia didn't wake until two in the afternoon. The shock of Jimmy's kidnapping, plus that of her fall, had left her body spent. Ivy was seated at her bedside when she awakened. Her eyes were swollen from the tears she'd shed when she'd learned from Nanine about Jimmy. With the child gone, Ivy resumed looking after Virginia. She drew her bath, helped her dress, and tied her hair back with a ribbon. Virginia couldn't sit still long enough to have it fashioned, and Ivy understood.

Downstairs, Ivy brought Virginia's breakfast into the dining room and hovered over her while she ate. When she finished, Ivy told her that her sisters awaited her in the library. She went there directly.

Nanine and Phoebe embraced her and Phoebe poured three small glasses of sherry. "It will help us think and also relax us."

"Would you prefer the drawing room?" Nanine asked.

"I like this room," Virginia said. "It's small and has the warmth of family in it. I can even feel Papa's comforting presence."

"I feel the same way," Nanine said.

"So do I," Phoebe said. "This is the room where Papa acknowledged me as his daughter and told me he'd had a fondness for my mama and had taken care of her."

Phoebe went over and closed the door.

Virginia, noticing, said, "It would be cooler with it open. There's a pleasant breeze blowing through the hall."

"We know," Phoebe said. "But we want privacy, and we must keep our voices lowered."

"In heaven's name, why?" Virginia asked.

"We're going to discuss the matter of a suspect who could be feeding information to Brad. And who might still do so if given the chance."

Virginia looked puzzled. "Do you mean it could be someone in the house?"

"It could be," Phoebe said.

"Not Ivy, I hope," Virginia exclaimed. "I've grown fond of the girl."

"Not Ivy," Phoebe replied. "Someone who's given us a lot of grief, but whose loyalty we never questioned."

"Belle?" Virginia looked astonished.

Nanine said, "Marcus came from the mainland this morning with a note telling us that Chris had visited Lieutenant Johnson and what the lieutenant's theory was regarding the kidnapping. Of course, he's incorrect. Chris also said that he'd stopped by the Colonel's early this morning and told Mama and the Colonel that you and I had returned to Valcour. He added that you—" She broke off. "Oh, Phoebe, let Virgie read it."

Phoebe removed the letter from her bosom and offered it to Virginia.

Virginia waved it aside. "You've already told me the contents."

"Not everything," Nanine said. "Chris also said that he convinced Lieutenant Johnson not to come to the island because the appearance of a man in uniform would only serve to antagonize Brad if he has someone posted here to keep an eye on our comings and goings."

"Did Lieutenant Johnson agree?" Virginia asked.

"Yes."

"Good." Virginia looked relieved. "Now, since there's no news of Jimmy, I'd like to know why you suspect Belle."

"I'll let Phoebe give you her reason first."

Phoebe told her about Belle's behavior in the kitchen that morning when she brought Marcus there to be fed.

"That's really no proof," Virginia said. "To me, that's normal behavior for her."

"I sat outside and wrote Chris a note while waiting for

Marcus to come out," Phoebe went on. "When he did, I walked down to the dock with him. I asked him if Belle had behaved, and he said she had sulked more than anything, but had given him two large servings of dessert, adding that he believed she had a reason. She got real nice then and started asking him questions."

"About what?" Virginia asked.

"What Chris was doing, how things were on the plantation, and if there was any excitement in town."

"Did he tell her about Jimmy?"

"He swore he didn't, and he said she didn't ask about the boy."

"She's the most logical suspect," Nanine reasoned. "She's been going to Charleston. She also went with you, saying that she wanted to buy some things for herself."

"She talked Mama into that," Virginia said reflectively. "Mama was in such a good mood that Belle could have talked her into anything."

Nanine nodded. "Also, Phoebe went down to the fields after Marcus left and questioned the men who take us over to Charleston. One of them told Phoebe that he took Belle to the city the day that the dark-skinned gentleman with the mustache went back. That they went together. The oarsman further identified Carlos when he said that the man was the one who had brought the seedlings."

"I can't believe she'd betray us," Virginia said.

"You should be the first to believe it after the way she's treated you," Phoebe said.

"And now she's turned against you," Virginia replied.

"She's so bold and rebellious, there's no doubt in my mind that she's the spy and also that she's being well paid for her information," Phoebe reasoned.

"She certainly relayed the information to Brad about Mama, Jimmy, Ivy, and I going to the Colonel's."

"She must have found out from the maid who went

upstairs to help Mama pack," Nanine said. "You know, Mama would have no reason for secrecy. She was so excited at the prospect of going that she could scarcely contain herself."

Phoebe raised a finger. "Another thing. Marcus told me that when he closed the library door this morning, Minnie was just outside it. When he surprised her by sticking his head out, she grabbed her apron and pretended that she was wiping dust off the table."

"She was ready to eavesdrop," Nanine said. "I recall before when we were talking, she had a way of coming in to ask if we would like something to eat."

Virginia nodded. "I remember that also."

"Does Moses know about Jimmy?"

"No. He came this morning, but I told him that when you got up we would send for him," Nanine said. "I suggest we send Ivy to fetch him."

Phoebe headed for the door. "I'll tell her."

After the door closed, Virginia said, "We'll tell Moses first and talk with him. After that, we'll summon Belle. I need a few moments to calm down. I feel like strangling her."

"Thus far, we have only suspicions," Nanine reminded her.

"I'll hold my temper," Virginia said. "But if she's guilty—and before she leaves this room, we're going to know—she'll be off the island before nightfall."

Moses entered the library and paused just inside the door. The somber expressions on the faces of the three sisters assured him that there was trouble.

"Knows somethin' gone wrong, Miss Virginia. Yo' looked real bad early this mo'nin'. Now the three o' yo' looks bad."

"You're right. Jimmy was kidnapped last night," Virginia said.

Moses gasped in surprise. "Belle say yo' went to Colonel Spires'. The boy kidnap from theyuh?"

"No," Virginia replied: "He was kidnapped from our plantation."

"Belle don' tells me yo' goin' theyuh."

Virginia's smile was cold. "She didn't know it."

Moses heaved a great sigh. "Knows whut's comin', sho' 'nuff."

"Tell me," Virginia urged. "If you know anythin'"

"Belle!" he exclaimed. "My Lawd, that woman goin' to drive me outta my min'."

"Do you think she knows who might have kidnapped Jimmy?"

"Reckon she know. Reckon it break mah heart to say so, but I been wonderin' 'bout her fo' some time now."

"What made you wonder?"

"She been goin' to the mainlan' two, three times a week. An' she bringin' back new dresses an' hats an' shoes. She tol' me yo' been payin' her mo' lately an' she kin affo'd them things."

"We have not paid her anything extra."

"Yo' leaves the woman to me, missy, an' I gets her to tells me anythin' yo' wants to know."

"Not this time, Moses. We'll handle Belle. You can stay and help if you like, but we have to find out who paid her, how she met Bradley Culver, and where she reaches him when necessary. There's no doubt that she's been supplying him with information for some time. As soon as Nanine comes down, we'll send for Belle."

"Yes'm. Soon's yo' knows whut yo' wants, me an' Belle leaves the island. Sho' cain't stay heah."

"Moses, this is your home. We don't want you ever to leave. What Belle has done is not your fault. We wish you'd told us about all the money Belle has been spending, but even so, she gave you what you must have believed was an honest answer. We're sorry, but Belle cannot stay on Valcour."

"Miss Virginia, nevah wants to see that woman again. I stays, an' I thanks yo' fo' lettin' me, but that woman cain't live on Valcour. She ain' my woman no mo'. She comin' in heah now?"

"Yes. We must have it out with her now," Virginia said. "If she gets wind of the fact that we suspect her, she may get away. It's absolutely necessary that she stay here to tell us everything she knows about Brad."

"Moses," Phoebe said, "go fetch Belle. Don't tell her why we want to see her. If she suspects anything and tries to get away, make her come here."

"Goes now, missy, an' brings her back. Ain"t goin' to be no mistake 'bout that."

After Moses had left, Nanine said, "I'm going to scare Belle out of her wits. I'm very angry with her, and you'll likely see a side of me you never saw before. She'll be here in a minute, unless she slipped off before Moses reached her."

Belle hadn't. She entered the library, followed by Moses, who signaled that Belle had no idea she was under suspicion. Belle took up her usual belligerent stand.

"Moses say yo' wants to see me, an' I says heah an' now, you' goin' to give one mo' big soiree, I sho' ain't goin' to be heah to cook fo' it."

"That's not why we wanted to see you, Belle," Virginia said. "I understand you've been going to the mainland much oftener than usual and spending a great deal of money."

"Reckon I goes theyuh to gets mo' things fo' yo' to eat. An' if yo' says that ain't right, yo' knows what yo' kin do."

"You also bought a great many new clothes, Moses tells

us, and you informed him you had the money for this because we had been paying you more. That, of course, is a lie. Where did you get the money?"

"Ain't none o' yo' damn bizness."

"Did you steal those clothes?" Nanine asked.

"Nevah steal nothin' in my life."

"Did you charge them to us?"

Belle's worried face lightened. "Yes'm. Tha's whut I did. Says yo' tol' me to buy anythin' I wants an' yo' gets the bill."

"But we never got a bill," Virginia took over. "You're lying, Belle. Bradley Culver paid you well, didn't he?"

She blinked in surprise but quickly recovered her composure. "Don knows whut yo' talkin' 'bout. Who this heah Bradley Culver?"

"The man you kept informed about everything that happened on Valcour," Virginia persisted. "You rode with us to the mainland and told him where we took Jimmy. You got a note from him to put on the mirror in my room. You rode back to the mainland with Señor Cabrera and told Bradley Culver what train Señor Cabrera would be on. You listened to everything you could. You knew what was going on most of the time, and Bradley Culver paid you to tell him."

"There's no use in lying anymore." Nanine stood up and faced Belle. "We've treated you well, given you a better life than you would ever have had anywhere else, both before and after the war, and this is the way you repay us."

"Yo' kin kiss—"

Nanine struck her with her open palm, a hard blow to the face that sent Belle reeling back into Moses's arms. He shoved her away with an angry cry.

Virginia rose. She and Nanine faced the now-worried Belle, and Virginia said, "Bradley Culver is an outlaw, a man already sentenced to hang. Anyone who helps him, who does not turn him in, becomes as guilty as he. We can prove you met him and that he paid you, and that means when he hangs, you'll hang alongside him."

"Yo' tryin' to scare me," Belle said. "Yo' cain't prove I knows Mistah Culver. Cain't prove nothin'.'."

"Mr. Culver is going to be caught anytime now, and he'll tell how you helped him kidnap my son," Virginia said.

"Cain't do nuthin' to me 'cause I ain't done nothin'.'."

"Moses, are the whips still hanging in the old whipping shed?" Nanine asked.

"Yes'm, they's theyuh."

"There used to be two of them. One was a flat strap that gave a great deal of pain but didn't cut the flesh. The other was a snake with a metal tip that tore out big chunks of flesh."

"Sees it las' week, missy."

"Take Belle down there, tie her to the whipping post, and use the snake."

"Uses it till ain't nothin' lef' on her back but bones. Yo' comin' easy, Belle, or does I bus' yo' one an' drags yo' down?"

Belle stepped back, arms extended and palms upraised to fend him off. "Yo' ain't goin' to whup me. Yo' my man. Yo' cain't do this."

"Belle, I ain't yo' man no mo'. Wants nothin' mo' to do with yo', an' whuppin' yo' like nobody evah been whupped on this heah islan' befo' goin' to make me laugh an' feel mighty good."

"After you get through with her, drag her down to the dock and put her on a boat," Virginia ordered. "Take her directly to the Yankee garrison. We'll be there by then, and the officer in charge will know what to do with a treacherous woman who sold her heart and soul to an outlaw wanted for hanging. They'll have a rope ready for you, Belle, when Bradley Culver is caught."

Belle had backed away until she was against the wall and could retreat no farther. Moses faced her; Virginia was on one side of her, Nanine on the other. Belle's belligerent attitude had rapidly faded.

"Wants nice things," she said. "Like y'all gets. Nice dresses an' shoes an' hats. Craves them, I does, an' ain't no way I kin get 'em 'less'n I does what I does."

"Culver did pay you," Nanine accused. "Tell me truthfully, Belle, or we'll ask no more questions. You'll go to the whipping shed and you'll be turned over to the Yankees. It's your last chance."

"Your very last chance," Virginia added harshly. "And I'll be there when they hang you."

"Say he on'y goin' to play jokes on yo'," Belle said. "Say he ain't meanin' no mo' trouble'n that."

"He paid you to put that note in my bedroom, didn't he?" Virginia demanded.

"Give me ten dollahs, an' I sees no ha'm in doin' a li'l thing like that."

"You told him Jimmy had been taken to the mainland, didn't you?"

"Say he on'y wants to sees Jimmy." Belle began to regain some of her courage. "Reckon a man want to see his son, he sho' gots a right."

"You surely kept your ears open," Nanine commented. "Where did you meet Bradley Culver?"

Moses's ordinarily soft voice, grew harsh. "Talk, woman."

When her lips compressed, Virginia said, "Take her to the shed."

Moses secured a hard grasp on Belle's arm and spun her around to begin dragging her to the door.

"Yo' ain't goin' to whup me," she screamed, "Yo' cain't whup me."

"Show her we can, Moses," Nanine said. "We don't want to see her again."

"Not until she swings alongside Culver," Virginia added.

"Meets Mistah Culver at the back o' the hotel in Charleston. Whar yo' stays when yo' in the city."

"When they get Culver," Nanine said, "and they will, you'll hang for what you did."

"Mistah Culver say ain't no big fuss he'pin' a man get his own son. Reckon yo' been tryin' to skeer me, but yo' lyin' says I gets hung."

"Oh yes," Nanine said, "one more little thing. Did you tell Bradley Culver when Señor Cabrera was taking a train in Charleston?"

"Yes'm. Gots no reason to lie 'bout that. Even rode oveh wit' the señor. He don' likes me, I don' likes him."

"You're trying to tell us that you won't hang because you didn't turn Culver in?" Virginia said.

"Yes'm."

"Belle, Culver got on the train with the Mexican, and while they were traveling South, Mr. Culver killed him. Now, that makes you an accessory to murder. Accessory means you helped Culver kill the man. Do you think they won't hang you for that?"

Belle managed to reach a chair and sit down heavily.

"Sho' nuff?" she asked in fresh anxiety. Then, rejecting it, she said, "Don' b'lieves it."

"Ma'am," Moses said, "lets me takes her down an' whup the hell outta her. Wants to do it."

"In good time," Virginia said. "Belle, where did Culver take my son?"

"Don' knows. Nevah tells me."

"I think you know," Nanine said. "You must have been in contact with him often. Culver wouldn't dare stay in Charleston all this time. He wrote you and you picked up the mail at some address you gave him on the mainland. Don't lie about it. We can easily find out where his mail reached you."

"Nevah tells me," Belle insisted.

"Didn't he, though?" Nanine said. "We don't even have to ask. We only did to see if you would cooperate with us. If you had, we planned to let you go."

"Yo' tryin' to fool me, tha's whut yo' doin'."

"Belle, Mr. Culver lives in New Orleans. We're not trying to fool you. We were just trying to find out if you were worth saving from a hangman. Now we know you're not, so this ends it. Bradley Culver lives in New Orleans and you know that as well as we do."

Belle was again rocked by strong doubt. There was no question that they knew where Culver was. She knew her chances for getting out of this dwindled with every question. They knew everything anyway.

"Yes'm, lives in N'Orleans, he does. If I tells yo' jes' whar yo' kin fin' him, yo' lets me go?"

"We'll think about it," Virginia said.

"I tells him whar Missy Phoebe's mama run her big whorehouse, an' tha's whar he live."

Nanine sat down with a great sigh of relief. Virginia raised a hand to slap Belle across the face, but thought better of it and resumed her chair. Belle, terrified now, rose and backed up into Moses's firm grasp of her shoulders.

"Yo' says I goes free." She no longer had any trace of belligerency. "B'fo' God, yo' promises . . ."

"Moses," Nanine said, "take Belle to the dock, put her on a boat, and have two of our men take her to the mainland. Don't go with her. Don't let her take any of those new clothes she sold her soul for. Don't give her a thing. Just turn her loose. Belle, we never want to see you again."

"I goes quiet," Belle said. "But yo' comin' wif me, Moses."

"Like hell I am," Moses retorted.

"Yo' my husban'."

"Not any mo' I ain't. Does whut yo' says, Missy Nanine. An' mighty glad to get rid o' this heah woman. She b'long mo' to the devil than she b'long to me."

He dragged her out of the house and pushed her to the dock, calling for two men to row her to the mainland. But after he forced her aboard the boat, with orders that if she tried to fight she was to be thrown overboard, he couldn't check the tears as he watched the woman he had once loved being rowed across the intercoastal waterway to Charleston. He walked slowly back toward the mansion, skirted it, and went to the large cabin that he'd shared with Belle.

From the trunks and the clothes closet he unearthed the things Belle had bought with Culver's money. He gathered them all into one big pile, carried it down to the cabins where the workers and their families lived, and dropped it onto the grass beside the walk. To the amazed wives who watched him, he issued an invitation to help themselves, then he went back to his cabin while the women fought over Belle's fancy wardrobe.

He shut the door and shut Belle out of his life forever. He picked up a folded paper from the floor and thrust it into his pocket. Half an hour later he was in the fields, fussing about the condition of the cotton plants. He didn't want to worry Miss Virginia. She had enough on her mind. Yet, he knew he had to let her know. He'd noticed right after Belle had left for the mainland. He worried over it through the night. The next morning, he returned to the house.

When he entered the library, Virginia, Nanine, and Phoebe were there to greet him. He had already removed his straw hat, and he stood somewhat awkwardly in front of the desk.

"Sit down, Moses," Nanine invited.

"Yes'm. Feels like I bettah. Couldn' sleep las' night. Gots

to tell yo' somethin's happenin' I cain't 'splain. An' I sho' is s'pose' to be able to 'splain anythin' goin' on theyuh. 'Spesh'ly whut I gots charge o'."

"What's wrong?" Virginia asked. "Is someone making trouble?"

"Oh no, Miss Virginia. Ain't nothin' simple like that. Eve'ybody heah is mighty happy. It's got to do with the crop."

"The cotton? It seemed all right to me," Nanine said.

"Yes'm, looks real fine, till yo' gets on yo' han's and' knees an' yo' sees it ain't doin' so well. Don' knows whut's wrong."

"Is it the Mexican cotton?" Virginia asked.

"Yes'm, it's the Mexican cotton fo' sho', but that on'y looks wuss. All the cotton look like it sick. Blossoms should o' been twice as big. Seem like it's ailin' some. Kin a cotton plant get sick?"

Nanine arose. "We'd better have a look, Virgie."

"By all means," Virginia agreed. "Seems trouble comes all at once."

Moses led the three sisters to the patch where the Mexican cotton seedlings had been planted. At this time of year they should have been in full bloom, with the cottonballs large and still growing. The balls were little more than half the size they should have been, the fibers were limp and thin, and at the base of the blossoms there was a strange brown color.

"There surely is something wrong," Nanine agreed. "Let's look at our own plants."

These, too, were unhealthy-looking, but not as bad as the Mexican type.

Moses said "Reckon them Mex' plants are older. Yo' 'membahs they was seedlin's when we was plantin' jes' seed. Looks to me they dyin'."

"I'll look at Papa's papers about cotton and look in the

books we have on the subject," Nanine said. "There are pitifully few, and I don't think they're very good or up-to-date, but perhaps they'll tell us what's wrong here."

"Our big problem," Virginia said, "is that none of us ever did pay much attention to the crop itself, until it was harvested. Myself, I don't know anything about raising cotton, only about selling it."

"I sho' ought to knows whut's wrong heah," Moses said, "but nevah sees anythin' like this."

"Well," Nanine said, "the plants are still growing. It's weeks to harvest time. Perhaps they'll grow out of this. . . ." She leaned over and rolled one of the blossoms between her fingers. She flecked an insect off the blossom. "Pesty bugs," she said. "They get over everything on a plantation."

"Thank you, Moses, for calling this to our attention," Virginia said. "Watch carefully and let us know if it gets any worse."

The sisters walked slowly back to the mansion. "All we need is a crop failure," Virginia said. "Does it have anything to do with the weather, do you think?"

"How could it? The weather's been fine. Not too hot, surely not too cold, and there's been no more than the normal amount of rain. It looks to me like some kind of disease."

"What in the world can we do about it?"

"I don't know. I wonder if it's happening on the other plantations."

"The Tyler acres aren't far. Let's go over."

"That's a good idea. But if their plants look sick too, it would be best not to say anything until we know exactly what's wrong."

"How can we find out? If the books and Papa's papers don't say anything, how can we know?"

"There's a way," Nanine said. "Give our old enemies their due. Washington has a branch of government that studies all kinds of farm problems. We'll just forget they're Yankees and beg them for help."

"Reckon they owe us that much," Virginia said.

"We'll wait a reasonable amount of time. I wouldn't want to bring a Yankee down here right now," Nanine said.

"For the first time," Virginia said, "I wish my Yankee husband were here. He'd know exactly what to do. Don't misunderstand me, Nan. Under no circumstances would I ask him back. I just think it would be handy if he were here. Then again, he might be in the dark as much as we."

"I wonder if Chris could help," Nanine mused.

Virginia turned to Phoebe, who had been following in silence. "I'd like you to go to the plantation and talk to Chris about what we've seen. He may be familiar with this."

"It's worth a try," Phoebe said. "Besides, I'd like to see him. But I thought you and I were going to New Orleans."

"We are," Virginia said. "First, I must stop at the Colonel's and tell Mama about Jimmy. It isn't fair to keep it from her any longer, especially since we won't be here."

"How do you know Belle is telling the truth about Brad being at the brothel?" Nanine asked.

"I don't," Virginia replied. "And I hope and pray he wouldn't bring the child there, though I know that if it looks the way it did when Fannie ran it, it's high-class and spotless."

"Sam will keep it up," Phoebe said with assurance. "He really loved Mama. She even made him learn to speak like white folks."

"She was quite a woman," Virginia said.

"Mama had a college professor from the North live there for one year," Phoebe went on. "During the time he had the pick of any of the girls. The only requisite was that he teach her how to speak English properly. She didn't want me to be ashamed of her if we ever met. As if I would."

"We'll pack and go to the mainland," Virginia said. "You talk with Chris about the cotton. I'll stay at the Colonel's. Chris can drive us to the depot in Charleston the day after. You'll have a night with him. Or would you rather not?"

"I need it, Virgie," Phoebe said quietly. "I love him so, and he loves me."

"He told me. Make the most of your visit. I don't know what we'll meet up with in New Orleans. I don't even know if Brad is there, though I rather fancy he is. It's an easy city to hide in."

"If he's at Mama's place—or Sam's place now," Phoebe said, "our task won't be so hard. Though I rather doubt he's there."

"So do I," Virginia replied. "But we have to start somewhere."

Their mood was pensive as they packed for the trip. Virginia was doing her best to keep her emotions under control, but her nerves were jumping and she felt as if she had butterflies in her stomach.

Ivy accompanied them to the boat. The two oarsmen were just about to push off when they heard Moses calling to them. He was running toward the dock and waving to them. The oarsmen held the boat in place until he reached them. He was out of breath, but he handed them a folded piece of paper, telling them he'd found it on the floor of his cabin when he'd taken Belle's clothes from the closet. It contained nothing but a man's name, and it might have no meaning, but he felt they should have it.

Virginia thanked him and waved a farewell. She slipped it into her reticule and promptly forgot about it. Her mind was too taken up with thoughts of Jimmy, plus the added worry about the cotton.

*   *   *

Lenore and the Colonel were pleased to see Virginia, and once again she marveled at the change in her mother. Her voice was cheerful instead of forlorn, her manner warm and friendly.

However, she sobered when she learned the news about Jimmy.

"Why weren't the Colonel and I told?" Lenore asked.

"I returned to the island at once."

"Well," Lenore said, "at least Nan was with you.'

Virginia had almost forgotten the lie she'd told her mother about going to the plantation.

"Why would that outlaw do such a thing?" the Colonel asked.

"He wants a ransom." Virginia repeated Chris's story.

"But why pick you?"

"Lieutenant Johnson believes it's revenge against Elias for capturing him on Valcour and turning him over to the military."

"Don't forget, Zachary," Lenore said, "Elias was a Union officer."

"Culver is a lowly brigand," he retorted. "No man could stoop lower than to kidnap a child."

Virginia related the part Belle had played. Lenore was astonished to think Belle would betray the family and was relieved to learn that she was no longer on Valcour, though Moses had chosen to remain.

"He was always loyal and courteous," Lenore said. "Unlike Belle."

"Has the army made any progress in locating Culver?" the Colonel asked.

"Chris is maintaining contact with them. If there was any, he'd have come to the island, or he'll come here, now that he knows I'm here. Phoebe will tell him that I'm informing you of Jimmy's kidnapping."

"Do you think it proper for Phoebe to remain there overnight?" Lenore asked.

"Yes, Mama. She and Chris are betrothed."

"At least you brought one pleasant surprise." Her tone took on a note of worry. "I hope that horrible man won't harm Jimmy."

"I'm sure he won't, Mama," Virginia said calmly.

"How can you be so sure?"

"He's done a lot of terrible things," Virginia replied. "But I feel certain he'd never harm a child."

"I wish I could be as certain," Lenore said.

The Colonel reached over, caught Lenore's hand, and raised it to his lips. "Let us hope Virginia is right."

Lenore gave him an adoring smile.

Virginia joined Lenore and the Colonel for the evening meal, but there was little conversation. They were too worried about Jimmy. Virginia didn't tell them about the cotton crop on Valcour; there was no sense in alarming Lenore when they weren't yet certain what the problem was.

She managed an apologetic smile as she caught the Colonel and Lenore studying her. "I'm sorry I had to bring such bad news to you, but I felt you should know."

"We should, my dear," the Colonel replied kindly. "We're pleased you came, aren't we, Lenore?"

"Yes," she said. "It's too bad it takes a crisis to make us realize how important family is. I was too wrapped up in my own loneliness to be a proper mother to my daughters."

"We understood, Mama," Virginia protested. "You went through a great deal during the war."

"So did Nanine and Phoebe," Lenore countered. "I'd never have survived without the courage and determination of you three girls. Especially you, Virgie."

"Not me alone, Mama."

"Yes, you alone. Nan was too ill. You wouldn't accept Phoebe at first, but once you did, the two of you performed nobly."

Virginia laughed. "We had no choice."

"No matter," Lenore said firmly. "I haven't forgotten, even though I never referred to it." She regarded Virginia's surprised features across the table. "You can't believe it's your mama talking. I don't wonder."

The Colonel took up the story. "Lenore told me everything you girls did during the war. I also learned about Nan's illness, plus that of her husband, Miles."

"The Colonel knows how badly I behaved about not letting Nan bring him to the house," Lenore said sadly. "I'll always be ashamed of that."

"It's over, Mama. And Miles understood. He was a strong character."

"I'm glad he lies beside your brother, Marty," Lenore said. "Even though I raged about it at the time."

"I'm sure they're both quite content," Virginia said. "As for me, Phoebe and I are leaving for New Orleans in the morning, so I'd like you to excuse me."

"We'll be up early to see you off," Lenore said.

"Please don't. I'll be too nervous, and Phoebe will be here right after dawn."

"If that's what you want, my dear," the Colonel said. "Is there anything you would like us to do?"

"Just one thing, Colonel. Pray that we'll find Jimmy. We believe he might be there."

"Will you go to the police?" Lenore asked, worried. "I hope so."

"If necessary," Virginia said. "First we have to find Bradley Culver, then learn if he has Jimmy with him. He may have him hidden elsewhere. It's the child I want. Not the outlaw."

"We'll pray, Virginia," the Colonel assured her.

Virginia was about to put out the lamp when a soft knock sounded on her door and it opened a few inches.

"May I come in?" Lenore asked.

"Of course, Mama."

"I won't stay long."

She went over to the window where two small chairs flanked a table. Virginia followed and sat opposite her mother.

"What is it, Mama?"

"The Colonel has proposed marriage," she said.

Virginia was too stunned to reply

"Well?" Lenore asked. "Oh, I'm sorry, Virgie. I shouldn't have come in with news like that when you're going through such agony."

"You should, Mama." Virginia leaned over and squeezed her mother's hand gently. "It's wonderful news. Will you accept?"

"You act as if you think I shouldn't," Lenore said.

"It isn't that. It's just that marriage is more than a few light kisses and holding hands."

"My dear," Lenore said firmly, "I was married once and have had three children. I think I'm aware of what the marriage bed is."

"Is it what you want?" Virginia asked, still troubled by the news. "What I mean is, I'm sure the Colonel will expect more. . . . I had the feeling you didn't want anything like that."

Lenore regarded Virginia with open disapproval. "My dear daughter, I not only want it, I have already had it."

"Oh You mean you and the Colonel . . . ?"

"Exactly," she replied, with a firm nod of her head. "Last night. And just before I came upstairs, I asked him to join me tonight. While Nanine might be shocked, I don't believe you will be."

Virginia couldn't help but smile. "No, Mama. I guess you know me."

"I also know how to keep a secret."

"What do you mean?" Virginia asked cautiously.

"I had a sleepless night at Valcour—it was a little over two years ago. In fact, I had a lot of them, and would sit by the window to catch the cool night air and look out at the water. This night—or rather it was early morning, but long before dawn—I saw a man leave the house. He looked back and saw me in the window. There was a full moon, and when he paused and looked up at me, I had a perfect view of his features. He was handsome and smiled at me. A devil-may-care smile. And do you know what he said?"

"No, Mama." Virginia felt a wave of weakness flood her.

"His exact words were, 'She's quite a woman—your daughter.'"

"Bradley Culver." Virginia's voice was barely audible.

Lenore nodded. "I never told anyone. I never will. Not even the Colonel."

"You can tell him, Mama. You'll be his wife."

"No. The one I feel sorry for is Elias. That's why he left, isn't it?"

Virginia nodded. "When he went to Washington and had surgery to remove the bullet, he learned he could never father a child. On his return, he stopped at Dr. Hawley's with a letter to that effect from his surgeon. But before he had a chance to show it, Dr. Hawley told him he was going to become a father. As you know, he never came back to Valcour. But he told Dr. Hawley to tell me I could use his name for the child."

Lenore stood up, bent down, and put her arm around Virginia. "I'm sorry, my dear. I never knew for sure, and if I hadn't seen that man that night, I'd never even have wondered. You're so much like your papa. I know I turned away from him, but even when we were lovers, he was a philanderer."

"It was hard for you, too, Mama."

"Yes. Though your papa was discreet. He also took very good care of us."

"I don't regret my indiscretion, because it gave me Jimmy, and you know how much I love him."

"Why did that man kidnap the boy?"

"He wanted to have him for six months. I refused. Then he sent me a note demanding that I meet him on the mainland. He threatened me with exposure, saying he'd reveal Jimmy's true paternity if I didn't let him have the child for that length of time. Again I refused. But he said he'd get him somehow. And now he has."

"Belle kept him informed?"

Virginia nodded.

"Thank heavens, that woman is off the island. Have you any idea of where to find him?"

"Belle said he's at the brothel that belonged to Phoebe's mama. A man named Sam owns it now. Phoebe and I are going there first. I can't believe Brad would take Jimmy there. I do think he may have told Belle that. Probably more to anger me, knowing we'd seek out the spy once he'd gotten Jimmy."

"Well, my dear, I know better than to attempt to persuade you not to go," Lenore said. "But do take care. That man is desperate."

"We'll be careful," Virginia said. "But now you know why I'm not worried about him hurting Jimmy—he's his son."

"Yes." Lenore straightened. "Yes. I'll pray that you and Phoebe get Jimmy. Then I'll pray that the army will capture Bradley Culver. And what you just told me will never cross my lips."

"Thank you, Mama," Virginia said. "I have to tell you one thing more. Chris knows about Jimmy. I had to tell him. I brought Jimmy there after I received a note from

Nan. She didn't come to the mainland. I said that because I feared you might not let me go there unchaperoned."

"I could scarcely reprimand you now. Go on."

"I was afraid that if Brad was watching us, he knew we were here at the Colonel's. He did. You know I asked for a carriage to take Ivy back to Valcour. The real reason was that she carried a bundle that resembled a sleeping child. Obviously, Brad had the Colonel's under surveillance, but went to the island when Ivy was observed leaving here. He broke into the house and confronted Nan. He was furious not to find the child."

Virginia went on to relate that after she'd told Chris the reason for her being there, he expressed doubt that Culver would kidnap a child. To convince him, she had to tell him the truth. Brad had taken the child when she'd made the mistake of leaving the house to ask Chris for a gun.

When she ended her story, she stood up, and the two women embraced.

"Mama, I think we've been closer tonight than at any time in our lives."

Lenore nodded. "We'll keep it that way."

"And, Mama," Virginia said as she accompanied her mother to the door, "I'm pleased you and the Colonel will marry."

"We won't immediately, because of Jimmy," Lenore said.

"I wish you would," Virginia replied, "unless you want a large wedding."

Lenore laughed. "The discussion never got that far. Well, we'll see. It's just that the Colonel wants to make me respectable, and I'm old-fashioned enough that I want to be."

"Then make it legal and binding," Virginia urged. She kissed her mother good night, then closed the door.

She couldn't sleep and decided to walk out into the hall. She was barefoot so as not to disturb her mother or the

Colonel. However, the sound of muted laughter reached her and she saw a light beneath the door of the room her mother occupied. She smiled and returned to her room, pleased that her mother would once again have a mate. Virginia thought of Elias, and for the first time, she didn't damn him. She wondered if she would ever again know the protecting feel of a man's arms holding her close.

Back in her room, she paced restlessly, then sat down, wondering how to locate Brad. If he wasn't at the brothel and Sam could offer no clues, they would have to start over again. But where? It was possible that Belle, out of spite, had lied about his being at the brothel. Brad might not even be in New Orleans.

She knew there was an early-morning train out of Charleston. They'd get a private compartment so that they could talk freely. Fortunately, she had brought plenty of money—her reticule bulged with the bills. It didn't look very attractive. Certainly nothing a lady would carry.

A soft cry escaped her as she recalled the slip of paper Moses had handed her at the dock. She snatched her bag off the table and pulled roughly at the cords in her haste to open it. The paper was near the top.

The paper was folded just once. Virginia held it to the lamplight and read a man's name.

"Bernard Caldwell," she said aloud. "Bernard Caldwell."

Her mind strained to recall such a person. Then she noticed the first and last initial. Her brow creased thoughtfully. Bradley Culver, alias Bernard Caldwell. Could it be? Dare she hope?

She wondered why he'd entrust the name on paper to Belle. The answer came easily. She would never remember Bernard Caldwell. Yet, it didn't explain why he had given it to her. Virginia mulled that over for several minutes. Could it be that he stayed at the Charleston Hotel more frequently than anyone knew? If so, Belle could have made contact

with him there. Perhaps that explained her frequent trips
to the mainland. She would only have had to go to the rear
of the hotel and show the name on the paper, and they
would summon Brad.

It was worth taking the time to go to the hotel first and
make inquiries. She would be discreet, but she was known
there, and they'd not be suspicious of her.

Virginia slipped the piece of paper back into her reticule
and put out the lamps except for the one at her bedside,
which she turned low. She prayed for Jimmy's safety and
for success in finding him. If she could get the address of
Bernard Caldwell from the hotel, her mission would be
easier. With that thought in mind, she drifted off to sleep,
though she woke long before daylight.

To her surprise, the cook was in the kitchen when she
went downstairs. She ate a hearty breakfast, knowing that
she wouldn't bother at the depot. Once she was on her
way, she would be too nervous even to think of food. The
only blessing was that Phoebe would be with her. She ate
hastily and was on the porch when Phoebe and Chris
drove up. He placed her baggage under the backseat,
helped her in, then resumed his seat in front with Phoebe.

"Hold on," he said. "I want to make time."

"I want you to," Virginia replied. "We have to stop at
the hotel first."

"Better not dally there," he warned. "We're calling it
close as it is."

It was impossible to carry on even a shouted conversation.
Chris forced the animals into a gallop and she and Phoebe
held on for dear life. Virginia was relieved when they
reached the outskirts of the city and he had to slow down.
Fortunately, the streets were almost empty, so they suffered
no delay.

Virginia didn't wait for Chris to get out and assist her

from the carriage. With a curt, "Be ready to move when I come out," she jumped to the street and ran into the lobby.

The desk clerk greeted her with recognition.

"I came to pick up a Mr. Bernard Caldwell. He's to visit a friend of mine on Valcour."

"Mr. Caldwell checked out a few days ago. He may be coming back today, but he hasn't arrived yet."

"Oh dear," Virginia said. "I wonder if he might have gone directly to the dock and is awaiting me. I came in from our plantation."

"That could be, Mrs. Birch."

"At least they described him to me. Would you agree with it? They said he's over six feet tall, has a healthy head of unruly hair and a full beard, and is fashionably dressed."

The clerk beamed. "That's him."

"And he's from New Orleans?"

"Correct again, Mrs. Birch."

"I don't have his street address," Virginia said in mock chagrin.

"We don't either," the clerk replied. "I recall he left something here once, and I suggested he leave his address in case it should happen again. he said that the next time he left something here, whoever found it could keep it. But he never left anything again."

Virginia laughed. "Well, thank you. I'll see if he's at the dock."

"I'm sure you'll find him there."

Chris lost no time getting to the station. He carried their baggage into the depot and waited while Virginia purchased a compartment. There, a porter took over. Chris gave Phoebe a lingering kiss and Virginia moved along with the porter. Phoebe soon caught up.

"I have something to tell you," she said breathlessly.

"*I* have something to tell *you*, Virginia replied, smiling at Phoebe's flushed face. "Let's get settled first. I think we're the last ones on the train."

The porter looked over his shoulder. "Hurry, ladies. Train 'bouts ready to pulls out."

They did no more talking until they were seated in their compartment. But once the train started, both started to talk at once. Virginia held up a hand for silence.

"Very well, Virgie," Phoebe said. "You first."

"No," Virginia countered. "I'll listen, because what I have to talk about will take time."

"This won't," Phoebe assured her. "Chris and I were married last night."

"How did you accomplish that?"

"It was very simple. There was a Negro minister there visiting the servants. He married us."

"Is it really legal?"

"So far as Chris and I are concerned, it is."

"Then it's legal," Virginia said firmly.

"Let's be practical," Phoebe went on. "I'm part Negro and I doubt I'll ever be allowed to completely forget it. Frankly, I don't want to. But there will be times when it's going to present difficulties. I know it and so does Chris, but he'll never walk away from me."

"I know that," Virginia said. "He talked with me about you and he made it very plain that if the problem of color should become too much for both of you here, you'd move to California."

Phoebe nodded and held up her left hand, revealing the wedding ring. "I'm respectable now."

Virginia embraced Phoebe and wished her happiness, then said, "Mama's also going to be married."

Phoebe beamed. "Good. Too bad you had to tell her about Jimmy."

"She said they'd not marry until he was back safely with us, but I insisted she go ahead with it. She said the Colonel wanted everything to be respectable—especially for Mama."

"Chris said the same thing," Phoebe confided. "Are you still concerned that she won't make the Colonel happy?"

"No," Virginia said with quiet firmness. "I talked with her about that last night and she put me in my place. They've already consummated their relationship, so I imagine that when we return, we'll learn that they've married."

"That is good news."

"Yes," Virginia agreed. "But that isn't the surprise I mentioned."

"While we're on the subject of your mother, Chris wants me to tell you that he'll look in on her and the Colonel and also tell them the instant he learns any news of Brad's whereabouts. Or Jimmy's recovery."

"Thanks, Phoebe, Virginia said. "My news concerns a clue as to Brad's whereabouts."

She brought out the slip of paper and handed it to Phoebe.

Phoebe read the name aloud. "Bernard Caldwell. I never heard of him."

"I didn't either," Virginia replied. "But after I studied the name and spoke it aloud several times, almost like a streak of lightning an idea came. Notice the first initial of the first and last name. *B* for Bradley, *C* for Culver."

"Do you think so?" Phoebe exclaimed.

"I hope so," Virginia replied. "It's all we have to go on."

"We'll go to Sam's first—just in case Belle was telling the truth. If Brad isn't there, perhaps this name will have some meaning to Sam. If it doesn't, he may be in a position to find out."

"What a blessing that would be."

"Even if we discover where Jimmy is being held, how can we get him free?"

"I have no idea," Virginia admitted. "But if my son is in New Orleans with Brad, I'll not leave without him."

Virginia sighed and sat back, her eyes closed. When

Phoebe saw a tear trickling down Virginia's cheek, she switched the conversation to the cotton.

"I told Chris what we found in the cotton and how sickly it looks. I also described the bugs. He has no idea what they could be, or if they're responsible for the cotton looking as it does."

"I wish I'd thought to have you ask him to go over to Valcour and look at it."

"He's going," Phoebe said. "He's as concerned as we are."

"That's good news. It will also be good for Nanine to have a visitor. One she needn't fear."

"That was a dreadful thing Brad did," Phoebe said. "Terrifying poor Nan that way. She's such a gentle person."

"I know," Virginia agreed. "I think she may be right about his mind having been affected by the war."

"It wasn't affected that much," Phoebe countered. "You're too quick to defend him."

"I admit I don't think too rationally where he's concerned. I know it's because he fathered Jimmy. I may as well be honest: I don't want him captured. I don't want my son's father to hang."

"But you have to be sensible, Virgie. I wouldn't say he's a menace if he hadn't taken the boy. But he did, and I have no sympathy for him."

Virginia said, "Would you like something to eat? I'm not hungry."

"I'm starved, even though I had a big breakfast." Phoebe's smile was a little self-conscious.

"Making love always helps one build up an appetite. So run along to the dining car. I'll watch the scenery."

"Try to nap a little," Phoebe said gently.

They reached the depot in New Orleans the next morning. A porter carried their bags to the street and secured a driver for them. Phoebe gave the address of the brothel but had the driver stop a block away from it. They walked the remaining distance. Phoebe led Virginia through a back street to an alley.

"We'll go in the back door. I still have a key, and I doubt anyone's stirring yet."

Phoebe unlocked a wooden door set in the high brick wall. They entered, and she relocked it. The same key opened the kitchen door. Once inside, Virginia was struck by the silence. Obviously, Phoebe knew what she was talking about. Common sense would dictate that activity here didn't start until late afternoon.

Phoebe led Virginia through the house to what had once been her mother's office. Virginia was struck by its size and opulence. The dominating color was red. The deep-pile rug was maroon. The large desk was of teakwood, its top inlaid with leather. Chairs were upholstered in red damask. Colorful shawls were thrown over twin lounges.

"Stay here," Phoebe said. "I'm going upstairs and wake Sam. I imagine he's sleeping in Mama's room. But I know the house and you don't. I'll close the door just in case someone's about."

Virginia sat down, trying to still her rapidly beating heart. She wondered if her son was upstairs. She wanted him to be, and yet the thought of him being sheltered in such a place was sickening.

Phoebe returned and told her that Sam would be down presently. After she'd awakened him, he'd awakened his sleeping companion and told her to dress and make them breakfast.

"I'm glad Sam found someone," Phoebe said. "Mama would have wanted him to. This woman is mature and quiet-spoken."

In a matter of minutes, Sam appeared. He greeted

Virginia and asked their mission. Virginia let Phoebe tell the story.

"No Bradley Culver here, Miss Virginia," he said when Phoebe finished. "I know about him. Guess everyone in the South does. Sure an awful thing he did—kidnap a baby."

Virginia handed Sam the paper with the name Bernard Caldwell on it. "Did you ever hear of this man?"

"Is he important?" Sam asked.

"I don't know," Virginia replied. "We've no idea who he is. But our cook maintained contact with Bradley Culver and kept him informed of our comings and goings so that he could kidnap my son. She kept the paper in her dress pocket."

"Hate to ask you this question, Miss Virginia, but do you think your son is still alive?"

"I pray to God he is."

"Tell you what," Sam said. "After I have breakfast, Lissa and I will go and question folks in the Quarter. Maybe this man has servants who come in by the day. Lots of folks do that now."

A soft knock sounded on the door and it opened halfway. A Negro in her early thirties put her head in and, with a friendly smile, announced that breakfast was ready.

They repaired to a small room off the kitchen. Virginia wasn't surprised to see china, silver, and crystal of the finest quality. She wondered if her father had donated any or all of it. No matter. Fannie had wanted the best and had gotten it. For Phoebe's sake, Virginia was glad.

Lissa had a voice as soft as velvet. She wasn't a hand-some woman, but her eyes had a lively sparkle and her mouth a ready smile. She grew serious when Sam intro-duced her as his woman now that Fannie was gone, and she listened carefully when he asked her if she knew anyone by the name of Bernard Caldwell. She gave a low shake of her head.

"Don' mean nothin', Sam, 'cause I nevah kep' a lis' o' high-class genulmen's. No cause to."

"Ever hear the name mentioned, Lissa? Maybe at the quarters where the day help live?"

"Nevah."

"Are you familiar with the neighborhood?"

"You knows I is," she replied. "Lives theyah tills yo' took me in."

"Took you in because you act like a lady."

"My mama taught me that," Lissa said, with a proud tilt of her head. "Mama was the mis'tiss o' the highest city 'ficial in this heah city."

"You're an attractive woman, Lissa," Phoebe said. "Why are you doing cleaning work?"

"'Cause it r'spec'ible. Will houseclean in a cathouse, but won' wuk at it. Got too much se'f-r'spec'."

Sam beamed. "Guess I got myself a lady."

"You really have, Sam," Phoebe said.

"Know you ladies are impatient to find out about this Bernard Caldwell, so Lissa and I will set out right away. The ladies will be coming down shortly. Don't pay them no mind. Would be better if you stayed in the office. They're not allowed in there unless they're summoned." He got up. "We'll do our best to find out what we can. Be back as soon as possible. Get in your glad rags, Lissa, and we'll be on our way."

"Couldn't we go with you?" Virginia started to rise.

"Better if you didn't," Sam said. "Our people will talk with us—maybe. With you along, they wouldn't open their mouths."

Sam and Lissa didn't return until late afternoon. The day maid had brought Virginia and Phoebe sandwiches and coffee. After eating, they went out to the small garden behind the house. They worked off some of their nervousness by walking and discussing the flowers. Virginia grew more and more uneasy as the afternoon waned and there was no sign of Sam and Lissa.

It was after four when they finally came back. The sisters had returned to the office and continued their restless pacing. For a time they'd amused themselves commenting on the framed nudes in various poses—most of them suggestive—that almost completely covered the four walls. But even that palled after a while.

Sam came directly to the office. "We asked an awful lot of questions, and were about to give up, when we found a lady who worked for a few days for a man by that name."

"Does she know the name of the street where she worked?"

Sam smiled. "It's called Magnolia Lane. It's not in the heart of the city, but it's not too far on the outskirts. Very fine homes there."

"Did she ever see her employer?" Virginia asked.

"Yes. She described him for us. Dark hair and lots of it. A full beard. Fancy dresser, brown eyes. Tall and strong." Sam paused, then added thoughtfully, "Sound a little frightening."

"Yes," Virginia admitted. "He's ruthless."

"Then we'll have to be careful," Sam said.

"You've done enough," Virginia said. "We're grateful. We can't let you risk your life."

He pointed a finger at Virginia. "Now you listen to me, Miss Virginia. One day I'm going to pass through those pearly gates and I'll be coming face to face with Fannie. Do you think I want her to chastise me before all my people for not looking after her little girl? No sir! I'd never be let through those golden gates. I go with you. We have to find your little boy. Let's hope this is the same man.

And let's hope he has the child. I want to send you both back where you belong."

"Thanks, Sam." Phoebe put her arms around him and planted a kiss on each cheek. He beamed.

"Notice you're wearing a wedding band, honey. Is he white?"

Phoebe nodded. "He's overseer on the Hammond plantation."

"That's you, ain't it?" he asked. "Fannie always said her daughter was a Hammond."

"Yes, Sam. There are three of us, and we're very close."

"And their mama?" he asked.

"She treats me as if I'm her daughter too," Phoebe assured him.

"That's all I wanted to know. I'll tell Fannie when I see her. We're going to Magnolia Lane tonight. I know the exact house. But we can't start out until after dark—just in case you're being watched."

It was almost eleven o'clock when they left the house from the rear. The place was beginning to liven up. The girls were in the parlors, thinly garbed and smelling heavily of eau de toilette. A cigar-smoking piano player was banging out ragtime on a grand piano, while one of the girls warbled songs in perfect beat.

Sam had a carriage waiting on the next street. The driver was as big and burly as Sam was.

The girls sat in the back, their faces heavily veiled. That was Sam's suggestion. He'd shown Phoebe where Fannie had kept her finery, which he hadn't disposed of.

It took them twenty minutes to reach the place. Sam had the driver pass the house and continue the short distance to the end of the street to let them out. He gave the driver orders to return to the front entrance once they

disappeared, but to approach it slowly. If there were any
other carriages about, he was to keep going, then return.

Sam turned to the girls and said, "We're going around to
the back. Not likely to attract attention that way. We'll
have to climb the wall, and it's a high one, but there are
bricks that stick out on each side of the door to give you a
foothold."

"What about the entrance to the front?" Virginia asked.

"That looks easier. There's no keyhole there—I imagine
there are bolts holding it shut. I'll pull them back before
we enter the house, so we can get out quickly."

"If we're able to enter it," Virginia said worriedly.

"We have to. Now," Sam said, "a large patio surrounds
the entire house. There's a lot of shrubbery and small
trees. That makes it a little easier for us to get into the
house. We'll try the back door. First, though, once we get
over the fence, you two conceal yourselves until I unbolt the
front-wall door and come back."

"How do you know so much about this place?" Phoebe
asked.

"Lissa and I came here earlier and I looked the place
over. There are trees outside the fence and I climbed one
and had a good view of the patio and rear of the house.
There wasn't a soul stirring."

"It doesn't sound very encouraging," Virginia said. "But
I won't rest until I know."

"Let's go," Sam said. "I'll climb over first. You can
make it on this side easily. You'll have to let yourself down
by holding on to the top. I'll lift you down then. It's a
mighty high fence. And take off your veils so you can see
better. You won't need them now. And no more talking.
Once you reach the place, I'll hold up my hand."

Sam walked ahead, then turned into a wooded lane for
several feet. He made a right turn and they were at the

rear of the row of fine homes enclosed by high walls. There was nothing but open fields on the other side.

Sam made a steady, noiseless, cautious advance. Virginia and Phoebe walked soundlessly on the grass beside the slate walk. When Sam raised his arm and moved close to the high wall, the girls slipped off their veils and followed.

Sam made a small gesture and began the climb to the top of the wall. Phoebe went next. Once, she lost her footing, but she was low enough that Virginia was able to brace her until she regained her balance and continued. She knelt on top of the wall for a few seconds, then carefully got a grip with both hands and edged over it. Finally, all Virginia could see were Phoebe's hands holding on to the wall. Then they disappeared. Virginia went up the wall without any trouble. She edged over the top as Phoebe had done and felt Sam's large, strong hands grasp her waist. She released her hold and let him lower her to the ground.

They waited under a low-branched tree while he went to the door at the front of the patio and loosened the bolts. When he returned, they followed him cautiously to the back door. It opened when Sam turned the knob. They entered soundlessly and he closed it behind them.

He led them through a large, dimly lit reception hall. The floor was marble, so they had to move cautiously. They looked into twin drawing rooms on either side of the hall; they, too, were only dimly lit. The stairway, directly in the center, was almost in darkness, though they could see dim light above. The steps and balustrade were also of marble. They ascended in silence and stood at the landing, looking about to get oriented. There were several doors on both sides of the hall, which was in half-darkness.

Sam motioned for them to follow. The room behind the first door he opened was in darkness. He listened, then shook his head. The second had a faint glow. Sam opened it and heard gentle snoring. He glanced into the room, then closed the door.

He turned to Virginia and Phoebe, who stood behind him. "Bradley Culver."

"Are you sure?" Virginia exclaimed, forgetting the whisper. He placed a forefinger to his lips for silence and nodded. He motioned them on and he opened the next door. Soft light came from that room also. He glanced in, then opened the door wider. He released the knob carefully, turned, and mouthed the name "Jimmy." Virginia started to move, but he caught her arm and pointed into the room. Both she and Phoebe stood in the doorway and observed a woman in a snow-white uniform and lace cap seated in a chair beside a crib. She was sleeping, her head rested against the high-backed rocking chair.

Sam whispered for them to stay where they were while he looked into the crib. It seemed certain that the child would be there, but the woman's form obstructed their view. He entered the room as quietly as he had moved through the house. When he reached the crib and had a full view of it, he turned and nodded to the girls, but raised a hand, palm upward. They remained motionless. He bent slowly to pick up the child, careful not to wake him. But when he started to lift Jimmy, the baby whimpered.

The maid woke, and when she saw the form over the crib, she screamed and started out of the chair, but she was still half-asleep and her movements were slow. Sam turned and gave her a short clip on the jaw, cutting off her screams. She fell in a heap. Jimmy started crying. Both Phoebe and Virginia ran to the crib, with just one thought in mind. Sam picked up the child, gave him to Phoebe, and told Virginia to get out as fast as she could.

Brad's angry voice reached them as he shouted, "What the hell's going on?"

They heard the pad of his feet as he approached. Phoebe

ducked into the closet. Sam hid behind the bedroom door. Virginia ran into the hall, hoping to head him off.

"You bitch!" he exclaimed. He was wearing a silk robe over his nightshirt.

She doubled her fists to fight him, but he caught her wrists, pulled them behind her back, lifted her up, and continued to the nursery. He looked in, heard the baby crying and saw the maid on the floor, and stood motionless, trying to locate the source of the cries, which were now hysterical.

He threw Virginia from him and she landed in a heap on the floor. Then suddenly Sam stepped out of the closet and moved close to him.

"Turn around, Mr. Culver," he said.

Brad spun around. He held a gun aimed directly at Sam. "You filthy nig—"

He never got the word out. Virginia had gotten to her knees, without touching him, she sank her teeth into his wrist. The gun dropped at the moment that Sam's fist made contact with Brad's jaw. He flew back, struck the wall, and slid to the floor.

"Come out, Phoebe," Sam called. "Let's get the hell out of here. The police will be here any minute."

Sam took Jimmy in his arms and the three left the house. Brad still lay on the floor. It would take him a few minutes to regain consciousness; by that time, they hoped to be away from there.

Once they were in the carriage, Virginia said, "What do you mean—the police?"

"I told Lissa to inform the police that Bradley Culver, alias Bernard Caldwell, was living here. She left the house about fifteen minutes after us. Is there a reward out for him?"

"Several thousand dollars," Phoebe volunteered.

"Good. It will give Lissa a nest egg. The best tonic she

could have to give her the respectability she craves. All she talks about."

Before they reached the end of the street, two wagon-loads of police came toward them, the horses galloping. Virginia felt a heavy weight in her heart. She hadn't wanted Brad to be captured; she'd only wanted her son back. She voiced that to Phoebe, who replied that it was the only way to guarantee that Brad not take Jimmy from her again. She knew Phoebe was right. She drew her son closer. He was quiet now that he was in her arms. Small as he was, he knew he was safe. Virginia kissed him tenderly.

TWELVE

Following their rescue of Jimmy, they returned to the brothel, but remained in the kitchen. Sam told them there was a late train leaving New Orleans and he wanted them both on it as soon as they learned if Brad had been captured. Sam then informed them that Lissa had gone back to Brad's house to observe what happened.

It was almost midnight when Lissa returned. She reported that both the maid and Bradley Culver had been put in the police wagon. The police had had to carry him from the house because he had spancels on his wrists and ankles. She did not know whether he was conscious. Virginia recalled him falling on the floor and striking his head. She knew he was unconscious before he fell, however, because Sam had struck a hard blow to Brad's temple.

She felt no triumph that he'd been captured, though she knew she would have no peace of mind as long as he was free. After what she'd done, he would be enraged at her, and his humiliation would be complete because a Negro had bested him. She felt sorry for the maid, who must have been completely unaware that the baby she was minding had been kidnapped. Lissa reported that the maid was crying hysterically when the police took her from the house.

Phoebe, Virginia, and Jimmy left New Orleans shortly before midnight. It was a long ride, but Jimmy slept through most of it. Phoebe and Virginia took turns holding him for he was heavy, but neither gave a thought to it, so overjoyed were they to have him in their arms.

When they reached Charleston, Phoebe sent a letter by messenger to Chris. In it, she related in detail everything that had happened. She told him she was returning to the island with Virginia, in case Brad escaped again. She asked Chris to get word to Lenore and the Colonel immediately and to send word to the island as soon as he knew that Brad was in the army's hands.

A joyful Ivy took Jimmy in her arms the moment the boat docked. He seemed just as delighted to see her, for he immediately started his happy babbling. For the first time, Virginia and Phoebe gave in to their travel fatigue. Ivy had long since disappeared from view when they reached the house, where Nanine awaited them.

They had to bathe and change before they could talk with Nanine. And even then, their story was brief, for they were both exhausted. Nanine, ever tolerant, smiled and told them to get their sleep. They could talk later. All she cared about was that they and Jimmy had returned safely.

It was early evening when they retired; they slept until seven the next morning. The three sisters breakfasted together, Nanine listening quietly as they related the story.

"It's wonderful to be back and eating at our own table again. This egg-and-ham omelet is delicious," Virginia said.

Nanine smiled. "Ivy took over in the kitchen. She selected a woman named Daisy to take Belle's place. Believe it or not, she's a better cook than Belle."

"These biscuits have pecans in them," Phoebe said.

"Right." Nanine smiled. "Daisy asked for a few minutes with me each morning to discuss the menu. Ivy told her that's the way it should be done."

Virginia brightened. "Has Ivy taken over the entire household?"

'She's a blessing," Nanine said. "Of course, I was the only one here, but Chris came over to the island yesterday. He checked the cotton, and I'm sorry to have to tell you it's a total loss, and so is everyone else's."

"Oh, dear," Virginia said. "I was hoping some of it could be salvaged. Did he recognize the insects?"

"No. He'd never seen anything like them before. So, I'm leaving for Washington this afternoon. I'd have gone sooner, but I couldn't leave without knowing what had happened in New Orleans."

"Does Chris know if any of the plantations on the mainland have been affected?"

"No. He'd never seen anything like them before. So, there's another thing. Mama and the Colonel are married. Chris took me back to the mainland with him because they wanted me to be matron of honor and Chris the best man. They were married in Charleston. Then the four of us returned to the Colonel's for a wedding supper. Chris brought me back here afterward. Mama wanted me to stay overnight, but I wanted to be here when you returned."

"Does Mama know about the cotton?"

"No," Nanine replied. "Chris and I figured that Jimmy's kidnapping was enough for her to have on her mind at this time."

Virginia and Phoebe nodded agreement.

"Phoebe, you should return to the mainland," Virginia said. "It isn't fair to Chris."

"Not until we know definitely that Brad is still either in the custody of the police in New Orleans or had been turned over to the army."

"I appreciate your thoughtfulness," Virginia said. "I feel guilty, though."

"Don't," Phoebe said. "Chris and I have the rest of our lives to be together."

"I'm pleased you're remaining," Nanine said, "because I'm leaving for Washington this afternoon. I don't dare let another day pass without seeing what we can learn about what's happening to our cotton."

"It's good of you to go, Nan," Virginia said. "I just don't feel safe in leaving Jimmy at this time. Are you certain you're not timid about traveling alone?"

"Strange as it may seem, I believe I'll enjoy getting away. I'm sorry it's for such a reason, but I like feeling I'm on a responsible mission."

"You are indeed," Virginia said. "I hope someone there knows how to wipe out this pesky bug."

"What if they don't?" Phoebe asked fearfully.

"I don't dare think about that now," Virginia said worriedly. "Certainly I'll feel the wrath of the islanders."

"Well," Nanine said, "let's not start worrying until we know there's no hope."

"We will pray fervently," Phoebe said. "Virgie, I changed my mind. I am going back to the mainland farm when Nan leaves; I want to make certain Chris hasn't developed the same problem. I'll return immediately to be with you."

"So I'll not be alone when they hang Brad? No, I can face that. I have Jimmy back. That, my dear sisters, is the greatest asset I have now. I doubt Brad will get away this time. I feel quite safe here."

"But Nan won't be here," Phoebe protested.

"She'll only be gone a few days," Virginia argued. I have enough work to keep me busy. For the present, I'll ignore the complaints of the neighbors until I figure out what to do. I must notify our customers that there will be no Valcour cotton on the market this year."

"Elias had to be notified also," Nanine said.

"I'll leave that to you. I want no contact with him."

"He'll still have the mainland cotton to sell," Nanine said. "Which is a profitable venture. I must pack now.'

"How long will you be gone?" Virginia asked.

"I'm not sure. It depends on how the Yankees receive a Johnny Reb asking for help. The memory of the war years is still too fresh in everyone's mind not to recognize that fact. I'll do my best and try to bring someone back to find out what's going on here."

"Virgie, why don't you and Jimmy come back with Chris and me for a while?"

"Thank you, Phoebe, but I have too much to do here."

"Then I insist on returning to Valcour so you'll not be alone when they bring Brad back."

"It isn't necessary. I told you that," Virginia said.

"I know what you told me," Phoebe said. "As soon as I find out when he's back, I'll return. You shouldn't be alone when—it happens."

"I'll welcome you. It isn't going to be easy." She turned to Nanine. "How is Moses?"

"He's bearing up well. He's been hurt by what Belle did, but I've little doubt he'll get over it. She didn't give him too good a life. He gave away all the clothing, shoes, hats—everything she'd bought with the money Brad gave her for spying on us. He's cleared out the cabin of everything that would remind him of her."

In the early afternoon, Virginia, holding Jimmy, accompanied Phoebe and Nanine to the dock. Once the boat pulled away, heading for Charleston, pangs of loneliness hit her. She started a slow walk back to the mansion. Halfway, she paused and set Jimmy down. He ran and shouted and she played in the grass with him until some of the loneliness left her. She dreaded the approach of darkness, when she'd be alone.

*   *   *

The night after Phoebe and Nanine left, Virginia invited Ivy downstairs for a talk. The girl sat somewhat nervously on the edge of a chair facing the library desk.

"Sit back, Ivy, and relax. I want to talk to you about a few things."

"Yes, Miss Virginia."

"How old are you?"

"Eighteen."

"It's time you did something more than being nursemaid to Jimmy."

"I like being nursemaid to Jimmy."

"Your devotion to him is one reason I intend to help you. He won't always be a baby, you know. I want you to have a future of your own. So I'm going to send you to the mainland in the fall to begin higher-grade schooling than we have on the island. A private school for Negroes, paid for by private individuals. I want you to think carefully about what you want to be."

"I'd like to do what I told you." Ivy's voice warmed with enthusiasm. "I never thought it was worth thinking about because there'd be no chance."

"There might well be. Miss Nan told me you took over in the kitchen and did very well. Certainly your choice of Daisy as the cook to replace Belle was an excellent one."

"Thank you." Ivy's smile revealed her pleasure. "I know now I'd like to have charge of a large hotel."

"Oh my," Virginia exclaimed in dismay. "That's quite an ambition."

"I know it could never be," Ivy said philosophically.

"But that's what I'd like to do."

"Well," Virginia said, "It's something to strive for. And if you can't get something as big as that, I'm sure you'll settle for something less."

"I will, Miss Virginia," Ivy said happily. "Just so I can

be doing something. It may not be important, but if it's important to me, I'll be satisfied."

"Good." Virginia smiled. "You have a lot of common sense. That should see you through life."

After Ivy returned to the nursery, Virginia spent some time looking over the books. She estimated what it would cost to replant with some new type of cotton if it was suspected that the old kind could not survive another onslaught of bugs or disease. She wished she knew which had caused the crop failure. There had always been insect pests in cotton farming, but not the kind that now infested the fields.

She stopped by the nursery to look in on Jimmy. Ivy sat beside the sleeping child, her expression thoughtful. It was apparent that she was still overwhelmed by what Virginia had promised her.

Phoebe returned late the following morning. Virginia was out for a stroll and went down to the dock to meet her.

"They've brought him back," she reported. "It seems he wasn't that badly hurt."

Virginia nodded slowly. "Tomorrow they'll kill him."

"I had a glimpse of the gallows they're building," Phoebe said. "It made me ill."

"It makes me ill to think about it," Virginia said. "I'm doing my best not to. Tell me about Chris and the plantation. Are there any signs of disease or those damned insects?"

"None. Chris also made a number of discreet inquires about it and found no one who had any knowledge of the infestation. The news of it seems not to have been spread beyond Valcour."

"That's a bit of good news in an otherwise gloomy day. Did you accompany Nan to the depot? I wonder how she's getting on in Washington, coping with the Yankees. She's so lovable I'm sure she'll have no trouble convincing them we have a severe problem here."

"I hope she can find someone who can get to the root of this problem. It frightens me. If we can't raise cotton on Valcour, what in the world will happen to our lovely island?"

"I've wondered about that too," Virginia said. "And I'm just as frightened as you are."

"Have you been in contact with any of the neighbors?"

"No, they've not come near me, and you may be assured I stayed away from them. I did see Moses this morning; he's like a man who has lost everything he ever cherished. I can't make up my mind if it's because he lost Belle or because he's losing the cotton crop."

"Raising cotton has been his life," Phoebe said. "It's more likely that."

"I believe you're right. Have you seen Mama?"

"I stopped there on my way home." Phoebe paused and smiled self-consciously. "That still sounds strange to me."

"It won't after a while," Virginia assured her, returning the smile.

"Lenore is radiant. The change in her is astonishing. She embraced me when I came and when I left. She's in love with the world and so am I."

"I envy you both, but I'm happy for you both. How is the Colonel?"

"They're like young lovers. They can't keep their eyes off each other. They remind me of Chris and me."

"I know what you mean," Virginia said wistfully. Then, her voice brisk, she changed the subject. "I'm sending Ivy to that private school in Charleston."

"How nice, Virgie. I'd like to help her too."

"Give a donation to the school."

"We do that anyway."

"You give another."

"Very well. Is there any special thing she wants to do?"

"Yes. Manage a hotel."

"My God," Phoebe exclaimed, aghast. "Not even a white woman could find such a position."

Virginia laughed. "I as much as told her, but she said she'd settle for less."

"I hope so. Anyway, I'm sure we can find something that will satisfy her—if nothing more than overseeing the three houses. This one, our mainland plantation; and the Colonel's. I'm sure he'd be amenable."

Virginia was enthusiastic. "I like that idea."

"To get back to your mama—I told them everything that happened. Of course, the story of Brad's capture is in the newspapers. There's one in my suitcase."

"I'm really afraid to ask this, but is there any mention of the kidnapping?"

"None. You look as surprised as I was. I have a feeling Brad did some quick thinking."

"He's resourceful," Virginia agreed. "But I am astonished. I won't be relieved until I know for certain the story didn't come out."

"It hasn't so far," Phoebe said. "Virgie, would you mind if I went upstairs for a nap? I had little sleep with Chris, but I loved every moment."

Virginia laughed. "Judging from the handful of mail you're holding, I'll have enough to keep me busy for a while. Run along. Leave the newspaper on the table in the hall."

"No," Phoebe said, "you run along to the house. I want to say hello to Moses first. I'll leave the newspaper in the hall downstairs."

Virginia became so absorbed in business letters that she was unaware that a visitor had arrived on the island. He had to announce himself by using the door pull. She hastened into the reception hall before the maid came from the kitchen. She wasn't surprised to see Lieutenant Johnson.

"Do you remember me, Mrs. Birch?"

"Yes, Lieutenant Johnson. Please come in. What brings you here this time?"

"An unpleasantness, I'm sorry to say."

For a moment, fear mounted swiftly. "Has Bradley Culver escaped again?"

"Oh no, ma'am. He won't escape this time. He begged me to come here and ask you, as a favor, to pay him a visit."

"Did he say why?"

"No, but I'm inclined to believe he wants to set things right before —they hang him."

"I don't know," she said doubtfully. "After all, what he did . . ."

"I know, I know, Mrs. Birch. I said I'd ask you, but I didn't expect you to agree."

"I don't have much time to think about this, do I?"

"None, practically. You'll have to return with me. Before long he'll be denied visitors. Did you read the newspaper story?"

"A short time ago. My sister brought it to me. I noticed there was no mention of the kidnapping."

Lieutenant Johnson nodded. "Are you sorry?"

"Good heavens, no. I just never dared hope for such a thing."

"It was Bradley Culver's quick thinking. Since there was no child in the crib, once he got to the station and his head cleared, he told the police that he had hired the woman to care for the child of a friend of his and the child had been picked up an hour earlier. He'd been sleeping when someone got in with the idea of robbing the house. He couldn't see who it was, and being groggy from sleep, he was no match for his assailant. However, the woman he'd hired screamed so loud that she frightened the would-be robber away. The police fell for it."

"Would you have?"

"With the file we have on him, I doubt it. But with an empty crib, it sounded logical to the police, and of course, until they captured him, they had no idea of his identity."

"Didn't the maid give the story away?"

"For all she knew, it could have been a true story. Culver told me she had no idea he'd kidnapped the child. Besides, she was so terrified she couldn't talk, other than to say that a Negro man struck her."

"Did Brad give a reason for his behavior?" Virginia asked fearfully.

"Yes. Ransom. He felt you sisters could well afford to supply him with money. He added that he felt you owed it to him. He's a strange character."

"Very," Virginia agreed.

"Well, Mrs. Birch," the lieutenant asked, "will you come?"

"Very well," she said. "I'll waken my sister and inform her I'll be going to the mainland and then I'll accompany you ashore. I cannot find it in me to deny a dying man this request."

"I'll be waiting at the dock," the lieutenant said."

Virginia hurried upstairs and awakened Phoebe.

"Brad sent word, through an officer of the garrison, that he wants to see me. I must go back with the lieutenant at once."

Phoebe came fully awake at the news. While Virginia changed her clothes, they talked.

"Is it wise, do you think?" Phoebe asked.

"How can I refuse him?"

"What can he want?"

"I can't think. But Bradley Culver never did anything without a reason."

"If you go to see him, won't someone suspect you favor him? Are in love with him?"

"I don't care. I must go."

"Or," Phoebe reasoned, "is he going to demand that you try to stop the hanging? His arrogance knows no bounds."

"How could I do that?" Virginia asked with fresh worry.

"I don't know, but he might try to force you by threatening to make a gallows speech. About Jimmy's paternity."

"He wouldn't," Virginia said fearfully. "No, I won't believe that of him now. Not for my sake, but for Jimmy's."

"But what if the news leaks out? What will people think? I don't like it."

"The lieutenant thinks that Brad wants to see me to apologize for kidnapping Jimmy, along with all the other things he did to us. According to the lieutenant's theory, that might make Brad feel a little better before he dies. Also, the lieutenant told me that Brad kept the kidnapping a secret."

"He does have some decency," Phoebe said. "As you say, you must go."

"I'll get back here by dark somehow. I don't want to be—close by in the morning when it happens."

Virginia finished dressing hastily, kissed her sleeping son, and hurried down to the dock. The lieutenant and two soldiers greeted her and helped her into the large and fairly comfortable craft. They shoved off immediately.

"I'm glad you agreed to see the man," Lieutenant Johnson said. "I've talked to him and he isn't a bad fellow. He's well educated, too. It's all in the file."

"I understand that he comes of a fine family."

"Yes, though his parents are dead. So he has no one."

"Is he despondent?"

"I wouldn't say so. He's somber, but taking it well, I'd say."

"He's a strange man," Virginia said.

"That was a very brave and daring act you and your sister performed. Even though I don't approve of what you did."

"We had to do it, Lieutenant," Virginia said. "We knew where he was. Despite the risk, we were successful."

"You should have notified us so we could have gotten word to New Orleans and had him arrested. It could have been mighty dangerous for you, Mrs. Birch."

"We were more concerned about the danger to my son if the police or the military interfered. We wished only to get the boy back safely."

"Oh, I must tell you this, Mrs. Birch, in case you think we always behave in such an unethical fashion."

"What do you mean 'unethical'?" Virginia asked.

"The fact that we didn't become openly involved in the kidnapping of your son and it never became public. We looked for clues but could find nothing. He's clever, that man. However, what I'm getting at is that before Captain Delaney was transferred North, he informed me that if you should, at any time, need help, we were to cooperate in every way possible. He never forgot that your husband captured Culver on Valcour. Even though he got away, it was a brave thing Mr. Birch did. As you well know, Culver was considered a dangerous man. He still is, and we're taking every precaution to see that he'll not be rescued by his band of thugs again."

"It's kind of you to give me such consideration," Virginia replied. "I didn't want it to come out that my son was kidnapped. I didn't want him to have to grow up in any kind of fear. I want him to be brave and strong—like his father."

"He will be, Mrs. Birch. He will be," the lieutenant said with quiet assurance.

"Thank you, Lieutenant."

"As you know, the hanging is tomorrow. I hate the thought of being there. I just wish the scoundrel weren't so likable."

As if sensing that she found the subject of the execution

unnerving, he grew silent. That gave her a chance to think. What, she asked herself, could Brad want? What could make him ask her to see him? Was he still enraged that she'd finally outsmarted him? Was he planning to make a final threat? It certainly couldn't be that he feared dying; he was too strong a man for that.

She was still dwelling on the likely motives when the boat reached Charleston and she was escorted to a waiting carriage. She wasn't aware of anything during the ride to the military prison. Her fears and her sadness prevailed over everything else.

She was introduced to a Yankee major whose name she remembered for no more than a minute. The lieutenant led her into a small room through one door. The second door was barred.

He said, "I don't relish submitting you to any indignity, Mrs. Birch, but it is a rule here that whoever visits a prisoner, especially one condemned, must be searched, and if the visitor is a lady, her reticule must be also searched and left on the table in this room."

"I understand, Lieutenant," she said.

He went to the barred door and signaled. A woman, sturdily built, but kindly, searched Virginia quickly but efficiently. She then led Virginia down a dismal, dark gray hallway lined with cell doors. At the end of the corridor was a larger cell, this one with a door that was solid, not barred. A small, barred window was set high in this door. The woman inserted a key and swung the door open, and Virginia entered hesitantly.

Brad, stretched out on a bunk supplied with a thin mattress, sat up. Behind Virginia, the door closed with a resounding clang.

"Hello, Mrs. Birch," he said. "It was good of you to come."

"Hello, Mr. Culver." It was an effort to keep her voice steady. The sight of him left her thoroughly shaken.

"Please sit down, Mrs. Birch, and don't ask which chair because there's only one. I'll sit on the edge of the bunk."

"Why did you send for me?" she asked as she seated herself.

"That will come later. They've given us unlimited time." He rose and held out both hands. She hesitated for a moment, then extended her hands and rose, and they stood, hands clasped for a minute or two, neither one speaking.

Virginia didn't know how she felt. Here was a man, the father of her son, who had kidnapped the boy and threatened to keep him. Here was a man who had served well in the Rebel army and then turned into a notorious outlaw.

Yet, she had been in this man's arms and had reveled in his lovemaking. She had laughed with him, wept because of him, and many of her woes could be traced directly to Bradley Culver.

Now he was soon to die, at the end of a hangman's rope. For the father of her son to die that way saddened her beyond belief. She looked directly into his eyes. His face was immobile. She couldn't fathom what he was thinking.

He spoke rather loudly, she thought. "I'm glad you agreed to see me, Mrs. Birch. I could not allow this to end without an apology from me. I'm sorry I kidnapped your son, but you can readily understand my desperate need for money. With enough of it I could have escaped, gone abroad to live. I know how wealthy you and your sisters are, so—I picked your son as the means of saving my life."

"Still," she said somewhat stiffly, because she was following his strange attitude, which she sensed was necessary, "you gave me more heartache than I ever experienced. I would have preferred that you came to me and asked for the money."

"My dear lady," he said with a curt laugh, "I was wanted for murder and already sentenced to death. How could I come begging under those conditions?"

He still held her hands and he drew her closer. His voice dropped to a whisper. "They're listening. They do that every hour or so. Afraid I'll take my own life. If I hadn't been caught off guard, I would have. They'll go away soon."

"I can't say what I would have done if you had come asking for money," she said in a normal voice. "But stealing my son was unforgivable."

He let go of her hands and moved quietly to the door. He pressed an ear against it, nodded, and returned to her side. "They've gone."

"How can you be sure of that?"

"When you're in a place like this, you learn the routine quickly. I've been here before and gotten away. Not this time, though. Virgie, do I have your forgiveness? I must have it before . . ."

"Don't say it, Brad. After those awful moments in New Orleans, I despised you. I'm not sure how I feel now. I cannot forgive you for stealing Jimmy. I can see why you did it, but I'll not forgive that."

"What of the other things I've done to you?"

"What you did to Nanine was worse."

"I'm sorry I terrified her. I was furious because you'd outsmarted me. How did you learn my alias and where I was?"

"We fired Belle and banished her from the island. Moses disposed of her clothes. The name was in one of her pockets."

Brad nodded. "Who was the big Negro?"

"He owns the brothel my papa bought for Phoebe's mama. Papa was Phoebe's father."

Once again he nodded. but he didn't speak. He kept looking into Virginia's eyes.

"Brad, stop talking around the reason why you asked me to come here. What is your real reason?"

"First, there's my hope that you'll forgive me. A forlorn hope, no doubt. There is another reason. We'll get to that in a moment. As for time, they'll give you all we require. For a man about to die, they're treating me very well indeed."

"What is the second reason? Please, Brad, don't play games with me."

"I wanted to hold you in my arms once more. If only for a second or two. That is what I desire, almost most of all."

"Almost?" she asked.

"Yes. There's a third reason, but let's take them one at a time. I want to hold you, to tell you that all this time I've loved you. The only woman in my life I really loved."

"Don't, Brad," she cried out, turning away from him so he wouldn't see her tears.

He placed a hand on her shoulder, tightened the grasp, and turned her around until she faced him. She cried out in grief and went into his arms. He held her for a long time. They didn't speak. Both knew that this was their final farewell. There was no joy in it, but they felt a certain satisfaction, vague though it was.

"I'm going to say something I have never said before," he told her. "Worse luck for me that I didn't, but I never found the one woman to whom I could say 'I love you.' Not until I met you, and then it was too late. It's always been too late for me. Now it's finished, ended, every dream gone, and there'll be no more. I love you, Virgie. I don't expect to hear you say that to me. Not after the heartache I caused you. But at least, forgive me."

"If that is what you wish to hear, I do forgive you, Brad."

"I'll not ask for more."

"I'm confused," she admitted. "I've wanted you as much as you wanted me. I have no regrets for what we did. It was wrong, but I enjoyed it and it filled a need for both of us. As for love, I think I was madly infatuated with you. You gave me Jimmy. Do you love him?"

"Oh God, yes. Will you take good care of my son? Don't ever let him learn what sort of scoundrel his father was."

"I promise."

"Thank you. Please sit down. We still have plenty of time. My appointment isn't until dawn. You see, I can joke about it. That makes me a brave man. I could relish that—if it were true."

"Tell me how you moved around so freely and even took a new name when every policeman and Yankee soldier was looking for you."

He smiled. "You're going to try to occupy my mind so I won't think. At least for the little while you'll be here."

"Brad, it mustn't be for too long or they'll become suspicious."

"I know, but let's be reckless. Just once more. Let's just talk and damn the consequences!" He gave a hollow laugh. "That's not entirely fair. For me there'll be no consequences; but you'll have to bear them all. I'll finish shortly. I knew what I was risking when I came back to Charleston. When I heard of that soiree, it seemed to me a splendid opportunity to see my son at last. That's what drove me, Virgie. For the first time in my life, I felt like an important human being. I had a son!"

Virginia nodded understanding but made no reply.

"Once I laid eyes on him, I wanted him. I'd already purchased that house, given myself a new name, and set about finding a way to get him away from you. When I wanted something, I went after it and I didn't care whom I hurt in the process. I met Belle. She was very receptive to the idea of making some money and at the same time satisfying her hatred for you and everybody else in your house. Yes, she met me often. Both on the island and in Charleston. I gave her the name on a slip of paper. That was a mistake."

"So you and Belle were meeting a long time before things came to a head. We knew that she was arrogant, that she disliked me, but we never suspected she was in touch with you. We never believed she would betray us."

"I was quite sure you'd never guess she was involved. She let me into the house the night I frightened Nan. I saw Ivy return and thought she was carrying Jimmy. Was that your idea?"

"Yes."

He smiled. "I should have known. You're a damn clever woman. As resourceful as I am, we'd have made a good pair."

Virginia didn't agree, but she remained silent about that. "How did you get into the house on our mainland plantation?"

"Belle informed me that Nan had sent you a letter. I knew you were at Colonel Spires's with your mama. I also knew that Jimmy must be there with you. Oh yes—Belle used to feed me when I hid on the island—which I did frequently after our son was born. And I lied to you when I pretended that the soiree was the first time I'd laid eyes on him. I watched him from a distance several times. I ached to go into the open and pick him up. You did right in coming after him. I doubt you'd ever have seen him again if I'd had a chance to make my escape."

"I knew that," Virginia said. "That's why I was determined to get him back. I couldn't let him grow up with a father who always had to hide from the law and the army."

"You're right, of course. I don't blame you. I only wish

you could have said you loved me. But then, it might be easier with you not loving me."

Virginia felt growing apprehension. "What are you talking about?"

"Excuse me a moment." He rose and pressed his ear against the door. The barred window was too high to look out of. He returned and sat on the edge of the bunk.

"Do you consider me brave, Virgie?"

"Brave?" She puzzled. "I suppose I do. I'm not sure if you could be called brave when you and those men in your outlaw band were burning and pilfering. But right now, the way you're facing this—yes, I think you're brave."

"I'm the most frightened, terrified man in this world, Virgie. Right now I'm on the verge of slamming my fists against the wall and screaming and not stopping until they choke off my breath."

"Brad." She spoke his name with compassion. His admission shocked her.

"There was always but one thing in life that I feared above all else. That was being hanged. I'd risk a knife, a gunshot, a club, any other way of dying. The thought of the rope is enough to drive me mad."

"What can I say?" Virginia asked helplessly. "I can do nothing."

"Yes, you can. Virgie, if they lead me out of here and make me walk to the gallows, I'll scream my head off. I'll fight them every step. I'll die screaming. I'll likely wind up in hell still screaming. I don't want to die a coward. I have a son. I'd never rest in peace, fearing he might one day learn of it."

"He never will. I promise."

"I can't risk it. That's one thing you cannot talk me out of. Right now I'm trembling inside. Shaking with the terror of what's to come in the morning. Don't let me die a coward. That's the main reason I asked you to come see me. I want to show you something."

He rose, took her hand, and led her to the barred window. He spoke softly now, in case someone was listening at the door.

"Look out there! Beyond this building there's nothing but tall grass. Nobody ever goes there. It's open land, useless."

She was more puzzled than ever. "What about it?"

"I'm going to ask you to do something for a man who caused you nothing but misery, who kidnapped your son with the intent of never giving him back to you. Yet, you never needed to fear me as you did. I always loved you, even when I denied it. How could I kill the one woman— the only woman—I loved? I couldn't. But now I'm going to ask, entreat, beg that you kill me."

She stepped away from him, aghast, too stunned to reply.

"Tonight they'll supply me with a lamp," he went on earnestly. "At three in the morning, or close to it, is the time I'll set. I have no watch, but they'll tell me what time it is, knowing how precious time is to me tonight."

"What are you getting at?" she asked, fearful of what he would say.

"At three o'clock I'll move this small table back toward the door. I'll place the lamp on it, turned up as high as it will go. I want you to be out there, hiding in the tall grass. When I step to the window I will be clearly silhouetted with the lamplight behind me. I want you to come here with a rifle. I want you to wait until you see me in outline at this window. I want you to take very careful aim and pull the trigger."

"Are you mad?" she asked. "How could I do such a thing?"

"Because you must. For my sake and yours, but mainly because of our son."

"What in the world has he to do with this?"

"I told you, I can't face hanging. I'll have to be carried out, and when I reach the gallows and they ask me if I wish to say anything, I know I will beg for mercy. I won't be able to help myself. I will beg them not to hang me because of our son. I know I'll use that as an excuse. I won't be able to restrain myself. I'll be clinging to any kind of hope that will spare me from dropping through that trap. Do you understand?"

He seized her shoulders and shook her roughly. "Do you understand, Virgie?"

"Yes, but I could not. It's impossible. I want to go now."

"I knew I'd shock you, but you're my last resort. I have no one else. I hoped, in view of what we have been to each other, that you would do this last thing for me. I know you're a crack shot. I know you have modern rifles that will do the trick neatly and painlessly. I beg of you, do this for me."

"How could I?" Suddenly she threw her arms around him and buried her face against his chest. "I could never pull that trigger. Never!"

"I think you could. I pray you will. It's my last hope, my last chance. I'm not asking for my sake, but for Jimmy's. I know I'll break down and bring him into it. I don't want to die that way. You'll make it quick and clean. When I stand at that window, my head and chest will be in plain sight. You can't miss. And you'll have my gratitude, even if it's in death."

She kissed him. Then she let him go. "Goodbye, Brad. If I don't go now, I'll be in such a condition that Lieutenant Johnson will know there's more to our meeting than just your asking forgiveness."

He nodded, crossed the cell to the door, and pounded lustily against it. She followed him.

"I beg of you, once more," he said. "Do this for me. Spare me and our son. It's the only way. At about three, I'll stand in the window. Aim well, my darling Virgie. Here they come."

"I have tried to make my peace with you, Mrs. Birch," he said loudly enough to be heard beyond the door. "I know I was wrong, but no harm was done except to me. I cannot see why you will not forgive me. I beg of you, let me die knowing you've forgiven me."

She didn't answer. When the key turned in the door and she was free to go, she kept her head down. The door clanged shut behind her. She realized it would open next when they were to lead him out.

The woman who had searched her now took her elbow gently. "He's a bad one, that man. I wonder why they let him ask you to come see him."

"He—has no one," Virginia managed. "I didn't relish the ordeal. I, too, think it was unnecessary. But my conscience is clear. I only hope I helped him."

"I can guarantee he won't bother you again," she said. "Here's your reticule, Mrs. Birch. I'm sorry we had to search you. He'll not be granted any more visitors. Go home and try to forget tonight."

Virginia doubted she ever would.

The same soldiers who had brought her to the mainland rowed her back to Valcour. They helped her ashore and promptly shoved off. Halfway up the slope, Phoebe met her.

"It's a relief to see you," Phoebe said. "I was worried from the moment you left."

"I was safe enough," Virginia said. "I had the Union army with me."

"I know. But I feared that Brad's band of brigands might have been up to something. They outsmarted the army once before, you know. I was terrified they might try to kidnap you."

"Nothing to fear on that score," Virginia assured her. "Brad is resigned to his fate. And you may be assured he's well guarded. Even I was searched by a matron before I was allowed to see him. And I had to leave my reticule on a table in another room."

"May I ask what Brad wanted?"

"Forgiveness. He talked about Jimmy. About his fear of being hanged. The rope terrifies him. I believe he wanted me to come because I might lend him some strength to face the morning. I'm very dispirited. I feel completely responsible for everything that's happened."

"You're not. Brad brought it on himself."

"If I hadn't succumbed to him, he would never have returned to the island."

"You can't be sure," Phoebe reasoned. "Anyway, it's too late to think about that."

"What time is it?" Virginia asked.

"Four, a little after. You must be tired."

"I am. Unnerved, too. I think Brad asked to see me so he wouldn't be alone. He apologized for taking Jimmy, though he admitted I'd never have gotten my son back if he had been able to get away. He did ask how we found him. I told him we had Moses to thank for that."

"Belle may have helped him, but she proved his undoing, too," Phoebe said.

When they reached the veranda, Virginia turned and looked out over the water. Trying to get her thoughts off Brad, she said, "I wonder how Nan is doing in Washington. Seems to me our family is always in turmoil. And I'm the cause of it all."

"Let me get you a sleeping draft," Phoebe said. "It will

help you stop this brooding. You've been through a great deal these last few days."

"So have you," Virginia said solemnly. "This should be a glorious time for you. Once again, it's my fault."

"It isn't," Phoebe contradicted. "If I didn't wish to be here, I wouldn't be. Want me to go upstairs with you?"

"No, thanks. And I won't need a sleeping draft. I'll stop by and see Jimmy."

"An excellent idea. He should brighten your spirits."

Virginia nodded, embraced Phoebe, and went upstairs. She stopped by the nursery and her heart lifted temporarily when Jimmy exclaimed happily as she entered the room. He made his unsteady way to her and she swooped him up in her arms and covered his face with kisses. Then she set him down and said to Ivy, "Thank you for giving him such good care."

"You look tired, Miss Virginia. Better get some rest."

"I'm going to. It's time for Jimmy's nap, too. You needn't remain in the nursery now when he's asleep. He's no longer in any danger."

"Thank you, Miss Virginia. I'm glad to hear it. I'll go down in the yard and read."

Virginia went to her room, removed her shoes, dress, and corset, and lay down, but she couldn't sleep. Her mind was back in that cell with Brad. She could easily cry for him, but she could not love him. On her part, theirs had been an affair of passion, a physical need for him. That is, until her pregnancy had complicated things. She diverted her thoughts to Elias, granting to herself that the abrupt way he'd left had been the kindest way possible. He'd asked for no explanation, given no hint of the reason for his departure, and he'd saved her an embarrassment that could have wrecked her life and that of her son.

If only once he would write a letter instead of a report. Why didn't he ask her how she was, or tell her something about his life in England? She'd often told herself that he must be having affairs with many women, but she knew she was only being vindictive.

But those thoughts didn't quell the one important and dreadful idea in her mind. Brad wanted her to kill him. It seemed so completely mad, so impossible to consider, that it became quite unreal. Except that she knew he meant it. He depended on her. What he was asking was something only a person with great mental strength and determination would even consider. She wondered if she possessed that much fortitude.

What he asked was logical, she thought. There was sense to it, and there was ample reason why she should comply with his dying request. She would bring an end to his fear of the rope. She would ensure that he would never blurt out the truth about Jimmy in a fit of terror as they made ready to draw the black hood over his head.

She sat up, bunching the pillows behind her. Suddenly she realized that she was thinking in terms of performing such an act. Then she slid down in the bed, buried her face in the pillow, and wept bitterly, for knew she could never do such a thing.

How could she accomplish it, anyway? It was two hours of strenuous rowing to reach the mainland, and two hours back. By night the journey was hazardous. Storms came up quickly at this season. There were fishermen afloat all the time. She might easily be detected, and she could give no logical reason for rowing to the mainland, or back, at this hour of the night.

Even if she reached shore without being seen, there was the question of reaching the prison. She'd be carrying a rifle, not easy to conceal. There would be people on the streets, law officers, military police. She was known in Charleston; she might easily be recognized. It was impossible. She firmly made up her mind about that.

Five minutes later, she wondered how she would ever sleep again knowing that Brad had died screaming in horror. How would she ever free herself of the thought that she could have saved him that, and prevented the risk of having Jimmy revealed as her illegitimate son, fathered by Bradley Culver?

Once again she sat up; this time, she swung her legs off the bed. Jimmy must never know. That was the strongest motive of all. She bent her head, not in shame or sorrow, but to think. How could she do this final act for Brad?

Still in her underclothes, though wearing slippers now, she padded down the hall to Phoebe's room. She prayed that Phoebe would not be there and was relieved to find the suite empty. She made her way to the closets where Phoebe kept the articles she seldom used. Among them was a cosmetics case containing the creams, powders, rouges, and lip colorings she had used as an actress. There was one jar Virginia sought. She found it easily, for the white metal lid was stained black.

She carried this back to her own rooms, sat in the parlor, and opened the jar. It contained a black greasepaint that Phoebe had used when she was part of a minstrel show. Phoebe used to laugh heartily when she told her sisters how she, with Negro blood, had to blacken her face to pretend to be a Negro.

The cream was soft, still usable. Virginia concealed it in one of her bureau drawers. When she sat down again, she knew she was going to fulfill Brad's last request. Somehow, she was going to do it, despite the enormous risk.

Once the decision was made, it was easier to face, though nonetheless fearful. There were so many things that could go wrong. The slightest slip, the merest stroke of bad luck, and it would become something horrible. Yet, the chance had to be taken.

She feared, most of all, the moment when she must pull

the trigger. As Brad had said, he would be a perfect target, and Virginia had grown up with guns. In her early teens she'd become as good a shot as her father and brother. Later, she had often bested them. But she knew that at the moment she would pull the trigger, her nerves would be stretched to their utmost.

She slipped into her shoes and dress, went downstairs, and ate a quiet dinner with Phoebe. They talked briefly about the islanders and their irritation toward Virginia because of what had happened to their crop. She admitted her blame, but she refused to dwell on it until Nan returned from Washington and they heard what she'd learned. Phoebe made no comment, not wishing to lower Virginia's spirits any more than they already were, though admitting silently that Virginia's fortitude seemed to have strengthened with her rest.

Phoebe sent Virginia back upstairs to the nursery and closed and locked the house for the night. Virginia brightened at sight of her son, who was playing with a ball. She sent Ivy downstairs to have her supper and waited for her to bring Jimmy's back. When the girl returned with the tray, Virginia placed Jimmy in his high chair and fed him herself, relishing every moment. She knew they were what made the thing she was going to do a necessity and worth the danger and anguish that she would have to endure.

She went to bed at the usual time. She was glad Nanine was away, for it made the risk of detection that much less. She dozed, forcing herself not to drift into a deep sleep. There would be only one chance to accomplish this grim business, and it had to be tonight.

Shortly before twelve, Virginia stepped into the hallway. Everything was quiet. A walk along the corridor revealed that no lights gleamed beneath the doors. The household was asleep. Returning to her room, she dressed quickly, except for the black dress she would wear. Seated before the mirror, she opened the jar of black makeup and applied it liberally to her face and neck. Her hands would be covered with black leather gloves. She made sure that when fully dressed, no white skin would show.

This done, she finished preparing for the journey. Thick leather gloves would protect her hands when rowed, to be replaced with thinner ones so that she might use the rifle properly. She made her way downstairs in the dark. Once in the library, she lit a lamp so she might select the proper gun and load it.

The rifle was akin to a sharpshooter's weapon, though it was heavier and fired a larger bullet. It was a repeater. She filled the magazine, though she realized she might have only one shot without being detected. One would do, she knew very well.

She had provided herself with a hooded black cloak, which she now put on. She practiced carrying the rifle concealed beneath the cloak. Finally, she left the house. There was a problem about locking the door—it could not be done from the outside. The bolt would have to remain open. She planned to return before daylight, and she could slip into the house, bolt the door, and reach her rooms without being seen or heard. If her luck held out.

At the dock, she untied a rowboat and placed the rifle under the seat. With one oar she pushed free, then drifted a bit until she had the oars in place.

The stars provided enough light for her to steer by, and it was no novelty, for she had made the trip by night before. She knew how to stay on course, how to row quietly if it became necessary, or not row at all if danger was closing in. Still, the rowing was hard. It took every bit of her energy, for she was handicapped by lack of sleep and by worry and fear. There was also the ceaseless wild pounding of her heart. It seemed endless, this ride through the dark. Fortunately, the sea was calm. If there had been a storm, she'd have been in trouble, for she knew she would have attempted the journey in spite of it.

Her attitude now was that her mission had to be fulfilled. The bloody grimness of it took no part in her planning. She had wisely estimated her chances, planning every detail, praying that she would succeed. A strange praying, for if it came true, she would kill a man she had once felt a mad fascination for and who had fathered her son.

At last she saw the dim lights in the harbor, and the agony in her arms and shoulders lessened. She managed to maneuver the boat to a well-used part of the dock where there were many boats of the same kind. If hers was seen, it could scarcely be identified as having come from Valcour.

Now began the more dangerous part of her task. Before she lifted the rifle out of the boat after tying up, she climbed the stairs to the harbor street and looked about. At two-thirty in the morning, Charleston was as deserted as a small town.

She lifted the rifle from the boat, thrust it under her cloak, and held it firmly against her with one arm. She began walking down the street. She would have to walk all the way and back, for hiring a carriage was out of the question, even had there been one to hire at this time of night. Once she saw what seemed to be a uniformed man in the distance, and she promptly stepped back into a dark alley between buildings.

When she was sure the man had vanished, she emerged from the alley and, keeping close to the buildings, moved quickly along. Twice she had to move for cover and await the passage of a policeman. In both instances she acted swiftly and she knew she'd not been seen.

Then she came to the prison, and she skirted it only to discover she was heading straight for the scaffold that awaited Brad. Shuddering, she strengthened her resolve to carry out his last wish.

It was strange how little fear she felt now. She did not even think about the madness she would soon perform. It was something that had to be done, like selling last year's cotton crop. It was a task that must be accomplished, no matter what the peril or the consequences.

She passed the scaffold, averting her head. She was wearing her lapel watch under the cloak, but in the darkness she couldn't see the time. She was certain there were few minutes, one way or the other, from the time Brad had set. She headed out into the tall grass and shrubs at the back of the prison. She knelt in the tallest of the weeds, which concealed her well. She began to crawl toward a spot directly opposite the window where Brad would stand. All the windows at this side of the prison were dark, except for the window of the cell where Brad was being held.

She took the rifle out from under her cloak. She made certain a bullet was ready to be fired, then she parted the tall grass so she might watch the window.

At no time did she try to talk herself out of this awful thing. In fact, she gave no thought to it. Her heart had a steady, calm beat. She was cold and calculating, as if it were no more than an ordinary unpleasant thing she had to do.

Her knees were getting stiff and cold. She wrapped the cloak around her more tightly. She knew without a doubt that if anyone passed close by, she would not be seen. The black cloak and her blackened face made her almost invisible. She began to worry. She looked at her watch but was still unable to read the dial. It must be close to three o'clock. She began to wonder if her resolve would last beyond that. Her hands were beginning to shake.

The light in the cell seemed to grow stronger, brighter, as if Brad had kept the flame low and now turned it all the way up. Virginia raised the rifle and aimed it at the window. Her finger remained loose on the trigger. She knew she had the window, and anyone in it, framed precisely in the rifle sight.

Then the shadow appeared. That was all she could see, the form that filled the window frame. She envisioned him there, pressed against the bars, his arms outflung, waiting for the welcoming bullet that would end his ordeal.

She pulled the trigger slowly. To her the explosion seemed like that of a ship's cannon, but it couldn't have been heard even in the prison. The form in the window vanished and did not reappear.

She thrust the gun under her cloak and crept out of the brush. She would have to move quickly now, for the closer it came to dawn, the more likely someone might see her.

She walked boldly, not like the criminal she suddenly knew she was. Twice she passed milk wagons, but neither driver paid heed to her. At the dock, she stood for a moment, peering about in the darkness. No one was abroad; the streets were still deserted.

She descended the steps to where her boat was tied up. She placed the rifle quietly on the bottom of the craft, untied it, got aboard, and began rowing. As the mainland lights faded and the darkness engulfed her, she felt easier. Now all she had to do was avoid being seen by anyone on Valcour. She rowed on through the dark, every stroke bringing her nearer home. She was still shivering with cold. She gave no thought to the actual crime she had committed. When she saw the outline of Valcour, she was surprised, for she'd been unaware of the time that had elapsed.

Tying the boat was simple. Again concealing the rifle under her cloak, she hurried along the path to the mansion. It was still dark. She mounted the porch steps quietly, let herself in, bolted the door, and breathed a sigh of relief. She made her way to the library and again lit a lamp. She opened the gun cabinet and replaced the rifle, not even bothering to unload it. She would clean the weapon later if she could do so undetected. If not, it would wait. No one ever touched any of the guns anymore.

She carried the library lamp upstairs, tiptoed along the hall to her suite, and immediately went to work washing off the black makeup. She rolled up the soiled towels in old newspapers and concealed them in a corner of her closet for later disposal.

She undressed and inspected herself in front of the mirror to be sure no traces of black paint remained. Then she slipped on a nightgown, got into bed, and blew out the light.

Now, slowly, she felt the tension leave her and, with it, the calm chill with which she had performed this deed. She closed her eyes and thought about killing a man who had once been in her arms. Eager, demanding arms. The man who was the father of her son. She was struck hard by the enormity of what she had done. She felt ill, as if she would vomit. A fierce pain stabbed at her stomach, and her body shook uncontrollably. The shock of what she'd done weighed heavily on her mind, even though it was what Brad had wanted. She closed her eyes tightly and prayed that the bullet had been true and that Brad had died instantly.

It was well after daylight when Virginia finally managed to fall asleep. The turmoil within her and the energy she had used in performing her task provided a weariness that made her sleep as if drugged.

It was late in the morning when Phoebe awakened her, shaking her lightly and speaking her name softly so that she would not be alarmed. Virginia opened her eyes, her mind blank for a few seconds. Slowly, the events of the previous night flooded her mind. She propped herself up on one elbow.

"Good morning," she said. "Have I slept late?"

"Quite late," Phoebe said soberly.

"I'm glad. It must be over by now."

"I would imagine so, but still I'm not sure. I woke you because there are some Yankee soldiers nearing the island. I caught sight of them in Papa's old glass."

Virginia swung her legs off the bed. "Perhaps they're coming to tell us that Brad was granted a reprieve."

"I doubt it. More likely they've come to inform us he's dead."

"Either way, I've got to dress. Please ask them to be patient. I'll be ready as soon as I can."

"Of course. I'll do my best to delay them a bit if you wish."

"That won't be necessary."

Virginia bathed and dressed carefully, and all the while she maintained her wits, certain she'd not give way when the Yankees delivered their message. She wondered why they'd come, then decided that the way Brad had died was something they felt they should impart to her. Unless he was not dead. She stifled the horror of that idea.

She was on her way down the stairs when Phoebe admitted Lieutenant Johnson. She greeted him with an extended hand as he approached. He gravely saluted, then bowed over her hand.

"Good morning, Lieutenant," she said with a calmness she was far from feeling. If anything had gone wrong, she might be in serious trouble.

"Mrs. Birch," he said. "Mrs. Savard." He bowed again. "I've some rather startling news, and I've been ordered to make a formal request of you, Mrs. Birch."

"Good heavens, you sound very grave, Lieutenant. I

believed you'd come to inform me that Mr. Culver has been executed."

"No, ma'am, he was not hanged."

"Not hanged?" Phoebe and Virginia asked in unison.

"He was murdered! Someone shot him to death."

"Please come into the drawing room, Lieutenant," Virginia said. "I'm beginning to feel quite faint."

"How could a condemned prisoner be shot?" Phoebe asked on their way to the drawing room. "How could anyone reach him, let alone shoot him?"

They sat down. "Sometime during the night," the lieutenant explained, "someone crept up to the window of Culver's cell. We don't know the circumstances by which this could have been arranged, but Culver apparently positioned himself in the window of his cell, and the person outside fired a bullet through his head."

Virginia looked horrified. "Why would anyone do such a thing?"

"For my part," Phoebe added, "I'm sure he'd rather have died like that than to have been hanged in public."

"You mentioned something about a formal request," Virginia said.

"Yes. We think this killing was premeditated. Whoever was on the outside waited until Culver presented himself at the window to be killed, surely by his own wish. He had dragged a table to the far side of the cell and placed a lamp on it. That brought him in full silhouette at the window. We believe it happened somewhere between two-thirty and three-thirty. Mr. Culver kept asking the guard for the time. The guard believed he was keeping track of the hours before dawn, when he was due to be executed, but we think it was planned that Culver would stand in the window at a certain time."

"What's all that got to do with this request you mentioned?"

Phoebe asked, while Virginia held her breath, for she
sensed what was coming.

"You see," the lieutenant said almost regretfully, "you,
Mrs. Birch, were not only the last outsider to see him
alive—but also the only visitor he had since being brought
back from New Orleans."

Virginia felt her nerve beginning to crack, but she
managed to portray disbelief. "Are you accusing me?" she
asked.

"Please, Mrs. Birch, I accuse no one, but it is necessary
that an investigation be conducted. We have no other
reason than your visit to Culver to incriminate you in any
way. Culver kidnapped your son, and that automatically
places you under suspicion because of that motive. Are
you familiar with firing a gun?"

"All of us here know how to shoot a gun," Phoebe broke
in. "We are quite isolated and feel the need to keep guns
for our protection."

Virginia felt herself turning pale and dizzy with sudden
apprehension. Phoebe should not have mentioned guns.
The rifle she had used was in the gun rack, still loaded,
and with evidence that it had recently been fired. She had
an urge to grow angry and refuse to permit a search if the
lieutenant suggested one, or to exhibit such intense rage as
to dissuade him from attempting such a search. Instead,
she said nothing, but she hoped her anxiety was not
outwardly visible.

"I dislike what I must ask next," the lieutenant said,
"but may I inspect those guns? Now?"

Phoebe rose. "Certainly. The gun rack is in the library,
if you will please follow me. Virgie, there's no need for
you to come along."

"I—would like to," Virginia replied stiffly.

Lieutenant Johnson opened the gun rack and inspected
the four rifles and the shotgun. He sniffed the end of the

barrel of each gun and replaced it. Virginia almost cried out in relief, for when Lieutenant Johnson opened the rack, she saw that the rifle she had used was not there.

He turned around with a smile. "Of course, I knew this search would produce nothing. Suspecting you of killing Culver, with his consent, was unbelievable, although you had good reason to want to. We know what happened in New Orleans. Thank you, ladies. I shall report that as far as you are involved, Mrs. Birch, the case is closed, and we shall look for the murderer among those of his old band of outlaws. It is possible he gave them instructions on what to do in the event of his capture."

"It sounds reasonable to assume that!" Virginia managed.

"At any rate," Lieutenant Johnson said as they neared the front door, "the man is now dead, and whatever problems he presented to you are gone. I thank you once again, and I apologize for the trouble I caused you. And most emphatically I apologize for even this hint of suspicion against you, Mrs. Birch. Oh," he raised a forefinger, "your husband and I keep in constant touch, Mrs. Savard."

Two soldiers waited outside the door. Virginia shuddered at how close she'd come to being arrested. The presence of those soldiers, obviously on guard against anyone trying to escape from the house, was visible evidence that even the lieutenant had some measure of doubt. They followed him onto the porch and watched him leave after his usual formal salute. Then Virginia turned to Phoebe.

"Do you think he actually suspected me of shooting Brad?"

"I think he was under orders to make certain you had not. It must have been only a routine measure. Who could ever believe that any of us would have done such a thing?"

Virginia was on the verge of asking Phoebe if she had removed the rifle, but she hesitated. Perhaps Phoebe had

protected Virginia by removing the gun and wanted no
more reference to it. Virginia embraced Phoebe warmly.

"I wonder how I'd ever have managed without you," she
said.

"Quite well, I'm sure," Phoebe said with a smile. "In
fact, I'm positive of it. Now let's do our best to push this
tragic incident from our minds. Bury our memories of
Bradley Culver as much as we can. All I'm afraid of now is
what Nan is coming back with from Washington. Virgie,
our entire crop is ruined. Moses is almost in tears over it.
And everybody on the island has suffered this loss along
with us."

Virginia realized then that if Phoebe had anything to do
with the disappearance of the rifle, she wished nothing
more to be said about it. There must be a tacit understanding between the two sisters that whatever had happened
was for the best. It would remain a secret between them.

Virginia said, "I'm sure the neighbors are angrier than
ever with us. Especially me, because I let Carlos persuade
me to plant the seeds—and later, the seedlings—believing I
was getting a bargain. I should have known that when he
lied to me regarding his marital status, he couldn't be
trusted."

"You let your emotions overrule your judgment," Phoebe reasoned.

"That's always been my weakness," Virginia said
regretfully. "We've paid for it. The entire island has paid
for my poor judgment. Carlos was angry because I with-
held payment on the check. I know now what he meant
when he told Brad he would fix us. The seedlings were his
way of getting revenge. We paid for it with our crops."

"He paid for it with his life," Phoebe reminded her.
"Bradley Culver must have loved you to do what he did.
Not that he hadn't taken a life before, but he went out of

his way to find Carlos and make him pay for what he'd done to you."

"I doubt Belle would have told Brad of Carlos's visit to the island if she had thought we would end up with our cotton crop ruined."

"Yes, she would have," Phoebe contradicted. "She was getting well paid, I'm sure."

Virginia nodded. "There was nothing cheap about Brad. He paid for what he wanted, even when it concerned information."

"I may as well tell you, Virgie, I think we'd better prepare ourselves for some troublesome visits from the islanders."

"I'm sure they'll be here—and soon," Virginia agreed. "Let's go take a look at the fields and find out how extensive the damage is, though I don't see how it could get any worse. I'd just like to breathe some fresh air and shut out Lieutenant Johnson's visit."

They found it much worse. Those plants that had shown some signs of resistance to the epidemic or to the ravages of the strange insects were now as wilted as the others. No plant was spared. The crop was completely ruined. The loss would be heavy.

"I don't like to bring up the subject, but Elias should be informed about this so he won't sell cotton we can't deliver," Phoebe said.

"Nan can take care of it," Virginia said curtly. "Just keep hoping that the mainland isn't infected. At least we have that, and the crop there will enable us at least to break even this year. Next year will be something else."

"If growing cotton on Valcour isn't permanently lost," Phoebe commented.

"That would be the end of Valcour," Virginia said. "If cotton won't grow here, what's left?"

"Only a lovely island where I hope we can spend the

rest of our lives in peace and quiet. You sometimes forget, dear Virgie, that we are wealthy enough that nothing can really spoil Valcour for us. Even if the Hammond sisters are the only ones left here."

They toured the fields, accompanied by Moses, who was at his wits' end. The field hands stood about with nothing to do. Many spent their time at home with their families. Virginia had notified the help that they would be paid as usual, regardless of the conditions.

"Been raisin' cotton all my life," Moses said sadly. "Nevah sees anythin' like this. Breaks my heart 'cause all this heah wuk goin' to waste. Yo' reckon we kin grow cotton nex' yeah, Miss Virginia?"

"I hope so. I pray so," Virginia said. "But whatever occurs, Moses, you have nothing to worry about. You're part of the island, of the family. It's time you began to take it easy anyway."

"Cain't," Moses said glumly. "Wouldn' know whut to do with myse'f."

"Do you miss Belle?" Phoebe asked.

Moses scowled. "Misses her I does, Miss Phoebe. Misses all the cussin' she done an' the cheatin' an' the totin' from yo' kitchen. Used to tote a whole ham sometime an' sells it li'l bit at a time to her frien's. Takin' money fo' stealin'. When I lays my haid down fo' sleep, misses nuthin'."

"We could bring her back," Virginia offered.

"Don' do that fo' me. Nevah wants to see her again, I kin he'p it."

"I think you're wise," Phoebe said. "Belle isn't a woman who could ever change. Tomorrow Nan will be back from Washington, and then we'll have news, good or bad."

"Yes'm. Yo' calls me, please, so's I kin know."

"Of course. We'll let you know what she learned as soon as we do."

"Thanks yo', missy. Goes now. Don' knows whut to do. Sho' cain't mess with dead plants."

He wandered off, unsure of himself for the first time in his life. Phoebe and Virginia returned to the mansion. Virginia, still tired from her ordeal of the night before, went to visit with Jimmy for a time, then had a nap.

When she came downstairs for supper, she went into the library. She glanced at the gun rack. The rifle she'd used was back in its place, cleaned and smelling of fresh oil. Mentally Virginia thanked Phoebe, but at supper she made no reference to the return of the gun.

They had just seated themselves in the drawing room when they heard the approach of horses. Phoebe went to the window.

"It's Mr. Damon and Mr. Langan," she said.

"I think we can guess what they want," Virginia said. "I'll let them in."

Langan, a white-haired, portly man, greeted Virginia with a chilly glance. Damon, younger, a hard-working man with a large family, took Virginia's hand with a grave smile.

Phoebe joined them as they sat down in the drawing room. Virginia indicated the silver coffee service on a nearby table.

"Would you gentlemen care for coffee?" she asked. "I'm sure it's still hot."

"We didn't come here to socialize," Langan said curtly. "We want to know what's being done about the cotton crop."

"We represent all the other folks on the island, Mrs. Birch," Damon said in a calmer tone. "I don't believe we're going to get a single ball of cotton off any of the plants this year."

"We had a meeting," Langan said, "and we decided you're to blame for this. We've lost everything."

"So have we." Virginia kept her tone gracious. "Whatever caused this catastrophe didn't miss us either."

"Nan is now in Washington," Phoebe explained, "where

she's been talking about our problem with specialists in this sort of epidemic. We expect her to return tomorrow."

"We hope she'll have information on how to handle this," Virginia added.

"Washington!" Langan scoffed. "Do you think the Yankees will help us? What would they know about growing cotton?"

"They have men who specialize in agricultural problems," Phoebe said. "That's more than we have."

"I wouldn't believe a thing they said," Langan persisted. "And that's got nothing to do with the purpose of our visit. What are you going to do about this?"

"I told you," Virginia said with growing heat. "We'll know far better when Nan returns. You surely can wait until tomorrow."

"Every day makes it harder," Damon said in a reasonable tone. "We're not able to stand up under this loss, and day by day it gets worse. If we can't harvest our cotton, we can't pay the banks on the money we borrowed. You know when you have one crop a year, you live on credit most of the time, and we won't be able to get any. It's a very serious situation for us, Mrs. Birch."

"I can't even advise you," Virginia said, her tone apologetic. "We're as worried as you."

"What've you got to worry about?" Langan demanded. "You got half the money in the world."

Virginia rose. "I must conclude this discussion, Mr. Langan. We'll advise you as quickly as we get news. Good evening, gentlemen."

Phoebe had already reached the door to hold it open. Langan went by with a scowl. Damon followed, quickening his step to catch up with Langan, whose rapid footsteps matched his anger. Phoebe closed the door.

"We're going to have trouble," she said. "We'll be blamed for what happened."

"I'm as worried as they are, Phoebe. The only resource this island has is cotton."

"Would you be annoyed if Nan or I wrote to Elias about what has happened?"

"Yes. He's to have nothing to do with this."

"Very well, Virgie. For now, I'll obey your wishes. However, if things don't improve, or if we don't learn what the problem is, we may have to outvote you. Certainly you remember that Elias, during his stay on the island, even before you married him, became an expert on growing cotton. We can't afford to let any chance of recovering our plantation go by. I'd also like to remind you that he started the plantation on the mainland again."

"You don't need to remind me of what Elias said. I'm well aware of it. Besides, what makes you think he'd come back?"

"I didn't say anything about him coming back," Phoebe replied, looking directly at Virginia, who averted her eyes.

"I wouldn't let him if he offered," Virginia replied. "Besides, his interest lies in only one thing—selling our crop. Other than that, he's not even mildly interested in what goes on here or on the mainland."

"You can't make that statement in good faith because you don't know."

"I know I didn't order him off the island," Virginia retorted. "He left of his own accord."

"Do you blame him?"

"Of course not," Virginia said impatiently. "I know what I did. I know what it must have done to him. I also know he's made me pay for it."

"Just don't blame him for walking out on you," Phoebe said. "Especially since you've never written him a personal letter. You never asked his forgiveness—or did you?"

"Never," Virginia said boldly. "Nor will I."

"Very well then. Try not to feel such bitterness toward him."

"And I did write him a personal letter once," Virginia countered. "I asked him what I should do with the jewelry he sent me from Washington. The pendant and earrings he had made up specially for me."

Phoebe repressed a smile. "He replied to that."

"Briefly."

"You never sent them back to him. That's not like you."

"Only because they're very beautiful. Besides, he bought them for me."

"Yes, he did, and it shows where his thoughts were when he was away from you—even when he went to Washington for surgery."

Virginia bit her lower lip. "You've never spoken like this to me before, Phoebe."

"It's my opinion that you're being very unfair to him."

Virginia turned and crossed the drawing room in angry strides. Before she reached the reception-hall doorway, she turned and ran back to where Phoebe stood. She embraced her tightly. "I'm a fool. A stubborn, obstinate idiot. I know what you did for me. If you hadn't removed that rifle, I'd be in jail right now, very likely. I've treated you shabbily, and I hate myself for it. Forgive me, Phoebe. Please."

"We're sisters. We're bound to disagree and quarrel now and then. But we love each other. Because of that, we can resolve our differences."

"Thank you. And forgive me."

"As for this talk about my saving you from some terrible thing because of what happened to Brad, I don't know what you're talking about, and I don't want to know."

"I'll not refer to it again."

"Then let's go up to see Jimmy. It's time we devoted ourselves to him for a change. He can always make us forget our problems and brighten our spirits."

THIRTEEN

"Who in the world has Nan got with her?" Virginia asked.

"I'm sure I don't know," Phoebe said. "I've never seen him before."

They stood on the dock waiting for the boat to move in. Both were filled with an overpowering anxiety and a feeling of despair. Earlier in the morning they'd gone back to the fields and wept at the sight. The plants, which should now have been white with blooms, were dead stalks.

The man in the boat had rowed with strong arms, sending the craft through the water at a remarkable speed. When the boat bumped against the dock, Nan stood up and threw a rope ashore, and Phoebe quickly tied it up.

The man stepped out first, then helped Nan ashore. He was at least six feet two, towering like a tall, thin giant beside the sisters. He was lanky, almost awkward. He had red hair, a freckled face, and bronzed skin. His arms seemed to be too long even for his height, but he was anything but ungainly.

He bowed to Virginia and Phoebe. "I am pleased to be in the company of such attractive ladies. My name is Adam Farley. I'm a Yankee in the presence of fair Rebels, and I'm glad to be here. Nan has, of course, told me all about you and about the island."

"Adam is an entomologist," Nanine explained even before she embraced her sisters. "He works for the government, and they very kindly sent him here to find out what's wrong."

"Then you are indeed welcome," Virginia said. "By the time you've freshened up, Daisy, our cook, will have food on the table for you."

"I'd rather see the fields," Adam Farley said. "At once!"

Virginia, startled at the man's insistence, began walking toward the fields. Phoebe joined her. On the dock, Adam unloaded Nanine's suitcase and a bulging canvas dufflebag initialed U.S.A. He swung this over his shoulder, then picked up Nanine's suitcase with one hand, and when Phoebe turned to look back, she saw Nanine put her arm around his free one.

"Nan's hanging on to him as if she's afraid he'll disappear," Phoebe said, curious.

"I don't understand what she sees in that brusque Yankee. He sounds as if we've committed a crime."

"Maybe we have," Phoebe said with a light laugh. "I have a feeling we'll soon find out."

"If he can find out what's causing this ruin on Valcour, I don't care how he acts. He's overwhelming, but a forceful individual."

"I find him quite fascinating," Phoebe said. "I think Nan does, too."

"We'll begin by showing him the section where we planted the seedlings Carlos brought. That seems to be about the worst spot. Probably where it all began."

Nanine and Adam caught up with them as they reached the field. Adam dropped the suitcase and slipped the dufflebag off his shoulder. "When did all this start?" he asked.

"When did what start?" Virginia asked.

"Did the wilting begin here? Is this where you planted first? The Mexican seedlings Nan told me about?"

"Yes. These plants were given to us by—"

"Jesus Christ!" Adam cried out. "It's come!"

"What are you talking—?"

"How many Negroes you got working here?"

"Enough to take care of the fields."

"How many?" He towered over Virginia. He seized her shoulders and shook her hard. "I asked you, how many?"

"Let go of me!" she said indignantly. "Who do you think you are?"

"Dammit, will somebody tell me?" He released Virginia and turned to Nanine.

"Two hundred permanently," Nanine said.

"Somebody get them assembled. As fast as you can. I want every last one here as soon as possible. Nan, you're the only one here who seems to have your wits about you. Do you have any oil, pitch—kerosene—anything that burns?"

"We keep kerosene—" Nanine began.

"Have somebody get it out here. All there is."

Phoebe, now alarmed, spoke up. "Please—what are you going to do?"

"Just stand aside," he said matter-of-factly. "Don't get in the way."

Virginia faced him. "I'll not move a muscle until you tell me what in the world you're talking about. Why you want all the workers here and all the kerosene..."

Adam bent down, picked at the stalk of a dead plant, and deposited one of the tiny insects into the palm of his hand. It lay there as if dead.

"This," he announced, "is known as *Anthonomus grandis*. Known in English as a boll weevil. Ever hear of it?"

"No," Phoebe confessed.

"Nor I," Virginia added, somewhat mollified by Adam's apparent knowledge of what he was talking about.

"This is the first invasion ever in the United States. It's all over Mexico. . . ."

"Mexico," Virginia repeated. "These plants came from

there. We were using them in an experiment to better our grade of cotton."

"Of all the damn fools!" Adam exploded. "Have you any idea of what you did? Have you the slightest idea?"

"Now you heed the way you talk to me," Virginia said, then stopped when Adam bent over and brought his face level with hers.

"I said you are a damn fool. In fact, you're a hell of a lot worse than a damn fool. You're a goddamn fool!"

Virginia looked about for Nanine, but she'd bustled off to comply with Adam's orders. Phoebe stood aside, taking no part in the argument, though she seemed quite taken by Adam's manner.

"Let me enlighten you, Mrs. Birch," Adam said. He held out his hand with the tiny insect in it. "This little bug eats cotton buds. Eats them so it can produce a little worm that finishes dining on the plant. Look on the ground. There never were any buds on your plants. They fell to the ground when these weevils got through dining on them. They're real smart little fellas. I'll show you. This one looks like I squeezed it to death. Watch."

He knelt and deposited the insect on the ground. It lay there apparently dead. After a few moments it suddenly came to life and scurried off into the soft earth around the plant.

"Now let me show you something else."

Adam pulled up one plant, roots and all. He broke the stalk, opened it to the seeds, and exposed a tiny white grub moving slowly. "The weevil starts the destruction. This little devil finishes it. What you have here could be the most dangerous thing that ever happened to the South. The war that ended a couple of years ago wasn't much worse than this bug and the damage it can do."

"Do you mean that we've lost this crop? That I can endure, but what of next year?"

"I'll talk about that later. Tonight, if you'll put me up. Tomorrow I go back to Washington. I must get word there as soon as possible about this bug."

"We do have telegraph facilities," Virginia said with a trace of sarcasm.

"If I sent what I have to say over the wires, the South would be in a frenzy by tomorrow. This has to be a secret for now. Even the Negroes who work here mustn't know why I'm going to do what is necessary. What of the rest of the island? Is that planted in cotton too?"

"We grow the finest cotton in the world on this island," Virginia said. "All of us depend on it for our livelihood."

"Is it infested too?"

"Yes. As bad as it is here."

"I want one thing understood here and now. I'm in charge. I give the orders, and they'll be carried out, even if I have to go to the mainland and bring back a regiment of Northern troops."

"The island was invaded before," Virginia said. "I know we can do nothing to stop another invasion. But I resent you and your methods, Mr. Farley."

He eyed her grimly. "Wait'll you hear what I'm going to do. As for you, Mrs. Birch, keep your mouth shut and obey any order I give."

"Just what do you have in mind, Mr. Farley?" Phoebe asked.

"Wait until your help gets here. Is there any way to send word to the other plantations on the island? Immediately!"

"We can send messages," Phoebe replied.

"I'll assign some of your help to warn the other planters."

Virginia said sharply, "Mr. Farley, whatever you are, whatever position you hold, this is not your island, not your plantation. Before we do whatever you order us to do, we're entitled to a full explanation of your dictatorial manner. Apparently you intend to do something drastic to our plants. I want to know what that will be."

Adam gave a curt nod. "Nan's coming back and she's herded a goodly number of Negroes. I'll tell you at the same time I tell them what is to be done."

He moved away, approaching the hundred or more workers who had assembled. He called out for them to form a group and to come closer. Nanine returned to stand beside Phoebe and Virginia, who was seething with anger.

"Nan, what kind of a tyrant did you bring us?" Virginia said.

"He knows what he's doing, Virgie. He's well versed in the science of—"

"Bugs!" Virginia said sarcastically. "That's a fine vocation for a man. I've about had enough of him."

"Virgie, he's dedicated. He feared something like this."

"He's loathsome. I can't see one thing in his favor. He's so tall he's ungainly. He's so ugly. . . ."

"He is not ugly."

"What do you call that red hair, or whatever strange shade it happens to be? And his face looks as if he's been drinking too much."

"He spends almost all his time outdoors, in fields such as ours. And he's not a drinking man . . . well, not much, anyway. I think he's quite handsome."

"What do you think about him?" Virginia asked Phoebe.

"I'll withhold judgment until I find out what he's about to do. I think I know what it is, but I don't want to believe it. While you and Nan were discussing him, he sent half-a-dozen men to bring all the old rags they could find and anything they could tie the rags to."

"Nan!" Virginia cried in horror. "He told you to bring kerosene. . . ."

"He's going to burn the crop," Phoebe said.

"What good will that do? It's dead anyway," Virginia

said. "I don't think I'll give him permission to do any such thing."

"You won't have to," Nanine said quietly. "Adam can do whatever he thinks best, and you can't stop him."

"He may burn the houses, too . . ." Virginia said. "No, he's not going to burn anything!"

Four men carrying large tins of kerosene appeared and placed the cans on the ground. Adam ordered them to bring buckets, barrels, anything that would hold the kerosene. Three men scampered away to obey his commands, even seeming eager to do so. None of the Negroes hesitated. They recognized authority and jumped to answer it. Only Moses stood aside, his black face wrinkled in worry. Phoebe, watching him, thought he knew exactly what was going to happen.

In a surprisingly short time, everything was ready. Adam walked back to join them. "Now you're going to hear what I have to do. Nan, assign enough men to carry the word to every planter and their families on the island. Have them told that I'm going to burn everything on the island. Plants, brush, bushes, flowers—every growing thing is going to be put to the torch. Now! At once!"

"Now see here," Virginia began.

"*You* see here, Mrs. Birch. Unless these bugs are burned out, they'll be back next year. Maybe even burning them won't help much, but if this isn't done, you won't have a crop next year either."

"He's right, Virgie," Nanine said.

"Has anyone ever thought to ask if this trouble has traveled to the mainland?" he asked.

"Adam," Nanine said, "as I told you, we have a large plantation on the mainland, and the last I knew, there was no infestation. Virgie, have you heard about any? Phoebe?"

"No," Virginia said shortly.

"My husband runs the mainland farm, Mr. Farley,"

Phoebe said. "There is no infestation there, and I don't believe any other plantations are affected either."

"We can thank heaven for that," Adam said earnestly. "It's worried me nigh unto death. Now—I want all planters to be warned that we're coming through with torches. They are to stay in their houses. The Negroes will stay in their cabins. Nobody's going to be hurt if I'm obeyed. If I'm not, they'll have to accept the consequences. I do not intend to burn any houses or outbuildings. And that's all I have to say. As soon as things are ready, the burning begins."

"May I ask why the hurry? Can't it wait a few days?" Virginia asked.

"I'll postpone it for no more than ten minutes," Adam said. "These bugs are now foraging at their utmost to provide themselves with enough fat to last out the winter and hold them until the appearance of spring. They'll eat as much as they can, which means there'll be nothing left. The bugs have almost finished their work. What we have to do is burn them out now, without wasting any more time. In a day or two, they'll begin burrowing into the ground or crawl beneath leaves and bark. Anywhere to hide during the cold season. Now do you understand?"

Moses, who had quietly moved up, seized one of the stout branches brought by the men. He tied a thick layer of cloth around it, dipped it into a vat of kerosene, and shouted orders for his men to follow his example. Soon two hundred oil-soaked firebrands were ready for lighting.

"Reckon this heah man sho' knows whut he talkin' 'bout," Moses said. "This heah yo' plantation, Miss Virginia, Miss Nan, an' Miss Phoebe. Yo' gives the word an' we stahts burnin'."

"It seems I can't stop this," Virginia said. "If Miss Nan and Miss Phoebe agree, you may begin whenever Mr. Farley says so."

"Right now," Farley said. He clapped Moses on the shoulder. "Miss Nan told me about you, Moses. You've got more sense than these others. Dip your torch and begin right here. Send your men each end of the island and spare nothing except trees. All brush, bushes, flower gardens, and everything else is to be burned to ashes."

Moses had two men gather a few scraps of wood, douse them with kerosene, and get the small fire going. Moses then plunged his torch into the blaze. When it caught, he began moving about the plants, applying the flame as an example for the others to follow.

Virginia suddenly seized a torch from one man and stepped into the midst of the plants that Carlos had brought from Mexico. She applied the torch, nearly setting her dress on fire as she did so, then hurled the torch into the middle of that section.

"At least I'll get some some pleasure out of it," she announced.

Gradually, as the men spread out, so did the fires, and a heavy pall of smoke began to rise. A number of other planters and their families came quietly toward the mansion to stand and watch the wholesale destruction.

Adam moved efficiently among the men, directing the application of firebrands to places not burned enough to suit him. Virginia finally walked slowly to the mansion and went inside. She proceeded directly to the library and sat down. She stared straight ahead for a few moments, then burst into tears. Her weeping didn't last long. She heard Ivy hurrying down the stairs.

As she entered the library, her face was frantic with fear. "What's happening, Miss Virginia?"

"It's all right, Ivy," Virginia said. "It's become necessary to destroy all the cotton fields on the island. They're being burned out because that's the only way to get rid of those awful insects that have been killing our plants."

"But what will you do if there's no cotton?" Ivy asked.

"The man Miss Nanine brought back from Washington ordered the burning," Virginia explained. "It seems he has authority to do that, and I suppose it had to be done before those insects spread to the mainland." She paused. "I'm not so worried about us—we can weather this—but everybody else on the island is going to lose this year's crop, and for some, that could be a heavy blow. We were coming along so well here on Valcour. Let's pray we can resume next year."

"I'm sorry, Miss Virginia. I hope you can plant again next year."

"We'll know more at supper, when this man from Washington tells us what to expect and what we have to do. I'm almost afraid to hear him speak."

Ivy returned upstairs to the nursery.

Smoke had seeped into the mansion despite the fact that the doors and windows had been shut tightly by the servants. Soon Phoebe and Nanine, their dresses smudged with ashes, entered the library, pulled up chairs to face the desk, and sat down wearily.

"I hope this destruction of our crop was necessary," Virginia said.

"What crop?" Nanine asked. "There wasn't anything left. It would have had to be dug up and buried anyway."

"But in an orderly fashion. Not like this. Setting fire to the whole island. I wonder how long it will be before people from the mainland come out here to see what's going on. There's enough smoke to reach Washington—I hope."

"I expect Chris will arrive any moment," Phoebe said. "I'll be happy to see him."

"You know this had to be done," Nanine said. "There was no other way. If the weevils weren't destroyed now, they'd likely be here forever. Adam says it will be the worst blight ever to hit this nation if the insects spread to the mainland."

"Adam, Adam, is he all you can talk about?" Virginia snapped.

"One day you'll appreciate what he had to do," Nanine said firmly. "You don't have to act as if he's destroying everything on a whim. He hates to do this as much as we hate having it done."

"By the look on his face when the burning began, I didn't get that impression," Virginia commented.

"He was in the process of exterminating those insects and that must have pleased him. He wasn't happy that every plant on the island had to be destroyed. Virgie, have a little more patience."

"I agree with that," Phoebe said. "He told me he'd explain the whole thing after supper."

"What's there to explain?" Virginia asked. "Everything is burned out—destroyed. We'll be lucky if some of the buildings don't catch fire."

"You know what worries me most?" Nanine said. "It's our friends and neighbors. This is going to be very hard on them."

"They're already complaining," Virginia said. "Even before this burning they blamed me."

"In a way, they're right," Phoebe said. "It did begin here on our plantation."

Virginia rested her head against the back of her chair behind the desk and regarded the ceiling. "I wonder if we could ever have crossed one brand of cotton with another."

"It's a little late to wonder about that," Nanine said.

"In my opinion," Phoebe said, "we were the victims of a very smooth medicine man selling us an idea that was impossible to carry out."

They heard a maid open the door for Adam. He was

shown into the library, followed by Daisy, who announced
that supper would begin in ten minutes."

"Will someone show me where to wash up?" Adam said.
"I'll be down in time. God knows, I'm hungry enough."

He was smeared with soot and ash, his clothing impreg-
nated with smoke and badly soiled. Nanine brought him
to one of the guest rooms.

The sisters were seated at the supper table by the time
he came down, freshly washed and shaved and dressed in
clean clothes. He sat down and smiled warmly at Nanine.
Virginia rang the bell to summon the maid who served
them.

Afterward, in the drawing room, where coffee was
served, Adam settled down and gave them a brief education on the boll weevil.

"This," he began, "is an insidious little beast. So small
he's there before you know it. These insects wiped out
crops in early Egypt and, I suspect, in other parts of the
world. By some freak of nature, the weevils never reached
the United States."

"Until now," Virginia added grimly.

"Maybe it's confined to this island," Adam went on. "If
that's so, we're very, very lucky. It's prevalent enough in
Mexico. When I return to Washington, I'm going to send
out inspectors to comb the border states where cotton is
grown and begin a hard search for more of these pests."

"Adam," Nanine asked, "will we be able to grow a crop
next year?"

He shook his head. "Right now, I'd say you won't be
able to plant next year. It's even possible you'll never be
permitted to grow cotton on Valcour again. The risk is too
great. You'll learn that from Washington. All I can do is
submit a report."

"All because of a bug so small you can barely see it," Phoebe said.

"This is a very resourceful bug," Adam explained. "When you look casually at one of them, you can't easily notice that it has wings. They're covered while they work destroying our crops. But when they want to, they can fly. Fifty or more miles, looking for more food. They have snouts that can drill into flower buds and eat the juices inside. But it's even worse when the female lays an egg into the puncture they created. The egg hatches into a grub that eats the heart out of the bolls; when the bolls drop to the ground, that's the end of the plant, for it produces no seed and no cotton."

"There are so many plants, so many buds," Virginia argued.

"Mrs. Birch, a weevil larva becomes an adult in twenty days. And each female lays hundreds of eggs. If they ever cross the border, I swear they'll spread like—like the fires we just lit. And nothing can stop them. A few hundred— or less—can multiply to thousands in a few weeks. There's no stopping them."

"Will fire stop them?" Phoebe asked.

"It's the only recourse we have. Now, I've studied these insects. I know a great deal about them. I won't bore you with the details, but I'll explain the reason I had to burn everything so quickly. As I told you, the weevil has to hibernate in cold weather. But before that happens, it has to eat enough to provide fat to see it through the winter. So, if we burn them now, before they disappear until spring, we can eradicate most of them. On an island like this, I hope we eradicated all of them. But we can't be sure. Whether or not you can ever grow cotton here again is problematical. The odds are against it for a long time."

"Adam explained most of this to me in Washington," Nanine said. "The trouble is that some of the weevils will get away, will hide somewhere and last the winter. If there are only a few, they will emerge in warm weather, when the plants are in bed, and start eating again."

"And proliferating again, like wildfire," Adam added. "That's why I can't promise you'll be able to grow another crop. Perhaps never. I'm sorry, but that's the way it is. Believe me, whoever gave you those infested plants didn't do you any favors."

"How well I know," Virginia said. "I'm resigned to it, but I'm certain the neighbors aren't."

Phoebe nodded. "We'll be hearing from them tomorrow."

"We had no choice," Nanine said. "We've done the only thing possible. Thank God I went to Washington. If we'd let it go, the mainland would have been affected."

"Let's hope it hasn't been," Virginia said.

Adam finished his coffee. "I'd best take a tour of the island now, to look for sparks or untouched places. I'll need a lantern, if you'll be so kind."

"We'll need two lanterns," Nanine said. "I'm going along."

Adam gave Nanine a broad smile. "I was hoping you would."

Phoebe and Virginia watched them leave the room. In the hall, they saw Adam look down and give Nanine an adoring smile. His arm went around her shoulders as they headed for the service pantry where the lanterns were kept.

The two sisters exchanged knowing looks.

"Do you think we have a romance in the making?" Phoebe asked.

Virginia's smile was almost envious. "I'd say a torrid one. Nanine isn't even shy with him. And she was eager to have him to herself."

Phoebe nodded. "She deserves happiness. She's given so much of herself to others."

Virginia looked thoughtful. "Did you ever see two sisters as different as Nanine and me?"

"No," Phoebe admitted. "Nor did I ever see two as loyal. It balances out."

"You must miss Chris terribly," Virginia said.

"I do. But he understands this is a very trying time for you."

"No need for you to remain here now," Virginia said. "The crisis—or crises—are over."

"Not quite. I want to be here when the islanders confront you. And I'm certain they'll lose no time in doing it. Now, I'm going to bed. I'm exhausted. It's been quite a day."

"Quite a day," Virginia repeated. "I guess I like Adam after all."

Phoebe laughed. "You may as well. He'll be around for a long time. Or if not here, at least in the family."

"I hope so," Virginia said. "I want Nanine to feel the completeness of love."

Phoebe gave her a startled look. "Completeness?"

"Fulfillment," Virginia said quietly. "Miles was much too ill. He was reluctant to marry Nan because of that. I told him that for her, the marriage would be consummated when he placed the ring on her finger."

Phoebe looked at her in surprise. "She's practically a saint."

Virginia smiled. "I think with Adam she'll be quite a woman. Quite a woman. I'm going upstairs, too. Nan will lock up the house for the night. Besides, it will be nicer for them to come in and be alone together."

At first, Nanine and Adam walked down the worn path toward the dock. Each carried a lighted lantern. The night was sultry, heavy with the acrid smell of ash. But the moonlight was bright, its glow revealing the destruction.

The beauty of Valcour had ceased to exist. Everywhere there was ash, blackened earth, trees with their lower branches seared. Where lovely gardens had bloomed there was now only a heap of twisted, half-consumed branches, stouter than those that had succumbed to the flames.

Adam stopped and looked around. "It looks like the entrance to hell," he said. "Nan, you have no idea how much it pained me to do this."

"I know," she said. "But it is . . . sad. Will there be a next year for us on Valcour? Please be honest."

"The weevil is a hardy bug. Even with all this destruction, some will survive. It requires very few to produce another generation, which will only destroy everything again."

"I don't know what we'll do. Oh, not us so much, but the others who live here and depend on cotton for a living."

"They'll have to be told," Adam said. He took Nanine's elbow gently and they continued their slow walk to the dock. "Under no circumstances can the government allow cotton to be grown when there is danger that the weevil will multiply. If the few left are confined to this island, in another year they'll have starved to death. That is the theory we have. Yet, we might be wrong. They might survive. If they do, there's always the chance that some might get to the mainland. Perhaps in something you ship there, or on clothing; they might even establish themselves as passengers on the many boats tied up around the island. You have no comprehension of what would happen if only a few migrated. The way they multiply, they'd overrun the mainland in two or three years. The damage they'd do can't be calculated. It would be a catastrophe. Washington will not permit that."

"I've thought of that, Adam. I suppose, sooner or later, the weevils will cross the border."

"I've repeatedly warned of that. I'm only half-believed, but it's coming."

"Then I can see your reluctance to allow more cotton to be grown here. It's to the benefit of the South that you not permit it."

Adam came to stop. He faced Nanine. "What do you mean?"

"The war ended with the South in ruins. Cotton will restore us, bring back at least a portion of what the South used to be. We need time for that. A few years while cotton-growing flourishes. We need time, and cotton, to get back on our feet."

"Well said. You're an amazing woman, Nanine."

"It's just common sense."

"Yes, but you have more of it than average. I must confess that Valcour looked enchanting when we approached it today. It's one of the loveliest places I've ever seen. Or was," he added ruefully, "before I set it on fire."

"It was necessary. In fact, when everybody gets used to what happened and understands the reasons why, they'll be glad to endure this, whatever is in store."

"Next year," he said, "the island will be green again, there'll be flowers and shrubs. The dwellings may need painting. The smoke and ash didn't do them any good."

"But there will be no cotton."

"No cotton," Adam repeated soberly.

"What must be, must be," Nanine said. "Are we going to look for sparks, perhaps small fires?"

"That was an excuse to get you out here with me. Just the two of us. There are no sparks, no fires."

"I see." Nanine studied Adam's face in the moonlight. "Is there a purpose to this?"

"Haven't you guessed, Nan?"

She nodded slowly. "I suppose I have, but I can't believe it."

"I'm an ornery, outspoken cuss," he said. "I don't hesitate to say what I mean, and I mean what I say. I fell in love with you the moment you were escorted into my office. I don't know why I knew it then, ten seconds after I laid eyes on you. They say it happens that way sometimes. Rarely, I suppose."

"Rarely," Nanine agreed. "Very rarely, Adam. That's why I have a hard time believing it."

"Oh," he said with a resigned sigh.

She reached up and cupped his face with her hands. "But I do believe it, Adam."

He stared at her. "Really? You do?"

"When you took my hand for the first time, greeting me, I fell in love with you."

"I'll be damned," he said, unable to think of anything else.

"I'd rather you felt blessed, not damned," she said. "It's come to me late in life. I'm already into my thirties. But I welcome it as I've welcomed nothing before. Adam, if you don't take me in your arms and kiss me, I'll have to kiss you. I prefer that you make the first gesture of affection."

His arms enclosed her, gently at first, and his kiss was almost shy. Not because of himself, but because, despite her maturity, there was a sweet innocence about her.

Still holding her, he stepped back. "Isn't there someplace we can go? There's not even a place to sit down here."

"Come." She took his hand and, with each of them still holding a lantern, led him down the incline to the boathouse. "There's a room in here that used to be Papa's. He used to come here to engage in liaisons with slaves. For some reason, I had one of the house servants keep it up. I don't think even Virginia and Phoebe are aware of the room, or at least that it's been kept up."

"What made you do it?"

Nanine laughed softly. "I could say I knew that one day

a gentleman would ask me if there was someplace he could bring me and I'd have it ready. But that wouldn't be the truth. The truth is, I just wanted to. Despite his weaknesses, Papa was good and kind and generous—to his family and to his slaves."

"I'm eager to see it," Adam said.

The main room contained a low bench, some tools, and scraps of lumber. Nanine lifted her lantern and led Adam to the next room. It was a narrow room, holding only a bed, a few chairs, and a small table on which were twin lamps. There were no wall decorations, but a small braided rug covered the floor in front of the bed.

Adam closed the door and looked at her. "I didn't expect this."

"Have I shocked you?" she asked.

"No. I want you desperately. My body is crying out for you. Are you offended?"

"No, Adam," she said quietly. "Because mine hungers for love. The love of a good man."

"Oh, Nanine, I love you madly."

He took the lantern from her and set them both on the floor close to the door. His arms enclosed her again and he drew her to him, firmly this time. Her face raised for his kiss and her arms went around his neck. This time their embrace was demanding and his hands moved down to her buttocks. He pressed her so close that she could feel the maleness of him. A soft cry escaped her. He moaned in reply. Then he lifted her gently onto the bed and began fumbling with her clothes. Her half-laugh was almost a cry of impatience, for she was as eager as he.

She removed her garments as quickly as he did his, and she lay there, arms extended, waiting for his body to cover her. His hands caressed her bare skin and his mouth moved over her face, her neck, and down to her breasts.

He had aroused her so that her body was moving ceaselessly against his and she spoke his name repeatedly.

Her hands were exploring, seeking, and finally, when she felt she could no longer stand the waiting, she arched her body and, hands against his buttocks, pressed him to her. As he closed the distance between them, his mouth covered hers. When he penetrated her, she stifled her cry, moaning instead, then gave herself up to the ecstasy of their passion. For a moment he paused, but he could no more hold back than she, and their cries and moans mingled until their passion was spent.

Only then, after he'd turned her so that her body rested on top of his, did he speak.

"My God, Nan! You were a virgin!"

"Yes. I suppose I should have told you."

"Why didn't you? Nan, for God's sake . . . !"

"Don't be alarmed, my darling Adam. I didn't tell you because I was afraid you might—not take me. I ached to have you. I wanted the wonderful feeling of being a complete woman. To know what it is like to be possessed by a man. A man I love. Even if you don't love me. It doesn't matter. I know now, and it was the most wonderful, most beautiful experience I've ever known."

His hands held her head and his eyes devoured her. "I know I'm sane. I know what happened—what I did. And I do love you. But you told me you were a widow."

"I am, Adam. I married a man I loved with all my heart. He was dying when I met him, dying when I married him, and after a few short months he did die."

"I don't know what to say."

"If in doubt, just say you love me," she said with a smile. "It was so strange, Adam. I guess I loved him in a special way because he was dying of a sickness that almost killed me. I was lucky. A cure came in time for me, but too late for him. Oh yes, I loved him, even though he killed my brother, Marty."

"He . . . killed your brother?"

"It does sound weird, doesn't it? Miles, my husband, fought a duel with my brother. Miles sought the duel because he wanted someone to kill him, he was that ill. My brother was fighting for something called pride. My brother fired first. I'm sure he missed on purpose, but some say he was suffering from a hangover so severe that his hand was shaking. Miles definitely intended to miss. He moved his pistol to one side of the target. My brother moved at the same instant, directly into the line of fire. It wasn't murder, it wasn't a duelist's bullet that killed him. It was an accident."

"My God, you're quite a family."

"Does it frighten you? Do I frighten you?"

"No to both questions. I want to marry you. The quicker the better."

"The quicker the better for me, too," Nanine replied, kissing him.

"Lady, if you have anything more to tell me, you'd better stop that," he cautioned.

"Very well." She laughed. "I'll tell you, then we'll start over again."

"Are you sure? After all, it's the first time and that . . ."

"No excuses from you. All the first time did was make me want the second, third, fourth, and—on and on and on."

"Start talking," Adam pleaded, "or the on and on and on will start."

She laughed, then grew serious as she told him about Phoebe's life.

"I thought I recognized her!" Adam exclaimed. "I saw her perform in New York and enjoyed it. She is gifted."

"She's married now to Chris Savard, who runs our

plantation on the mainland. Phoebe stayed here with Virgie because Virgie's son was kidnapped by a man who has just been hanged. Bradley Culver, the outlaw."

"Everyone's heard of him. Now, what's outrageous about Virgie? There must be something. This family is so full of surprises my head is spinning."

"Virginia loves too much, too often, and recklessly. Then there's Mama, who has just married Colonel Zachary Spires, whose plantation on the mainland adjoins ours."

"Oh, Lord," he said, "how are you ever going to leave them?"

"Leave?" She became instantly serious.

"My work is in Washington and all around the country. I keep moving."

"You could give it up, Adam. You'd be surprised how much money there is in this family."

"No," he said. "We'll not talk about that. I like my job and I like the experience I'm getting, because I do have ambition for something more than to hunt bugs."

"And what might that be? Not that I care a hoot, as long as it's something you want to do."

"I'm going to become a landscaping engineer. I want to design great estates and public parks. I want to create beauty. Mainly because I'm no beauty myself. Are you positive you want to marry me?"

"You're handsome," she said, lighthearted again. "The most handsome man in the world. And I wonder what you see in me. I used to be called an old maid, and there were moments when I felt like one. I never dared dream that one day I'd have a family. Now I can dare hope."

"I still don't know what to say. I need time."

"How long will you stay on Valcour?"

"Not long. Only long enough to go over the island and look for any weevils that may have hidden away and escaped the flames. If I find many, I'll have to go back immediately and help prepare some substance with which to poison them."

"I hope you'll be back soon, Adam. I want to be with you."

"Oh, you will. From now on, every day and night. Always."

"But you said you had to go back."

"We'll be married first and you can come with me."

Nanine rested her head against his chest. "I always dreamed of being married on Valcour, with lots of people, flowers, everything pretty and fresh. Oh, Adam, you shouldn't have burned everything first."

"I had to, even if I'd had any idea that this was going to happen. Our marriage must be hasty. It's what I want more than anything. I hope you do, too."

"Oh, I do, my darling. I can't wait. And we're talking too much."

"Are you sure you want to? After all, it's the first time."

"I don't want to stop there. I've waited so long."

Nanine raised herself and kissed him passionately as her hands moved down to his groin.

He moaned and turned her onto her back, covering her again.

They lay there another hour, making love and making plans. They decided to be married in Charleston so that Nanine could return to Washington with him. Nanine suggested that Lenore and the Colonel be witnesses to their wedding. Chris and Phoebe would attend also. In that way, Adam could meet the entire family, except for Elias and Jimmy.

Nanine said, "Maybe we ought to walk about some, with the lanterns. By now my sisters must be wondering what's happened to us. We don't want to surprise them too much, do we, Adam?"

"I agree we should do some inspection of the island. I'm

sorry I had to destroy its beauty. How I hated those insects! But I don't mind them now. Can you imagine two people falling in love because bugs brought them together?"

They picked up their lanterns and left the boathouse. They walked back toward the mansion, then skirted it and took another path. Adam stopped, peeled bark off a tree trunk, and held up his lantern to study the bared spot.

"Full of 'em," he said.

Nanine peered at the spot. "They must be smaller than usual."

"You can't see them? They have to be there, my dear Nan. They must be there, because if they're not, what excuse can I give to come back to Valcour?"

"I see them now," she said. "It's alive with them."

"We'll leave for Washington tomorrow and stop at Charleston to get married. I'll make my report and then we'll come back."

"Is there any special hurry tonight?" she asked.

"Not that I know of."

"Couldn't we go back to the boathouse again?"

"There is a certain charm to that place," he said sharply.

Though Adam's baggage had been placed in Lenore's suite, he spent the night in Nanine's room. As Nanine expressed it, "There's no need for us to be hypocritical, and besides, we're going to be married in the morning."

Neither Virginia nor Phoebe was surprised when Nanine broke the news at the breakfast table the next morning. Both Virginia and Phoebe kissed Nanine and expressed their happiness.

"I thought it would be nice to have Mama and the Colonel as matron of honor and best man," Nanine said. "We'd like it also, Phoebe, if you and Chris could attend."

"I'm sure he'll be as eager to be there as I am," Phoebe

replied enthusiastically. "I just wish you could come too, Virgie."

"So do I," she replied. "But I expect trouble here later today. I just wish you didn't have to leave so soon for Washington."

"I must, Virgie," Adam said. "The Farm Bureau must be informed of this as soon as possible. They'll want to organize an immediate search for boll weevils along the border. That's of the utmost importance."

"Have you any special instructions for us on Valcour now that the burning is over?" she asked.

"None, other than to keep an eye out for stray plants that were not burned. Destroy them at once."

"May we plant in the spring? That's what I really want to know. At least, with that news I'd have some hope for the islanders when they come here."

"I wouldn't advise it. In fact, Virgie, I may have to issue a formal order prohibiting replanting. I'm sorry, but I think by now you realize what a problem these weevils can be. They could destroy the financial status of the South as much as the war did. And you do have your mainland plantation to consider."

"Yes," Virginia admitted. "We understand."

"Good." Adam looked relieved at her common-sense attitude. "Nan and I will be off as soon as I finish this coffee. It's damn good. So was the breakfast. I was starved."

"So was I," Nanine said, giving Adam an angelic smile. He bent down and kissed her brow.

Virginia and Phoebe smiled knowingly, for they understood the real reason behind Nanine's and Adam's voracious appetites. They'd had second helpings of everything. Adam was now on his fourth cup of coffee, Nanine on her second.

He had just taken a final sip of coffee and was about to stand when the sound of voices reached them.

"Oh dear," Virginia said, rising. "It's happening sooner than I expected. Excuse me."

"Is it the neighbors?" Adam asked.

Virginia nodded.

"Then I'll accompany you outside. They'll have to obey my orders."

"I suggest the four of us go outside," Nanine said.

They walked briskly out to the veranda, where the neighbors were gathering below the steps. The four stood patiently until those who were trailing behind joined the group. Mr. Langan, who had been an unsettling influence on Virginia since he'd complained about the weevils, took command.

He looked around to make certain he had everyone's attention, then turned to face the four on the veranda. "We're all here," he announced, "and I don't mind saying that we're damn angry. We want a full explanation."

"We've lost almost everything," Mrs. Damon added, but not belligerently. "There's nothing left but our homes."

"How do we support them?" Mrs. Langan was as antagonistic as her husband. "Where's the money coming from with you people ruining the crop? Burning it, no less."

"It was ruined before we burned it." Adam glanced at Nanine and Virginia and received their nods of assent. "The weevils destroyed the crop, not the fire. That destroyed the weevils, we hope and pray."

"What do we do now? Just wait until next year?" Langan demanded. There was some muttering from the group.

"There will be little to wait for," Adam explained. "You cannot plant cotton next year. Not for several years, perhaps. And I officially make that an order. If my order is disobeyed, I'll haul any offender into court."

"What right do you have to give orders?" Langan demanded.

Adam could hear whispers including the word *Yankee*. He held up his hands for attention. "I'm an official of the Farm Bureau in Washington. You might also recall that Washington is the capital of our country. We have in mind only what is good for you and for the nation. Cotton grown here can present a terrible hazard if the weevils spread. So, if any remain, they must be confined to the island."

Mr. Damon spoke up. "We don't take to that very kindly. How do we know those damned bugs are dangerous?"

Virginia attempted to reason with the angry group. "Have you folks forgotten what your cotton plants looked like before they were burned? They were dead—no blossoms, no cotton. Just dead stalks. And the same thing likely will happen next year if you plant."

"If you do," Adam added, "I'll be back and burn you out again. This is a most serious matter and my orders are not to be disobeyed. Nor even trifled with. There is to be no experimentation to see if the weevils are still here. Not one cotton plant can be grown. That's an order. I'll be back to make sure it's obeyed."

"Bear with us," Virginia said. "We've been through a lot together. We're friends. We've known one another most of our lives. We can't let a thing like this break us up."

"Ain't nothing left to break up," Langan called out.

"Give us a little time to plan, to look into the future," Virginia pleaded. "Mr. Farley and Nanine are going to Washington to report. And we would like all of you to know that Nanine and Mr. Farley are going to be married."

"Now that's the ultimate!" Langan called out. "Nanine is marrying the man who destroyed the island."

"Adam saved this island," Virginia said heatedly. "He didn't bring the weevils here. He came to destroy them."

"We know that," Langan persisted. "We know who brought the bugs. We know who brought that Mexican here. And you can bet your life we're not taking any blame for what happened. And we're not going to just let it all go, either."

"Come back tomorrow," Virginia said. "All of you. Or we'll meet in the schoolhouse if you like. Then we'll discuss the situation and try to find a sensible solution. I'm sorry, but Nan and Mr. Farley must leave now."

The meeting ended reluctantly, with the neighbors talking among themselves, some with considerable anger. Not until after the last one had turned away did the four on the veranda go into the house.

"It isn't fair that you remain here and share their enmity by yourself," Nanine said to Virginia.

"I'm reponsible for it," Virginia replied. "I'll feel better facing up to them alone. Don't worry about it. If you think you'll not be back shortly, I'll write you and keep you informed."

"Adam may not know until he returns to Washington and gets his instructions. Please come upstairs with me, Virgie. I have a little gift I brought Jimmy back from Washington."

Phoebe and Adam had moved into the drawing room, where they were discussing the altercation that had occurred outside. Upstairs, in Nanine's suite, her bag on the floor beside Adam's knapsack, Nanine handed Virginia a box wrapped in fancy paper and tied with ribbon.

"This was thoughtful of you, Nan," Virginia said, "but when were you ever otherwise?"

"No need to open it now. It's a silver cup. I really had another reason for asking you up here. Adam and I didn't go outside last night to look for boll weevils. We wanted to be alone. We went to the boathouse."

"You don't have to explain. Don't you suppose I've been through that?"

"I have to ask you to have Daisy change the bed linen in

the boathouse," Nanine said. "We used the room Papa used for his liaisons with his slaves."

"My God!" Virginia exclaimed. "I'd forgotten about that room. I'll see that it's taken care of."

"Thanks," Nanine said. "I always had it kept up. Daisy took care of it. I'm glad she's in the house now. We can trust her."

"Yes," Virginia said. "I may give her the responsibility of Jimmy. I'm sending Ivy to the private school we helped to endow. I want her to have a higher education."

"That's good of you," Nanine said. "Does she know what she wants to do?"

"Run a hotel," Virginia said, then laughed at Nanine's stunned expression. "Don't worry, she'll settle for less."

"That's a relief," Nanine said, joining Virginia in laughter. "As for Daisy, I don't think she'll want to relinquish her position in the kitchen. She's quite proud of that. And she's good."

"Then she can select one of the young girls to look after Jimmy, though I'd like her to sleep in the playroom adjoining the nursery."

"Are you still worried?" Nanine asked. "About Jimmy's safety?"

"Not a bit. At least that crisis is ended."

"Things will work out," Nanine said. "I'm as sorry as you about what happened to our cotton."

"It's a bitter pill to swallow," Virginia said. "It's a cruel realization I have to confront myself with—that Valcour might never again grow cotton."

"Try not to be too discouraged," Nanine said. "It might be for the best."

"I'd like to think that, Nan." Virginia tried to keep her tone light. "But I'm responsible for what happened here. I made a fool of myself, and in doing so I've hurt you,

Mama, and Phoebe. We've lost the income we got from the cotton grown here."

"Will you write Elias about it?"

"Phoebe asked me the same question. The answer is no. I told her to do it."

"Can't you swallow your pride?" Nanine asked gently. "One can be very lonely with nothing but pride to see them through day after day."

"Has Elias expressed the slightest desire to see me?" she asked.

"No. But then, he's never written to me at all."

"He hasn't to me either—not really. Just business letters."

"You can't expect him to take the first step," Nanine replied.

"Please, I don't want to talk about him."

Nanine nodded understandingly and changed the subject. "Do you know, I haven't seen Mama since she went to visit the Colonel. I'm really looking forward to it."

"You'll be amazed at the change in her," Virginia said. "She's not like the Mama we knew. She laughs a lot, she's vivacious, and she has a much greater interest in clothes. The Colonel is as happy as she. I imagine he indulges her slightest whim."

"Do you think she'll be upset with me for making such a hasty marriage?"

"It's no more hasty than her own. And I'll tell you something that may amuse you. I attempted to dissuade her from marrying, because I believed she would not want to fulfill her vows. She not only reminded me that she'd had three children, but said that she and the Colonel had already made love!"

"I'm afraid we misjudged Mama," Nanine said.

"No matter. She's happy now and so is the Colonel. They're like two lovebirds. So don't have any misgivings that she'll start scolding you."

Nanine laughed. "That's good news. To think we believed we got our lustiness from Papa. No doubt Mama contributed her share."

"I'm sure of it." Virginia reached for a parasol that lay on the bed. "I'll carry this down for you."

Ivy stepped into the room and smiled at Nanine. "Miss Phoebe just told me the good news. I came to wish you happiness, Miss Nanine, and to carry down the baggage."

"One of the boatmen can do that, Ivy," Virginia said.

"They're down at the dock already. Please let me."

"Thank you, Ivy," Nanine said. "I'd like you at the dock to wave me off."

Virginia and Nanine followed Ivy from the room. Nanine said, "I must tell you that Adam and I won't be living here or on the mainland."

"Why not?" Virginia's tone revealed her shock at the news.

"He wants to be a landscape engineer. To lay out the grounds of huge estates and museums and public parks. He said it would take us all over the world. However, we'll be back for visits."

"I hope so," Virginia said soberly. "When will we see you again?"

"Oh, I'm speaking of the future. Until it's certain that the boll-weevil threat is eradicated, Adam will remain with the Farm Bureau."

"That's a relief. I couldn't bear the thought of not seeing you for any length of time. Not just now. Too much has happened."

Nanine cast a sideways glance at her sister. She wanted to take her in her arms and comfort her, but she felt that was the last thing Virginia wanted. She couldn't help but feel left out of things, with Phoebe newly married and Nanine about to be. Even their mother, had found a mate. Nanine knew that Virginia was an intelligent woman, even a resourceful one. She'd proved that during the war years. But she was a highly passionate woman, one who desperately needed a man's love. There was nothing Nanine could say that would lift Virginia's spirits.

They reached the dock and saw Moses there; he had come to bid them farewell. He approached Nanine first.

"Missy Nan, I jes' heerd the news 'bout yo' marryin' Mistuh Adam. Miss Phoebe done tol' me. Wishes yo' all the luck yo' gots comin' to you'. An' that all the luck in the worl'."

"Thank you, Moses." Nanine hugged him and Adam shook his hand. Nanine and Virginia embraced, then Virginia embraced Phoebe, and Adam helped them onto the boat.

Phoebe called, "I'll be back soon and we'll work things out. Take care now."

Virginia and Moses stood on the dock and watched the boat move into the intercoastal waterway. Phoebe looked back and waved.

"Somehow," Virginia said, 'I have a feeling that Valcour is never going to be the same again, Moses."

"Reckon tha's the way I been thinkin', Miss Virginia. "Yo' reckon it goin' to be good o' bad?"

"With your help, Moses, it's not going to be all bad. We'll think of something."

"Ain't goin' to be easy." They began their walk back to the mansion. "All I knows is how to grow cotton."

"What worries me is what we are going to do with the help. Without the fields to tend, we surely don't need many hired hands here now."

"They's thinkin' that too," Moses said. "Got 'em mighty worried. An' reckon yo' knows the white folks gettin' mad 'cause they crops burned. Reckon they goin' to make trouble?"

"I know it. And I dread it. But we'll think of a way out of this trouble. Maybe we ought to grow something else."

"Eatin' crops, ma'am? Reckon we kin grow 'em, but they ain't much o' a money crop."

"We grew exceptional cotton here," Virginia said. "You know that. We'd never have been as prosperous with ordinary cotton. With farm crops, the competition will be so severe we'd barely make ends meet. We're in for some hard times, Moses."

"Reckon so, missy, but we sho' had 'em while the wah goin' on, an' we hurts some, but we sho' got through it mighty fine. O' course, Mistuh Elias he'p mos'. Got a head on his shoulders. Wukked till he 'bout ready to drop. Sho' misses him. Reckon he evah comes back?"

"Reckon not, Moses. He likes where he is. Anyway, I don't want him back."

"Whut 'bout Mastuh Jimmy?" Moses ventured. "He need a papa."

"I'll have to be both mama and papa to him."

"If it the way you say, reckon yo' will."

"Don't be too discouraged about Valcour. Tell the help they'll be paid on time and in full, even if they don't have to work. When we decide if there's something we can do, we'll let them know. We hope they can stay here, but we can't promise them anything until we know ourselves."

"Yes'm. Reckon they knows that. Tells 'em soon's I gets down to the qua'ters. Puts 'em to cleanin' fo' now. I thanks yo', missy, fo' whut yo' doin' fo' all o' us."

"You deserve it."

Moses tipped his hat and went off to dispense the news. Virginia entered the house and for a few moments stood in the middle of the drawing room. The silence of the house bore down on her and she felt surrounded by loneliness. She'd never known anything like it before. It was an unsettling experience.

The house had always been filled with laughter and good times, until the war. She sat down slowly on one of the chairs and thought back to the days when she was seventeen. When she was delighted to flirt with every good-looking boy who came along—and there were plenty of them. She recalled her father and almost wept for him. She remembered Marty, her brother. The memories were too bitter. She went into the library, but there the loneliness was even worse. For a time she tried to catch up with some of the bookwork, but she couldn't put her mind to it. She took a walk around the island for an hour, but the acrid odor that still filled the air only increased her despondency. She walked down to the water and spotted the boathouse, went inside, and saw the bed in disarray.

She recalled Nanine's request that she ask Daisy to change the bed linen there. She went back to the house and found Daisy alone in the kitchen. Her face brightened at the sight of Virginia.

"Be glad to, Miss Virgie," Daisy said when Virginia asked her to change the linen. "Haven't had a chance to tell yo' befo' that I real happy to have charge in the kitchen. Allus wanted to, an' yo' papa done tol' me that one day I would. Loves cookin' an' loves watchin' oveh yo' an' yo' sistuhs an' yo' li'l boy. Mastuh Jimmy a real sharp youngstuh."

"Why didn't you start working in the kitchen when Papa told you that you could?" Virginia asked.

"That Belle, she got nex' to yo' mama, an' I guesses that yo' papa don' wants no troubles. It all right. I gots in when they was parties. But that Belle, she real jealous an' mean. Don' lets her fool yo', Miss Virgie. She loved it heah 'cause she the queen, an' she nevah thought she would have to leaves, 'spite o' all her fussin'."

"Well, she's gone now, Daisy, and we're very pleased with your cooking. You're better than Belle."

"Knows it even iffen I says so. But I'm happy to be in the house fo' all time."

"Oh, Ivy may be going to school on the mainland, and I'll want you to sleep in the playroom that adjoins Jimmy's nursery."

Daisy beamed. "That be the very nices' thing yo' could let me do. Do I still stays in the kitchen?"

"You do. And you and Ivy can talk about another girl to look after my son in the daytime."

"Be glad to, Miss Virgie. Real glad to. I'll ten' to the boathouse right away. Miss Nanine real sentimental 'bout that room, an' I changes that bed eve'y othuh week. Nevah tol' a livin' soul."

Daisy left the house to perform her chore and Virginia went upstairs to Jimmy's room. Her heart soared when he extended his arms to her when she entered the nursery. She excused Ivy because she wanted to enjoy her son in privacy. He was a delight. He couldn't talk yet, but he babbled happily. This was no lonely world for him. He was learning to walk, and his antics gave her something to smile about, something to watch and store in her mind.

However, he finally tired and began to doze off. She undressed him, placed him in his crib, and watched him as sleep crept over him. He did resemble Brad. She shuddered inwardly as she thought of him. She'd avoided thinking about him, and despite the dreadful discovery Adam had made, at least her mind had been so occupied that she'd not had time to think of what she'd done.

When Ivy returned, Virginia remained for a time, trying to think of things to talk about with the pretty ex-slave. She asked Ivy about the books she was reading, and the girl talked excitedly about them, but even that subject exhausted itself. Then she mentioned that she thought Ivy should start school in the autumn. In a way, Virginia dreaded it, because the house would be lonelier than ever.

She met Daisy in the hall when she went downstairs. "I put some food on the table fo' yo', Miss Virgie. I knows yo' is lonely an' the house awful quiet, but yo' gots to eat."

"Thanks, Daisy, I will." She went to the table but found she had no appetite. She returned to the library and worked there until it was time for supper. Daisy had prepared a delicious chicken stew. Virginia ate a fair amount so as not to disappoint Daisy, then closed and locked the house and went upstairs.

She was in bed before ten. She turned down the bedside lamp and settled herself for sleep, but it refused to come. She blew out the lamp and tried again. At last she began to doze, and then came sleep and with it a dream that turned into a nightmare.

She saw a man standing at a barred window with his arms outstretched and his face tense, waiting for a bullet. It was so real, so frightening. She saw him rear back, his face bullet pierced and bloody, his features contorted into a red mask of horror.

She tried to wake up, to escape the dream, but it went on. He was standing at the barred window again, looking at her with a silent plea in his eyes. Then the blood again, the horror, and she thought she screamed, but she wasn't sure. She had to get away from this nightmare, but she seemed to be frozen there, seeing the face and the eyes again and again, watching the features smashed by a bullet she had fired. She moaned aloud and there was a crash. She sat up, befuddled by the nightmare; but the crash hadn't seemed a part of it.

She was badly frightened, and she almost screamed, holding back only because it would wake Ivy and she'd be unable to explain why she had screamed.

Yet, the crashing sound seemed far more real than the nightmare. She swung her legs off the bed, found a match, and lit the lamp. She sat there listening intently. She heard voices and then another crashing sound. This time she knew what it was. Someone had hurled something through one of the downstairs windows. She hastily slipped into a robe and slippers. Seizing the lamp, she hurried along the upstairs corridor. below, she heard the excited voices of servants who had been awakened in their downstairs rooms.

Daisy met Virginia at the bottom of the staircase.

"What's going on, Daisy?" Virginia asked.

"Don' rightly know, Miss Virgie. Two windows been busted. I fin's this heah rock on the flo'."

She held up a large stone. "Busted 'nothuh window. Ain't looked theah fo' a stone, but reckon that's whut busted the second window."

Virginia hurried into the library and opened the gun rack. She grabbed the rifle with which she'd killed Brad, it felt white-hot to the touch. She dropped it as if her hands had been burned. She turned away from the gun rack and, with as much resolution as before, went out to the veranda where she peered into the dark and listened intently.

There was no one in sight; not a sound disturbed the quiet of the night. She called out, "You cowards! If you've something to say in your anger, come to me and say it. Come now! If you have the courage to do so.."

Silence answered her. She stood there a few more minutes shivering in the night chill before she turned away. The cook and one of the maids were at work picking up the shards of glass. The cook displayed a second stone.

"I'll have someone repair the windows in the morning," Virginia said. "Thank you for helping me."

The racket had awakened Ivy. She was in a nightgown and robe, standing outside the nursery.

"Go back to bed," Virginia told her. "It was just some of the neighbors telling me they didn't like the burning of their crops. Some people have strange ways to deliver a message."

"Yes, Miss Virginia," Ivy said softly. "They scared me some. But Master Jimmy didn't wake up."

"They scared me, too," Virginia said. To herself she admitted that the stoning of the house was a blessing, for it had awakened her from that horrible dream.

Now she was afraid to go back to sleep, fearing that the nightmare would return. She sat in a chair and tried to read. At dawn she was still in the chair, dozing. Mercifully, the dream had not returned, but as she woke she wondered if this would be a nightly occurrence. If this was what being lonely would bring, she feared it. Or was it what she had done? Was it her conscience smiting her? Why had Brad chosen her to kill him, when he still had his band of outlaws who would do it for him? Was it his way of punishing her?

She bathed and dressed, taking her time, every motion studied. There was no need to hurry. No one would be waiting downstairs. Virginia grimaced at the sight of the broken dining-room windows. She went out to the veranda and stood there for a time, waiting for someone to come by. She was angry and wanted someone on which to vent her anger, but it seemed that the neighbors were staying away, just as angry as she. She couldn't really blame them. She smiled bitterly.

Elias certainly had his revenge. She'd paid dearly for her gamble with Carlos. And now the islanders were paying also. She'd restored the island only to end up destroying it.

Carlos had known about the boll weevils. That's what he'd meant when he told Brad he would get even with them. She wondered if she would ever have peace of mind. If she would ever know tranquility again.

Back in the dining room, the morning air coming through the broken windows made the room cold and uncomfortable. She arranged to have a small breakfast served in the library.

With the tray finally on the desk, she ate a few hot biscuits, but pushed aside the eggs and settled for coffee. Eating alone was an ordeal. Especially since she was still shaken by her nightmare and the crash of broken windows.

She raised her coffee cup like a wineglass. "Goddamn the war. Goddamn the weevils. Goddamn people who are cowards. Goddamn . . ." She had almost said Elias, but her tongue stumbled on her husband's name.

FOURTEEN

Virginia arranged with Moses to have the windows repaired. When she returned to the dining room for her midday meal, the sense of loneliness again asserted itself. More than once she almost addressed the empty chairs where Nanine and Phoebe usually sat. She was still angry at the neighbors who had broken the windows, though she was glad it had happened, for the sound had broken her awful nightmare of pained faces, bloody faces. Even now, on this bright summer morning, she shuddered at the memory of it.

She decided to call an afternoon meeting at the schoolhouse and asked Moses to send men to invite every resident of the island. She spent the rest of the morning with Jimmy and Ivy. She was slowly recovering from her anger, and by the time set for the meeting she was calm, unafraid to face the censure she knew was coming, and determined to find a way out of this predicament.

She walked down to the schoolhouse. As she passed the row of old slave cabins, now updated into comfortable dwellings, she stopped often to talk to the ex-slaves; they, too, were concerned with the future, now that the cotton crop had failed. Virginia did her best to reassure them, though there were moments when she doubted what she told them. But this was no time to upset them. The white population was enough of a challenge.

She was proud of the schoolhouse. It was large,

comfortable, and had all the facilities of a city school, and likely more than that. The Negro children on Valcour were now getting a good education. She acknowledged that the Yankee occupation forces had built the school, but she and her sisters had certainly improved it.

The schoolroom was already filled when Virginia arrived. She seated herself on the edge of the teacher's desk, which was set on a raised platform. She studied the group and was sure there were no absentees.

"Last night," she began, "someone threw rocks through two of the windows of my home. In the middle of the night, depending on the darkness to hide their cowardice. I *will not tolerate* a repetition of this incident without reporting it to the proper authorities."

"How do you think we feel?" It was Langan who spoke out.

"I appreciate how you feel, which is why I called this meeting. As you know, our crop has been demolished by insects and the flames that killed them. Or most of them. That is where the problem lies. If there are any weevils left, hibernating as they do, they'll reappear in the spring as soon as our plants begin to bud. Then the same thing will happen again. I hope you understand that."

"I guess those damn bugs have to be controlled," Mr. Alcorn, another neighbor, conceded. "What worries us is what are we going to do?"

"You're to blame for it," Langan called out. "It wasn't any of our doing. So what are you going to do about it? That's what we want to know."

"I'm wide open to any suggestions," Virginia said, controlling her anger. "Speak up if you have any ideas."

There was only silence. Virginia nodded. "You see? None of you has any notion of how to handle this, so don't blame me if I can't supply the answers either. But I'm going to try."

"It better be good," Langan shouted.

"I would like it if you'd wait until Mr. Farley and Nanine returned from Washington. I assure you it won't be long."

"Well, we won't!" Langan held on to his leadership among the most discontented. "What good can that damned Yankee do anyway? What the hell does he care what happens to us? We're just Rebels they think they've defeated."

"If most of you have that attitude," Virginia said, "there's little I can do except arrange for all of you to leave Valcour."

That brought gasps of astonishment and some shouted refusals to leave. Alcorn, the more moderate of the dissenters, stood up.

"Miss Virginia, I can sympathize with your problems, but I don't believe our leaving the island will remedy anything. Except to get rid of some of the loud-mouthed discontents.

"If you mean me, we can settle this—"

"I mean you, Langan. We'd get on with this in a more sensible manner if you'd shut up."

There was a generous amount of applause at that statement, and Langan kept quiet for a brief period.

"You know that my sisters are not here," Virginia said. "If they were, we could come to a conclusion much faster. However, all of you are angry, all of you are nervous about the situation, and I don't blame you. So I'm going to make a suggestion that I hope you will at least think about."

"Go ahead and make it. That's what we came to hear," someone said.

Virginia spoke quietly now, giving voice to a plan not yet completely clear to her. She'd had little time to probe its value, but something had to be said to satisfy these people that she was making an effort to find a resolution to the problem.

"Very well. Let's face facts as we know them. In all likelihood, there will never be cotton grown on this island again. That's the gist of what I've learned about weevils so far. They are almost impossible to get rid of. Unless they are completely eradicated, the land becomes unfit for cotton. Without a money crop, not many of you can afford to keep living here. A food crop would not pay your bills. So, with the agreement of my sisters and my mother, I propose that my family buy your homes for exactly the price you paid for them after the Yankee carpetbaggers and troops left. I realize what you lose through the destruction of this year's crop; with the agreement of the rest of my family, I'll see that you are recompensed for that, too."

"You'll pay what it cost us to reclaim our homes after the war?" Langan asked, a trifle more calmly this time, for in such a deal he saw some cash being offered.

"I'll pay the same sum paid to the Yankee tax collectors and auctioneers who sold the homes to us. As you may know, we had to buy back ours as well."

"What are you talking about?" It was Damon who exploded in wrath this time. "Our homes are now worth ten times more."

"I'm aware of that," Virginia said.

"Then why take them from us with so damn little payment?"

"Because, while we're not poor, we are not wealthy enough to pay what your homes are really worth."

"What kind of an offer is that?" Damon demanded.

"Not a bad one, under the circumstances. Especially since you paid nothing for these homes, except the payments on your mortgages for the last two years. Don't forget, my family and I had already purchased your homes from the Yankees; you moved in with no payment whatsoever. We also granted all of you full title, with no payments except on the mortgages you instituted to get enough money to begin planting and hiring help. You've lost nothing, you've profited for two years with little investment in the way of money."

"The whole thing is crazy," someone on Langan's side shouted. "We ain't selling our houses for what you offer."

"It's your choice," Virginia said. "I assure you, the banks will foreclose and you'll get nothing. I offer you some reward, even if it isn't much. Because if you do sell to us, what are we to do with empty houses? That's why I asked for your ideas, but none were forthcoming. This is the only way out that I know of now."

"You got some scheme in mind," Langan accused. "You ain't doing this just for our good. Anyway, you caused this to happen. You and your damn Mexican plants."

"I shall amend what I just told you," Virginia said. "The offer I made applies to all of you except Mr. Langan. He can dispose of his property as he sees fit. He can take his chances with the banks. I'll have none of him. And he will not risk planting cotton. I think we have concluded this meeting. When I call another, my entire family will be here. Perhaps there will be a new offer, or some changes in the one I just made. But this matter has to be settled soon, or you will all lose your homes. I further suggest that you immediately send most of your workers back to the mainland. You cannot support them any longer, and without the growing of cotton, there will never again be a place for them here. That is what worries me most. They will have a hard time of it. Good afternoon."

She walked out and headed back to the mansion. She was afraid some might follow her with arguments, or even violence, but no one else left the schoolhouse. At least she had set them to community thinking about her offer.

Virginia spent the rest of the day with Jimmy, playing with him on a small patch of grass that had somehow escaped the ravages of the fire. But Jimmy insisted on crawling beyond the grass onto the ash-covered earth, which necessitated a change of clothing and a bath, which Ivy attended to.

For Virginia it was an exceedingly boring evening. She went from room to room, seeking something to do. She dreaded the thought of sleep, even though by ten o'clock she was exhausted. She had spent considerable time at the library desk, trying to estimate what it would cost to buy out all the householders. The amount was staggering and not an inducement for sleep. So she spent another two hours estimating what it would cost to operate the mansion and the empty fields and how many hands were needed to maintain the place. Without an income from cotton, that alone would amount to an uncomfortable sum.

When she finally went to bed, her mind was filled with discouraging figures and plans for Valcour. She told herself that tonight she would not dream. She told herself over and over that what she had done was an act of mercy, begged for by Brad.

She fell into a restless sleep and the blood-seared face reappeared. Once again she saw the shadowy figure at the barred window. She was raising the rifle, tightening her finger on the trigger, aiming carefully, and the sound of the shot was like the roar of a cannon. Once again she saw the man at the window hurled back by the force of the bullet. She saw him fall backward. Then the dream changed abruptly and she was standing in the night, still holding the rifle, and looming above her was the scaffold prepared for the hanging of Bradley Culver. She stood with her legs planted firmly apart, her back arched, her head thrown back, while she laughed hysterically at the rope and the rough wooden framework. She even pointed the rifle at it and fired again and again. The empty noose swung crazily and the trap fell but without a victim.

She woke with a start and a cry, which she hoped hadn't

awakened the household. She rose, wrapped a comforter around her, and spent the rest of the long night in a chair, with every lamp in the room at its highest flame.

She sat there huddled in the chair, wondering if this was going to happen for the rest of her life. Perhaps, she thought, she would see that bloody, exploded face again and again, night after night. She would see the man fall backward. Perhaps even the cheated gallows would come back to haunt her.

"Oh, Brad," she said aloud, "if only you knew what you've done to me. If only you knew that what you asked would haunt me like a vengeful ghost. If only you knew."

It didn't help. She was still sitting in the chair after dawn when, like the night before, a commotion awakened her. This time it was not the sound of shattering glass, but of a multitude of voices.

She rose and went to the window. Standing there, she saw a line of Negroes, the men toting huge bundles of household goods, the women laden with children and packages. The exodus was beginning. The neighbors hadn't waited. Virginia wondered how many of the ex-slaves had been paid. She shook her head and felt a surge of sorrow that brought her, finally, to tears.

Outside the mansion, her house servants and some of her field hands were watching the others depart, no doubt wondering how long it would be before they too would have to leave. Very soon, boat after boat dotted the sea. Many of the craft had been brought to Virginia's dock, most likely by intent so that she wouldn't miss the sad scene. It reminded her of the time when guns had been heard and all the planters on the island seized whatever could be carried and dashed for their boats to clear out before the Yankee soldiers arrived and took them prisoner. Only this time it was the result of preying insects and a double-dealing Mexican.

Virginia turned from the window, went into the bathroom, and washed hastily. She dressed, pinned on her hat, seized her reticule, and hurried down to the dining room. Daisy and the kitchen maids had heard her stirring and breakfast was on the table. Without sitting down, she hastily ate a biscuit and drank half a cup of coffee. Then she heard Moses at the front of the house and had him summon men to row her ashore.

She knew she couldn't cope with this alone. She was waiting impatiently for the appearance of the oarsmen when she saw four people approaching the mansion. She went to the head of the veranda stairs and soon recognized two of those approaching as Alice Benson and her husband, Robert. With them were a man and a woman whom Virginia thought she'd met before.

She was in a hurry, but only to get off the island and find solace in Phoebe's company. Actually, there was no vital need for her haste.

"Good morning, Virginia," Lorraine Farrel said as they arrived at the foot of the veranda stairs.

"We weren't sure if you'd be up this early," Alice Benson said. "Do you remember Douglas Farrel and Lorraine? They were our guests a while ago."

"Of course. Please come in. I also recall there was a husband and wife—let me think—yes, their name was Bishop."

"You have a remarkable memory, Mrs. Birch," Douglas Farrel said. "We came to offer our condolences for what has happened to this lovely island."

"We're going to stay," Alice Benson said. "Fortunately, we can afford it. Robert and I will never leave here."

"And," her husband added, "we're not angry as most of the others are. Mary Lou and Alan Cartwright are going to stay also. They're expecting their friends from Oklahoma in a few days. They're coming back, too."

"We were planning a trip abroad," Lorraine Farrel explained, "but we changed our minds. I think Valcour is the loveliest place I've ever visited."

"I second that," her husband added. "And the fishing is good, too. If my business permitted it, I'd like to move here and stay."

"It's true," Alice Benson said. "I don't know what we'd do if we had to leave here."

"Thank you," Virginia said. "You've no idea how much I needed a kind word. Alice, I shall immediately assign some of my field hands to clean up your estate. To seed the land, plant flowers, whatever is necessary to make your property pretty again."

Douglas Farrel laughed. "Even with all the burning and the ash and everything else, Valcour looks wonderful to me. Of course it will grow back and be as lovely as before. That won't take much time."

"I'm so happy you stopped by," Virginia said. "I'm on my way to visit Phoebe at our mainland plantation. Nanine, as you know, is in Washington. I pray she'll soon return. Perhaps she will have some good news for a change."

"I'm sure she will," Robert Benson said. "Having him burn everything was a blow, to be sure, but I liked the man. He knew what he was doing, and he hated doing it. Someday maybe we'll grow cotton again. Until then, we'll just stay and enjoy ourselves."

"It's like a paradise here," Alice remarked.

"For a vacation it can't be equaled," Mr. Farrel said.

Virginia found it possible to laugh again. "It's more like the outer limits of hell, with all this blackened earth and ash. But it will come back. You're right about that. And it will be paradise again, I promise you."

They chatted a few more minutes and then her guests wandered off. Virginia walked briskly to the waiting boat at the dock. It was wonderful how those few kind words had changed her attitude.

She settled herself in the large boat, the men cast off, and the rowing began. She wasn't thinking about Brad now, or the ghoulish nightmares, or the burning. She was thinking about what her visitors had said. It was so true. Valcour was one of the most beautiful spots on earth. She'd heard that before, but not quite as forcefully as the Bensons and the Farrels had spoken of it.

Suddenly Virginia threw back her head and, to the consternation and surprise of the two oarsmen, shouted with glee. With hope! With pleasure! Her spinning mind was already at work on the new project.

"Row faster," she urged the men. "Please! It's so important. Five silver dollars to spend if you get me there faster than usual."

The oars began to dip at a remarkable rate.

FIFTEEN

Virginia paid the carriage driver and ran into the house. Phoebe and Chris were just about to have their midday meal. Virginia greeted them enthusiastically, then flung her arms into the air and pirouetted several times, emitting whoops of glee.

Chris laughed. "Enlighten us, please. After what happened on Valcour, I can't think of anything that could make you shout with joy."

"What is it, Virgie?" Phoebe pleaded. "Calm down so you can tell us what's turned you into a cyclone of happiness."

"I have something to tell you. I'm going to need your advice, though I hope it's the kind I want to hear."

"If it isn't, you'll ignore it," Phoebe said philosophically.

"If only Nan were here," Virginia said. "We won't make any decisions without her."

"Your wish is granted," Phoebe said. "She sent us a telegram asking that Chris meet her and Adam."

"Of, forgive me," Virginia said, suddenly contrite. "Did Mama and the Colonel meet Adam? And did she approve of the marriage on such short notice?"

"They did and were witnesses at the wedding," Phoebe said. "Chris and I were there, too. It was a gala affair, except that Mama wished to have a soiree, but Adam explained to her satisfaction why they must return to

Washington, though they had a wedding dinner at the hotel. The Colonel was the host."

"Mama's changed, hasn't she?"

"In every way," Phoebe replied. "Even Nan was astonished."

"I wish I could hold back what I want to tell you until she and Adam arrive, but I can't. Just now I'm starved. I'll talk while we eat." Virginia turned to Chris. "You poor man. You haven't been able to get a word in edgewise."

"I'm perfectly content watching you," Chris said. "I've never seen you so filled with enthusiasm."

They went into the dining room, where lunch awaited them. Tessa served, after greeting Virginia with enthusiasm. For a few moments Virginia was reluctant to broach the subject until Nanine arrived, but she was unable to restrain herself.

"To begin with, this morning I felt awful. Depressed and lonely. I decided to come here to visit, hopeful that my spirits would lift. On my way to the dock, I met the Bensons and their guests from New York. All they talked about was the loveliness of Valcour."

"We can concur in that," Chris said.

"The Bensons are going to stay. So are the Cartwrights."

"Wonderful," Phoebe said. "They're good people. But what has that to do with your newfound joy?"

"Very simple. Here were those people talking about the beauty of the island when it looked like a burned-out ruin. They spoke of Valcour as a place to vacation. That's the word. *Vacation!*"

Chris, in sudden realization, struck the table with the flat of his hand. "That's it! A vacation spot! A place for people to come and enjoy."

Phoebe looked puzzled. "But . . . how will that take the place of a money crop of cotton?"

"We'll build places for guests to stay. Maybe a hotel,

maybe cottages. It's not *how* we'll do it. It's making up our minds that it must be done."

"A hotel." Phoebe's face lit up with joy. "Virgie, what an idea!"

"I haven't had time to figure anything out, but it's worth thinking about, and I'm as excited over it as I would be over a bumper crop of cotton."

"It's going to be mighty expensive," Chris said.

"Just sitting on Valcour doing nothing would be expensive. Phoebe, let's go with Chris to meet Nan and Adam. We'll have supper at our favorite hotel and talk this out. Nan really knows more about Valcour than we do. And, unlike me, she has a level head on her shoulders."

"What of the folks who live there now?" Phoebe asked.

"I'll tell you about it at supper. That's already settled."

"I can't wait," Phoebe said. "There's so much to talk about."

"Don't get your hopes too high," Chris warned. "This is a mighty big project. You could build a hotel—do all sorts of things to the island—but what if nobody came? How many folks ever heard of Valcour except for those on the mainland close by?"

"Advertise," Phoebe said promptly. "That's how to do it. When I was in the theater, I learned that a show would get nowhere unless it was well advertised. Why shouldn't it work with an island?"

They were at the depot half an hour early, still very excited by the new, tantalizing idea. Nanine, in a new dress obviously from Paris, stepped off the train first and showed her surprise when she was met by her sisters and Chris. Adam, too, expressed joy and surprise.

"Nan, you look like the beautiful bride you are," Phoebe said.

"That's because I'm still on a honeymoon," Nanine replied happily. She studied Phoebe's face for a moment, then turned to Virginia. "You two have something on your minds. That's why you met me."

"We're going to have supper at the hotel and stay overnight," Virginia said. "We've made all the arrangements."

"What's the idea?" Adam asked. "Not that I'm against supper and staying overnight."

"First," Virginia said, "we wish to know what you found out in Washington. About the eventual fate of Valcour."

"I can tell you that in mighty few words," Adam said.

"Save them for supper. If you have nothing but bad news, we may have something to counter it. Isn't that right, Phoebe?"

"I hope so. It sounds very good to me. Even better than growing cotton."

They took a carriage to the hotel, and while Nanine and Adam rested and cleaned up from their journey, Phoebe and Virginia decided to go on a shopping spree.

"It's been so long since we did anything like that," Phoebe said. "It will be fun."

"I was hoping you'd agree," Virginia said. "I'm sure it will be a tonic for me. We'll stop by and see what Mrs. Keefe has."

They tried to talk Chris into joining them, but he refused. "A better idea would be for me to go to the bank and talk with Henry Tyler about your plans. Get his thoughts on it and how we should begin. That will save some time, because I have an idea that when Nan hears about it, she'll be as raring to go as you two are."

"Provided Adam doesn't have to return to Washington immediately," Virginia said worriedly.

"Maybe he won't go back," Chris said. "We'll meet at the hotel for supper."

"Get back in time to change," Phoebe cautioned. "I packed another suit for you, dear."

On their way to the couturier, Phoebe said, "I received a

letter from Sam. Poor Lissa didn't get her reward. She
didn't even dare claim it. Sam sent me an article from the
paper that stated that the army presented the New Orleans
police with a check for their clever detective work."

"Then we'll send her a check for the reward money—
only we'll triple it. Three thousand."

"I already did exactly that," Phoebe said. "I knew you'd
feel the same way I did. I know Nan will, too. Lissa
certainly deserves the money, after what she did. And
she'll have the security that she so desperately wants."

The rest of the afternoon was spent buying clothes.
When Virginia and Phoebe returned to the hotel, it was
almost suppertime. At seven the group was seated around
a reserved table set in a back corner and surrounded by
potted palms to ensure privacy.

Virginia ordered champagne. They ate and drank and
filled one another in on happenings since they'd last been
together. It wasn't until the coffee and brandy were served
that Virginia opened the serious conversation.

"Adam, please tell us what happened in Washington and
what you believe is in store for Valcour."

"It's not pleasant, Virgie. There's no doubt that the
island is still infested, even after the burning. I have orders
to announce no more planting of cotton on Valcour for
some years."

"Well now," Virginia smiled, "fancy that."

Adam looked at Nanine. "She's certainly taking this in
good spirits."

"She has reason to," Phoebe said. "Virgie, tell them."

"Yesterday I called a meeting of every property owner
on Valcour. We held it at the schoolhouse. I did this
because the night before, some of our good neighbors
threw rocks through our dining-room windows. I knew
something had to be done."

"You did the right thing, Virgie," Nanine said. "Imagine

them breaking windows. We're taking all the blame, I suspect."

"All of it," Virginia conceded. "In fairness, what happened to the cotton is my fault. Now, this may make you jump a little: I told them we would buy their homes and plantations for the same sum that was paid to the Yankee tax collectors at the end of the war."

"Money we paid," Nanine reminded them. "Our neighbors spent only what was required to establish themselves there and start the planting again."

"A small item I'm afraid some of them forgot. Early this morning, they discharged almost all of their workers. I believe they're going to take up my offer."

"What about our workers?" Nanine asked.

"I'll come to that in a few moments. After that meeting, I was depressed to tears. All I could see was the end of Valcour. But the Bensons came by with guests from New York. They regard Valcour as a vacation island. They think it's the most beautiful place on earth."

"Which it is," Chris cut in.

"Go on, Virginia, tell them," Phoebe urged, with a broad smile.

"With your approval, and if it can be done, I hope to build a hotel on Valcour and advertise for vacation guests. But there's more to it than that. I've only told you the mere beginning."

"Turning the island into a resort," Adam said dreamily. "All my life I've wanted to create a paradise out of some large property. An island is the ideal place, and Valcour can be landscaped to resemble a jewel in an exquisite setting. Please, may I humbly ask for that job?"

"Adam, what a thought!" Virginia cried out. "Of course. But it won't be a job—it will be a partnership. Nan, what do you think?"

"I have to study it further," Nanine said, ever the

practical member of the family. "It sounds very good. But it will take a great deal of money."

"I talked to Henry Tyler at the bank this afternoon," Chris said. "He says it's the best idea he's ever heard. The bank is willing to finance it."

"That would be financing it with our own money," Nanine said with a smile. "We're the heaviest investors in that bank. But it was a generous offer."

"Tyler also said we'd need an architect to handle it," Chris said. "He gave me the name of the one he considers the best in Charleston."

"Of course, someone will have to do the planning," Nanine admitted.

"Then let's hire him," Virginia said promptly.

"Well," Phoebe asked, "how about it, Nan?"

Nanine sat back and raised her brandy snifter. "Here's to the Hotel Valcour, the new vacation resort of the South. I hope and pray our dream becomes a reality."

After that, the conversation came from all directions, as ideas were offered, discarded, set aside for further study, or enthusiastically endorsed. They were still in the dining room at closing time. Virginia was the last to go upstairs. She purchased a newspaper and *Godey's* magazine. As she ascended the staircase, she realized how alone she was. Chris and Phoebe were in their room; Adam and Nanine were in theirs. But she was doomed to sleep alone, in a room filled with loneliness. Even though her sisters and their husbands were close by, she was almost in tears. There was only one good feature about this day: it had so occupied her that she had not once thought of Brad. And now, at bedtime, she was so exhausted that she slept well, without her ghastly dreams.

They met again at breakfast. Chris, Phoebe, and Adam decided to return to Valcour at once to make plans. Nanine and Virginia had already made an appointment to see

Alexander Murray, the architect recommended by Henry Tyler. Afterward, they would visit Mama and the Colonel and inform them of the plans for Valcour.

Murray's office was downtown, in a building recently restored after the ravages of the war.

When they entered the reception room of his office, there was no one to greet them. The secretary's desk was unoccupied. However; in seconds the door to the private office opened and a tall man stepped out. He had brilliant blue eyes, and his blond hair was worn rather long, with copious sideburns. There was no doubt that he was an unusually handsome man, six feet tall, slender but sturdy, like a man who keeps in fine trim and prides himself on his appearance.

"Welcome, ladies." He bowed, and his tone was warm, and he had a deep, masculine voice that Virginia found had sensual appeal. At least to her.

"I'm Mrs. Elias Birch," she said, "and this is my sister Mrs. Adam Farley. I believe Mr. Tyler has already contacted you about a project we have in mind."

"Yes, indeed. Please come in. My secretary has the day off, but we won't be interrupted. I canceled all other engagements. Henry told me what your plans are, and I believe they can turn your island into the wonderland of the South. I would be greatly honored to take over the project."

"That's what my sister and I came to discuss," Virginia said.

Nanine favored Virginia with a sideways glance. Though Virginia's smile was decorous, she was slipping a few loose strands of hair back in place. Nanine knew the signs. Virginia was already falling under the spell of Alexander Murray.

They talked with him at length, and it was late morning

when they granted him the task of designing the Hotel Valcour.

Nanine and Virginia took a carriage from the architect's office to the Colonel's, where they were greeted warmly. The Colonel and Lenore listened first with amazement, then with an enthusiasm that equaled Virginia's and Nanine's as they related their plan to save Valcour.

"How delightful," Lenore exclaimed. "We can have small soirees here and large ones at the Hotel Valcour. I love the name."

"Only this time, Mama," Virginia said pointedly, "the guests will have to pay."

"Who's the architect?" the Colonel asked.

"Alexander Murray," Nanine replied.

"Hmmm." The Colonel rubbed his chin reflectively. "I've never seen anything he's done himself. Usually he has someone come from New Orleans—or even Washington."

"Isn't he competent?" Nanine asked with concern.

"I can't answer that. As I say, I've never seen anything he designed himself."

"In that case," Virginia said, "we'll exercise extreme caution and study carefully whatever plans he shows us."

"Henry Tyler recommended him," Nanine said.

"Alex happens to be married to Henry Tyler's niece," the Colonel informed them.

"Exercise extreme caution, girls," Lenore warned.

"That would be wise," the Colonel said. "And keep us informed. We're as pleased with this solution as you are."

Lenore and the Colonel stood on the veranda, arms around each other's waist, and waved farewell to the girls.

They arrived back at Valcour late in the day. As the three sisters stood on the veranda, studying the devastation the fire had wrought, Nanine sighed heavily.

"Wait until Mr. Murray gets his teeth into this," Virginia said. "It's going to be more beautiful than ever before."

"I'm sure it will," Nanine said dully.

Virginia was surprised at Nanine's lack of enthusiasm. "Weren't you impressed with his suggestions?"

"I'll be more impressed when I see his plans."

"What's troubling you?" Virginia asked, studying Nanine's somber features.

"You," Nanine said bluntly. Then she sighed again. "Virgie, I have eyes. I could see you were falling under Mr. Murray's spell only minutes after we met him."

"How ridiculous," Virginia said indignantly. "Naturally, I admire the man. Certainly you won't deny that he's handsome, with a splendid build."

"Exactly," Nanine said flatly. "You missed none of his attributes, including, I'm certain, his deep-blue eyes."

"An asset, certainly," Virginia replied testily. "As in his voice. Deep, masculine, and sensual."

"You see?" Nanine said firmly. "You know all his assets."

Virginia restrained her impatience. "Nanine, don't you think I've learned my lesson from my mistakes?"

"I hope you've learned, Vigie," Nanine said patiently "But, I know how lonely you must be. Do exercise caution. Find out something about this Mr. Murray before you let him mesmerize you."

"Don't worry, dear sister," Virginia said blithely. "I shall be much too busy to engage in any liaisons with the handsome Mr. Murray."

"There's so much to be done," Nanine said. "We have to take care of the folks who wish to leave. Those arrangements will take time. Then we have to get the island cleaned up. Virginia, I would advise against letting any of our help go."

"I've the same idea. Moses will be delighted."

"Moses can well become part of this," Phoebe said.

"Perhaps an official greeter. Or he can have charge of the grounds employees."

"We'll talk of it later on, " Nanine said. "Tomorrow we'll actually begin with this enterprise. Adam is going to give up his Washington job. His heart is set on making the island a beauty spot. And he can do it."

"I'm so glad," Virginia said. "You've no idea how lonely this island can be."

"Chris will keep the big plantation going," Phoebe said. "But he'll come to the island as often as possible. I'll likely spend a great deal of my time here. Chris said he'll try to stand it."

There was so much on Virginia's mind that night that she never once gave any thought to the grisly memories that caused her nightmares. As she prepared for bed, she felt better than she had in many days. A long playtime with Jimmy helped, as did the remembrance of the way Alexander Murray had gently squeezed her hand as they said goodbye. And the way he'd looked at her. No one had betrayed that much warmth toward her in a long time. She'd been attracted to him instantly. Yes, she thought dreamily, the way she'd been attracted to Carlos and Brad and, long ago, to a boy going to war. It had even happened with Elias, despite the natural animosity between a Rebel and a Yankee during the war.

She gave her hair its usual brushing and blew out the lamps, with the exception of the one at her bedside. She propped herself against her pillows and read *Godey's* until her eyes were heavy-lidded. She set the magazine aside, blew out the lamp, slid down under the covers, and was fast asleep in minutes.

Then she was kneeling in the tall grass again, staring at the whitewashed walls of the military jail. Once more she saw the shadowy form of a man at the window, his arms flung outward while he pressed himself against the bars and waited for the bullet that was still in her rifle. She felt herself raising the gun. The figure was in plain sight now. She must aim for the head, to make the bullet certain. She heard the explosion of the gun. Now she was close to the cell window as the bullet struck. She saw the transformation of a white face into one crimson with blood.

Once again she saw the man fall backward, but suddenly there was a change. She was back on Valcour and someone was slowly approaching her. In his hand he was swinging a hangman's noose. As he came closer, she saw that it was Lieutenant Johnson, the young Yankee officer who had searched the house for the rifle. His smiling, gentle face now contorted into something akin to madness, he held out the rope closer to her, dangling it in front of her face, closer and closer until it threatened to go over her head.

She didn't know that she screamed. She awakened abruptly, in a panic of terror, her face covered with perspiration and her heart beating madly.

The door opened. Phoebe came in first, then Nanine, followed by Chris. She sank back against the pillow and tried to smile.

"Did I wake everyone? I was having a nightmare. It scared me half to death. Please forgive me."

"Are you all right?" Nanine asked. "It was a mighty lusty scream."

"I was frightened, Nan."

"Well, I'm glad it was only a dream. If you can't sleep, knock on my door and I'll stay up the rest of the night with you."

"It was only a dream," Virginia assured them. "I'm fine. I'll sleep as soundly as Jimmy does. Don't worry about me, please."

They left her alone. As the door closed, Virginia turned, buried her face in the pillow, and wept. She cried for a

long time, and she knew the dream would come again—
and again. Perhaps for as long as she lived.

In the corridor, Phoebe asked Nan to join her downstairs
for a glass of milk.

Nanine was about to reject the invitation, but the way
Phoebe looked at her made her change her mind.

"You go back to bed," Phoebe told Chris. "I'll be along
in a few minutes."

Chris, yawning, had no objection. Downstairs, Nanine
and Phoebe went to the kitchen. Phoebe poured two glasses
of milk and carried them into the library.

"There's something on your mind, Phoebe," Nanine
said. "It has to be about Virgie. What is it?"

"I never intended to tell you this, Nan. It was to be my
secret, shared with no one. But now I find I must tell you.
It's the most painful thing imaginable."

"Good heavens, what is it? Something Virgie . . . ?"

"Yes, it's about Virgie. You know she falls in love too
easily. And now it's happened again."

"You weren't even there when we talked to Mr. Murray.
How do you know she's attracted to him?"

"By the way she talked about him. When Virgie becomes infatuated, it shows on her like the headlight of a
steam train. She's heading for trouble again."

"What can we do about it? You know how quickly she
makes up her mind about men."

"Too well, Nan. But it's not her infatuations that haunt
me. It's the problems that result from them."

Nanine nodded. "You're referring to Brad—and Carlos."

"Yes. That, and more." She paused. "Nan, you must
promise me that you will never reveal this. Especially that
you will never give Virgie even the slightest hint that you
know. She'd never forgive me."

"Yes, I promise," Nan said gravely.

Phoebe took a long breath. "Virgie killed Brad."

Nanine gasped. "Phoebe, what a thing to say!"

"It's true. And after hearing her scream tonight, I know it is still with her. It's beginning to haunt her."

"Why are you so sure?"

"You were in Washington when Brad was shot. The day before Brad was to be hanged, Lieutenant Johnson came here with a message that Brad wanted to see Virgie before he died. Brad claimed he wished to apologize to her for all the agony he had caused. Tell me, Nan, if you were in her place, would you have gone?"

"I don't know. You said there were extenuating circumstances."

"Indeed there were. She was in such a hurry to obey that she went back to the mainland with Lieutenant Johnson and the man who had rowed him over. When she returned, she wouldn't say much about her visit. But that night I was awakened from a deep sleep. It was almost dawn—the sky was beginning to lighten—when I heard someone. You know how you often step on dry twigs or leaves along the path to the dock. In the middle of the night such small sounds seem louder. I went to my window. Virgie, wrapped in a cloak, and carrying something cumbersome under it, was running toward the house. I went to the head of the stairs to see what was wrong. She'd beaten me to it and was already in the library. I heard the door to the gun rack open. I heard her put a weapon inside and then close the door. I didn't know what had happened, and it wasn't until later that day that I learned Brad had been shot by someone outside the military jail. Apparently he had stood on a table in front of the window, facing it, waiting to be killed."

Nanine had turned very pale. She gestured nervously. "Are you sure you didn't dream this? I mean, it sounds like a nightmare."

"Nan, I went back to my room and shut the door. Virgie

entered her room. After a while I went down to the library and opened the gun rack. The sharpshooter's rifle had been fired. I could still smell the powder. I even smudged my finger when I rubbed it against the opening of the barrel. It had been fired recently."

"Oh, Phoebe, what an awful thing."

"I took the rifle out the gun rack and hid it. Lucky I did. Later that day, Lieutenant Johnson came to the island to tell us that Brad had been murdered. He said his superiors wanted him to question Virgie because she was the last civilian to see him alive. In fact, she was the only person who had talked to him."

"Virgie must have been terrified."

"No doubt. The lieutenant wanted to know if we kept any weapons in the house. Virgie had to tell him there was a gun rack. I can imagine how she felt when the lieutenant opened the rack and examined the rifles. The others hadn't been fired in months. Later, I cleaned the gun and replaced it. Virgie must know I did this, but she has never mentioned it—except in a roundabout way. She thanked me for what I did and said she'd never forget it. I pretended ignorance and told her that I had no idea what she was talking about, nor did I want to know."

"Didn't she say anything more?"

"There was nothing more for her to say. We made a tacit agreement and it will never be mentioned again."

"Why did she do it?"

"She mentioned that Brad had told her he was terrified of being hanged."

"So he made her shoot him," Nanine mused. "I wonder what threat he used."

"She was terrified that in his fear of being hanged, he might reveal that he was Jimmy's true father."

"My God!" Nanine cried. "Would he really have done such a thing?"

"Who knows? In any event, it was a risk Virgie wasn't about to take. So, she did as he requested. Perhaps he even ordered her. We'll never know, because I don't want her to talk about it."

"If she could tell someone, it might help her to be rid of the nightmares. Having to keep that secret must be a terrible burdon on her conscience."

"I don't know," Phoebe said worriedly. "But I don't feel we're the right ones for her to tell it to. She'd worry about our being burdened by it."

"I agree with your reasoning," Nanine said. "But she must be going through a private hell."

"I prefer to regard this as Brad committing suicide," Phoebe said. "I keep telling myself that."

"I understand. I'm also somewhat relieved."

"Why?"

"If she'd loved him, she couldn't have done it."

"If only she could learn to control her emotions. Her passionate nature is such that each affair has ended in violence."

"It's my opinion that she's loved only one man," Nanine said.

"Elias." Phoebe spoke the name without hesitation.

Nanine nodded. "She'll never swallow her pride and write to him. Let's hope and pray that turning Valcour into a resort will keep her so busy that in time she'll forget. And the nightmare will fade."

"Could you forget?"

"I'm sure I could not. But I hope Virgie can. She's strong—and no matter what she did, we'll stand behind her. We'll support her. Thank you for confiding in me."

"You know, Nan, I think she did a brave thing. Yes, I'm sure of it. I wish I could tell her so."

"But of course you won't."

"Never! But I'll continue to pray that one day she will

forget, or at least that the nightmare will fade. Right now I feel sorry for her. Damn, I wish Elias would come back. Why does she have to be so stubborn? I know she loves him. Deep in her heart there's never been anyone else. And he loves her. It's their damn pride that keeps them apart."

"I know. But she'll not countenance interference on our part."

"True. I fear it's something only she can resolve."

"She never will, Phoebe. She'd die first."

SIXTEEN

Alexander Murray arrived on Valcour the following morning to begin his assignment as architect of the hotel. Virginia was at the dock to greet him, and she did so graciously, but with no evidence that her interest extended beyond business. Yet, she had looked forward to his coming.

"Welcome, Mr. Murray," she said as he stepped ashore.

"Good morning, Mrs. Birch." His smile was as reserved as hers. He looked up, studying the mansion at the top of the knoll. "I trust you won't want me to recommend razing that beautiful home."

"That's Willowbrook," she said. "It goes back some generations in my family, although we enlarged it following the war. If changing the island meant destroying that house, the island would never be changed, sir."

"I'm glad to hear that." He took her arm, carrying a large portfolio in his other hand, and they began walking up the path. "I studied the island as we approached it and I'm sure we can do great things with it."

"We're just as certain of that, Mr. Murray. Even if I do sound vain."

He laughed. "Well, with all this burned-out landscape—no brush, gardens, or even lawns—at this moment it does not present its best face."

"You have to look beyond the ash," Virginia said lightly. "You also have to consider the climate, the isolation, and the beauty that lies under the ashes. I'll be very interested to hear your ideas, even the tentative ones."

"I have several," he said. "Is the rest of your family here?"

"No. My sister Nanine and her husband had to leave early this morning. He's with the Farm Bureau in Washington, and he's on an inspection tour of the South, checking the cotton plantations for boll-weevil infestation."

"Is that what wrecked your beautiful island?"

Virginia nodded. "We had to put the torch to every growing thing. It was heartbreaking, but there was no help for it."

"I've heard of them. And I've read a little about them. They destroy any plantation they infest."

"And nothing can be grown there for several years. You can imagine what would become of the South if that happened. After all, we're just beginning to get back on our feet."

"It was good of you to allow Mr. Farley to do what he did."

"We had no choice. It was an order from his superiors in the government. However, as soon as he has completed this assignment, he's going to transfer his talents to this island."

"What do you mean?" Alex looked puzzled.

"His ambition is to landscape the grounds of large estates, museums, and public parks. This will be his first assignment. He's delighted to have an entire island for his first project."

"I thought I was to oversee the planting. After all, that is part of what an architect does. He lays out the entire area—in this case, not only the hotel but the small buildings for changing to swimming clothes or tennis clothes— even a bandstand. I have several ideas for these things."

"I can see you do," Virginia said, enthused by his suggestions. "Don't worry about Adam. He's strong willed, but I'm sure he'll respect your opinions."

"That's good to hear, but will he follow my instructions? After all, there can't be two bosses on a single project."

"Don't worry about Adam," Virginia repeated. "Anyway, I'm sure you'll find him amenable to whatever plans you decide on."

"I hope so," Alex replied dubiously. "I don't like friction of any kind."

"You may find him excellent to work with and very knowledgeable."

Alex laughed. "You've convinced me, Mrs. Birch."

"I hope so, Mr. Murray, because we're a closely-knit family. This project could mean Adam's career. He's resigning his post with the Farm Bureau when he completes his present assignment."

"Then he'll be living here?"

"For the time being, yes. Though I don't know how long it will be before he returns. But then, you're not ready for landscaping yet, are you?"

"Indeed not, Mrs. Birch. And while we're on the subject of names, would you mind being less formal? Since we'll be having frequent consultations, I think it would be easier—in fact, more comfortable—if we worked on a first-name basis. My friends call me Alex."

"Then Alex it will be. And my family calls me Virgie."

"I prefer Virginia. It's such a beautiful name."

"Thank you. I also have another sister, who will help me with the interior decorations. I have my own ideas about that."

"I'm sure they're excellent. You may be certain I'll not interfere. That's not my field. Does this other sister live here?"

"No. She's married to Mr. Christopher Savard, the overseer on our mainland plantation. That's where they live."

"Then, except for your son, you are alone here?" he asked in surprise.

"Yes. My mother was recently married to Colonel Zachary Spires. They live on the mainland."

Alex brought her to an abrupt stop, let go of her arm, and made a sweeping gesture toward the land south of the mansion. "Right there! That's where we'll construct the hotel. I can see it now. Oh yes, I've ideas—many of them—and I'm sure you'll approve."

"After lunch, we'll tour the island," she said. "Or most of it. The island extends for quite a distance, but the main use has been on this end of it. Our beaches are not very good, because there are so many rocks. But our view of the ocean is beautiful."

"We'll discuss that during our tour."

"We have horses," she said, "if you'd like to ride."

"I'd prefer to walk, if you don't mind. I can see more at a slower pace."

A tour of the mansion aroused Alex's interest, and when she brought him into Jimmy's room, he exhibited the fact that he could charm anyone, of any age. Jimmy gurgled and hugged him, and Virginia's heart warmed to the man.

Touring the island took the entire afternoon and most of the next day. Virginia put him up in one of the bedrooms well down the hall from her suite. It was a pleasant, nicely decorated room and he complimented her on it. In fact, he issued so many compliments during his stay that Virginia came to wonder just how much of his praise was genuine and not just flattery. Still, it didn't lessen her liking for him. He was friendly to the Negroes and made a favorable impression on Moses. It was a lovely two days. On the second night, he and Virginia went into a detailed discussion of his ideas. Following supper, they settled in the library, he with a glass of brandy.

"I can turn this island into one that will attract wealthy

people. After all, unless your guests are wealthy, you'll never make much of a profit."

"We're not so concerned with profit as with preserving the island so that its natural beauty will never be lost, and so that it will lend itself to the enjoyment of all who come here. That's what we're after. Naturally, we want the project to pay for itself, but we don't wish to gouge the public."

"I'm sure you want to make money out of it," he said. "I have to be sure of that. If it's being done only to satisfy the whims of you and your family, then I would do it much differently."

"We wish a profit, of course," she said. "I only wished to stress how much we love Valcour."

"Then let me say that I have already visualized a long, one-story structure, spartan in appearance, but exactly suited to the island. I can lay out a garden, not too large, a few arbors, fine lawns. Mostly lawns. I can bring in some trees. Magnolias, mostly, because you will expect many folks from the North, and they regard magnolias as the symbol of the South."

"It sounds quite spartan, Mr. Murray. I had in mind something that held an air of enchantment. So did my sisters and my mother."

"You'll change your mind when I show you a drawing I'll make as soon as I return to the mainland. I want lengthy views of the island. I intend to leave in the morning."

"I'll have someone row you across."

"That brings to mind another thing. Rowing back and forth over that long distance won't be very acceptable to guests."

"What can we do? Steamships would be far too large."

"I'll look into the matter. But enough trade talk. I'm a man who likes to relax when the day's work is done. My brain is already reeling."

"This planning is tentative, anyway," she said. "I've enjoyed our conversation. How long have you been engaged in this profession?"

"Ever since I was graduated from Princeton," he said loftily. "I've always wanted to plan things, to use my imagination, and I do have an eye for beauty. This island is a perfect complement to you, Virginia."

"Thank you. I suppose this project will continue during the winter?"

"And beyond. May I ask where your husband is? You haven't mentioned him."

"He's in England, where he takes care of our foreign trade in cotton."

"But you're not growing cotton, so he'll be returning soon, of course?"

"No, Alex. We're—separated. We have been for a long time."

"I'm sorry. I know how you feel, though. My marriage has resulted in the same situation. It's not easy to bear."

"It's mighty lonely, I can testify to that," Virginia admitted.

"I know. Perhaps that's why we seem to get along so well. We enjoy each other's company."

"We do, as far as our discussions on the project are concerned." She realized that he was leading up to something a bit more friendly than business.

"I'll be back the day after tomorrow. Will that be all right with you?"

"I'll be happy to see you again."

"I have to look up the materials we'll need and make an estimate of what this will cost. You'll want the best, I imagine."

"The very best. If it's expensive, we can adjust to that."

"Good. This is going to be great fun, doing an island

over. I have thought about a race track. There's room for one."

"That's something that never entered my mind, Alex."

"I'll get all the information on it."

He continued with his ideas, many of which he seemed to contrive in his head as he talked. Nonetheless, Virginia realized that many of them were worth considering. It was quite late when they decided to end the day. As they stood at the foot of the staircase, he embraced her lightly and with no show of passion. She thought he was going to kiss her, but he refrained, and she was pleased that he wasn't the type to move too fast. Or to take a woman for granted.

She saw to it that the house was secure for the night, then glanced into Jimmy's room, where Ivy placed a finger to her lips, indicating the boy was asleep. As Virginia entered her suite, she glanced down the hall. There was light below Alex's door. She was glad she'd taken the precaution of putting him up as far from her bedroom as possible. She prayed that he'd not be awakened by her screaming, which had become a permanent part of the nightmares that still haunted her.

She lay awake for a long time, partly because she feared sleep, but because she felt also unsettled by Alex Murray. She liked him. He might be a trifle overbearing at times, but he was pleasant and courtly. She found herself wondering what kind of lover he would be.

That annoyed her, because she'd not thought in those terms since she'd bedded with Brad in the hotel in Falmouth, but she couldn't help herself. As she thought about that, she fell asleep. There was the nightmare again. It never failed, but tonight it wasn't so intense. It seemed as if there were a wall of mist, or fog, between herself and the grisly thing she usually saw so plainly. Upon awakening, she doubted that she'd screamed, and she wondered if the presence of Alex was responsible.

She hoped so as she dressed, and she was even more sure of it when she joined him at breakfast and afterward walked with him to the dock. Their conversation had not concerned business for the most part, but a lively discussion of how the South was faring since the war and what its future might be.

Alex believed that the North was biding its time and would invoke some harsh measures before the thing was done with. Virginia didn't concur.

"I'm sure they don't mean to impose any more conditions on us than they already have, and I must say those have not been too severe."

"They'll make up for it," Alex said. "Mark my words."

"Alex, I married a Yankee officer. My sister just married a Yankee government man. Even if my husband is living abroad, I think he and my brother-in-law are good examples of the average Northerner, and I'm sure they have no evil intentions toward us just because we left the Union and lost the war."

"It remains to be seen," Alex said. "Though I hope you're right. At any rate, that won't interfere with what we have planned, except to worry if any Northerners will come to the South on vacation."

"There are a couple from New York on the island now, on vacation," she told him. "They're visiting one of the two families who have elected to remain on Valcour."

He took her hands. "We're disputing something that probably won't happen. As you say, we'll get along with it anyway. I'll be back tomorrow, early. Will your sisters have returned?"

"No. Phoebe won't be back for a few more days. Nanine said they needed at least a week to settle Adam's affairs in Washington. And they're traveling through the South now."

"Until tomorrow, you lovely girl."

He kissed her, quite impulsively she was sure, but it

stirred the banked fires in her. She would have liked to embrace him hard, kiss him with vigor and passion, and feel his response.

Instead, she waved him off and waited until he was almost out of sight. She turned and walked slowly back to the mansion, wondering what a long, stark, one-story building would look like against the lush beauty of Valcour. She couldn't see it, but perhaps the plans he would draw might change her mind. She was sure of one thing. She was glad he was coming back soon—and glad that Phoebe and Nanine would not be present. Her body was aflame with desire.

Virginia hated having her meals alone at the large table, but she knew Daisy prided herself on her cooking. As usual, after supper Virginia relieved Ivy and spent a few hours with Jimmy. He was growing at a remarkable rate and he'd soon begin to talk and to walk with more confidence. And, as Ivy said, begin getting into mischief.

Tonight the dream came back. It was always the same—the man at the barred window, the way he was hurled back when the bullet struck, the way his face turned crimson with blood, the way he fell.

Tonight she tried to defeat the terror that stayed with her after the dream by thinking of Alex Murray. Of his obvious affection for her, not yet openly expressed. If he was with her, she would not have that again. Somehow she was sure of that. In his arms she would find the comfort she sought. With him she'd be content, warm in his embrace, protected by his love for her. On the wave of these thoughts, she drifted off and slept peacefully. In the morning she recalled that, and was more convinced than ever that she would never again sleep peacefully unless a man she loved was beside her. Nothing else would stop those dreams, and now there was a good chance that Alex might be the one to accomplish this. If he seemed in the least reluctant, she would change his mind. She knew the allure she held for men and she knew how to arouse them. Alex Murray was going to become her salvation.

He returned earlier than she had expected and she took this as a good sign. He was armed with drawings he'd made during the all-but-sleepless night, he told her.

He unrolled the tentative drawing of the hotel he had in mind. It was stark. Majestic, but in a cold way, while she had visualized something softer, more inviting. This hotel would be almost forbidding—and cold. The rooms, she thought, were too small.

"But, my dear Virginia," he complained, "with smaller rooms you make more money, and, after all, profit is what it's all about. Besides, people on vacation don't stay in their rooms long, and they don't expect all the comforts they have in their own homes."

"Perhaps you're right," she admitted. But in her heart she knew Nanine and Phoebe would object. He would have to win them over without her help, for she wasn't certain she would approve the plans either.

He also laid out an elaborate sketch for the landscaping that Adam must accept—and likely would not. There was too much lawn, too few flowers and bushes. In their place he had sketched in statutes, walls, and pools. He'd done nothing about the beaches or, at the far end of the island, the forest, the riding trails, and the animals. There was no place reserved for children. He'd never thought of that.

"Well," she asked, "what do you think?"

"I don't know, Alex. My sisters and their husbands will have to be consulted."

"Now see here," he said severely, "I don't want to be subjected to the criticisms and ideas of a great many people. The more I must please, the more difficult it becomes, and there are changes after changes. The project won't get started for months and then it will be subject to more alterations. I was of the opinion that you made the final decisions."

"No, Alex, I do not make the decisions, final or otherwise. This island is owned by all of us and we share in whatever plans must be made. I also notice that you have decided to raze most of the old homes that have been here so many years. They're lovely homes."

"Of course they are, but who's going to live in them now that they've been abandoned? A vacation island must serve to please the paying guests, and antiquated houses can be an eyesore, without value."

"We disagree on that," she said. "But let's wait and find out how the others regard it. Besides, I want you to see some of these old places you call eyesores. One, in particular, was left fully furnished when the owners moved out. We paid them for the furniture they didn't want to take with them. You'll change your mind."

"I'd love to see it," Alex said. "Right now is as good a time as any."

The house was located some distance away, so Virginia sent one of the maids to the stables to order horses saddled and ready. She and Alex held hands as they walked down to the stables; he'd caught her hand in his as they walked down the porch steps. She reveled in this close contact, and she hoped he would change his plans for the hotel and grounds to conform better with what she had in mind.

They rode down to the house, not talking much. Once inside the two-story, plantation-type dwelling, Alex seemed impressed. He agreed that the long veranda with its graceful white-painted pillars was handsome, and the tall, narrow windows fitted the architecture well. Inside, the Southern way of life seemed perfectly exemplified in the large ballroom, which served as the drawing room as well. And the dining room was no intimate arrangement, but one that would seat fifty people at the long, polished mahogany table with its leather-backed chairs and hand-carved sideboards. The kitchen, too, was large; banquets could easily be prepared there. Outside was an ample estate, still blackened by the fire, but obviously offering space and, when green again, great beauty.

She led him upstairs to the bedrooms. There were two bedroom suites and eight single bedrooms. Each had a private bath and some had small dressing rooms. The master suite was large, the parlor furnished in mahogany, with a long, wide chaise longue. It was upholstered with luxurious light blue velvet and was the most prominent, most beautiful piece in the room. Also, it was most inviting. The walls were covered with paintings of nudes of both sexes in poses meant to arouse fleshly desires.

Alex studied it all, then glanced at Virginia. "With your head resting on that huge pillow, you'd resemble Aphrodite, the love goddess. Especially with your golden tresses touching your slender, fair-skinned shoulders."

"Good heavens, Alex, you've never seen them. I'm wearing a riding habit."

"And a hat," he replied blandly, studying her face and letting her eyes slowly move down her form. "But I see you without your hat and your riding habit. I see your lovely breasts, straining to be free of your garments."

"We must go," Virginia said, stirred by his words.

"We must not go, my darling." Alex stepped in front of her, blocking her path. "Don't be haughty—or cold."

"I'm not, Alex, but I'm a married woman."

"So was Aphrodite, but she gave her favors to others. Do you know how she was created?"

"Papa didn't raise three stupid young ladies," Virginia said, with a proud tilt of her head. "And I do know. Though I'm not about to give you a lesson in Greek mythology."

His deep, throaty laughter mocked her. "You don't really know."

Her eyes flashed defiance. "Aphrodite was a Greek goddess who rose from the foam of the sea, created by Uranus's sex organ, which fell into the sea after he'd been mutilated by Cronus."

"Ah." Alex's eyes teased her. "So you do know."

"I also know that Aphrodite Urania was worshipped as a celestial goddess—the goddess of pure and spiritual love."

"And Aphrodite Pandemos?"

"The goddess of marriage and family life," Virginia replied, though her voice had softened.

Alex completed the definition. "Which is the essence of earthly or sensual love. And that is the most satisfying, the most uplifting, the most maddening, and the most ecstatic."

As he spoke, he removed her hat, slipped the onyx pins from her hair, and opened the jacket of her riding habit. His hands moved around her waist as her hair fell in a tumbled heap. His mouth covered hers and, despite herself, she moaned. His fingers skilfully unbuttoned the skirt of her riding habit and it dropped to the floor. Before she could protest, he lifted her and deposited her on the chaise and began pulling off her boots.

"Oh, my God, Alex, let's get out of here." She tried to raise herself, but he pressed her back and continued undressing her until she lay nude. She no longer protested; she couldn't. Her heart was pounding madly, her breathing was rapid, and her hands were now unbuttoning his trousers.

He slipped free of her. "Not here, my darling. There's a bed in the next room larger than any I've ever seen. Whoever lived here enjoyed the comforts of life and, from the furnishings in these two rooms, reveled in carnal pleasures. Good for them!"

He lifted her in his arms and carried her effortlessly into

the bedroom. He deposited her on the bed, removed his
boots, and undressed. Virginia didn't take her eyes off
him. She wanted his lips, his hands, his body. She wanted
him to possess her and she wanted to madden him with
her womanly wiles.

Her arms were outstretched to him as he walked over to
the bed. He was as fascinated by her lovemaking as she
was thrilled by his. The room echoed with their cries, and
their bodies and hands were in constant movement. Despite their hunger for fulfillment, they delayed as long as
possible, reveling in the throes of passion. Once their love
peaked, they clung to each other, still trying to hold on to
the wild magic of the final moments.

Neither knew how much time had passed before they
released their hold on each other and lay on their backs.

Alex spoke first. "If you say you have any regrets, I'll
shoot you first and then myself. I've never experienced
anything like that in my life. Have you, Virginia?"

She gave him a smile that told him nothing and served
only to torment him.

"Dammit, Virginia, answer me! That was . . . that was
. . . oh, Christ, I don't know how to describe it."

"We made love," Virginia said quietly, now in complete
control of her emotions. "I love making love. I put everything I have into it."

"And you have everything," Alex said, covering her
mouth with his. "Say you love me."

"No," she replied, now thoroughly relaxed, "because I
don't. You gave me what I wanted—what I needed.
Obviously, you needed it too. What more do you want?"

"You, dammit! Your body, your mind, your soul."

"You had it for a few minutes. Aren't you content with
that?"

"No! I want you for always. Let me rule this island with
you. You're lovely. I'm lonely."

"And we're both married."

"We can get divorces," he said.

"I may not want one," she said. She was shocked the moment she uttered the statement. Such a thought hadn't crossed her mind until then.

He was silent for a while, then a cynical smile touched his mouth. "I see. For you, your wedding ring is your protection against adventurers."

"Adventurers or philanderers," Virginia said, taking no offense. "That isn't true, though. The fact is, I was lonely for the love of a man, but I'm not a harlot."

"I think the name Aphrodite suits you," Alex said. "And I think I should do as Paris did—present you with the apple of discord. She was instrumental in starting the Trojan War."

"Paris was also known as Alexander. He had a violent ending," Virginia said. "Do you really wish me ill?"

"No, my darling." His arms enclosed her and he drew her close. "Let's not waste any more time. I need you again."

"Perhaps I need you more than I realize, Alexander," she said, closing the distance between them. "Just now, let's not talk any more."

He freed her lips long enough to ask, "Will you think about what you just said? About needing me?"

"Yes, my darling Alexander," came her muffled reply as he covered her mouth with his.

Their passion soared again, but this time it lacked the madness of before. Afterward, they lay quietly for a few minutes, then dressed and went out to their horses.

On the way back, they talked about the other homes they passed, and while Alex had been impressed with the one she'd shown him, where they'd consummated their physical attraction for each other, the rest of the houses bored him with their old-fashioned cupolas, tall windows,

ample verandas, and large entranceways. The war had
changed things for the better, he argued. She didn't agree
with him, but she left that for later, when she would
discuss it with Phoebe and Nanine.

Later, in the library, she wrote a substantial check. He
went behind the desk, grasped her upper arms, and lifted
her from the chair. He held her to him again, tightly,
passionately, his hands fondling her as his kisses grew
warmer.

"Day after tomorrow," he said, "when I return, we'll
inspect that old house again. I confess I didn't see much of
it. I can't even remember what the bedroom looked like,
and I want to see it again—with you. We can make it our
own—until we marry."

"You're mad," Virginia replied, though she was flattered
by what he'd said.

"I'm mad for your body," he finished. "Virginia, it will
be wonderful."

She went down to the dock with him. There he kissed
her a bit more chastely, in case the servants were looking
on.

She didn't return to the mansion after the boat had
vanished from sight. She walked slowly, still embraced by
his warmth. Once again she knew that with him beside
her, she'd never again have to endure those terrible dreams.
In his arms she'd be protected from the memory of Bradley
Culver. She felt as if she were walking on a cloud. She
hugged herself, threw back her head, and danced a few
steps while she laughed softly, all in the memory of his
kisses and his love and how wonderful it all was. And it
would be repeated soon. She wondered if she could wait.
Yes, she'd assuaged her pent-up passion, and he felt a sense
of relief.

Before morning, she realized she could not wait. That

night her dream was terrifyingly cruel. This time Brad seemed to be calling out to her. She could hear him shouting, "Shoot! For God's sake, shoot!" But the rifle she held weighed heavily and she couldn't bring it to bear on the man at the window, waiting to die. And it was repeated, again and again, until she woke near dawn in a sweat and trembling with fear.

She was out of bed and dressed long before breakfast was due to be served and she had to wake Daisy to prepare something. At the table, she told Daisy to inform Ivy that it was necessary that she go to the mainland to see Mr. Murray to discuss some changes she wished to be made in the hotel plans. She added that it might take so long that she'd remain in town overnight.

The trip to the mainland seemed overly tedious. She was impatient and eager. The mere thought of Alex aroused a sensation of great pleasure within her. She wanted to be with him, partly because of her need for companionship, but mainly because she wanted to spend the night with him. A night devoid of nightmares. A fresh thrill of desire went through her as she thought of their sexual union.

She took a carriage from the waterfront to her favorite hotel. She engaged a room and had her suitcase carried up, then she unpacked it and held up her nightgown, all but transparent and very low cut. If she couldn't seduce Alex with this, she deserved to lose him. She laughed aloud as she hung it in the closet.

She repaired the damage the ocean breeze had done to her hair, added a bit more powder, removed her bonnet, and pinned on her Paris hat, a beribboned straw with an ostrich plume. She walked to Alex's office with a light, leisurely step, for she had all day. She even thought that Alex's drawing of the hotel might be proper. Tastes were changing since the war, and perhaps a starkness of architecture was the coming thing.

She entered the building, walked up the stairs, and paused at the door to his office to take a long breath. She would walk into his private office unannounced, for she wanted to feel the thrill of surprising him. She even visualized his eyes touching hers with a knowing intimacy.

To her chagrin, the outer office was occupied by a middle-aged woman, slim, handsome in a sleek manner, with black hair and an oval face and eyes that seemed to sparkle with good humor. She was busy writing in a big ledger, but she looked up at Virginia's entrance.

"Good morning," she said. "May I help you?"

"I—I'm Mrs. Elias Birch, from Valcour."

"Oh, yes." The woman rose and extended her hand. "I'm so glad you came. Alex isn't here. He's working on a project at Lake Moultrie. He'll be very disappointed."

Virginia knew that the woman was speaking, but she heard no more than a few of the words, for she was staring at a large oil painting on the wall behind the woman. She was positive it had not been there during her last visit to the office. It was a well-done portrait of the woman now facing her, seated, with a boy of about four standing beside her while she held an infant on her lap. Standing on the other side of her was Alex, posing somewhat stiffly.

The woman noted Virginia's amazement and turned her head to glance at the portrait. She looked back at Virginia with a sigh.

"Yes, I'm Elizabeth Murray, Alex is my husband. Those are our children. It's rather awkward of Alex, isn't it? I don't mean the way he poses, though he does look a bit stodgy. Did he—compromise you, Mrs. Birch? I hope not."

Virginia was tempted to turn and run, but instead she lowered her gaze from the portrait to the woman. "The portrait wasn't there when I was here before with my sister."

"Alex usually removes it when he knows a lady is coming for an appointment. He says he can handle a lady client much better if she doesn't know he's married."

"He told me that he was married, but—not living with his wife."

"Sometimes he swears I'm dead," she said. "Mrs. Birch, don't feel badly. He's tricked so many women I can scarcely keep count."

"Yes," Virginia said, "I suppose he has. Why do you put up with it?"

"Two reasons, my dear. The children and the fact that I love him, despite his infidelity. I insist on serving as his secretary so I can be here when someone he's misled comes in. I try to ease their pain. You see, I'm quite wealthy. I don't want my family broken up, so I tolerate his peccadilloes—or worse. He knows I love him and will support him, and on occasion he makes love to me. He's an amazing bedfellow."

Virginia wondered how she could maintain such a calmness when her emotions felt as if they were going to tear her apart. "I imagine that when he's found out by his female clients, an agreement does suffer changes."

"I'll tell him you've canceled your order for his services. I will even give you back the check you gave him as an advance on expenses." She opened a drawer and removed the check. Virginia accepted it, still in shock.

"Thank you, Mrs. Murray," she said. "You're very kind."

"This does my heart good," Elizabeth Murray said. "For once he was found out in time. I'm glad I was here today, before he convinced you I was an ogre. It will deflate his ego some, though not much, for his ego is enormous."

"I'm—sorry," Virginia said, still holding the check. She didn't know what else to say.

"Don't be sorry, Mrs. Birch. Alex is not a very good architect, you know. He just makes people think he is. And he gets away with it. I told him the sketch he made of the hotel for your island was abominable. It looks more like a large bank than a hotel. You may have it, if you like."

"Thank you," Virginia said. "For everything, especially your frankness. You may have saved me from making a fool of myself. Frankly, I didn't like the sketch, either."

"And you came today to tell him." Mrs. Murray smiled. "I'm glad I'll have that opportunity. He needs something like that every so often to deflate his ego. Then, until he has another beautiful client, I'm the queen in his life. I console him, sympathize with him, and pretend that his clients were stupid and inconsiderate. You see, I play a little game, too."

Virginia extended her hand and Mrs. Murray grasped it and smiled warmly.

Virginia walked aimless for an hour, expending the energy she wanted to use in screaming her rage. Finally, she returned to the hotel and went to her room. She recalled another incident so similar as to be uncanny. She'd returned to a hotel room after learning that Carlos was a cheating scoundrel. That time, she'd cried the anger and sorrow out of her system. This time, she had no inclination to cry. she was more angry with herself than sad. She'd been made a fool of for the second time. The first may have been excusable, but not the second. It was her own fault for being too eager, too obsessed with a desire to be loved, cursed with a body that was highly passionate, and frightened by dreams that she hoped love would banish.

She thought about taking a carriage to the mainland plantation and visiting Phoebe and Chris but decided against it quickly enough. She'd made enough of a fool of herself with Chris, but she knew he was man enough to keep it to himself.

Virginia felt her cheeks flush with shame as she recalled that night. Was she really a harlot? That foolish Aphrodite bit that Alex had pulled on her was enough to make her think so. She knew Aphrodite took on lovers, even though she was married. However, that was mythology. There was nothing mythical about Virginia's escapades.

Strangely, Elias came to mind, and she thought of what she'd said the previous afternoon about not wanting a divorce. Of course, it wasn't true. It was just that she was aware of Alex's conceit and the fact that he'd had his way with her. She hadn't wanted him to think he meant that much to her.

She thought of visiting her mother and the Colonel and rejected that also. She'd never had the slightest suspicion that her mother knew of her liaisons with Brad. She didn't want to blight her mother's happiness by having her even suspect that she had once again been indiscreet. Worse than that, she'd broken her marriage vows for a third time.

She wished her sisters would come back. She missed them and needed them. But she couldn't summon Phoebe; her place was with Chris. They were newlyweds still reveling in their happiness.

So she was back on Valcour late in the afternoon. She tore up the check she'd given Alex, then spread his sketch on the desk and studied it for a moment. Laughing, she realized that it did look more like a bank than a hotel. It would have been so out-of-place on Valcour as to wreck everything else they might have constructed. Showing the sketch to Phoebe and Nanine and their husbands would cause them readily to approve her dismissing Alex from the project.

That night she took a sleeping draft. If she dreamed

again about Brad, she didn't remember it the next morning.
She awoke refreshed and ready for the day. The first
decision she made was to get Ivy enrolled in the private
school on the mainland. It might well be that she could
serve in the hotel in some capacity. Not as manager, but
with diligence she might work up to it one day.

Nanine and Adam returned a week later. Phoebe and
Chris came a day following their arrival. The five of them
were gathered in the library and had studied the sketch
carefully.

Nanine said, "Obviously, the only reason Henry Tyler
recommended Alexander Murray was because he's Mrs.
Murray's uncle. This is the wildest idea for a resort hotel
I've ever seen."

"He really isn't good, but his charm makes people think
he is," Virginia said.

"He certainly uses something other than talent," Phoebe
added. "Nan and Adam were discussing the project while
we were being rowed to the island. Their ideas make
sense."

"Virgie, what do you have in mind?" Adam asked.

"Something that will captivate the eye and match the
beauty of the island. Something that will make visitors
glad that they came and reluctant to leave. We can provide
all kinds of entertainment and recreation—optional, of
course."

"Then listen to Adam," Nanine urged.

"This is our idea" Adam said. "A three- or even a
four-story building with a hundred rooms and suites.
Maybe more if we feel it's needed. We can build with the
idea of adding onto it. But it isn't to look like a hotel. It
will resemble a Southern mansion, but on a much larger
scale. It will have wide verandas running around three
sides of the building. It will have white pillars with arches

between them. Over the doors—there'll be more than one, for we'll have entrances on each side—will be fan lights of colored glass and side windows of the same kind. Everything on the outside will be painted white, except for wicker furniture, which will be painted green."

"With upholstered seat and back cushions."

"If you can draw like you can describe," Virginia said, "please start making a sketch. We've so much planning to do."

"I forgot to mention," Adam added, "if there are three or four stories we'll have an elevator. They've proven very successful in Washington."

Adam switched his attention to Chris. "What do you and Phoebe have to offer?"

"I could only work with the interior," Phoebe said. "The walls should have bright colors. First, though, we'd have to see the plans for the rooms. My suggestion is that each one be different, even to the furnishings—or at least with the furnishings varied, but with Southern decor in mind. Virgie, Nan, and I should be able to make an outstanding place of it."

"I agree," Chris said. "You three work well together. Adam and I will concentrate on the outside—with Adam the idea man—and as we go along, he can make plans for you and find the contractors we need. If the winter is mild, we can have a great deal finished by spring and possibly open in summer."

"I suggest that we engage another architect immediately to draw the plans and find the contractors we'll need," Nanine said.

"Let's make summer a definite date," Virginia said. "I'm getting carried away with all these plans. I agree with Nan—let's go to work at once. We'll leave the choice of architect up to Adam and Chris."

The transformation of Valcour began with the cleanup

from the fires. As none of the field hands had been discharged, there was sufficient labor to get the work done quickly and, under the supervision of Moses, done well.

The early autumn months were warm, and there was the usual amount of rain, so the grass grew quickly. Bushes flourished almost as soon as they were planted. Each day, someone had a fresh idea. Adam came back from Washington with rough plans for tennis courts, a golf course, croquet layouts, and long docks to be built well out into the ocean for deep-sea fishing. All manner of boats were to be had for pleasure sailing. And Chris and Phoebe had plans to clear the beaches of rocks and replace them with sand brought in by barges. Bath houses near the beach were to resemble small cottages.

The foundation for the hotel was in place well before the cold weather set in. And it remained clear, with few storms and very little snow that winter, enabling carpenters to work without pause. Soon after the first of the year, the structure took on shape and they could see how attractive it was going to be. Chris kept in touch with Lenore and the Colonel, keeping them abreast of the work being done.

Sometimes the waterways between the mainland and the island seemed to be bridged with barges, rowboats, and sailboats bringing supplies and help. Some of the houses, none of which had been razed, provided shelter for the workmen. The island became busier than it had ever been. There were times, however, when the family relaxed and enjoyed the future plans that now seemed certain of fruition.

Chris was also kept busy on the mainland, and for days he and Phoebe were apart while she remained on Valcour. Everything went smoothly and the progress surprised everyone.

Adam had gone back to Washington and engaged an architect to draw up the final plans. He had been stationed on Valcour during the war and was familiar with it, so it presented no problem when he stated that it would be impossible for him to come to Valcour to oversee the project. Adam was more than willing to make frequent trips to Washington, and Chris agreed to accompany him to present his ideas for the landscaping of the grounds.

Virginia suggested to Phoebe and Nanine that they refurbish the houses on the island with the idea that some guests with families might prefer to rent a house completely furnished, even with servants. The idea was greeted with enthusiasm and they went to work on that.

The day Adam returned from Washington with the plans for the hotel proper, the five of them bent over the large table in the outbuilding that had been erected for Chris and Adam, where they had conferences with their foremen on the various projects. Since they wanted the hotel for the summer, they would have to work fast and hope for a mild winter. They were delighted with the plans, which included small cottages on the outskirts of the hotel. Nanine, always practical, planned small stores whose architecture would follow that of the hotel and be found in tree-shaded areas. There, special foods, candy, and souvenirs would be sold. Surrounding the circular lobby, which would be centered with potted palms and flowering plants, would be small, fashionable shops whose show windows would display their tasteful and colorful merchandise.

One night Virginia, highly elated over the way everything was going, sat down and wrote Elias a letter. She told him of the ruined crop, destroyed through her foolishness. She told him, in detail, what had happened to the islanders and how she had hit upon the idea for the hotel.

She revealed that they were already at work on the project and that Nanine's and Phoebe's husbands were as much involved as she, Nanine, and Phoebe. She asked, hopefully, if he might have some suggestions for improvements to their plans and if he would write her of them at his convenience. She finished with the hope that she would hear from him and the statement that she was sorry for the anguish she had caused him, and she asked if he could find it in his heart to forgive her.

She didn't ask him to return, but she hoped he would know that that was what she wanted. She went to the mainland to mail it so that no one in her family would know. To her chagrin, an answer never came. She knew then that it was over. Possibly he had met someone else. If so, she hoped he'd found happiness. From then on, she feared the mail, lest there be a letter from him asking for a divorce. She had only one consolation—she knew he would never reveal to anyone the true reason why he had walked out.

Virginia's nightmares didn't come as often, for usually she was too tired to dream. She kept busy, drove herself purposely to exhaustion. It didn't always work, but when it did, she had sound, healthy sleep.

But she knew this was due solely to the work in which she was now involved. When that ceased, the dreams would return as vividly and as horribly as before. The thought terrified her, and what made it worse was that she had no one to help her through the agonizing nights.

Adam returned from a journey to Washington with a fresh idea from the architect for improving the roads and creating new ones from one end of the island to the other, and to provide riding horses for the refurnished stable, and carriages for those who did not ride but wished to see all of the island and enjoy its scenic beauty. This led Phoebe to suggest forest trails and, perhaps, the import of a few more deer and game birds.

Things began to take shape. There were endless

conferences, trips to the mainland, trips to Atlanta for furniture they wanted, even two journeys by Phoebe and Chris to New York for decorations unobtainable in the South.

Lenore got into the swing of the preparations and glowed with joy at the results. She'd made lists of people she would invite, and she had to be reminded that most of the time, those who came would have to pay. The easy days on Valcour were over.

All of this made Virginia more and more tired. The island seemed to swarm with tradesmen and workers. In the spring, the seeded grounds where the grass had been burned came out greener than ever, the bushes prospered, and the flower gardens took on a magnificent display. They were almost ready for the grand opening.

At the supper table a week before they hoped guests would arrive, Virginia looked down the long table at Phoebe and Chris and Nanine and Adam.

"I have a confession to make," Virginia said. "After I've made it, I want no comments. I wrote to Elias and told him what we are doing and why it was necessary to do it. I asked for his forgiveness. I never received a reply."

"Has there been time?" Nanine asked.

"I did it months ago," Virginia said. "So much for that. I mention it so you'll never again suggest that I write to Elias. It's over. I don't blame him. Only myself. I'll make one more confession. I still love him. It was always Elias and it always will be. Now I feel better. It's just that seeing the four of you at this table, I realize how much your marriage vows mean to you, and I'm grateful you've found happiness. That goes for Mama also. I hope she and the Colonel will come the day we open."

"They wouldn't miss it," Phoebe said. "Chris and I have kept them informed of our progress."

"One thing worries me—transportation."

"I'm sorry, Virgie," Chris said. "I forgot to tell you that Adam and I have taken care of that. Everything's under control. So try to relax."

"How can I? Everytime I turn around I either see something that needs doing or I think of something. I walk around with a note pad."

"So do we," Phoebe said. "Even the men have pencils tucked behind their ears."

"Small wonder," Nanine said. "We open this Sunday."

Virginia didn't sleep the night before the event. She was troubled because of her tension and what would likely happen when she lacked it. Tension was a heavy cross to bear, but when that was gone, the nightmares would come back. They returned that night, and she awakened in a cold sweat and a wave of searing apprehension.

Everyone arose early, ate a hurried breakfast, and took care to dress well for the occasion. Then they had the help line up in the lobby for inspection. First they checked the kitchen help, recruited from the regular Negro workers who had been well trained by Daisy and had passed inspection from chefs imported from New Orleans and Atlanta. Next they checked the maids who would clean the rooms. Their uniforms were dove gray, with white lace aprons and lace caps. The houseboys wore red uniforms with caps that were held on by gold cords tucked under their chins. Their white cotton gloves were spotless. Men who had worked the fields were now gardeners, guides, janitors, carpenters, and plumbers.

By mid-morning, the five of them went down to the dock, turned around, and looked back at the results of their labors. The hotel, four stories tall, met every specification they had ordered. The elevator, a gaudy, gold-plated cage, went up and down with a smoothness that enticed the help to try it over and over, under Moses's supervision.

The new kitchen, many times larger than the old, was under the control of women who had fine reputations for their skills, and, over all, a French chef who had been recruited from one of the best restaurants in New York. Fortunately, he and Daisy got along beautifully. Nothing was lacking. No guest would complain that his vacation would not be interesting. They would be wined and dined in an imperial manner, but no guest-filled boats were in sight.

The first delegation was due about noontime, but Virginia, back on the veranda, saw no signs of any incoming boats, although, according to Chris and Adam, the transportation was in hand and would serve any number of guests.

Virginia, her nerves nearly out of control, made one final inspection inside. As she entered one of the fourth-floor bedrooms, she was startled by the sound of a loud whistle. It sounded like the new steamboats coming into Charleston. She stepped quickly to the window and saw a large vessel, painted white, with flags, bunting, and banners stiff in the breeze created by the speed of the boat. It seemed to be alive with people, all craning their necks for a first glimpse of Valcour.

Virginia ran downstairs. The others were already on the veranda. Uniformed bellboys and workers lined both sides of the road from the enlarged dock. It was no longer a path, but a broad, paved, tree-shaded route from dock to hotel, with a narrower path veering off to the mansion.

"Something has been kept from me," Virginia said. "Chris, Adam, is this the form of transportation you assured me would be ready?"

"Know what that is?" Adam asked gleefully. "It's a steam yacht. That's what we transformed it into. It can make the run from the mainland to the island in a little more than three-quarters of an hour, and it's a pleasant way to travel."

"It was used during the war when small Rebel boats would put out to sea by night and meet British ships carrying arms and ammunition for our forces," Nanine explained. "Tha Yankees had nothing that could catch this ship."

"You might also be interested to know that it's packed with as many guests as this hotel can accommodate," Phoebe said. "This is our surprise to you, Virgie. Elias drew up the plans for the hotel and outbuildings."

Virginia cried a little, kissed each of them, and then prepared herself to face what looked like an army of visitors. When they had assembled for the march to the hotel, the guests gave way to a man wearing a white yachting cap, a blue jacket with gold buttons, and white trousers, who then led them. Virginia didn't utter a sound. She went slowly down the veranda stairs, continued on for a few steps at a steady pace, and then, with a cry of joy, she began to run. The man ran too, until they met in an embrace during which she was swept off her feet and whirled about in a mad circle while she clung to Elias and wept.

She finally was able to lead him to the mansion, while the guests continued on, every one of them strangers to Virginia, but all acting as if they'd known her for years while they cheered Elias on. Chris and Phoebe led the way to the hotel, with Adam, Nanine, Lenore, and the Colonel following them, to greet the guests. Virginia stood on the veranda, her arm around Elias while she waved and smiled and tried to stem her tears.

"Did you see that red-faced man and the buxom woman with him?" Elias asked. "He's an earl; the woman, who is his sister, is a duchess. Her husband is somewhere in the crowd. They're all British, you know."

"British," she said. "Yes, of course, British," as if the word were foreign to her.

"I recruited them," Elias explained. "Some were our customers, but most were looking for a nice place to spend a vacation. I talked them into visiting Valcour."

"But how did you know what we were doing?" She faced him squarely. "I wrote you a letter baring my heart. You never acknowledged it."

He smiled. "I came instead. I was the Washington architect."

"Even so, why didn't you let me know you'd forgiven me? At least, I hope you have."

"I have, my darling. But we have a few things to talk about."

His expression was somber, and she felt a trickle of fear. Perhaps she'd taken too much for granted. He had come back, but perhaps only to help her make the hotel a success. He'd certainly done his part by drawing the plans, then by bringing a boatload of people. The list of guests would be in newspapers all around the world. Americans who were hungry to meet royalty would flock here.

"Perhaps we'd better go inside," she said.

"I'd like that.

"I would too, Elias."

They gave a final glance at the hotel, now bustling with activity, and moved briskly into the house. Moses, wearing a dark green silk suit with knee breeches, white silk stockings, and black buckled patent leather shoes, met them at the door. He gave an exclamation of delight. Elias embraced him and asked what he was doing all gussied up. His proud reply was that he was in charge of the elevator and all the houseboys and he wished he could stop to talk, but he had to get to the hotel.

Elias laughed and waved him off.

Virginia said, "We gave Moses the choice of any job he wanted. He just told you what it was."

"It's a pretty big order."

"He's up to it," Virginia said. "Did you know about Belle?"

"Yes, Virgie. Nan kept me informed. Let's go up to your suite so we can talk."

Once there, Virginia set down her parasol and removed her gloves. Elias motioned her to the settee, closed the door to the hall, and returned to sit beside her.

"You're as beautiful as ever," he said. "Your afternoon gown is exquisite. I love lavender on you. It picks up the violet of your eyes. I love you, Virgie. I always will, but I must say this—don't ever be unfaithful to me again. If you are, I'll walk out, because I'll not be cuckolded. The next time—and God forbid there'll be a next time—I'll not come back. I swear it."

"Perhaps you'll walk out without my being unfaithful to you," she said seriously.

"Nonsense."

"Don't be too sure," she said. "I have something to tell you. Something terrible. You know the bad things I've done. Did you know about Jimmy's being kidnapped by Brad?"

"I know everything that happened here," Elias said kindly. "Nan wrote me in detail. I received your letter asking forgiveness. I forgave you long ago. I missed you terribly. I hope you missed me. I'll ask you no questions and I don't want you to ask me any. This is a fresh start—for both of us."

"Not yet, Elias. I still haven't talked."

"I said that Nan told me everything."

"Nan doesn't know what I'm about to tell you," Virginia said.

He reached over and took her hand, but Virginia pulled it free.

At his look of surprise, she said, "I don't mean to hurt you, Elias. I love you dearly. I want you to know that first.

I've always loved you. And you said this is a fresh start for both of us. I hope so, but you must be the judge of that. Now I'll tell you."

"Make it brief, my love. Except I do want to say one thing. Thank you for wearing the jewelry I sent you from Washington."

She touched the pendant. "I love it. You have exquisite taste."

"And you're still wearing the same perfume. Whenever the fragrance drifted my way, I hungered for you."

"Thank you for telling me. Now let me talk. I did a dreadful thing. I'm sure Nan wrote you in detail about Brad's kidnapping Jimmy."

At Elias's nod, she continued. "Brad sent for me the final afternoon of his life. He dreaded the hangman and he—asked me to—come back in the middle of the night—to kill him."

"My God! What a horrible thing for you to have to do."

She nodded and felt her heartbeat quicken with the fear that Elias's revulsion at what she'd done would be stronger than his love and he would leave. Nonetheless, she had to know.

"I told Brad I couldn't do it. He told me how he would make himself an easy target. That beyond the prison, tall grass grew and I could hide there until three in the morning. At that hour, he would stand on a table and present himself as a target in the high window. The light behind him would silhouette him. I told him again I couldn't do it. He said I must because he feared that he would blurt out the only thing that might save him. That he was Jimmy's father. He said if I loved the boy enough, I'd do it. I left him, still refusing.

"I agonized over it after I returned, but of course I did it."

Virginia paused, then looked directly into his eyes. "I

murdered a man. Do you still love me? Do you still want to begin anew?"

"Have you gotten over the shock of it?" Elias asked.

"No. I'll have nightmares the rest of my life. It's been terrifying."

"From now on, whenever they come, wake me. I'll hold you and comfort you and love you. I will always love you, my darling. What you did took courage. Now, take me to see our son. I always wanted one. You did that for me."

He raised her to her feet and their lips met. It was a tender kiss, filled with trust and understanding. Then Elias placed his arm around her waist. They went into the corridor toward Jimmy's room, their eyes filled with the wonder of their love.